PEAK
PERFORMANCE

PEAK PERFORMANCE

DEMONIC MAGICIAN
BOOK ONE

Kleggt

Published in 2025 by Podium Publishing
www.podiumentertainment.com

Podium

PEAK
PERFORMANCE

CHAPTER ONE

Behind the Curtain

The greatest showman on the continent! At least, that's what the flyers said. For several years, I had held a firm grasp on fake it till you make it, and I had wrung out every last drop that I had the strength to. It wasn't so much of a lie—I mean, of course you had to suspend some disbelief anyway, seeing as it was a *magic* show. What was a little fluff around the edges?

Before the print run, I had already had the argument with my manager about whether it should be *continent* or *globe*. Although, at this stage, I couldn't remember which of us was for or against which option.

I gave my final bow for the night. The bright lights overhead had been melting me for the last half an hour, and I was sure to find my purple suit permanently affixed to me once I managed to shy away to the dressing room. A show expertly performed, just as rehearsed. The applause of the crowd was heartwarming, and even if I couldn't see their individual faces due to the near-blinding illumination beating down on the stage, their blobby appreciation for my act was enough dopamine to carry me home.

My cut of the ticket price certainly helped but wasn't exactly my main motivation. The figures just vanished—as if by magic—into an intangible space to be used when needed.

As the lights dimmed and the various stagehands scurried across to collect the spent equipment, the curtains began to separate my two worlds. The permanent smile across my face faded and lethargy sunk in as the shade blocked me from view of the roving throng.

"Great show, boss." One of the assistants nodded to me as he passed. I recognized him—his thick mustache and flatcap had been backstage at most of my current tour events.

"Greatest one on the continent, Larry." I returned the smile despite my heart not being in it. It was a mediocre show, in the grand scheme of things. How I had managed to turn amusing family and friends into a career of fame, I still was unsure. The people needed entertainment, and it made me feel complete, so who was I to judge?

I slid my way off the side of the stage, trying to find the corridor that led to my quiet resting place. Nods and faux assurances to all that passed. It wasn't that I didn't appreciate them or the work—it was just the facade that came with the job tended to wear me down quicker than I liked these days.

Of course, that was the whole thing, anyone with the know-how and enough practice could pull off most of what I could do—it was just the spectacle of it that made the difference. Let the people turn off their brains and be dazzled by the sparkles so they wouldn't be wondering if I had just moved the ball to my pocket or a hidden compartment.

Dark gray corridors filled my vision as I found my way through the depths of the building. No need for pomp and pageantry back here—the plain brickwork and barely safety-standard wiring would be for those with eyes already behind the curtain. Racks of costumes and large containers filled with props and who knew what else lined the sides of the passageways to my salvation.

My doorway loomed ahead of me—yet the day was not over. One last obstacle lay in my path. A portly man of dark skin and graying goatee stood next to his daughter, a young girl with a long ponytail and nerves in her bright eyes.

They saw me approach—although how could they not? Dressed in a shimmering purple suit with matching top hat, I was halfway sure I could be spotted from space if the clouds were clear. My dour expression beneath messy brown hair turned to a radiant smile before they even clocked it.

"Ah! Maximilian, I hope you don't mind, but—ah, Reggie said it would be fine for us to ask for an autograph?"

The slight nerves in his request comforted me. When a fan felt they were putting you out, they were usually much more sympathetic. The ones that acted as though you owed them your time and energy were the worst.

"Of course!" I beamed at them both with arms raised. "Always fantastic to meet a fan." Reggie was my manager and was usually pretty good at keeping the hordes away from me—these two would have passed his basic test to determine if they were worthy taking up my time. At least, in his mind.

"Anna here has been following you since the early days." The man nudged the girl forward. "She's quite the budding magician herself."

"Oh, really?" I tilted my head as she produced a top hat of her own for me to sign. She seemed more nervous than her father, and shy. Pretty normal reaction to meeting your hero—as dubious as that title may be.

I slipped a silver marker from my back pocket and twirled it between my fingers. The hat was a simple thing—black with a white ribbon encircling it. One with a false layer to hide things under when held out and some wear around the edges from loving use. I popped the cap from the pen and wrote on the inside of the hat—my signature long enough to scrawl the full diameter of the inside. It amused me as it made it look like some manner of runes or an odd spell. Magic by another name.

With a smile, I handed it back to her. "Anna was it? Do you have a new hat that you are using already?"

She shook her head. "No, I really like this one."

"Ah!" I gave her a brief bow. A favored item was always more precious, and I felt slightly guilty to have marred it with my own name even if at their request. "Here—I think the shop is still open." I ruffled around inside jacket and withdrew a gift card. Perhaps the least magical thing on my person—but it did allow the wielder to acquire some of my overpriced junk. Well, not all of it was junk, but merchandise was purely a Reggie thing.

"Thank you, Max." She grinned, clutching at it.

"We really appreciate it." Her father extended his hand, which I shook.

"The pleasure is all mine." My smiling muscles were starting to cramp, despite how much earnest emotion I put into them.

"Before we let you go—I'm sure you're tired," he continued, "is there any advice you can give to Anna?"

I paused and clicked my tongue. Truly, quite an open-ended question that had a multitude of answers depending on how jaded or *truly* helpful I wanted to be. Internally, I sighed.

"As cliché as it is, I have often found the best advice"—I raised a finger in the air—"whether in life or in magic, is that the show must go on. Whatever setbacks or mistakes you make, you have to keep your chin up and take it in stride."

And avoid getting into show business. Probably don't get into a career that revolves around dazzling people with sleight of hand and sparkly lights, only to have your soul drained away. "Oh," I added, "and keep smiling."

She did smile at me. Her father nodded his thanks again, and then they left. I stood and watched them go and turn the corner down the hallway before my face sunk and I deflated once more.

The door relented to body weight as I slunk against it, and the dimly lit room beyond welcomed me with cool but stale air. My temporary place of solitude for this leg of the tour. One show every night for a week, and then I'd be off to some other nameless city that had a slightly different flavor from the last. Not that I'd ever know, between the blinding stage lights and darkened corridors. It was almost as though they just changed the outside world, but I played the same arena every day.

Light flickered around the room as I hit the switch on a lamp, closing the door behind me with the intent of keeping the rest of the world at bay. Jacket off— straight onto a hanger. Slacks off next. As dazzling as the suit was, it was not made for lounging. And that is what the rest of my schedule had me booked in for.

Without ceremony, I sank into the leather chair that faced away from the wall mirror. I preferred my introspection without the judgment of my reflection. I wasn't vain—although it was hard to fake so much grandeur without admiring the scent of it. Staring at my own tired face was definitely a line in the sand I had yet to cross. My career hadn't waned that far.

The leather cooled my bare legs as I tried to shove the echoes of the night's noises from my head. A dull replay of all the cheers, minor explosions, and flashes of light danced inside my tired brain. It left me feeling withdrawn. Perhaps a part of the dopamine and adrenaline wearing off. Did I adore it and crave it? To some degree, sure. It's what kept me constantly performing.

I was an entertainer. Always had been. A bit of a trickster, smart with the tongue, and quick with my hands. I could have turned to pickpocketing, or stand-up comedy, although I truly had neither the stomach nor charisma for either. I could put on a show where people just had to watch and follow along— give me the occasional gasp or applause . . . but actively interacting . . .

With a sigh, I rubbed at my face. Two more nights in this city. Four more cities—and then down for the season. Then it'd be practicing new things, research and development of new tech and routines. A few months of practice, and then back at it again. Some merch deals or occasional one-offs to keep the pot filled up. For the most part, I just had to smile and nod, do my little tricks.

Reggie was . . . affable enough. Had the scent of business firmly sussed out and liked to keep me lining his pockets. Not particularly unfair on the distribution of wealth, I couldn't label him as predatory. Shrewd, yes, and quite the taskmaster when it came to it. But he kept the wheels rolling when sometimes I'd want to hit the brakes.

"The show must go on," I murmured to myself, repeating the mantra he'd always tell me. What they *all* told me.

And *it did*. I grinned from ear to ear and greeted every blurred face that cared to give me the time of day like I was *their* biggest fan. Behind the curtains, I was solitary. No real friends, little family, and no close relationships. I was friends with the road. The show was my family. Magic was my lover. All things Reggie had drilled into me right from the start, and I had lapped it up—wanting a taste of the full experience.

Now, five years on, had he been wrong? I was easily in the top twenty best-known magicians in the world . . . which was no easy feat despite how ridiculous that now sounded in my head. Is this what I had wanted? That was a more interesting question, closer to the point—the sharp edge of reality.

The chair groaned as I sank farther, and my eyes lazily moved to the poster on the wall. It wasn't a current one—probably from last year's tour. I had no clue why they thought I'd want my dressing room plastered with my own advertisements.

Maybe so that I could look upon them in moments such as this and have some confidence in what I had achieved.

My mouth had become parched, and I wasn't keen on letting my brain share a similar fate ruminating about my life. I stood from the chair with a grunt, knocking off a deck of cards from the arm. My intention was to stand and have a reaffirming internal monologue about what a great magician and showman I was, and the handful of cards ejected from the small rectangle box put a dampener on that notion.

I knelt and pawed them together. It was my favorite deck—one I usually practiced with in my dressing room but didn't use on stage. By now, this one was a little worn, and I'd need a fresh deck soon enough. There had always been something about this specific design that brought me comfort. A white rabbit was depicted on the box art and card backs, atop an etched purple-and-white pattern.

Back into the sleeve they went. I stood again, but something caught my eye.

Over by the door, on the floor, looking as if it had been pushed under the slight gap.

An aged piece of paper, the color of sand, folded neatly.

CHAPTER TWO

Suspension of Disbelief

How to start this journal? Magic was something I once thought was anything but. Tricks of the hand or carefully orchestrated illusions that had a set pattern and answer, just overlaid with the art of performance. It was a show, and the audience was just as much a part of it as the magician—for without their disbelief, there was no magic. Just riddles or puzzles that left you guessing. Without the show, nothing could go on.

I tilted my head at the offending page. There would be very few reasons for a message to find its way underneath my door. An assistant that didn't want to disturb me? Something from Reggie—or dare I consider some hastily delivered fan mail? As much as my life was steeped in the illusion of mystery, it wouldn't do for me to stand around and postulate.

Not wanting to drop the rabbit cards anywhere else by accident, I stowed them in the breast pocket of my shirt. I probably should have changed by now, but I hadn't the necessary willpower for buttons. Once again I knelt, this time to retrieve the paper that had managed to derail my whole train of thought.

The texture of it was . . . odd. Familiar. Very old. I allowed myself a little patience to return to the comfortable chair before daring to unfold the creases and reveal the disappointment. It reminded me of the faux old letters I had made as a child, using tea bags to stain the paper brown. But it felt more authentic than that.

I shuffled down into the seat and sighed deeply. Why I allowed myself to put such weight on the reveal I didn't know. Gingerly, I unfolded it.

And gasped.

Memories came flooding back. One of the first books I had read that had made me interested in magic—an ancient tome my grandparents kept. Yellowed, dusty, somewhat illegible—and with pages missing. While I hadn't learned any magic from it as such, it had painted my imagination with the things that could be possible. A whole new world that was beyond the technical application of my craft.

This looked to be a missing page—or at least most of one. Part of it was worn, but there—yes! The style of illustration was exactly the same. A stone archway with a doorway of luminous pink, wavy as if made of fluttering cloth. The words around the page I didn't quite understand, but the sensory stimulation was nigh overwhelming.

I still had that book too—it would be over at . . . Wait. So caught up in the prospect of reuniting this lost page to its rightful place, I had not considered who had left it or why it had come into my possession.

Grasping the paper tightly, I turned my gaze back to the door—as if expecting narrative reveal of the perpetrator. Silence, as reality didn't seem to have the same amount of flare I had expected. The more I thought about it—the stranger it seemed. If this was a specific missing page from the exact book my grandparents used to have, who would have had access to it?

My hotel room was a ten-minute cab ride away. Their house was almost two hours, by my rough estimation. Not that they lived in it currently, of course— they had passed on a good handful of years ago. How time flew. My father had inherited it, but he was working overseas for a few months. Quite the shame, seeing as my tour took me so close by. It would have been nice to see his blurred face out in the crowd. Ships in the night, we had only seen each other a handful of times since my grandmother's funeral.

I idly tapped at the armrest, unsure of how to proceed. Grueling day tomorrow—some rest and relaxation would be nice. Yet . . . Something intended to lead me on the trail of mystery—a little aftershow special. A wry grin cracked the side of my mouth—the show *must* go on, of course.

The chair complained as I left the indentation perfectly made for me. We traveled with it—much to the ire of some of the poor chaps who had to get it through doorways and into every new venue. There was something about always having it just where I needed it that kept me grounded. I pulled on my purple suit once more—better to be properly dressed if there was some game afoot here.

My phone illuminated my face with a pale glow. No new messages—actually, no—there was one from Reggie. He was feeling under the weather tonight, so would grumble at me in the morning. His actual words, not mine. I tried to filter through the events of the evening to try to remember if there were any big enough issues that he might chew me out for. Nothing exceptional—it was a pretty tight performance, given we ran it five nights in a row.

In my early years, I had been hailed for my nonstop shows, the enticed masses wondering how I had the energy for it and didn't get burned out. Well, *the show must go on*, for starters—I repeated the mantra at risk of it becoming trite—and secondly, I had held my feet to the fire for so long the heat comforted me. I'm sure that would look great engraved on my urn. There was time enough for future Max to worry about other problems, and I had yet to meet the man.

I hit the buttons on the technology to arrange for a cab to come and collect me. The true magic was modern innovation, for sure. There was nobody to witness it, but I spun the phone into darkness with a flourish—pocketed away for safekeeping. I would get chewed out by a handful of people if I were seen leaving the premises with my suit still on, but . . .

Even with my resignation to endure a brief rest, I had left my top hat on. So used to it that it no longer itched at my scalp or brought discomfort by overheating my brain. It was a part of me almost, a visual representation of my inability to separate myself from the job. *No*, it was a way of life. I lived and breathed the show.

Thankfully, most of the others working the performance had the invisible strings of other commitments dragging them away from my route out of the building. An almost abnormal absence of interlopers, in fact. For them, it was just a job. Clock out and go see friends, spend time with family, celebrate . . . holidays? Had I really fallen so far as to forget what normal people got up to? Even Reggie didn't breathe the business the same way I did—but that was okay.

I hailed my driver and got into the back seat. A bright smile widened across my face as the twinkle of recognition played in his eyes. The others may be just cogs in the machine that allowed me to perform, but they were important, and I understood their necessity and drive. While the passion was mine, they helped make it into a spectacle. I knew of other magicians who treated those supposedly beneath them with contempt, and it was no surprise to hear of their technical or theatrical blunders along the circuit.

"Off to the Legun Hotel then, Max? If I can call you that?" The driver brimmed with excitement, as if I held the cure for what ailed him.

I raised an eyebrow and gave him a brief nod. It was my given name, after all. There was a pause as I decided whether I wanted to change my intended destination. The driver would want to chat with me, and I would be too polite to decline the conversation. Ten minutes to the hotel would be a lot less stress on my tired psyche, rather than two hours . . . But I could endure one fan to satisfy my curiosity over the piece of paper now safely placed in my card deck, secure in my jacket pocket.

Thus, I gave him the address of my grandparents' old house. And the questions began. Some of them repetitions of previous interviews, and I could easily reel off a concise answer with ease, my face enigmatic and animated. Others required a little thought, but every response was delivered with as much joy and sparkle of mystique as I could manage. The darkened trip through the night went by quicker than expected, which I might have been thankful for were my mouth not dry and eyes aching.

As the cab door shut behind me, I turned to give him a generous tip, despite already doing the minimum through the app. To a cynic, it probably seemed like a gimmick to increase public relations—but he was genuine and a nice enough fellow despite the inability to see through my front and know when to shush. And I couldn't fault him for that. I was a master of illusion, after all.

He drove away, contented. A job well done, and a story to tell his friends and family. Even other passengers in the near future. Adoration and fame could act like a firework—one small spark and the crackling lights that illuminated your career burst out with wide reach to dazzle all. I just had to ignore the smell of gunpowder and appreciate the spectacle while it lasted.

I turned to face the building. A pleasant and modest home that my brain had painted eggshell blue and slightly off-white—comforting colors under the glow of springtime. Currently, it was just dark and foreboding. Now the corpse of a happier place since the original owners passed, as if the shell had shared the same fate. My father had kept it in good order—even in the shade of night and several months of absence, the shapes of it were at least prim and proper.

From my purple slacks, I withdrew my keys and tried to cycle through them under the dim glow of the nearest streetlamp. The one with the green tag. Located, I stepped across the gray slabs that led to the front door. Still the same wind chime that had a carved wooden dove atop it, and the welcome mat looked even more worn than I had remembered it—despite it being practically antique already when I was a child.

The key found the lock, and the door pushed open smoothly, although it pushed a small mountain of mail across the floor as it went. My finger found the light switch, just where it always had been—and a glow flooded the room after a brief hum. Dark wood and pale marbled surfaces. The flood of familiarity was overwhelming for a moment. Not much had changed—certainly some things had been replaced, but my father had opted to keep the authenticity of the original design, even if it was dated. It was all about the presentation, after all.

Door closed, I then passed through the open-plan kitchen and into the sitting room beside it, nostalgia both warming and saddening me. Picture frames hung on the wall, showing my grandparents from their early marriage, all the way up to old age. Full lives lived and now gone. With a sigh, I pushed past any reflective thoughts and a bead curtain into what my father liked to call the weird room.

They had always been into odd things. Magic, the occult, those supposed photos of fairies and ghosts that were popular before the advent of modern technology. The room was little more than a converted study. A door to the left led to the pitch-black garden, two bookshelves and a couple of cupboards arranged along the walls to loom over a small round table and two chairs.

My favorite place to be as a child.

Despite nobody else around to see it, a wide smile crossed my face, and I felt as though a weight had been lifted from my shoulders. I tipped my hat to Roger, the stuffed white rabbit that still sat on one of the shelves, and still felt a twinkle of excitement within me for all the charms, crystals, and other knickknacks decorating the place.

I knelt beside the various tomes that filled the bookcase—half expecting to spend the next hour constantly distracted by long-lost memories and renewed passion—but there it was, straightaway.

With a brief, pensive pause, I took the dark leather book in my hand and slowly slid it from its resting place. A lump formed in my throat as I felt as though I had just disturbed a grave.

One of the small chairs let out a surprised squeak as I sat. From my jacket, I withdrew the gifted page and placed it on the black table that was engraved with various runes and spiraled designs.

I brushed the dust from the front of the cover.

Demonic Rites and Foul Magicks, it read.

CHAPTER THREE

Not an Illusion

*Home. An interesting word. One that could house many meanings . . . But perhaps
I should use the sharpness of my wit to better beat back the unrelenting conflict I now
lived between, rather than box myself in and stroke my own ego through my . . .
memoirs? Diary? For me, home had become whatever grip of existence I could cling
to with tired hands in this new life—any normality that kept me grounded. Between
a sharp rock and whatever had lain before in my murky history, I had lost the tangible comfort of what the word had previously meant.*

I plucked through the aged pages slowly. Despite the banality of the action, my
heart rate had risen in my chest, and I briefly regretted not getting something to
eat or drink this evening. Every turn brought new symbols, odd diagrams, and
archaic scrawling. Some things familiar—particularly one about possession that
had a rather perturbed-looking devil bursting from the body of a woman.
Something that struck a nerve to my impressionable young mind. Perhaps there
was a trick for the show to work out there . . .

No. I shook the thoughts from my head. A bit too macabre for my shtick.
I turned another page, and there it was.

The missing space.

Unfolding the paper, I slowly placed it in the gap. Half expecting some world-
changing revelation and half anticipating the reveal of the person who had
labored me with this tiring journey to pop out from a corner and shout *surprise.*
Nothing of the sort happened either way. The page was a little easier to read now,
however . . .

With the picture fully formed, there was something about it that was starkly
familiar. It was an archway, made of a dark stone, with engravings along each brick.
I furrowed my brow as I traced one of the patterns—almost as though the texture
was something that I . . .

I stood, holding the book open with my left hand as I slowly walked toward the garden door. Narrowed eyes against the unrelenting darkness, my finger moved toward the lighting that should illuminate the pitch-black space—before my brain could start imagining all manner of other horrors that could be lurking back there.

A flash and what was darkness became shades of green and brown as the floodlight plunged the garden into false daylight. The grass recoiled in shock with the breeze, as the various bushes and closed-up flowers around the edge in different stages of dimming light remained impassive. The middle of the garden had been where they'd grown vegetables and had a walkway going through it that used to be covered by the most beautiful vines in spring.

I now stared at the entrance to this walkway and held up the book for comparison. It was as perfect a replica as you could get. My tongue felt around my teeth. Things were now getting slightly weirder. Again, I wondered when the page could have been taken from the book, and more importantly—by whom.

Curiosity once again got the best of me, and throwing caution to the wind, I unlatched the back door and was greeted by the cool night air. I stepped, gradually, over to this monolith of strange. Near perfect in mimicry. My shoes were soundless across the soft grass as I approached, allowing just my thudding heart and the rustle of leaves to be the only fanfare at the start of this show.

As I stood before it, I was in awe. I hadn't thought much of it as a child, not having the missing page, but it seemed they had this actually made at some point before it was torn out. You had to give it to them. They *knew* what they liked. The picture had a bright pinkish-purple glow in the center—I supposed they didn't have the time or LED technology to illuminate it as such back in their day.

I stepped up to it, placing myself in the threshold, and looked down at the book. There wasn't really much of a ritual here, or an explanation of what the supposed device was used for. Something about destiny and souls. My eyes rolled. I reached out my hand to feel around the engravings that I remembered.

Immediately my hand shot back as pink light encircled the groove. My mouth hung open. It looked as though someone might be playing a trick on me. Maybe a rival hoping to catch me on video, looking dumbfounded and out of my element. I stood taller—if they wanted a show, I would give them one.

With a smile, I snapped the book shut and placed my hand back on the arch. Pink energy once again flared where I touched and started to travel to the next brick and engraving above and below. I waited with a mix of boredom and smugness on my face, ready for the inevitable reveal—Maximilian would *not* be fooled by a simple—

As every brick became alight with energy, a flash filled my vision. Everything became pink, and I struggled to keep a grin masked over my displeasure at being briefly blinded. Vertigo struck me, and I dropped the book as a deep breath of cold air filled my lungs.

Then there was nothing but darkness.

My body felt numb against a firm surface.

Gradually, my senses took hold. Dried dirt thick with grass, my face wet with dew. No—as my aching arms lifted me up to be briefly blinded by the bright green, I saw with blurred vision that it wasn't dew dampening my face, but blood. I must have passed out. Slept all the way to the next morning . . .

A fist-sized stone stood proud, marred by the crimson once belonging to my throbbing forehead. It had come close to felling a giant, yet I persisted. Although . . . where I now came to be and my previous state of being were currently more muddied than my outfit. It wasn't hard to come to the conclusion that I wasn't at my grandparents' house . . . not at the . . . Hmm, my brain felt fuzzy.

I wiped down the purple suit. Very familiar to me, yet slightly off. A top hat in the same color lay on the grass a few feet away, but I was apprehensive to give it any due attention. My surroundings were vibrant in the greens and browns of spring, illuminated by midday sunshine. Very odd. My eyes closed to darken out the visual stimuli. One painfully concerning problem at a time. Something about a portal? Some manner of hell my mind wanted to escape?

With a deep sigh, I chose to investigate my head wound. Whatever I now knew, it included the knowledge that my soft brain was an important piece of the puzzle. Gingerly, I felt around in the darkness of my own making, allowing the bruised and tender flesh to tell me the tale. Nothing too dire—although I was not an expert on . . . this. Probably many other things that I had yet to address as well.

Soft hair of medium length, partially matted by dried blood. Clean-shaven face, and the usual nose and mouth that I found no discrepancies with. It was me. *I was me.*

Not as comforting a revelation as I had hoped.

I slowly turned to gauge the world that now lay around me. It appeared I was in a clearing in the middle of a forest. Very little else could be gleaned, other than it was objectively very pleasant. As I started to feel around my person for any clues, I noticed a glowing symbol on my left wrist.

As my fingers went to touch it, to see how real it was, a two-dimensional screen of blue flickered into my vision, white text blaring my name into my skull.

[Player: Maximilian Russet]
[Error—Unassigned Class]
[Error—Unexpected Soul Designation: Duplication]
[Scanning . . . Please stand by . . .]

I stood and waited. Half because I didn't care to sit upon the grass and dirt. Half because I was slightly taken aback as to what was occurring. For some reason, despite how strange this process was, it didn't move the panic needle much. Dissociation, perhaps. Either I was too far gone to believe this was anything more than a dream, or the part of me that was tethered to reality was off on holiday. An alien notion.

A second notification came up while the first sat in the background, doing whatever a scan was.

[Health Report]
[Severe stomach lacerations—Healed 100% (System)]
[Foot injury (Hole)—Healed 100% (System)]
[Light head injury (Blunt)—Healed 40% (Natural)]
[Soft Landing]

My stomach and foot felt just fine, other than the small amount of nerves keeping me on my toes. A little observation and light prodding determined I no longer had either of these supposed injuries. It seemed I had arrived here in less than one piece, and after being patched up good as new, I had shown my gratitude by immediately smashing my head open on the nearest hard surface.

Soft Landing didn't seem like an injury, but in focusing on it with a furrowed brow, it then brought up a secondary window to further berate me with details. No surprises that it wasn't referring to the harsh stone that had been my welcoming party.

[Soft Landing]
[Welcome to the System. You are refreshed and renewed.
Ready for adventure!]

With my head injury, it was hard to agree to some of the bright-white text. I did feel . . . relieved? The malaise and exhaustion that had painted my after-show evening were all but gone. Too soon to jump the gun and say I was ready for another show in whatever fever dream I had wound up in, but I couldn't deny there was the wriggling worm of renewed passion for my craft. It was just hidden behind a layer of brain fog and bemusement. Some part of me was comforted to be distant from my usual schedule, but I wasn't sure *adventure* was my second choice of vocations.

The needless factoid vanished away, and I resumed the search of my jacket and slack pockets for any convenient truths. My hands withdrew from my trouser pockets to find they were filled with a nominal amount of . . . ash? Whether these were useful items rent to dust from my transfer to this currently serene place or the dark powder was a sign of my last location—or vocation—wasn't really something for me to know.

My jacket, however, was a place of actual treasure—and my hand withdrew a thick rectangular object. A pack of cards. The cover was deep purple, etched with an intricate white pattern, the colors shifting and vibrant in the light of the day. On the front of one side was the simple logo of a white rabbit. This looked almost just like the card pack I had in real life but had the extra edge of . . . Well, it appeared to be brand-new instead of worn.

Any further musings were interrupted by the System, eager for my attention.

[Scan complete. Compromise found. Soul Merge partially accepted.]
[Assigning unique Class: Demonic Magician]
[Level set to <1>]
[New Ability: <Pick a Card>]
[New Passive: <Sleight of Hand>]
[New Passive: <Illusion Proficiency>]

Never in my life had *finding compromise* felt like a good phrase. Especially when it came to things pertaining to my apparent soul. *Max* didn't do compromise. I could remember that much. I had yet to decide on my feelings on what Classes were, but *unique* seemed like something with some pizzazz to it—so I let the rest of the internal-scream-inducing details slide for now.

[Magic item acquired: Unique Demonic Deck (Rabbit)]

The barrage of information continued, my apparent intrusion on whatever world I had become part of now trying to catch up with the paperwork lest I become untenable. Something about being a magician, having a rabbit deck of cards, and the top hat I was still trying to avoid told me it was at least accepting of my prior vocation—even if it had not heard of me. It was overly charitable to accept it just as it had accepted me, but maybe part of that was Soft Landing nudging my brain into staying put and suspending disbelief.

The System wasn't saying anything useful, but I at least wasn't subject to horrible dissociation. I still felt out of place, but part of me had begun to hope that if I just stayed put, then eventually something more realistic would cross my path. Although what *realistic* meant was neither here nor there—the grass and trees, even my stone nemesis—all looked and felt real. The breeze brought the smells of dirt and vegetation through my nose. Warmth radiated through my back, where the sun watched me eagerly. It would be comforting if I wasn't just wrenched from my previous life without explanation.

The glowing light of the System appeared as a star on my wrist, and tentatively I gave it a tap with my index finger. A rotating menu of words, each with the promise of more flickering screens of information. Easy enough to understand—I wasn't a total fossil when it came to technology. There was a Player screen, an Inventory, one for Quests, and even something to check the Skills I had just received. There seemed to be gaps for additional things, but I didn't worry myself with the horrors yet to be unlocked when there was plenty for my muddled mind to drown in currently.

First up, I chose to check out the Skills—the use of abilities seemed like something the old me used to do—like tricks at my disposal, maybe. This was familiar ground. Even if it had a totally different flavor to it, I found mentally consuming it palatable. Somehow.

Heartbeat pounding in my chest, it was time to see what I was capable of.

CHAPTER FOUR

Edge of the Deck

For all the beauty in the world, there was the constant presence of conflict. Few places were truly free of danger—and the System expected you to rise up and meet the challenge. Kill and grow, lest you become a stepping stone for those more ambitious and less scrupulous than yourself. And what was the reward for being at the top of the ladder, for surviving and slaying your way across the world to reach the highest apex? I did not know, even at this stage. Any glance of the truth I hoped to steal was buried among those who fell before reaching the pinnacle.

[<Pick a Card>: Ranged attack, (15) feet—100% INT Damage. Illusion Magic.]
[<Sleight of Hand>: Your Deception success chance increases with both INT and DEX]
[<Illusion Proficiency>: Effectiveness increased with skills that use this Magic School]

I tilted my head, trying to absorb the information. It sank into the back of my mind like a thick paste. All the words made sense, but the context was still beyond me. It might as well have been a recipe for lasagna for as clear as it was. Slowly, I massaged my tender head. I barely had the time to play video games in my actual life. I'm not sure why my mania had defaulted to this manner of setup.

But the show must go on . . . It was time to throw caution to the wind—and apparently some cards. The <Pick a Card> skill required a deck equipped—the System was keen to inform me. My feet moved stiffly across the soft grass. Either my muscles were reluctant to accept this new existence, or I had been lying on my rocky pillow with stars circling my head for longer than I had thought.

Distaste painting my impressionable mood, I grasped the top hat in my hand. My face wrinkled up, my features recoiling from the look. Instead of donning it myself, I gifted it to the one that nearly put me back in the ground—the bloodied rock. Perhaps it was the lingering concussion, but I thought it suited him.

Some life began to filter into my limbs in earnest. I stepped back to what I considered about twelve feet away from the dapper stone. With my deck in my left hand, I furrowed my brow.

For some reason, I had expected it to be a bit more effortless. A natural extension of my physical form. Where I dredged those aspirations from, I wasn't sure, but I felt confident enough to drag the lid back over that dirtied pool. Instead, I sighed and put my right index finger atop the magic deck.

I felt it before I saw it—the slight thrum of energy. The smallest of vibrations of the air, or rather, something within the air. White-and-purple light curved into existence to form a flat rectangle between my index and middle fingers. It felt . . . not exactly tangible, but it had a presence.

[<Pick a Card>]

I flicked my fingers forward, and it left my hand. The skill itself made manifest. It shot across the short gap and embedded into the hat, jostling it backward and leaving a narrow slice in the fabric with a lingering faint blur of purple. The breeze rustled through the clearing as I stood and stared at what I had done, the magical card fading from existence after a handful of seconds. Perhaps returning to the deck, as a quick rifle through didn't leave an obvious gap.

My first trick in this new world.

It didn't necessarily seem like something I could kill a man with, unless he were to walk around carelessly flaunting an exposed neck. But then again, I wasn't sure *why* I expected to have to murder when I was more of a showman. Perhaps I needed more INT—assuming it stood for Intelligence.

Clearly I didn't have enough, if I needed to assume that much.

Despite myself, a wry grin started to form across my face. *Magic.* Some manner of *actual* magic—this would work wonders for my performance. My eyes scanned the ground to see if the book had made the journey alongside me, but it seemed I'd made the trip solo. I wasn't sure how my skills of throwing cards would impress those local to this world, but the burgeoning weight of potential fame—of becoming this world's greatest showman—had started to sink into me.

Without wanting to get too far ahead of myself, I opened up the next menu to start me on my path to adoration and riches—Quests.

[Available Quests: 1]
[Welcome to Othea!]
[Travel north to Greenrest, defeating 10 Slimes along the way]
[Progress: 0/10 Slimes. Location not reached.]

Direction gave purpose, even if it didn't really clarify much. Perhaps answers lay at . . . *Greenrest*. Already the System expected violence of me, as if there were no choice in the matter. Become a killer or don't progress. I was slightly concerned that my reaction hadn't been obstinate panic at the suggestion.

I smiled and brushed my hair back, flakes of dark burgundy falling from my scabbed injury. Lucky for the System, I *had* been a killer—I could at least remember that much. Although, I stopped to run my brain past that last thought. I had been a *magician*, not a killer, surely? Untoward memories rose and faded just as quickly. Eyes among the shadows. Any true answer was fogged among mist in places my recovering mind couldn't reach. Strange.

"Keep the hat, rock. You earned it." I brushed down my suit once more, somewhat put off to hear my voice externally for the first time here. It *was* my voice, however. The System on my wrist had a small arrow illuminated, pointing in the direction I needed to travel. On second thought, I took the hat—it was part of the whole outfit, after all.

North. To exploration, conflict, and hopefully, answers.

I stopped after two steps, as a warmth began to radiate through the pack of cards. It was calling to me, in a manner of speaking. The familiarity it bore to something from my past felt even more real, as if a reassuring voice was whispering in my ear. No words sunk into my subconscious, but the message was clear. Grow stronger.

"I'm not crazy." I said this aloud as there was currently nobody else to reassure me. My internal voice would take an idea and run with it faster than I could catch them. But speaking my voice into the world made it more real, as if my life was worthy of dictation.

As my feet made headway through the woods under sunlight broken by the canopy above, I worked my jaw in contemplation. Puzzle pieces aligned, but I couldn't quite work out what picture I was supposed to be making. Part of me was familiar with the occult, the bizarre, and the untoward. The other part of me was as well—but in ways that weren't so flashy and painted by the recognition of fame. Where this world fell on that shifting scale, I was yet to fully absorb, but I was gaining a tentative grasp.

I felt like I had a rough enough understanding of the process. Do tasks to gain power and unlock better abilities to repeat the process. It seemed more like a hamster wheel than any real progress, but perhaps there was a path I could carve for myself. Gaining the power to escape seemed like an odd phrase—sure, I had come here from somewhere else . . . but would it be so simple to get back? Sparks of memories faded just as soon as they bloomed.

If anything, there was just a growing weight within me, knowing something terrible was going to happen. Great. If there was one sure bet to kill my mood, it would have to be bad omens. Both the System and I wanted to gain more power—but I didn't have the depth of knowledge to understand what that encompassed—would I just be throwing cards harder? Or were there more tricks up my sleeve that I required permission to use? If there was one thing the book left behind had taught me, it was that I wouldn't want to be someone unlucky enough to have destiny weighing down on my existence.

I stepped forth, northward, as the System commanded it. My body had gotten used to the prospect of living and being usable, which made the stroll through the forest entirely more pleasant. If it weren't for the odd feeling of not understanding my past and the constant reminder that I hadn't murdered ten souls yet, this would be a small slice of bliss compared to . . . whatever it was that I had come from. Some manner of hell.

The more I looked around and the farther I traveled, it seemed almost *too* picturesque. As though everything had been created from the same handful of near-immaculate set pieces. I supposed that wasn't too out of the realm of possibility, especially as—

My feet rooted in place at the sound of something nearby. The shuffling of bushes just ahead, to my right. I placed a tree between me and the offending movement, fingertips atop my magic deck.

A spherical object leaped wetly from among the foliage to land in an open space as if deliberately revealing itself to me. Despite its pink hue, it was slightly transparent, with two dark pits of eyes above an all-too-cute mouth. The System sought to hold my hand further, and a blue message flickered over the creature.

[New Monster: Slime <1>]

I daren't breathe just in case I scared away the Monster. It hadn't seemed to notice me so far. The simple thing content to squish around and watch the leaves of the surrounding trees wave about in the light breeze. I almost felt bad about the looming prospect of murdering the poor thing in cold blood. Almost.

With a wide step out from my hiding place, a card of purple energy formed between my fingers, and I threw it out at the surprised foe. Within a second, it struck it directly in what I would call the forehead. The rounded part over its eyes . . . which was the rest of it, really.

Briefly, it gave me a sad look as if I had labored upon it the worst kind of betrayal, despite not knowing it previously—and then it popped. A small spattering of pink slime dotted the area as its remains sunk into a thick, gel-like puddle on the ground.

"That was . . . underwhelming." I tilted my head, perhaps expecting a slight fanfare from the System for taking the first step on the route to being a mass murderer. Perhaps I shouldn't wish for greater hardship.

[Progress: 1/10 Slimes. Location not reached.]

The quest had updated, and I was one step closer to an unknown reward and perhaps some amount of exposition. I was being a bit presumptuous to assume I could bring any manner of further hardship to my journey that destiny hadn't already begun to put in motion. Often, once you started coming into some fortunate luck, the deck became further stacked against you until karma could deal you a terrible hand with a knowing smirk across its face.

"What now, then? Continue onward to the meeting point?" I worked my jaw again in having to talk aloud to myself, juggling with my sanity. My eyes fell down to the remains of my first victim.

Of course. It wasn't enough to take a life when you could also rifle the pockets of the deceased for anything of value. Although, whatever manner of valuables a living ball of slime might hold was as clear to me as was if they even had a soul to begin with. *Everything in stride*, I reminded myself.

As I crouched down beside the damp patch of mud and grass, I was somewhat surprised, but entirely whelmed to find that instead of having to delve my fingers into the essence of the Monster, a blue box had appeared to ask if I did indeed want to loot the body. My finger hovered in the air and somehow selected the confirmation of my intent.

[1 Gold]
[Slime Gel (1)]

"I suppose I could take it all. The Slime doesn't need it anymore." Text notifications filtered down through the side of my vision to inform that the ill-gotten proceeds were deposited in my Inventory.

Part of me assumed I would be getting some form of experience for my part in ending the near-defenseless Monster's life. Nothing had overtly pressed itself into my tiring eyes, but it was a decent assumption if I were to level. I seemed to have a firm grasp on things, which was more worrying than anything—not because I would prefer to be floundering in the new world, but because it only meant that harsher encounters would surely be leveled my way if I was doing well.

With a shrug, I returned to the task at hand—moving north toward the location my quest required of me. It was not long before I came across a second, then third, Slime and each one equally fell from a single thrown card. The fourth Slime I completely missed, and I almost died—of embarrassment—as the hapless creature just beamed up at me as if it wanted to be adopted. Cuteness didn't seem to be an evolutionary trait that was working out well for it today.

By the sixth Slime, I stopped to stretch out my fingers. It would have been nice of the System to allow me to function with the granted skills without getting cramps or throwing out my elbow—but perhaps these were just growing pains. I bent over, with a sigh, to loot this felled foe.

[2 Gold]
[Slime Gel (1)]
[Unidentified gloves]

"That's something new." I tilted my head.

Perhaps it was about time I investigated one of my other menus. Inventory popped up to show a grid of squares—two of which were filled. A stack of six pieces of slime and the newly acquired gloves. Gold seemed to just add to a counter—of which I now was the proud owner of ten pieces. How unusual to have things stored in this intangible space—although perhaps it was the same kind of magic flowing through the deck of cards?

[Identify?]

Without the necessary skill to do this on the regular, the System gave me a reminder that I could only identify uncommon items at my level or below. The green box around the gloves apparently indicated the rarity. A short bar of arbitrary time sped across my vision, and the task was complete—the briefest of jingles accompanying the successful process.

[Basic Gloves: +1 DEX]

Basic seemed a bit mean. Certainly, as I withdrew them from the two-dimensional space to pull onto my hands, they weren't ornate or expertly made . . . but they were functional and almost fit with my outfit. Dexterity would help with <Sleight of Hand>, so it's not like I could complain.

"Getting the hang of this now. Soon I'll be—"

I stopped mid-sentence as the sound of snapping twigs caught my attention. Coming from my left now, it was something bigger and heavier than a Slime.

Multiple footsteps and murmured voices.

My right eye twitched as I placed my fingers atop the card deck. Surely they wouldn't be foes? Most likely other . . . Players? The word felt odd even though that was what the System had called me. My heartbeat started to rise and thrum in my ears as the footfalls grew closer. Something potentially worse than adoring fans.

Muscles tensing, I stepped forward as two silhouettes came into view.

CHAPTER FIVE

First Audience

First impressions were everything, I knew this well. Especially in a world where violence was part of the populace's love language. In all my time here, despite the friends and enemies I had made (and the countless crushed beneath the weight of my self-deluded destiny) I still never really forgot the first people I had met. A quaint and amusing interaction viewed through the rose-tinted glasses on the other side of the mountain of trauma I now sat. At the time, however . . .

I paused as I stood out in the open, opposite the two approaching figures—both of them now mirrors of my awkward surprise.

Both of them male, mid- to late twenties if I were to guess—which I currently was. The first looked like he had spent most of his youth in brazen affront to the sun and had a deep tan that aged him beyond the life in his eyes. He wore a simple tunic of gray with a green waistcoat over the top—the color matching a headscarf covering light-brown hair and baggy slacks covering his modesty.

The second had leather armor in a rich brown color, well-worn but sturdy, over a deep-crimson undershirt. His black beard and shaved head drew contrast to his bright-green eyes. They appeared to be armed with melee weapons and held them in a casual manner that didn't seem any less threatening to me—the idiot standing there holding a pack of playing cards.

"Oh, who are you?" The man in green tilted his head, unsure of what to make of me.

"I am Max, the magician." I bowed—perhaps a foolish act, unless I wanted to invite a blunt object to open my cranium. The hope was that I could disarm them with my charm or the minute chance they had heard of me from the world I had once come from.

As I rose, the pair exchanged glances. I hadn't yet been informed by the System of whether Player-on-Player violence was even possible, let alone encouraged, but the looks in their eyes were a better tutorial than any floating bit of text. To them, I was perhaps no different than the Slimes.

"You're just level one, yeah?" Red asked me, almost on the verge of licking his lips, his intent being clear in his expression.

I nodded, considering what would make me look like less of an appetizing dish. "Still in the midst of learning what is on the inside of Slimes."

Once again, they exchanged a glance, and any tension held deflated as apprehension turned into annoyance.

"Not worth the trouble for a handful of gold," Green hissed at Red.

Curiosity got the better of me. I yearned for more knowledge to fill in the blanks, and it was only the dim view of my own abilities that stopped me from cracking their heads open to absorb everything they knew from their juicy brains. Metaphorically, of course. Monsters were one thing, but I hadn't yet signed up to being a murderer in this strange world.

"What level are you both, gentlemen?" I shot a pleasant smile and tried to look vacant, in the hope of appearing simple and less of a threat.

"Three," Red said plainly.

I worked my jaw, the wrong dialogue option worming its way from my mind. "So, are you purposefully searching out low levels to kill for easy loot, or is our meeting just an unfortunate circumstance?"

A two-level deficit might not mean much, or they might shrug off my attacks as if they *were* made of thrown cardboard. I narrowed my eyes as they chewed on their response . . . to see if they had easily accessible necks.

"Talking a lot of shit for a freshy." Red spat onto the grass.

"We don't need to kill easy marks, but we're opportunists." Green grinned, clearly proud about their pragmatism and more of a talker than the rougher Red. "Not everyone finds it easy to level, so we take what power we can."

I understood this, to a degree. Depending on how the world functioned, that might even be a very smart viewpoint. If you had to eke out any advantage to stay alive and functioning, then a little punching down at the expense of your morals made sense. Not that I agreed at this juncture.

Judging by the cute faces upon the Slimes and the vibrancy of my surroundings, it didn't appear to be that kind of world. Which meant these two gentlemen were nothing if not merciless killers. No doubt I wasn't their first mark. Whatever death led to in the System, I was not so keen to find out. Not enough answers to fully flesh out how I should feel about the pair. So far, they didn't look too keen on receiving my autograph.

There was a coldness in their eyes, the more they waited and stared at me. The realization that they might just be patrolling the area and I may run into them again in the near future—perhaps after the System had fattened me up a little—sank uncomfortably into my stomach. They would become my problem for certain if I didn't grow stronger, and quickly.

My thoughts echoed around my skull. I wasn't about to offer myself up to the wolves, but I would be selling myself short to continue to be unprepared. If they did crop up again in my adventures and wanted to try their luck—well, I hoped the System looked more favorably on self-defense.

"Understandable." I eventually nodded with a smile. "Well, don't let me keep you from your business—there're Slimes calling out for me to silence them."

"Right." Red nodded, his face twisting into some confused acceptance of my dismissal. "C'mon, Pozza, let's go find some business to attend to."

"*Business.*" Green grinned, an overtly obvious wink to his companion, the addition to his slobbering comment thick with their true intention.

Utilizing a strength brought from my previous life, I managed to hold a polite grin as they wandered off. After their footfalls and murmured chuckles eventually faded into the distance, I exhaled and deflated.

The decision came rattling through my tiring body—I did *not* like the pair. Somehow, I could sense my magic deck didn't either. It wouldn't do well to make enemies so soon, and perhaps there was another way I could win them over . . . but the prospect of having to go against them in combat chilled the part of me that just wanted their acceptance.

I shook my nerves off. Their unsaid threats had left a sour taste to the day, and I found myself annoyed at the supposed System I was now a prisoner of. "Seems underwhelming not to have some concise conclusion to an encounter," I murmured, perhaps still trying to fill an invisible audience in on my inner thoughts. I assured myself that becoming a corpse so soon would be an even more underwhelming outcome for both me and the world yet to bask upon a single show of mine.

My eyes rolled at my constant need to perform, but I had long accepted it. I wanted a sizable slice of this new pie, but biting off more than I could chew would leave me crushed by a weight I could no longer carry. Pick each battle as it came. Right now my equals seemed to be balls of contented gel—although they did die in only one hit.

I began my journey to the designated point once more—thankfully a different direction than my potential murderers—and happened by enough of the level-one Monsters to fulfill my quota. In fact, ever the overachiever, I slew another four along my travels. Mostly in the hope that they would drop me something more useful than money and goo—but it seemed I had used up all my luck in avoiding having my level-one brain cracked from my skull like an egg.

The surrounding trees thinned as I stepped out into a small clearing. A handful of wooden tables, ripe for a prepared picnic, sat sporadically in the space. Empty, save for the sparse dusting of loose green leaves from the surrounding canopy.

A noticeboard stood proud across the other side of the space, a name spelled out in bold beige text against the dark wood.

Greenrest, it announced.

Nothing immediately happened as I stood at the edge of the tree line. Perhaps my nerves were still a little on edge, and I had expected some manner of trap. That would be rather rude of the System to lure me into danger so soon into our relationship. It should at least butter me up with some undue powers first.

Clearly, I just needed to step closer. Maybe vocalizing this knowledge would settle my confusion. "I fully intend to go read the noticeboard and accept my ready reward for diligently murdering innocent creatures as demanded . . ." I rubbed at my forehead, still pretty sore from my rough arrival. There was just some apprehension, part of my gut hesitant to stride into the open so naively. Still, a fading hope that another doorway would spring up to take me home, or I'd wake from a coma into my more grounded life of illusion and show lights.

This had been my first step into the new world, and it was already lined with blood and corpses. Not quite what I had imagined, actually—but enough of a sobering thought that it prompted me to step forward. The grass didn't immediately immolate me, and assassins from the shadows didn't step forth to fill me with arrows and regret. Small victories. There wasn't even the sense of being watched, which was almost underwhelming, as if the System was going off script.

[Quest complete]
[10/10 Slimes killed. Location reached.]
[Receive Reward?]

I clicked the yes that was marked in green, as if I needed visual confirmation to do the right thing. Good brain, time for dopamine.

[Experience gained]
[30 Gold]
[Adventurer's Kit (3)]
[Health Potion (1)]

The items filtered into my intangible Inventory. More things to investigate and allow the knowledge to sink into me. In fact, I would have started immediately—if not for the System message on my wrist pulsing a golden glow. It would be rude to ignore it, so gingerly I reached out to press down.

[Level up—<2>]
[Stats increased]

[New Ability: <Summon Demon>]
[New Passive: <Mana Manipulation>]
[New Passive: <Demonic Magic>]

"Demons . . ." My thought process halted as I felt atop my head to where I was now apparently wearing a purple top hat. I lifted it down, a frown across my brow. I was sure I had left this behind with the rock. No, I had picked it back up—my brain seemed to be playing catch-up still.

It seemed natural enough to just dig my hand straight in—and I was rewarded by feeling . . . Well, nothing at this stage. Clearly I would have to do some magic the old-fashioned way if I were to woo and wow my way across the land. Where I would find the necessary equipment in what appeared to be a fantasy universe, I wasn't so sure.

Destiny. That's how I viewed it. Knowing that this was a completely different world didn't make my desires waver. The greatest showman across worlds—as soon as I had my bearings and some slice of civilization before me, I could perform once more. *The show would go on*, and I would be fulfilling my due purpose. The fact that my current skills might help me along that path was a boon rather than a distraction.

Exhaling through my nose, I brought up some of the information in the Skills window.

<Demonic Magic> seemed pretty straightforward, in that it allowed me proficiency or access to said school of magic. Similar to my already held Illusion Magic. Being a magician in my former life, one made more sense for me to have than the other, but apparently the System knew what it was doing. Perhaps something about the book had been dragged along for the ride after all?

<Mana Manipulation> allowed me . . . some manner of leeway with how I used my magic and the Mana used to power it. That was about as vague a description as I could imagine. At this stage, there was no explanation of what Mana or magic really was, so being able to manipulate it seemed as useful as being a Slime whisperer. Being that it was a Passive Skill, I was sure it would perhaps crop up during normal proceedings.

For <Summon Demon>, the flickering box of blue was a lot more information-heavy. I brought up the skill description and glazed over the duration and Mana requirements to note that I had two options that appeared as bonus passive abilities—a melee-focused Hellhound and a ranged support Imp. I could only have one out at a time.

No rabbit to pull from my hat yet. But the ability to bring forth hellish animals out of supposedly nowhere tickled me in a way that warmed my distant memories. I almost wished that I had an audience ready to test it out—but at least the System had made good on the earlier Class designation.

With a smile, I spun the menus around, feeling better about myself. "I guess I am a *Summoner* now, then."

"Oh, you're a Summoner, are you?" a familiar voice crooned from the tree line behind me.

CHAPTER SIX

Showstopping Entrance

Death would become a close companion on my adventures, in more ways than one. Taking the lives of monsters seemed vaguely guilt free even from the outset and would only numb with time. Avoiding my own demise was a rough road of occasional spikes that my boots were barely thick enough to tread through without some trauma. Taking the lives of other Players . . . Now that was something that still clings to my soul to this day, even as common as it became. A weight that would one day drag me to the depths if I allowed it.

I turned my head slowly and was not surprised to see the pair of Red and Green now standing at the mouth of the pathway that I had entered the clearing from. They were both slouched against trees, twinkles in their eyes now that they had found a morsel worth the risk. Perhaps I'd now learned the lesson of not speaking my thoughts out loud. Externalizing the process made it feel like I was pandering to an unseen crowd, but it looked like the current attendees had tickets for a different kind of show. A lesson hard learned for yours truly.

"Back so soon?" I asked with eyebrow raised as I glanced briefly at the empty clearing around me to see if there was an easy escape. No.

"We knew something was up with you," Red offered as they pushed themselves from their stoops and took their first steps into the clearing.

"Not just your smart tongue neither," Green added.

"And a Summoner always has a special item they use for their skills. Quite valuable usually."

Green licked his lips. *"Always."*

Their intentions laid bare. Part of me grew colder and steadfast. I held my hand up as they approached. "No closer."

They stopped, but even wider grins crossed their faces. Red drew a sword, and Green unhooked some kind of cudgel from his belt. Their next steps were written clear as day across their faces.

Unsure as to where my confidence had come from, I was more worried about how the System saw Player-on-Player violence, rather than questioning whether my life was at stake. Did I need to wait for them to make the first move to be seen as the aggressors? I doubted it took nuance into account.

I drew a card from my deck as their bodies tensed up, ready. It had a picture on it that I had never seen on a usual playing card—a dog of crimson fire. My arm extended to show them the small rectangle, and a circle of red started to spiral into existence in front of me.

<Summon Demon: Hellhound>.

A burst of red flame waylaid the assault of the two briefly surprised men as the demon crawled into existence. With the appearance of a Doberman who seemed to be constantly on fire, the beast then crouched down and growled at the assailants.

Red looked to be a duelist of some sort, intending to be the beater, while Green could flank and get opportune strikes in. Neither could be particularly skilled at only a level above me now but used the advantage of numbers to prey on the weak.

How my mangled brain managed to glean and scrawl that information into my skull so quickly, I did not know. The last true struggle I can remember was getting into my slacks before they had to be readjusted. Holiday season was hell. I wasn't sure I could even command my summon to do anything—but I at least thought really hard about what action I wanted it to take.

Attack the one in green while I deal with red.

Whether by chance or because it was how this actually worked, my demon started to angle toward facilitating my plan. I threw out a card at the man in red clothing, the purple energy of my magic scoring through the air as it struck him in the chest—leaving a brief mark across his leather.

"Ha! Maybe not so valuable after all." He grinned, briefly looking down to see the lack of damage sustained. "But now we'll kill you anyway."

He raised his sword as he sprinted toward me, brief panic shuddering through me at my lack of defenses. Green and the Hellhound were facing off, frustration in the man's face at not being able to assist his duo partner as my summon kept him at bay with the threat of sharp jaws.

How best to avoid a sword swing? I was woefully unprepared. I neither had the Agility to really dodge, nor anything sturdy enough to hold in the way of the blade. Accepting my fate seemed like a poor choice, but there wasn't a lot of illusion in my back pocket to deflect a sharpened hunk of metal.

His attack was heavily telegraphed, the intention to slam the sharp edge of his weapon straight into my torso almost so clear and to the point that he could have told me prior. I leaned away from it as my right hand went up, a handful of Slime Gel thrown and obscuring his vision just as his strike landed. The angle of his distracted slash was enough to bite through my suit and into my chest but not cut too deep.

"Asshole," he growled, wiping away the gel with the back of his arm. Enough time for me to withdraw a card. There was a rustle of leaves behind me. Hopefully a spooked wild animal and not a third Player come to knock my brains in.

At this short distance, I didn't have much choice where to fling it other than straight at him. With my hound tying up the other thug, I would only have a couple of chances before things turned in the favor of the one with an actual weapon. The purple light flicked out toward him as he stabilized himself, and he raised his sword to block the projectile. Illuminating the blade, the card hissed as it slid from the weapon and scored a line of crimson along the back of his forearm.

Not enough damage. He grimaced through the pain and lashed out with the hilt to punch at me. My arms raised, and I blocked it. Numbness flooded down my left forearm as I staggered backward. His eyes were now aglow with a predatory malice. With a flourish, his sword took on a red sheen. His body tensed, and then he leaped toward me.

The sound of air being cut tore through the clearing, a sharp sound moving at speed ever nearer to my position. I saw Red's eyes widen as I watched the glowing sword curve down toward me. The flash of pain across his face came as a shock to us both. He looked past me as his attack faltered and the color drained from his sword just as quickly as it did from his face.

A figure dropped down from one of the trees just to the back of me and rolled across the grass. In my peripheral, I saw them bring a bow up and pull back another arrow.

"Shit, it's that crazy bitch!" Green yelled. "Run!"

Red stumbled before me, falling short of introducing me to his blade as he looked down at the arrow lodged in his side. There was anger in his eyes as he looked back up at me but also indecision—this close to his quarry and yet having to escape. But *could* he escape now?

He would certainly try. His own life in this moment was worth more than whatever possessions I may hold.

Green stumbled over my Hellhound as he went to make his escape. In desperation, he tried to bat the demon away, but instead the dog latched on to his outstretched arm, tugging at his sleeve. Red turned from me and made the movements to run, but his body had become sluggish and unresponsive. The pulse of radiant energy flared across the clearing from the intruding figure to my right, and a glowing golden arrow struck the leather-armored man in the head, embedding through the back of his skull.

I may not have known much about how this System worked, but I knew that getting a solid object through the brain was a short sentence. Punctuated by death. Ah, my introspection was still a little rusty. For what was only a few short seconds, I had become a magician's rabbit caught in the stage lights and had barely moved an inch, yet bore fewer wounds from my indecision than was expected.

As my hound pulled on the man, blood ran down his hands as the demon found purchase—and then I saw it, the perfect opening. My hand touched the deck, and then a purple card was in the air, spinning almost as if in slow motion across the clearing.

Much greater than fifteen feet, but the card continued despite going beyond the signaled limitations. A twinge of pain ran down my fingers. Yet I watched, almost as though my will guided the projectile, as it slit across the man's exposed throat while he was busy trying to wrench away from the Hellhound. A crimson line grew from where the purple energy faded away.

Not an especially deep cut, but his shock caused him to grasp at the wound by reflex, allowing the demon to assail him unhindered. After tearing a shred from his arm, it leaped and latched on to his bloodied neck, the crunch of his windpipe soon following gurgles as he slumped to the ground, the hound growling all the while.

I turned to raise an eyebrow at my supposed savior to see if I was about to receive a pointed hello as well—but also to avoid having to stare at my demon eating through the freshly served corpse. Even if I was no stranger to violence in my previous life . . . one of my previous lives . . . it didn't mean I had to take any joy in it. Part of me knew I was contented by it. The thugs had chosen their part to play in the show, and although I wasn't center stage for the performance, their display had been admirable.

The figure stood up to scowl at me.

An . . . elfin woman, if what I knew about fantasy tropes held any weight. Radiant blonde hair and piercing blue eyes. Her leather armor of muted forest tones was padded and muddied—some leaves and errant twigs still stuck to it after bursting from her hiding place. I had not seen an elf before, of course, but from the pointy ears and other context clues, I felt confident at my assumption. Although, I never imagined them having so much tangible disdain to express.

"I owe you my thanks." I bowed. "Max, at your service."

"Manners don't get you anywhere in this life." She crossed her arms and glared at me, undeterred by my attempt to escape her ire.

"Perhaps not, but they are still freely given." I smiled, despite the daggers she continued to stare at me. Not aggressive—but still growing tired of my presence. A tough crowd, but I'd had a few in my life previously. "What do I call you, Miss . . ."

"I'd rather you didn't at all." She huffed and glanced over at my hound chewing through the would-be assassins. Sliding right past my question, she instead leveled her own statement. "Summoners *are* pretty rare."

As much as I wanted to take that as a compliment, that sounded much more like a warning. Surely if these two louts happened to want to pry my magic item from my cold dead hands, then they wouldn't be the only ones. The elf was hard to read at first, with the constant scowl, but she didn't seem interested in what I had. Or I would have been next on the list to be filled with an arrow. Something I was even less prepared to defend against.

Eventually I relented, as she didn't seem keen to fill more of the empty space in the conversation. "Apparently so. Worth killing over, it seems."

"A lot of things are; a lot of things aren't." She remained staring at my summon as if lost in some thought.

It would be nice to have an almost-friendly face show me the ropes, although it looked like it would be a hard sell. If I could gain some information, that would be the second-best thing, so I took my shot at the risk of annoying her away. "Why were you in the tree waiting for them?"

"They would have seen me if I were sitting at a table." She rolled her eyes and turned back to me. "Assholes have been a problem around here for a bit, so staking out some of the first Quest objectives seemed like the best way to catch them in the act."

"And they recognized you?"

"I'm not here to give you my life story, magic man." She sighed, her bright eyes burning through me. The first step in our parlay was reached, as she begrudgingly relented her name to me. ". . . Ren."

I nodded politely, not wanting to give her reason to regret divulging that information. "I'm rather new here. Is it too presumptuous to ask someone's level?"

"Four." She looked as though she would cross her arms if she weren't already doing it. "I could be higher, but . . ." Briefly her mouth opened and closed before she shook her head.

A strong ally would be worth their weight in gold, whether I was aiming for fame or escape. She was the highest level I had seen so far and not only saved my life but was engaging in . . . tense conversation without wanting to put an arrow through my neck. Practically best friends.

"I won't pry," I attempted to reassure her. "But I was looking for a group to Quest with."

She shook her head. "I work alone."

There was an air of finality to the statement. She bore some weight for that decision, and I wondered if that was the cause of her prickly nature. "There must be something I can trade for information though?"

She eyed me up, searching me for something that may be worth her time. "You just got Adventurer's Kits, correct?"

"Something you wanted from them?" I hadn't had the chance to check with the interruption of the two thugs. "Just received three."

"Yeah . . ." The words seemed to be held back briefly. "There's a type of cake you can only get in them, and I haven't had one for ages." Rather than appear embarrassed, she simply scowled at me harder.

"I'll give you all I have if you tell me your story, or at least some information."

I couldn't tell whether the growl that emanated from her was because of her ire or her hungry stomach's anticipation of the snack she craved. Her jaw worked in trying to decide if it was worth her time.

"Fine." She finally relented. "But the first time you interrupt me—I walk away."

With a grin, I spun open my Inventory window. "Deal."

CHAPTER SEVEN

Magic Words

Friendship was something that didn't come easily to me, despite the charm and manners I liked to ply to most that I met. I had been solitary in my life before. But this world required actual firm connections, not only to survive the horrors and challenges of the System's design, but also to retain your sanity and will to go on. Some relationships weren't meant to be. Betrayal or differing paths separating those that were once close. And some stood the test of time, became pillars of who I was, of who I needed to be to ascend.

We sat down at one of the benches opposite each other. She rested her bow beside her and caught me giving it a once-over.

"Rare." Her singularly worded sentence was meant to fill me in with all the questions I hadn't asked.

It looked nice, and I hadn't seen a bow in the flesh for . . . maybe a decade? It was hard to remember where or when I had actually last set eyes on one, but it had definitely not looked as well-made or ornate as Ren's. A vibrant wood with blue-and-silver detailing, small shapes resembling flowers in bloom along the body of the weapon.

Not wanting to frustrate the elf further, I swung through my Inventory to check out the Adventurer's Kits. They seemed to be some sort of pack that I was able to open from within this nether space, which seemed handier than making a mess all over the table. I tapped the Open All pop-up.

[45 Gold]
[Rope (2)]
[Bandage (4)]
[Random Armor Box (3)]
[Sweet Cake (6)]

"I received five cakes." I smiled at her.

"That's pretty lucky." Her resolve briefly faltered before her eyes narrowed at me again. "I think the drop is zero to two per kit."

I chose to ignore the rest of the items for now and focus on the problem that lay before me. Information needed gathering. "I'll give you three now and then the other two depending on how much I like your story."

"What?" She bared her teeth. "That wasn't part of the deal."

"I realize now I have the advantage in bargaining power, and the house always wins." I smiled and withdrew three of the cakes, amused to see the elf with a plate at the ready before her mouth could argue any further. They were a simple pastry in an almost cylindrical shape with white icing along the top. She seemed eager enough to get a taste that my transgression could slide.

She exhaled from her nose. "Alright, close that trap. My side of the deal still stands. Interrupt me or disrupt my enjoyment of the cakes in any way and I'm leaving, shrewd ass." She pulled the full plate toward her as she struggled to keep eye contact with me.

I nodded and allowed her the space she required.

The elf picked up the first cake in silence and bit into it. I averted my gaze to watch the Hellhound, now content with whatever it was able to eat from the fallen assailant, patter over to me. It sat on the ground beside me and whined.

Unsure what it really wanted, I patted it on the head and rubbed around its jaw. In my previous life, I had only had a few animal companions in my shows over the years. Some days, it was hard enough for me to stand before the lights and raucous cheers. I didn't want to force that on others who didn't have as much choice as I deluded myself into believing I had.

"It doesn't burn you?" Ren asked, peering over the table as she was onto the second cake.

I hadn't thought much about it, but I suppose it didn't for whatever reason. The hound still flickered in dark crimson as if he was permanently alight, and other than some human gore wetting my hand, I felt nothing. With a glance at the elf, I shook my head.

"You can answer direct questions."

"No, just feels like a normal dog." As I withdrew my hand from him, an arcane circle spun up underneath him, and he faded away into mist. None of the dogs I had known had done that before, but from an outside perspective, I had maybe played similar illusions. That gave me *ideas*.

I frowned up at the thought of the System I was now bound by. I had some questions for it when I wasn't so otherwise engaged and could find some manner of putting the words forth somewhere that would get me an answer. Another time perhaps.

Ren picked up the third cake and wagged it at me. "Why do you keep looking up into the air?"

"Thinking about how I can learn new tricks."

She narrowed her eyes. "You mean Abilities?"

"Those too." I rubbed at my chin as she continued to scowl, perhaps trying to decide if I had suffered some kind of concussion . . . I now realized that my visible head wound was on her side in regard to that idea. Silence fell between us as she tried to read my vacant face.

"Alright." She took a bite of the long cake and deflected with a sigh. "I came here a while back through a portal of pink energy. My memory is hazy. Nothing unique there, right?" She raised an accusatory eyebrow at me. "Probably similar to your own story? That seems to be the common theme for all the Players."

I nodded slowly. I couldn't fully remember the circumstance that led me to entering a portal, and the thought that this place was some melting pot of people who stumbled into the wrong dimensional doorway was odd. Like a net being dragged through the pond of existence.

"There's a reason why I'm still level four—and those two mangled corpses are part of it." She pointed the nub of the end of the cake toward Red and Green. "They were part of a gang who . . . are a problem here. So I've been trying to track them down and kill them. They deserve it, believe me."

She put the last of the cake into her mouth and paused to savor it. She closed her eyes and exhaled through her nose. "Hard to get Adventurer's Kits often." She returned to scowling at me, possibly remembering I had two more waiting if she gave me sufficient information. "Thing is, once you hit level five, you're out of here." She jerked a thumb backward.

Out of here seemed pretty vague, and the twist of excitement in my stomach was soon quelled when my sensible brain considered she meant the area rather than the System itself.

"This place is called New Forest." She rolled her eyes at the basic name. "It's a small island for the newcomers to get to grips with the System and world. Then the Quest at five takes you over to the main island."

I nodded again and bit my tongue. If she leveled up, then she would be whisked away from her revenge plot, and there would probably be no way of getting back. I admired the tenacity.

"With these two in the ground, it still leaves eight alive. Might sound like I've been resting on my laurels, huh?" She narrowed her eyes at me.

Despite it being a direct question, I shook my head to be on the safe side.

She paused briefly, as if trying to recall the taste of the cakes—or perhaps deliberating on whether she should even be sharing this information with me. "It's difficult, as they don't often travel alone, and the System isn't well-balanced for Player-on-Player attacks. It gets deadly, *very* quick."

Most likely why she was waiting and using me as bait. A little illusory trick where the true ploy was playing out in secret while all eyes were upon me.

"So I take what I can get, no matter how long I have to spend. I . . . appreciate your help even if you weren't party to the decision, and . . . I also appreciate the cakes." She crossed her arms and glared out to the forest. It looked like she was ready to leave but was allowing me to get a word in first.

Oh, more likely she was waiting for the extra cakes. The plate sat empty before her even as her gaze was looking away as if trying to avoid the obvious. Certainly that was plenty of information—more than I had expected, and while she hadn't told me what the dirty dozen had done to earn her ire, some secrets were allowed. That was part of the magic.

"Fair trade. I thank you, Ren." From my Inventory I withdrew two further cakes and placed them on her plate. I then withdrew the final one for myself.

Her eyes went to her plate and then up to me. "Fucker. Either you're terrible at math or there's something going on behind that silver tongue."

I shrugged. "Life has enough hardships without hard words." I took a bite of the cake. Maybe it was just that I hadn't eaten since my arrival—but it *was* delightful.

Ren gave a brief snort. "Good, right? Can only get them in the kits on this island—and they're either a rare drop or from Quests."

"And you can do neither as you don't want to level."

She nodded, somehow already halfway through the second cake. "So, what about you?"

"Same really. Weird portal, loss of memory. Unique Class—"

"Unique Class?" She actually paused her meal to stare at me. "You're not bullshitting?"

I shook my head with a smile. "I'd never bullshit you, Ren."

Her scowl could have cut me in half. "You literally just did with the number of cakes, you asshole. Unique is . . . something though. I've seen a couple of Summoners but none with demons."

My cake was now finished, and I was somewhat sad I hadn't tilted the scales a little more in my favor. Still, I could now add finding more of them to my to-do list. "So my goal is to get as powerful as possible, put on a good show, and escape the System."

I was surprised that she nodded in return.

"You and most that come through here. Well, apart from the show bit. A few change their tune before even leaving this island, but I have no idea how good or bad life is on the mainland." She was finished with her cakes now and had stowed her plate back in her Inventory.

I worked my jaw. Never had I been very proficient at asking for help. Not that I *needed* help, as such—I was sure I was competent enough to overcome anything . . . But it took more than one person to run a show. I could use an assistant. Although, I made the mental note to never call her that.

Instead, I had to offer her something she wanted. "Would you like some help with killing the eight?" *Murder* was a foul word, but I would dazzle all into the grave if it meant I got to dance upon it rather than rest below it.

Although she looked antsy to leave, she raised an eyebrow. "I told you I work alone."

"I can bribe you with further cakes if you please, but I'm offering you a far greater meal in getting your revenge sooner. Wouldn't that be sweeter?"

Ren clicked her tongue. "What's in it for you, trickster?"

"It's simple, m—Ren." I stood and avoided calling her *my dear* in case I was added to her kill list. "Allow me to assist in your revenge and prove my worth as a combatant. When we reach the mainland, I would then ask you to consider joining my Party to adventure further if it suited your ambitions."

Her jaw was clenched, and she slowly exhaled through her nose. "I'm . . . still not sure why you'd want to . . ."

"I admire your tenacity and strong will, and you have great taste in cakes." A little honesty could go a long way, even if I was laying it on thick. Briefly, I wondered if the System considered this Deception—even if I was being earnest.

Ren rubbed at the bridge of her nose. "Fine. Can't believe you talked me into this, you ass. But I have some ground rules."

"Naturally." I nodded.

"First, all dropped loot is shared equally. Second, you have to pull your own weight—so get to level four before making promises you can't keep." She drummed her fingers on the wooden table. "And third, no flirting with me or I'll pin you to a tree."

I opened my mouth.

"*With an arrow.*"

"Got it." I grinned. My effective power had at least tripled with my new ally, and the prospect of carving a path through this world seemed all the more doable. I could almost see my name in lights from here, down in the mud.

"Try not to smile so much too." She sighed and shook her head. "If the System sees that you are too happy, it'll find a way to ruin your day."

I pressed at the notification to see which Quests I now had available to me, the light illuminating my wide smile.

"Well then." I shot a brief glance toward my displeased companion. "We'd best stock up on cakes to cheer us up from that eventuality."

She shook her head, but her expression didn't seem to disagree. "What we need to do is go loot those two." Her eyes gestured over to the corpses I had a hand in creating.

It was something inevitable that I hadn't really let sink in so far. Sure, it stood to reason that Players could be looted the same as the Monsters I had been erasing from this world, but there was a thin curtain of my prior morality that dimmed my view of the process.

[32 Gold]
[Leather Bracers]
[Apple (1)]
[Bandage (4)]

I stopped for a moment, looking down at the shocked face with an arrow in the back of his head. There was an uncomfortable feeling, and not just because the System didn't seem to allow me to strip him completely. Perhaps it would be even more uncomfortable if I could. As much as I could have spent hours deliberating over what was worth taking, I chose to be pragmatic and not delay the elf further.

"Here." She stood from the thug with the torn-out throat. "Some linen trousers with damage absorption. You'll need that."

The sinking feeling in my stomach told me that was underselling the truth.

CHAPTER EIGHT

Sorry to Boar

The System liked to be . . . inconsistent when it came to how much danger a Quest should be for you. While the beginner ones were meant to hold your hand, once you had moved beyond the safety of the more pleasant climates it cared less about your well-being. Were the rewards even worth it? The number of things that were worth what I had endured on my travels was a short list. But those few may have well been chiseled in stone for how they kept me grounded.

D o you always breathe so loudly?"

I frowned at the elf. Sure, the trek through the woods on to the next Quest had been a bit more cardio than I was apparently used to—but I did have magician Stats, after all. Or something to that effect.

While the churlish nature of my companion had been amusing at first, the fact that her mood had gone unchanged was edging it closer to being worrying. While I was usually unflappable on a good day, the near-endless scowl of the supposed Ranger was having me doubt myself.

"The world I am from has a different atmosphere. I am still adjusting." I gave her a shrug.

"Do you always bullshit too?" She rolled her eyes and looked off into the distant woods.

I took a moment to consider the question. If I were honest with myself, then certainly—it seemed I was liable to lie or bend the truth to wiggle free of social discomfort—but there wasn't a malicious intent to it. Just part of my charms . . . which is something I at least believed I had, even if reality hadn't caught up to that fact.

"Are you always so grumpy?" Not the best example of my alleged charm.

"I am." She stopped and looked up at me. "Is that a problem?"

"Not really. I just wanted to make sure it was your default state and not an error of my making." I gave my best try at a polite smile.

"You're annoying, but it's not you. As self-centered as that makes you sound." She sighed and shrugged. "Pa always told me I had the temperament of a dwarf rather than an elf."

I barely remembered much beyond a small handful of things I had been. My father was . . . someplace not often present. "You remember much about your parents?"

Ren bit her lip, and her eyes unfocused, as if trying to reach inside her mind for the memories. "Occasionally. It's foggy and comes and goes." She snapped out of it and scowled at me. "Boars are nearby, trickster."

For all the confusion rolling around in the back of my mind, I was pretty sure I had parents too. Seemed natural. Something about a house . . . Lots of magic. A white rabbit . . . I knew I didn't like pigs, for whatever reason, and was slightly pleased that the next batch of murders the System commanded of me was to kill ten Boars.

Just two more levels and then we'd work on Ren's personal Quest. I had signed up for actual murder with little complaint, despite only hearing one side of the story. Was it because I owed the elf my life? Or because she had such conviction about the task? Maybe I didn't feel someone so easily won over by sweet pastry could have ill intent. Definitely wasn't those bright-blue eyes that drew me in.

"There." Ren pointed out to a clearing a few dozen feet out. Three Boars stood around, snuffling at the ground. "Two will flee when you attack one. I can't do much as I don't want to get any experience."

"Understood." I nodded. I rifled through my magic deck, and it seemed to be normal cards at first. No interesting pictures like when I had summoned a demon. This time, I would probably give the Imp a try.

"What are you doing?" Ren crossed her arms.

"Just wondering things. Are the demons I summon the same ones every time, or different?" I hummed and tapped my fingers at the top of the deck, as if an answer could resonate through it.

"What do *you* think?" Ren was tapping her foot now, clearly unimpressed about missing out on half the conversation I was having with myself.

"It's likely it's a different demon every time, but I suppose I'll know for sure once I use the ability more."

"Hmm." She nodded and relaxed her posture, looking back at the Boars ahead of us.

Perhaps she just wanted to know how things worked too or had a vested interest in demonology. Or dogs.

I narrowed my eyes and crept forward, unsure as to how close I could get without attracting the attention of the Monsters. The Slimes had been content enough to hop up to me as if we were friends, but I doubted things would be that easy going forward.

[New Monster: Boar <2>]

My hand drew a card from the deck—one with a picture of a spherical demon of crimson with a little pitchfork and pointy tail. I held it aloft and cast the spell.

<Summon Demon: Imp>.

An arcane circle swirled by my feet as the foot-and-a-half-tall Imp crawled out from hell. Much like the picture on the card, he had ruddy skin and was almost comically round in shape. Ears, nose, horns, and tail were all pointy in contrast—although he didn't hold a pitchfork.

"Alright, champ. We have some little piggies to cook." I gave him a nod, and he returned the gesture with a hint of excitement in his beady eyes.

I drew a purple rectangle for <Pick a Card> and held it ready. Despite the skill description having a fifteen-foot listed range, I seemed to be able to throw it almost double that. Perhaps it was more of an effective range than a hard limit. Testing would need to be done, and I had a feeling <Mana Manipulation> had something to do with it. The Imp watched me, waiting to see which target I would strike.

With a flick of my arm, my wrist snapped the card through the air—a slight arc to it as it curved past two trees and sliced along the flank of one of the grazing Boars. It turned to me with pain and anger in its eyes, as the two other beasts sprinted off in different directions in panic.

The Imp started gathering energy, creating a small fireball between his tiny hands. As I drew a second purple card, the flame was thrown forth toward the charging Boar. The bright amber of the fire attack left a glow across the forest floor before it struck the creature straight in the face.

With a shriek, the Boar stumbled, blinded by the burn across its face. Just enough distraction for my thrown card to strike it dead center in the skull—piercing it with a sharp crack. The creature took another step and then flopped over heavily.

"What was your plan if it got into melee range?" The scouring tone of Ren came from behind me.

"Probably get gored and spill out all that freshly eaten cake from my punctured insides." I turned my head back to her and wasn't surprised to find my casual attitude didn't soften her sharp edges.

She rolled her eyes. "You'll have to take things a little more seriously if you're going to help me."

While it was nice to hear again that she had accepted my help, I didn't feel it prudent to espouse my feelings on the benefit of having a joyous take on life, to deal with the rather ridiculous world I now found myself in. Instead, I just gave her a nod and turned to walk over to my prey.

[Progress: 1/10 Boars. 0/5 Boar Meats.]

"I can definitely see a lot of meat on this little piggy." I frowned toward my Imp, who had come to stand beside me and inspect the corpse as well. "How do you even quantify *five meats?*" It looked like two or three meats to me.

"It's a specific drop." Ren followed up behind us and leaned against a tree. "I realize how bizarre it is, believe me. You'd think you could just butcher and cook up the Boar as it is, and *you can*, but for the Quest, you need the specific Inventory-item drop."

I looked at the slot in between its eyes where my attack had struck it through the brain. "Well, we will just have to get lucky with the bacon, then." I gave the Imp a pat on the head. "Well done, bud."

One of the two boars that had run off had settled not too far from me. Rather unrealistic, I thought—although my knowledge of actual boars was probably rather limited. My fingers drew a card, and I held it briefly to feel the power of it. The magic had a vibration to it that I was manipulating with my ability. Perhaps if my Passive Skill was the cause of the extended range, I could do even more with that. If I could only work out how to make a show of it . . .

The card zipped through the air, swerving around a tree just before hitting the Boar. With the spark of fire, we played out the same couple of attacks for this Boar, and then two others. Each one fell from a card-fireball-card combo. Satisfyingly consistent—just like all good magic should be.

My Imp turned to me and waved a thin little arm at me, as an arcane circle started to glow around his feet. I gave him a quick bow as he descended into mist.

[Progress: 4/10 Boars. 1/5 Boar Meats.]

"Finally." I checked my Inventory to see the icon of some well-butchered Boar meats. "Hope the drop rate picks up."

"Did you open your random boxes yet?" Ren again hovered in the background, arms folded.

"Are they worth it?" I stood and brushed my suit down. "I already look pretty snazzy."

She rolled her eyes. "Don't be dense. Armor has Stats and actual defensive bonuses. Your . . . suit is just cosmetic."

"I did find gloves with Dexterity on them." I looked at my hands with furrowed brow in the realization that it didn't look like I was actually wearing them.

Seems there was both an equipment set that you could gain stats from and one that was on show. "Alright." I gave her a smile. "You've convinced me."

Fingers on the menus, I opened up the Inventory again to check the boxes. Knowing my luck, I might just get another three pairs of gloves. Open All saved me some intangible-button pressing.

[Basic Leather Boots]
[Basic Leather Boots]
[Basic Cloth Helm]

"I am thoroughly whelmed." I gave Ren a shrug as I equipped the various things that didn't even have Stats on them. It wouldn't let me put two pairs of boots on, or one of each—which was almost as disappointing as just getting only common-rarity gear.

"The rates are terrible, but you're slightly further away from having your intestines gored out."

"Now I'm truly living." I smiled out at the forest. Part of me hoped she would at least attempt to save me if it came to that—she couldn't be *totally* on the cusp of leveling out of being on the island.

With a stretch, I allowed myself a yawn. I wasn't sure what time of day I had arrived in this world, but it now looked to be in the postnoon period of sunshine. Assuming the sun rose and sank like in my previous world. Still, things had been more tiring here, with violence being the main activity. The socializing had been a strain as well.

"There's another Quest after this one, then you'll level up again most likely."

I couldn't wait. Despite the spot the cake had hit in my empty stomach, I was hungry for something greater. The desire for more power had sunk in behind my eyes, and the promise of furthering my demonic abilities was almost enough to put a spring in my step. Even more so because it would annoy Ren.

Doubly so, as ideas were popping in the back of my brain for ways to use my new Abilities as tricks in my next show. I'd need a pen and paper to really scour my intent into being, so the invention was on pause until we had rest in some town or city. Things seemed to be looking up for me, and I couldn't wait for what the future may bring.

Between two fingers, I drew the Hellhound card and grinned out at the world ahead that opposed me.

Two red eyes glared back at me. The snuffling of a nose bigger than a normal Boar, followed by the shaking of chains came from the dense bushes to my right.

CHAPTER NINE

Dire Situation

Some lessons were easily learned compared to others. It seemed that the ones that required you to be dragged bloodied and screaming into acceptance were the most important, however, if only so you didn't make the same mistake again. That was human nature though. To strive for a goal no matter how unreachable, all the while repeating terrible history over and over. You just had to hope your brain caught up with the acceptance before your folly dug a nice hole to lie down in, forever.

What is that?" I clenched my teeth together, gripped with panic as the creature came into view. My Hellhound sprung from the ground and immediately began growling.

[New Monster: Dire Boar <4>]

Oh, thank you, System, for having killed the intrigue of the encounter. It wasn't like I couldn't have assumed as much myself, although knowing the level was handy to comprehend how much danger I was in. As the crimson eyes loomed through the shadows, my quick glance told me that the current hound was a different one, although similar in appearance and just as eager to defend me.

The large monster stepped out from the bushes. Its short, coarse fur was a deep gray and its skin scarred from the supposed battles it had survived. Around the four stout legs were metal cuffs and short lengths of a broken chain.

"Not sure . . ." Ren seemed slightly hesitant. "Those aren't usually native to this area. The chains suggest an escapee."

"Pet of one of your friends that has escaped?" I put my hand to the deck and felt the hum of energy. Somehow I doubted a couple of cards would fell this beast.

"Somewhat likely. Are you going to flee?" Her voice was impassive, clearly intending to see what my course of action would be. Judging me for it.

The creature was worrying, certainly, but I wouldn't balk at such an early stage. Test or not, I was capable and confident. As the Dire Boar stopped to pad at the mud, ready to charge, I flung out my first card.

My Hellhound sprung forward, keen to meet the Monster and halt the attempted charge. The purple card struck along the edge of its face, a dark line burned through its thick fur. No blood that I could see. Second card was already being made manifest as the hound was halfway to our target.

The Boar rose up and then slammed into the ground, creating a shock wave around it that cracked the ground. I paused in surprise before sending the second card out. My hound was slightly stunned from the wave of force and wasn't able to move as the dire creature sprinted forward and struck the demon with his tusks.

As the Hellhound yelped and slid across the ground, spilling demonic blood, my card buzzed through the air where the Boar had once stood—completely missing. Anger burned through me at seeing my little friend injured.

I couldn't accept this. My magic tricks didn't miss. *Unforgivable.*

My fingers clenched together, and I took a grip on the energy flowing through my deck. The spinning card slowed in the air behind the Boar before reversing course and slashing into the back of one of its hind legs. It grunted in anger, but after glaring toward me, it turned its attention back to the injured demon.

A stinging sensation radiated around my hand. I ignored it and drew another card. Flinging it into the air higher than the opponent. As it blurred upward through the air, I pulled it down atop it—a spark of purple as it severed through part of the Boar's ear.

The Monster snapped at the air as if it expected the cause of the damage to be above it. The Hellhound leaped up from the prone position on a broken leg to snap against the exposed throat of the dire beast. Blood dripping from the puncture wound, the Boar kicked out and tried to shake the demon loose—but the demon was latched on tight.

With aching fingers I threw another card out, this one wide to the right. I circled it around in the air, awaiting an opening—and then with a flick of my wrist, it tore down into the Boar's right eye. I tensed my hand even as sharp pain flared through my bones, and the card remained present and spinning for a couple of seconds before fading.

I hadn't realized I had been holding my breath, and the air left my lungs so I could gasp deeply. Sweat was running down the side of my face, and my right arm felt numb. Still, my focus was entirely on the battle ahead. Eye on the prize. I even had a smile affixed to my face to impress the crowd.

The Boar had slowed now. As the limp body of my summon dangled unfettered from its neck, it was draining precious lifeblood. My next attempt to draw a card felt harder to realize—I was slowing too. No time to contemplate whether

I had expended my Mana reserves or had just physically worn myself down. I clenched my teeth in a grimaced grin as I forced another to appear.

It flew through the air without the energy of the previous attacks, and I didn't have a lot of hope it would do much with weaker power. It hit the back leg again, not really enough to score Damage but enough for the Boar to stumble and succumb to lethargy. The Hellhound dropped to the ground as the dire beast stopped moving.

Immediately, I ran over to him and scooped his blood-soaked head up into my hand. He had at least a broken leg and gored chest. It was hard to see any more through the flickering flame and Boar blood. I stroked his head and ears. "You did perfect, buddy. I'm proud. Go home and rest." I unsummoned him, and his form returned to a dissipating mist. He would heal back in hell. Knowledge I had, even though I wasn't sure where it came from or that it was even true. I had to believe it.

With a sharp, gurgling growl, the Boar reared up and leaped at me. A last-ditch attempt to mete out some anger it held with its tiny brain. Somehow I managed to grab onto the tusks, avoiding being impaled as it trampled atop me instead. Blood and saliva splattered down onto my face, the constantly leaking neck injury soaking my suit. It took all my strength to try to wrench the mouth away from my neck, and we rolled across the ground, its heavy weight briefly crushing me.

Muscles in my arms burned and shook as I found myself underneath the beast again. My body was in pain, but adrenaline kept me focused on the present danger. Warm air burst across my face as he breathed heavily and tried to destroy me in his death throes. Mentally, I focused and manipulated the Mana stream that I could feel from my deck several feet away in the mud. A card withdrew and, with difficulty, made it over to me.

I sent it up into the throat wound. Focused on nothing but my arms holding the tusks away and the card persisting and spinning. The world was dark around me as I danced with almost passing out. My opponent became lax, and with pained arms, I slowly gained enough ground to where I could push the still body off.

With bleary eyes, I stood and stumbled away. My chest was covered in blood, and my breathing was ragged. Pain flared in my skull as a headache barged in wearing heavy boots. Footsteps drew near as I doubled over, hands on knees, and I tried to keep those sweet cakes in.

"What did we learn today, then?" Ren admonished me, but there was the slightest soft edge to her words. Or perhaps that was wishful thinking.

"Blood tastes awful." I spat out a mouthful, undecided on whether I was hoping it was mine or the Boar's.

Pain started to wrack through my body as the wounds I had actually taken came by to make their presence known. My left shoulder had a gash through it, my legs a few scrapes and bruises, the thumb on my left hand was probably broken, and my right hand just burned as though I had stuck it in some fire.

I breathed deeply, which was also painful. Maybe broken ribs? Or just bruised. I didn't have a lot of experience with being put through a wringer. "I bet that was quite the show though?" Unfortunately, I couldn't raise my torso to shoot her a smile. I settled for coughing up a bit of agony and blood again.

"Stupid asshole, this isn't a game." I heard her sigh. "Here, but don't let this become a habit."

She pressed a hand against my sore shoulder, and immediately a wave of soothing energy passed through my whole body. I wiggled my hands, which were now pretty functional, if not just aching still. With a furrowed brow, I stood up straight, finding myself mostly put back together.

[Total Health—Healed 85% (Ren)]
[Full report?]

I chose to not review the full extent of my injuries. I was already thankful enough that I hadn't died beneath the large pig. What a way to go. Against the dirtied sleeve of my suit, I rubbed the sweat and blood from my forehead.

"Thank you, Ren. I owe you again." Tempted to bow, I didn't want my head to fall off my delicate shoulders just yet.

"Adventuring is a lot of dragging each other from the brink. As long as you reciprocate eventually, then it's nothing." She tilted her head, still disappointed in me but not as curt.

The amount of healing was a surprise. I had thought she was some manner of Ranger, and she would have a focus on bow attacks and survival abilities. Although the reasoning that had led to me to this conclusion had now vanished off into some nether inside my brain.

"What is your Class?" I wanted to ask in a less direct way, but my nerves were currently shot.

"Surprised by the healing?" She could read between the lines. "Yeah, I like to be underestimated and seen as just a Ranger." A scowl crossed her face. "I've actually . . ." She paused, briefly unsure if to give me the information. "I've got a rare Class called Oathwarden."

I nodded slowly, not really understanding what that meant. At least mine did what it said. I summoned demons. I did magic. I was a Demonic Magician. Did she ward oaths? Maybe I was just shaking a little too much to fully understand the basics. Perhaps I needed a quick nap—a sharp visit to my friendly floor rock again.

"It's a bit like a mix between a Ranger and a Paladin." Her eyes tried to read me, slight concern for my well-being behind them. "So, some healing, some defensive abilities, bow attacks . . ."

"Ah, you killed Red with something that had like a . . . radiant glow."

"Red? Oh, yeah. You can't see what Skills are called when other people use them, unless you have a certain Ability yourself—so it's been easy enough to keep my Class secret." She looked off into the woods.

"Well, your secret is safe with me. A rare and unique teaming up would be quite the force multiplier, huh?" This time, I did manage a smile. I opened up my Inventory to check those bandages found earlier—and was contented, if not bemused, to see that they healed a flat 15 percent of my Health.

"If you don't die first. You need to get some smarts knocked into you." She rolled her eyes at me.

She hadn't interfered, and I understood it. It had been my decision to engage instead of flee. In that moment, I had committed to my fate and had to either overcome or sink below. Had it been worth it? Well, I lived and had worked out what <Mana Manipulation> allowed me to do. Mostly destroy my hand in the process, but it was early days. I hadn't even needed to touch the deck to summon the card.

As I finished wrapping my arm in a bandage, a little meter went up—and I was just about good as new. I checked my shoulder and legs, and all cuts had healed over. My muscles were still achy, and I was sure to have bruises tomorrow—but I was about as far from death as I could possibly be.

My feet stumbled the rest of my body over to the Dire Boar's corpse, as I half expected it to rear up against me again like some kind of zombie. I would need to get something to protect me from close-range death. The Loot button appeared, and my eyebrows raised.

[46 Gold]
[Tusks (2)]
[Boar Meats (2)]
[Rare Chance Box]

Now that might have made the whole grueling performance worth it.

CHAPTER TEN

Hidden Coin

As things stood, my first brush with death wasn't the sobering event it should have been. Certainly, I have come closer to ceasing to exist many times in my travels, but the Dire Boar had a special place in my heart. Not one I enjoyed reliving of course, but there was something about the ferocity and feral nature of writhing for my life in the dirt against a terrible beast. It played to that part of me that desired to mete out violence and eagerly held hands with the other part of me that wanted to put on a good show.

Ren continued to glare at me. "Why not open it already?"

I imagined that her scowl would be a permanent companion for as long as we traveled together, and after staring at death in the slobbering maw a few hours earlier, her temperament no longer bothered me.

"Suspense is an important part of the show," I murmured, eyes slightly glazed over as I looked at the path ahead.

"This isn't a show. This is *real*." There was an element of actual annoyance in her statement this time.

"Shows are real too." I raised my eyebrow at her as my eyes focused. "I'll open it when we hand the Quest in, I promise."

The elf sighed. "Fine. I just . . . Sorry, I have no patience for unopened things."

On the other hand, I was not a fan of the Chance Boxes or any sort of randomly assigned loot. Give me a solid outcome, some known factors that I could work with and plan accordingly. "This one won't have cakes in, right?"

"No."

If I could trade it, I would probably give it to Ren. There was a chance it would be something I couldn't or didn't want to use anyway. Like a two-handed axe or plate armor. The System had already given me a unique weapon to match my Class, so that may be something I needn't worry about for the near future.

The Boars had been a bit more skittish after I had felled the dire one, as if word had gotten around that I was a dire portent of pork-ending malignancy. It hadn't stopped me from farming up enough of the required meat to be able to turn the Quest in. Apparently, this would be where I'd meet my first NPC—a non-player character that was wholly System-created. Like some kind of puppet come to life.

I was partially hesitant to start seeing more of the System laid bare. So far, everything had wanted to kill me. Especially things that I wasn't trying to kill. Any poeticism or further reflection was lost, as my brain had become too tired. It had been an eventful day for a man who had only just spawned in this world.

"The Dire Boar won't have caused me to jump up enough experience to level sooner, will he?"

"Probably not. Experience is geared toward Quests, mostly. You really have to grind Monsters to put a dent in it." She idly tapped at her belt. "I'm not sure how that translates past the island."

The whole world, beyond the island. It was hard to imagine, and I was thankful for the introductory space despite how bloody it had been. Not that it was any less of a shock compared to my existence previously, but at least they kept the wild differences to a minimum. I was walking alongside an *elf.* I could summon *demons.* I still couldn't get the taste of *Boar blood* from my tongue.

"I'll be honest with you, Ren. I am certainly missing the taste of those cakes."

"They must put something addictive in them." She shook her head.

"I bet you there's a shop that sells them all the time on the mainland." I smiled at her, and she rolled her eyes, her scowl briefly softening.

"Well, I try not to dream too big, trickster. But if there is, then you owe me the first handful."

"A dozen, at least." I narrowed my eyes out to the woods. The trees were starting to thin again, which usually meant some kind of hub or landmark was nearby. "I'm sure you'll have plenty of opportunity to save my life before then."

"Hopefully you'll start pulling more of your own weight."

"Ah." I turned back to her with a smile. "And you just said you try not to dream big."

I thought that I almost got a brief smile out of her—perhaps my most hard-fought and glorious victory so far—but no such luck. Although she had been pretty against the idea of our partnership, part of me suspected she was warming to the idea that not everyone was bad news. I would press her on what had happened with the twelve goons at some point, but for now, the boat didn't need to be rocked.

Whatever brief moment of camaraderie soon faded as she looked away. "You saw how quickly I dropped those two. You need to be more decisive and ruthless when it comes to fighting Players."

In my mind, I remember having killed one of them, but I understood her point. An actual person wouldn't be so simple or easy to wrestle with as a Boar. Not with Abilities. If we had to fight through another eight . . . Well, I hoped now that we could single them out. The actual weight of the matter hadn't truly sunk in yet. I had agreed to *murder* but had just as easily signed myself up to be erased instead.

Soon the tree line fell away and opened up to a small field. To our right was a log cabin of dark wood, a simple fence surrounding it. Out on the front porch, a man was sitting. Long gray beard, checkered shirt, and worn slacks. Bare feet, which I found as intriguing as I did impractical. I raised my eyebrow at the elf.

"Quest NPC." She gestured. "Created by the System. Go hand your meat to him—*Boar meat*—and he'll give you the next part. Completion will level you up."

I nodded and prepared myself for the potentially awkward conversation with the not-real person. Although, I wasn't sure where that line could be drawn. Rather than have an existential breakdown, I curled my mouth up into a smile, and approached the . . . person. Was Ren real? While being an elf seemingly stuck on the *glare* factory setting, I doubted something fake could have such dazzling eyes.

"Greetings!" I announced, stepping through the gate and onto his property. Normally not something I'd be so forward with, but after meeting my death a few times, my personal boundaries had been shaken a bit loose.

"Evening, friend. Looks like you have been out fighting Boars." The old man gave me a wink from his chair but didn't stand. "I don't suppose you have five Boar meat you could trade me?"

"Trade, huh?" I rubbed at my chin. "What do you have to give me?"

He leaned forward in his chair, not really getting that much closer, as I had opted for a safe dozen feet away. Just in case he suddenly developed large tusks and wanted to tussle. Could never fault me for not being prepared.

"I have the know-how to reach some hidden treasure." He winked. "Share half of whatever you find and we have a deal."

I clicked my tongue and shot a glance back to Ren, still at the road. She had her arms crossed and an impatient scowl across her face. Not really a useful read— I'd have to play this by ear. In turning back to the man, it appeared as though he was waiting for my response.

"There must be enough danger that you cannot retrieve it yourself, yet you trust me enough to return and not keep it fully for myself?"

"Part of the treasure is a family heirloom that belonged to my late wife." A sadness came over his wrinkled face.

Given that he wasn't . . . real, it wouldn't surprise me than many Players found no issue with running away with whatever they found—although, now that I considered it, if they couldn't complete the Quest without returning it, then that was an artificial reason to stick to the narrative.

"Consider it a done deal, my friend." I gave him a short bow and then retrieved the five meats from my Inventory. "For you."

"Thank you, kind adventurer. Here, let me mark the place on your Map." He shuffled toward me and made a motion in the air but still missed the mark by eleven feet.

[Map updated]
[New Quest: Retrieve Family Heirloom]
[Progress: 0/1 Heirloom]

"Consider it done." I beamed at him.

"You don't have the required item," he replied, a glum expression on his face.

I turned a quick one-eighty immediately, before the uncanny valley could crack at my psyche. The fact that Ren hadn't changed position or expression this whole time wasn't helping, but I was at least sure *she* was a real person . . . I thought. Asking her might be a bad idea. No, not might. It would certainly earn me an arrow for my troubles.

"How was it?" she asked as I made my way back to the road.

"My sanity was already wearing pretty thin, so I think I can move past it for now and scream into the void at a later date."

She nodded slowly, unsure how seriously to take me. "This next part might crack at your little skull too—you alright with spoilers?"

I worked my jaw. There was part of me that wanted to experience the vibrancy and authenticity of the world one step at a time, as the System intended. That small part of me had been squished into a box at the back of my mind with the lid nailed shut. Show me behind the curtain so that I may learn every trick and know the outcome of certain events. Familiarity bred competence.

"Go for it." I gestured with my hand for the beans to be spilled.

"The treasure is being guarded by Bandits—actual humans like that guy but also System-created." She jabbed an accusatory finger at the old man, who was now staring off into nothing.

This all made my brain itch, and I rubbed my head. "So . . . wild assumption here, but they come back to life—they respawn after some time? But we as Players do not?"

Ren nodded. "Huh, some smarts survived the Dire Boar then, trickster."

"I'm . . . halfway decent at working out the background of how things work." Somewhat true; it was part of being a magician, of course.

"That how you got <Mana Manipulation> to work so well already?" She tilted her head and narrowed her eyes as if I was hiding something more untoward in my backstory.

I shrugged. "It kind of hurts to use it. Perhaps I'm overextending what I should be capable of."

She stared at me for a couple more seconds before relenting and gesturing to the road ahead. "Sounds like the kind of bullshit a unique Class would do. We have a bit of time before night. I suggest we rest before the Quest."

"I submit to your more qualified knowledge." I looked off into the woods to avoid whatever glare she was giving me. It wouldn't do well to get caught out in the forest at dark. Already the late evening sun had started to depart, and the last thing I wanted was for one of the thugs to give me a quick death in my sleep.

She led on in silence, giving up on browbeating me for a while. The silence was somewhat nice—having someone almost at the edge of friendship was something new to me. As fun as it was to have someone to talk to, someone you didn't *need* to talk to was almost as good. There was no awkwardness to it, but perhaps my social walls had all been eroded by the trauma of the day.

Either way, I persisted, and a smile lay across my face, just as I had practiced for so many years.

"Here." Ren eventually gestured to the side of the woods.

I followed her through, and perhaps a hundred feet in, she stopped and pointed with her hand at a bush. My brows furrowed before realizing it was a camouflaged entrance. If she hadn't been pointing it out so sternly, I would have walked straight past. The sun had fallen behind the trees now, and only dim light graced our position—adding to the hidden den.

At her behest, I crouched down and wormed my way inside. A small alcove had been dug into the ground—and I did mean small. Briefly, I panicked that this was all a ruse, and I had just literally crawled into my own grave. Then what scant light could filter in was blocked as the elf followed.

"Move over, asshole. This was meant to be a one-person thing, so I suggest you keep your ego facing the other wall. I have two hidden knives in here."

I shuffled over and lay on my side facing the left dirt wall. Ren did the same facing the right. The dirt beneath me was rather cold, and her stern words did little to comfort me into easy sleep.

Still, after a few tense minutes expecting a knife in my back, I eventually relaxed my muscles. No sooner had I done so, my exhausted mind drew me straight into the darkness.

CHAPTER ELEVEN

A Light Grilling

Often, I found that brief interludes of my life spent in peace and contentedness were often just moments where I sat in the eye of the storm. It was important to have these spaces where you could catch your breath and remind yourself what happiness was. What you were struggling and bleeding for. Beyond the storm was a clear sky and warm sun to greet you, if only you could weather the hardship long enough before the next inclement disaster rolled around.

"Max? Hey, Max."

I opened my eyes and panicked, briefly disoriented as to where I had awoken. Dark and cold. Muddy. The dirt was uncomfortable, and I rolled onto my back to observe the daylight dimly illuminating the hiding place from one end.

"Wake up, trickster. You like bacon?"

Ren's voice came from just outside the hole, although I couldn't see her. "Yeah, sounds amazing, actually." I worked my jaw, the muscles down my side aching from the terrible sleep. Still, I had definitely needed it, if my oversleeping had been the result.

I relented to awkwardly pushing out of the hiding hole, born once more into this new world and scoured by sunlight. It took my eyes a moment to adjust from the glare, but I now saw the elf just a dozen feet off. She was standing by a miniature grill, pieces of uncooked meat starting to sizzle and pop. The smell hit me, and I almost melted on the spot.

"It's the last of the bacon I had, but I've got a couple bread rolls. No butter though." She tilted her head at me, and her scowl didn't have as much weight behind it this morning.

"That sounds divine, thank you." I stretched out and then rubbed my eyes. Never had been much for camping myself. Picking out a hotel with a nice enough bed had become one of my secret skills over the years. For all the good that did now.

Ren scrunched up her face. "I'm sorry for being so prickly last night. There's been a few fair-weather friends passing through whose compassion didn't extend further than their . . ." She wagged a pair of tongs at me.

"Understandable." I nodded politely.

She waited for a moment, either expecting for me to elaborate more or having something herself that she was considering saying. Eventually, she broke the silence. "I'm surprised you have some convictions, given that you look like a Bard's College reject."

I looked down at my muddied and bloodstained outfit. The sparkling purple had lost some of its luster, but I perhaps had to agree that I probably stood out among others. And the surroundings. "In truth, I've never been too good at the whole relationship thing anyway."

The elf raised an eyebrow as she brought out a pair of plates from her Inventory. "Is that so?"

"Too much of a workaholic." I rubbed at my chin, trying to find a way to skirt past this conversation. "All my time went to that. It's hard to form connections when most people I met were fans of my persona, rather than the real me."

She handed me a plate and placed an open bun on it. "A little common ground there for us then, trickster. There's plenty of elfin-princess fetishists that can't see past that in trying to befriend me."

I nodded, a smile across my face. "You're a princess?"

A scowl was leveled my way, but she instead focused on turning the meat over. The smell was making me salivate. "Not in the traditional sense." She sighed. "More of an heiress . . ."

"But not of a crown and untold wealth?"

"Inherited responsibility." She shook her head. "You have a lot of questions this morning, Max." The elf removed the meat from the small cooker and placed some in my awaiting bread before adding some to her own. The grill then vanished into her Inventory, taking with it the nice glow of warmth.

"You seemed as though you were in a good mood, so thought I'd press my luck." I smiled and gestured my thanks for the meal with the plate.

She glared at me but tilted her head. "As if you can tell."

Even with our brief time spent together, I had learned to look past her grouchy demeanor and pick up on the tells for her actual emotions. So I thought anyway. Wouldn't be the first time I was wrong, but I liked to think I happened to be a decent judge of a person.

It was part of the job—at least some of it. Not so useful on the big stage, but when you were doing the crowd work at smaller gigs, a little sleight of hand and social awareness could help you along. There was no need to labor her with my supposed qualities, so I just smiled, and we ate in silence. It was a little on the dry side, but having not eaten much aside from a cake the day prior—it felt lifesaving.

"Another thing I feel like I owe you for." I bowed as I returned the plate to her.

"Everyone needs to eat." She rolled her eyes. "You're no good to me dead. The portable grill you'll get during a level-three Quest—do you not have any food of your own?"

I brought up my Inventory to look at the Slime Gel and assorted boar parts. "No? Perhaps I should have done some normal butchery."

She sighed loudly. "You should have received some items during your introduction to the world."

With an apologetic shrug, I wasn't sure what else to tell her. My appearance had seemed like something even the System was a little surprised by, given that it had struggled to give me a Class at first. It must have skipped over some of the usual welcoming information while I was busy sleeping on the sharp rock.

"Here." She held out a dagger withdrawn from her own stash. "I feel like I can trust you enough now. Do *not* make me regret it." Her glare painted the picture of what would happen if I tried anything.

"Thank you." A dagger was pretty basic, but it at least gave me an option for when I had a large Boar trying to crush me to death. I found that I could equip it to my belt, in a leather sheath that I didn't have before. That was some convenience I could definitely appreciate.

"We'll get water from a stream that is on the way." She slung her bow over her shoulder. "Can't spend the morning drying out our tongues with inane chatter."

We most definitely could, but I nodded and tapped at my STAR. The glow of an arrow to point us in the direction of the treasure turned slightly to notify us it was to the left, through the forest. Ren knew the way already, of course, but it was probably a good idea I got used to using the System for all the benefits it had.

"It'll be quicker to circle back via the road, unless you have a desire to kill all the wildlife we come across?" Despite the tone used in saying this, she seemed open to the possibility.

"Road." I nodded, and we set off. As much as the idea of getting more practice with my Skills and looting some basic items sounded like an otherwise pleasant day, the sooner I could get these Quests done to catch up to Ren's level, the sooner we could kill the bad guys and progress.

I used the term *bad guys* to help smooth other the fact that we would be committing murder. It was nicer to believe that we were in the right and whatever ire they had invoked from the elf was worthy of such harsh punishment. She didn't seem like a particularly bad person and had shown me enough niceties to convince me of her nature.

Sleeping in a hole in the ground was a bit of a red flag, but if you were potentially hiding from a large group of people that wanted you dead, then it seemed pragmatic enough. I would perhaps kill for a decent bed, so our goals aligned perfectly.

"A lot on your mind, trickster?"

She roused me from my thoughts, and I realized we had already been walking down the road for a few handfuls of minutes. The day was beautiful, with hardly a cloud in the sky to prevent the sun from warming and illuminating all the vibrant greens, earthy browns, and light grays of our surroundings. It made my brush with death seem like a distant memory.

"Yeah." I worked my jaw in trying to think of how to best sum up everything that was whirling about in my mind without it becoming a constant stream of word salad.

"I was the same. It takes a few days to really accept and get used to." She looked out into the woods to our left. "Can't say it gets much easier . . . but it becomes *normal.*"

I grunted an acknowledgment. The world was nice enough, even if bizarre in ways. Heartbreaking and bone crushing in others. There wasn't a succinct way to sum up how I felt, nor did I wish to babble on with complete nonsense. I took everything in stride, after all, as the show continued to go on.

"How long have you been here?" Rather than falsely flaunt how much I was enjoying my time, I deflected with a question.

"A while. There's been one or two new Players every few days. It's been slower lately, not so many. A lot I don't get to meet. Most I choose not to meet."

"Some you wish you hadn't met, and some you wished had never left."

She turned to me with a scowl on her face, but some of the fire was gone from her bright eyes. "You should stay in your own head, trickster." With that, she began to walk slightly ahead of me. A nerve struck, perhaps.

After another ten minutes or so, the arrow illuminating the direction to my Quest told me to turn into the forest—almost at a ninety degree to us.

Ren held up a hand for us to stop and scoured our surroundings. I followed her gaze around, assuming four eyes were better than two, even if her eyesight was potentially better than mine. Probably checking for the shadows of those we were intending to erase from existence. I wasn't too sure how things worked around here, but it was safe to assume Red and Green's disappearance would have been noticed by now. Whatever conclusion the rest would come to was far beyond me.

"Alright, it's a little ways through here." She pointed a finger in the same direction as the STAR arrow was directing me. "I'm going to be shadowing you, but you'll mostly be on your own."

"More tough love?" I grimaced and peered into the depths of the trees.

She exhaled through her nose. "You need to learn aggro range and threat management. It's your choice to clear the camp or just take out the groups of Bandits that you need to. But if you fuck up, then you'll pull half the encounter."

I nodded, understanding most of it. The System-created seemed pretty dense and shortsighted most of the time, but I'd need to be cautious and not so flagrant with my attacks. Hellhound probably wasn't the best to lead the charge—perhaps picking small gatherings off with range would be a little more sensible.

Ren stepped up beside a tree and pulled a leaf off. She held it between her hands, and after a brief whisper, a radiant glow bloomed briefly in her grasp. As she extended the leaf toward me, I could now see that she had inscribed some manner of rune upon it. Gingerly, I took it from her, enthralled by the shifting golds of what magic she had emblazoned it with.

"Crush it for a twenty-five percent heal. It's the only way I can assist without drawing aggro myself." She turned to lead into the forest before pausing and looking back at me. "I'll be watching, and I'll pull your dumb ass from the fire *if* I can, but don't rely on it."

She stepped aside and gestured for me to go first.

Somehow, I managed a brief smile and headed inward beneath the canopy. It was cooling after being in the morning's sun for so long but made me apprehensive. As if every darkened trunk or thick bush could be holding any manner of danger ready and willing to leap up and tear my throat out.

Without realizing it, I had begun creeping and placing my feet carefully among the light vegetation and fallen sticks—as if to avoid the clichés on my approach.

And then, after a few minutes of tiring tension, I heard the murmur of voices and saw movement up ahead. For a few seconds, I stopped to check my arrow, and it told me I was in the right place.

Carefully withdrawing my deck, I tilted my gaze back to see that I had been walking alone.

CHAPTER TWELVE

Quick Hands

Although, as a magician, I was used to things being not as they seem. This world had a way of bringing about surprises that I could never have imagined. Deception and sleight of hand could only do so much when people had literal invisibility, the ability to conjure firestorms, or genuine telepathy. Had the System not granted me the Class that it did, I may have found myself overwhelmed and minute in the grand scheme of things. A unique Class meant I could feign who I really was—a skill well honed over most of my adult life.

My mouth ran dry as I stared out at the figures moving about just beyond the blocking foliage. How I managed to get myself into this situation, I had no idea. Well, that wasn't quite true—I had been present for all the events that had led to this moment. The surrealness of it had just caught up to me at this juncture.

Stalking through the bushes toward a group of supposed Bandits—who looked like real people but apparently were a close and limited approximation at best. To steal back some family artifact or heirloom, so that I could . . . level up and gain more power. All to convince an elfin not-princess that I was worthy of joining her murderous revenge tour. Hardly my usual audience.

More uncomfortable was the thought that I might be able to try some of my magic on them. Old magic, that is. How fooled would they be? I apparently had some bonus to being deceptive, but would the System-created humans be receptive to my attempts to charm or just stick me with a sword as soon as I showed my face?

The latter seemed more likely at this stage. Certainly if I wanted to test my capabilities, then something slightly lower stakes, such as the old man at the little farm, would be the more sensible option. I had to start small and build my audience up again. It bruised my ego in a way I didn't think possible—as if part of me was convinced going for the bigger haul of wowing all the Bandits at once would be the better option.

I took a deep breath to cool my nerves. Clearly I was letting things get to my head if I was just going to stand here like a statue and ruminate over things neither here nor there. Ren was probably watching me from a distance and scowling at my inaction. Or for any other reason.

Just to make sure I wasn't full rooted to the spot, I made a few steps closer to my quarry—and slightly to the right. If I could flank one edge of the camp, then perhaps I'd have less chance of bringing terrible danger upon my neck. Gradually, as I got closer, more of the situation became visually evident to me. I circled farther to the right, where a slight incline gave rise to some higher ground that bordered one edge of the campground.

Overselling my ability to move stealthily out in the open in a sparkling purple suit, I slithered on my front up onto this ledge and crawled toward an opening in the vegetative cover. One light-green branch shuffled slightly out of my face—and then there it was.

Three wagons of dark wood had been arranged in this clearing as a loose border to the camp proper. Two dozen tents sat around the wagons and farther afield from the stone bordered campfire directly in the middle. Several half-log benches were strewn around the inert fire and over by a makeshift table where they supposedly ate. Indeed, two Bandits seemed to be sitting there in idle conversation.

Each wagon had a group of three Bandits each, the fire had a group of four, and then there were three groups of two, some who seemed to be making patrols. Nineteen total, unless there were some in the tents. Best to operate under the assumption that there were and avoid them.

From here, it looked as though if I stood up and waved my hands, I could easily be seen by everyone present. Ren had said I needed to learn about aggro and threat, and the Boars had been pretty indifferent after the initial attack on their brethren. But where the piglets had run, these Bandits would come straight to attack.

The three at the wagon would be closest to me as long as I waited for one of the patrols to move away. Fighting three Bandits at once seemed like a bit of a step up from solo wildlife . . . but it was just something I had to get on with and learn. I had the feeling Ren was putting me through a bit of a trial of fire, but if I couldn't deal with some basic thugs, then how was I going to help chew through actual Players?

If things got too hairy, I'd have to run. I had the imbued leaf, along with some bandages to keep me alive. Still, there was the thought of staring death right in the eye that had my psyche recoiling. Part of me was used to it, although I wasn't sure why. There was more going on in the background than I truly understood.

I lifted the deck and withdrew the Imp card. Gradually I got up into a crouch and moved back as far as I could while still keeping a line of sight on all three enemies. If I didn't know any better, they passed as normal humans. Grubby looking, a mix of worn leathers and sun-scorched skin. Rough around the edges, but life was full of all sorts.

<Summon Demon: Imp> brought out a pudgy little caster beside me, and I tipped my hat toward him. Slightly different than my first one. I pointed my finger out toward my first intended target, a broader Bandit among the three with a dusty-brown bandanna covering his hair.

The Imp nodded and started preparing a fireball. My eyes darted back to the camp—thankfully, the patrol was away from our targets.

[New Monster: Bandit <2>]

A purple card hovered into my hand without my needing to touch the deck. It spun slowly as I waited for the right opportunity. Part of Bandanna's routine involved chuckling at some murmured joke. I imagined it was something completely unrelated to rough banditry—like something about baby chicks. Not that it made my next action any easier.

Magic card flew out, arcing through the air and slicing into his throat. My fingers twitched as I held it there and pushed it into the wound for a brief extra second before it faded away. Bandanna clutched at his neck as blood ran between his fingers. He then turned to face my direction, his eyes wide—just before he was struck by the thrown fireball of the Imp.

The other two turned and started after me, anger in their eyes as the bleeding one fell to the ground. A second card was already forming in my hand, and I aimed it for the closer enemy. His weapon dropped from his grip as my card sliced into his forearm. I didn't hold this one for long as I needed to cast a third with the next Bandit now bearing down on me.

Fire shot from my Imp and struck the third Bandit in the legs, scorched flesh and melted linens causing him to stumble and drop to his knees. I sent the card out to the second Bandit and spun toward the third, drawing the knife and stabbing into his throat as he collapsed.

I jumped back in brief shock at my own actions, and my eyes darted toward the second Bandit—the card had pierced through his shirt and straight into his heart.

The Imp did a joyous little dance as the bodies collapsed to the ground. I looked at the bloodied dagger. Surely sleight of hand skill didn't really translate over to melee combat? Perhaps this was just something I knew. Other Max smiled—which was possibly the worst sentence I had ever thought up. *Why tell myself that?*

Air escaped my nose as I exhaled and took to looting the two closest bodies. The third by the wagon would have to wait.

[30 Gold]
[Armor Chance Box (1)]
[Ration Box (1)]

Now, did the Quest say the heirloom was on one of the people here—or is there a chest or place it had been stowed away that I should be looking for? That was part of Ren's test. Could I complete the Quest without getting myself into trouble—or could I handle myself and clear the camp with no issue? Either option had merit, and based on that combat—the latter one might work out. More loot and chances for sweet cakes.

The patrol had now returned, and my eye twitched as they approached the dead body by the wagon.

"Hey, Hank here is dead."

"Let's search around."

They had reacted to finding it, which was one of my questions ticked off. Now, with weapons drawn, they were making an exaggerated effort to scour all the surroundings for any clue as to who had done the foul deed.

My first card gashed along the closest Bandit's head, severing half of his ear. His rush toward me was stalled as a fireball burst on his chest, burning through his shirt. The second was much quicker, and I barely got a card out before he was near me. A spurt of crimson followed the purple dash of magic as it missed his neck and struck along his collarbone.

I stepped away from his flat-footed swing of a sword, gripping the dagger tight in my right hand as I willed a card up from the deck in my left. Metal rang out as I deflected his follow-up with my shorter blade, although the warm stinging pain along my arm told me I didn't come out fully unscathed. With his next attack already in motion, I flung the card in panic—striking him in the mouth.

Blood and broken teeth sprayed across me as the man recoiled, grabbing at the shredded skin and gums. I stepped toward him and stabbed downward into his eye socket. The weight of him collapsing was surprising and caught me off guard—right before I was struck by something hard in my left upper arm.

I rolled to the ground, my deck bouncing twice on the soft earth. My arm was numb throughout—but not broken. As I went to stumble to my feet with bleary eyes, the shadow of the mace-wielding Bandit loomed over me, his weapon raised above his head. I knew this trick. He wanted to make my brains appear all over the ground.

As he went for the downward swing, he paused and swore—the Imp's fireball striking him on the back of one leg. I willed a card from the discarded deck through the air—gashing the back of his other knee and twirling it back into my left hand. I leaped atop him, knocking him to the ground. He tried to stop my dagger with his hand and received impalement for his efforts. While his attention was focused on that, I jammed the held card into the underside of his jaw, cutting both my own hand as well as his throat open before it vanished.

Dagger out of his hand. Into his neck. Twice. Three times. I just didn't want to hear that gurgling sound anymore.

I took two deep breaths. *The show was still going on. Put a smile on, Max. Finish the job.*

With a groan, I got to my feet. I could move my left arm now, but the upper half was numb and complained with bruised agony when moved. My right forearm had a gash down it that continued to drip blood. I felt pretty miserable, but that was neither a physical malady nor able to be healed by any of my items.

I stretched out my neck and spat some blood on the ground. Stepped toward my deck and retrieved it. Despite the roughhousing it had received the past few days, it still looked flawless. From my Inventory, I brought out a bandage and gave myself a little heal. Trial by fire meant getting used to enacting and being on the sharp end of violence. Dissociating from death . . . in which I was slightly uncomfortable at being halfway there already.

Without realizing it, as I watched the progress bar of my heal slowly increase, I started humming a little tune to myself. Continued as I looted through the bodies. *Fame and fortune*, the lyrics went. Fame and fortune, as I slew and looted.

My old show's intro song, still just as fitting all these years on.

CHAPTER THIRTEEN

In Hiding

Even as I sit here, so far beyond that day, I still remember it clearly. The time I grew tired of blood. Well, maybe not tired—but an uncomfortable acceptance for it became part of my repertoire. A necessity. You had to be cold to survive. That's why I needed to surround myself with things that warmed my heart and soul. Otherwise I'd just end up frozen and forgotten.

I drew heavy breaths as I applied another bandage. Wounds closed back up. The good weather didn't seem to bring me the same amount of contentedness anymore. My hands kept on bleeding despite the fact I could not see any cuts. Something to do with the Mana manipulation, no doubt. While the progress bar on my healing sauntered toward the finish line, I idly threw a card out.

After about fifteen feet, I curved it around to return to me—and I caught it from the air like a boomerang. With a twinge of pain down my arm, I put a pulse of power back into it, renewing its lifespan instead of letting it fade away.

Slowly and painfully, I was gaining better control. The magic deck now sat in the chest pocket of my purple jacket. Now that I could draw the cards without needing to touch them physically, it left one of my hands open.

I had managed to chew through half of the camp so far, and the inert corpses of those I had maimed were a quick ticket to trauma town. Even knowing they weren't truly *real*, they acted like it. Bled and died the same. I'm assuming anyway—what knowledge I had of death seemed to be locked away in the back of my brain next to my personal baggage on the subject.

One wagon group, the two at the table, and a pair on patrol were all that remained.

Humming to myself again, I conjured up another Imp card to replace the last who had returned to hell just prior. I had sent him off with a bow of gratitude, and as the new one crawled into existence from the magic circle, he looked in good enough spirits to assist. His tiny nose was a little stubbier and horns a little longer, but he was built the same as his brethren.

Now this was the harder part—the table was relatively close to the wagon, and I had a feeling that I would pull the whole group if I was sloppy. At this stage, I *was* feeling pretty sloppy. What had started out as a rough ride through some manner of video game world had become gritty and exhausting. Then again, this wasn't supposed to be a one-person job.

I had the feeling that groups—or Parties—were meant to be the default. It only made sense when you had Classes with different strengths and weaknesses. Put me behind a knight who could take a beating and this would have been a breeze. Perhaps Ren was just trying to get me killed without the blood being on her hands? I shook these thoughts from my head. Fruitless to injure myself when the Bandits were just as willing.

The clock was still running, and I still had time to put in. We had discussed respawning before, and if fresh Bandits started to appear into the empty spots, then I'd find myself in a lot of trouble.

Patrol first.

I waited till they were out of the way, putting myself back down closer to the side of the actual camp. From here, I could even smell the leathers, the fat used on the tents to waterproof them, the musk of charcoal briefly in the air . . . and a lot of body odor. No mystical scent of the heirloom, and the STAR just blindly pointed into the middle of the camp.

The card spun over my hand as I held it aloft, and then by my will it flew toward the two Bandits. As if steering it with my hands, I slammed it into the side of the throat of one, pulling it to the side like a blade to open up the arteries and windpipe. I dropped the card as my fingers ached and prepared to draw another—before my Imp let off his fireball.

This one was slightly different than the others, and as I watched it illuminate the path toward the second patrolling man, there was crackling red lightning arcing all over the ball of fire.

It struck the man and burst, the explosion easily double that of a normal attack. The heat escaped into the air with a puff of smoke as the Bandit dropped to his knees, his upper torso ablaze with flame.

"Hey, what's that?"

"We're under attack!"

The Imp looked up at me sheepishly as I scowled at him. "Overachieving is a fast track to ruin," I muttered to him. We started to back away, as the tents were blocking a proper view of the campsite—but it sounded like the table pair had noticed our impromptu firework display.

A card hovered in the air as they both rounded one of the tents and came into view. Each of them wielding Crossbows, which seemed remarkably unfair to me.

The Imp charged up another attack as my card went out—slightly wide due to my apprehension about the sharp ends of those projectiles.

The purple magic tore into the shoulder of the man on the left, only just disrupting his aim as they both fired. A warm pain radiated across my chest as the bolt struck one of my ribs, skirting around into the softer flesh of my flank instead of breaking bone. The second bolt was aimed true—and burst through the forehead of my Imp.

As he started to fade into mist, he held a hand up into the air—either for me to help him or in apology for bringing this on himself. A brief nod of acceptance and finality was all that I could offer him, alongside a beaming smile despite the burning anger within me.

The next card was out already, as one started to reload and the other dropped the ranged weapon to approach me with a sword. My left hand held my right wrist, and my hand shook from the pain. I hoped that the tight grip would at least stop my hand from bursting away from my body. With my eyes narrowed, I curved the glowing purple rectangle through the air, cutting at the back of the enemy's ankle before slashing across his other calf. As he started to drop to the ground, I moved the sharp magic card around him, zipping side to side until it reached his throat, leaving a zigzag of crimson to soak through his plain linens.

With a flick, I dispensed the card across and into the forehead of the crossbow Bandit, cracking and embedding into his skull just as he had done to my demon. I scowled as the blood soaked through my jacket, running in a stream from my hand. I wouldn't be able to do much more of this without causing myself actual ruin.

I sighed as the two bodies sank to the ground and my card dissipated. Now that my hands were slowly running out of use, I made the discovery that I could manipulate the STAR mentally with my willpower too. *Now* we were talking—briefly all manner of application circled through my mind, all the tricks I could do by accessing my Inventory in secret. In this instance, I actually went through the Health tab.

[Right hand—No recent injury]
[Left hand—No recent injury]

That didn't seem right, on account of the amount of blood I was currently losing from the two. Unless the blood was all in my head? Some by-product of using demonic magic? I would have to ask Ren next time I saw her. If I saw her again. Despite my trusting the elf, part of me did wonder if she had just dropped me off at Bandit day care so that she could go and do adult stuff. Like murder.

Only three Bandits left? I felt slightly silly for having to go through the whole camp to get what I came for—but none of them that I had looted had held the heirloom in their possession. When I had the high ground, I saw no obvious-looking treasure chests. I guess now it was time to head into the camp proper to search around.

I skirted between two of the tents, toward the central campfire, peering around to make sure I hadn't missed any groups. The last wagon group stood just off to the side in idle conversation. From my deck, I conjured the Imp card but was confused when it was monochrome—as though it was inert or spent. Perhaps I could only do so many in a certain time span—or it was because he had died and this was my punishment for allowing such a fate to befall my helper.

Well, the show must go on. <Summon Demon: Hellhound> it was then. The card burned away as a magic circle spun near my feet and the demonic canine rose from the beyond. I gave him a pet on the head, and he nuzzled into it.

Standing once more, I shook the pooled blood from my arm and drew a purple card. The Hellhound crouched low, ready to leap off into a sprint at my behest. There was some slight hesitation within me, as I didn't want him to get injured like the Imp, but I knew I couldn't stop him from eagerly doing his duty. I would just have to do my best.

I empowered my card, focusing my Mana on this single one—and was contented to see it glow brighter. Instead of spinning it, I pushed it flat, a trail of bright energy scoring the air behind it as it went at almost twice the speed. Just as it was about to collide with one of the Bandits, I pointed my fingers upward, and it corrected course. Now briefly going directly up before entering the underside of the man's chin.

While attacking the neck was getting pretty old, it seemed like the quickest way of encouraging the Bandits to shuffle off this mortal plane. Even if it didn't kill them outright, they'd still grasp at the wounds or struggle with the blood or breathing. Once they started wearing neck armor, then I'd need to be a little more inventive.

The Hellhound sprinted off to one of the others, mostly just keeping them at bay with growls and bared teeth. If they went to hit the hound, he would move away. If they started to come for me, my demon friend would start to nip at them. It was surprisingly effective and allowed me to whip round another card to slay one and humble the other enough to where the hound could bring him down and have a snack to eat.

I stumbled over to the bodies with a groan and looked through all the loot.

Still no heirloom. I looked down at the STAR, which just pointed me toward the campfire. With a sigh, I simply closed my eyes. So tired, despite it still being barely afternoon . . . maybe early afternoon at worst. As I opened my eyes again, something caught my attention.

Just past the inert campfire, nestled against some of the tents in a position that would have been blocked from the ridge above—was a chest.

Or at least some kind of wooden locker. Wearily, I approached it, allowing my hound to do whatever he liked. With iron struts and a lacquered wooden finish, it almost looked too pristine for a Bandit encampment—but perhaps it was stolen too. Bending over, I tried to grasp at the latch.

[Locked]

Ah. Typical, now where was I going to find a—

The growling of my hound distracted my thoughts. I turned at the sound of footsteps. Large furred boots, way too much exposed skin aside from a loincloth and bearskin cloak. A large two-handed axe, which was already on the upswing toward me.

[New Monster: Bandit Leader <3>]

Before I fully realized it, I was tumbling across the dirt. I didn't need the System to tell me that I had broken ribs and that the soft wet parts my hands were clutched against were probably meant to be inside my body.

"Trying to steal from me, eh? Nobody steals from me." The gruff voice of the leader was adamant I not retrieve the heirloom but didn't seem fazed I had just dismantled his whole gang.

The following crunch and whine told me my pup did no better against the axe. With pained determination, I brought forth the healing leaf and crushed it, a pulse of radiant light washing over me and healing over my wounds. No time to bandage while he was still alive, so this would have to do.

[Health critical—35%]

The leader flicked the blood from his axe as he stepped toward me, my own legs seemingly unable to offer the same support, cursing me to remain on the ground as his shadow loomed closer.

CHAPTER FOURTEEN

Treasured Memories

Violence often led to more violence. Something that was drilled into me with sharp screws again and again over time. Did the knowledge ever stop it from occurring? Sometimes, certainly. Knowing how to read a room was as useful when trying to ply trickery as it was gauging which people were likely to want to carve their name in your chest just to be heard. Infamy cast you as an empty whiteboard just dying for anyone with a marker to deface—and some of them were permanent.

I fought the urge to empty out my stomach as the Bandit Leader approached. Something about having half of my chest carved apart and then magically stitched back together hadn't sat well with my organs, who had to bear witness to the act. I hadn't eaten enough as of late to generously share with the ground.

Where had he even been hiding? Perhaps the System-created could just appear where they needed to be—on some trigger? Like part of a rehearsed show, he crawled out of the woodwork once I sought to meddle with his treasure chest. Not as big of a threat to a Party of adventurers, but to a distracted and wounded—

I rolled to my side, farther away from the camp as the axe bit into the soft dirt where I had been lying. Now wasn't really the time for prodding about the inner workings of the how the System did things—unless I wanted to find out what happened when you died. It turned out I did *not* want that.

Against aching muscles, I managed to roll back onto my feet, some long-forgotten muscle memory helping me with the amateur acrobatics. The Bandit Leader was fast, already winding up for a second swing. A card flared up in front of me, some pain from exerting myself preventing me from doing anything too fancy with it. I still had no idea what Mana was or how it worked, but a finite resource that was harder to grasp the more power I used seemed about on the mark. Going too far seemed to cause me pain rather than refusing to function outright, but even that had a limit.

He tried to block the flung card with his axe shaft, but I turned it at the last moment and cut into his chest. Wrong position and not deep enough for a heart shot. In his brief moment of pain, I leaped over some fallen stools and tried to circle around a couple of tents to buy time.

The Bandit kicked through the wooden items, sending their broken parts across the ground behind me, as he continued to advance.

I dropped a Hellhound card by the front of an open tent and moved to lure the leader closer to the center of the camp.

"Quit running and face me," he growled.

"Are you capable of going off script?" I asked as I backtracked closer to the inert campfire.

"Stop talking and die." The Bandit crouched and tensed his legs, looking like he was ready to leap forth toward me.

I wasn't sure if that answered my question or not. It could have gone either way. Not that I thought myself capable of dissuading him from parting my head from my neck—but extending their union worked in my favor. A card spun out in front of me.

He made his move, but just as he did—the Hellhound that had been waiting in silence jumped forward and bit him just above the ankle, causing him to falter and stop his intended sprint.

As he turned to strike at the latched-on canine, my card zipped through the air and struck him in the forearm. Not enough to stop his blow, but it rendered it inaccurate, and he sliced at the earth beside my summon. While he rose, another card slashed him on the side of the head. Blood ran down his face, but there was no fear or panic in his eyes—just anger. One of the few things that took me out of the encounter.

Calmly, I drew card after card—the Bandit now stuck between the hound he was unable to shift and the constant barrage of gashes from my magic deck. As if he couldn't decide whom was more worthy to attack first, he now just paused in confusion, until he could no longer hold the axe. Weakened from my relentless assault, one final card to his neck and he was as good as dead.

I clutched at my pained chest as his body fell, more blood soaking my suit as my hands were doing the whole bleeding thing again. Mentally, I made the note to add absorbent gloves to my shopping list. For when I had some place to shop that didn't mind my current appearance. I added getting a proper wash and change of clothing to my to-do list slightly higher than the gloves. Couldn't be seen in public this way; I had an image to build.

My Hellhound came over and sat before me. "Good boy," I said, "or girl. I haven't really been checking. You may go now. You did great." I gave the flaming canine some pats on the head and neck, and they faded away back to hell.

With a slight spring in my step and awkward gait due to my lethargy, I approached the Bandit Leader to loot him.

[75 Gold]
[Uncommon axe]
[Ration Box (2)]
[Supply Box (3)]
[Bandit Key]

As nice as the gold and weapon were, the Bandit key was the real winner here. My aching eyes went over the bloodied camp to see which Bandit it would open up. Oh, no—it was more likely for the treasure chest. Something to draw me toward Quest completion. I turned and approached the chest, wondering if I should use a bandage first . . . After a brief pause, I relented and used the two I had remaining. Greedy and reckless, maybe, but I also wanted to be as far from anything remotely death adjacent.

After two progress bars, I felt a little sharper and less like I was about to collapse into core parts on the ground. With key in hand, I opened the locked box.

[80 Gold]
[Antidote]
[Power Token]
[Family Heirloom]

A wide grin spread across my face as relief took grip of my soul, the desire to locate the heirloom glazing over whatever else I found. Any joy was briefly halted, however, as soft footsteps came from my side. Purple energy flared up into a card as I stood and turned. The magic dissipated as soon as I clocked the shape of the figure with piercing blue eyes, and I gave a glum nod to Ren.

"Got the Quest item?"

"Yeah, I did." I rubbed at my tattered suit where a sword had torn into my now mostly healed forearm.

She looked tired, and her usual glare was narrowed toward the ground. Maybe there was some guilt there for trying to feed her lamb to the wolves without intervening. If anything, I was more surprised and impressed she might have had regrets but still not intervened. Showed some strength of conviction, even if a little coldhearted.

"You look like shit," she said with an eventual sigh. "Let me heal you back up, at least."

Still wasn't giving me eye contact, which was a shame, but we'd get around to processing things once we were back in the clear away from all these bodies.

I hadn't realized it, but I had my show smile across my face since looting the box. The elf put her hand on my arm, and a radiant pulse of energy filled me, soothing my aches and pains.

"Don't get beaten up for a bit. You're still not at—" She stopped to turn to look behind me with wide eyes. "*Move!*"

I was shoved and hit the dirt, my head catching the side of the treasure chest. Sparks danced within my eyes as a flash of amber and yellow engulfed the elf. Radiant light flared from inside the vanishing fireball, leaving a scorched Ren grimacing and drawing her bow.

My head swam as my vision blurred and wobbled in the direction of the attack. Not Bandits. Three figures stood just at the edge of the bounds. Shaved head in a robe—some kind of Wizard. Dark-gray metallic armor that reflected the sun with a full plate helmet—looked to be a Knight. Third was a man in greens and browns holding a shortbow—an actual Ranger, I presumed.

Even as I struggled to my feet with lopsided balance, I threw out a Hellhound and mentally had them set their sights on the Ranger. The Wizard was building another fireball as Ren fired off an arrow. With a quick step, the Knight moved in front of it, batting it away with a plain iron shield.

"Kill the dog," the Wizard seethed, diverting the Ranger away from attacking us. My card was already in motion though, and with the plated man in the way, I swerved the projectile wide and brought it down into the robed figure, striking him in the hand and severing fingers.

He dropped the spell, shocked as his missing digits fell to the ground. While the System had been great at healing bodily damage, I had no idea if it was able to regrow missing appendages. He wouldn't have the chance to find out either.

Ren lit up her arrow with the flare of an ability—it didn't look like the radiant glow of before. This one had a green hue that danced with golden waves. As it flew through the air, it lit a trail across the camp, like a firework or streamer. A simple enough attack for the Knight to move in front of and block.

As the arrow struck his shield, it burst out in golden light. From the ground around the three, vines grew up and encircled their legs.

My Hellhound wasn't able to dodge the return fire, and an arrow struck him in the front between his chest and foreleg. He tumbled to the ground with a yelp as my card spun through the air above him. I clenched my teeth. Too slow to try to intercept the arrow and save my pup.

Instead, I whipped it around at the Ranger, going for the neck shot. Just as it went to strike him—he blurred, as if turning intangible briefly, and the purple rectangle went straight through him and struck the Knight. A flare of energy, but it did no damage to his suit of armor.

We scattered to each side now as the Ranger drew another arrow and the spell-caster began to charge something with his one good hand. I leaped over the chest and rolled between the two tents, unable to see how far Ren went. The first fireball had done quite some damage to her, but it looked as though she had healed through the worst of it. If she had Mana that worked the same way mine did, there might be a limit to how much more support she could provide.

From my Inventory, I withdrew the Health Potion and popped the cork. I couldn't entirely rely on the elf, and that treasure chest had left a dent in my head that threatened lightheadedness. Immediately I cupped at my mouth and avoided retching and drawing attention my way. It tasted horrible. Warm aniseed with the sharp bite of alcohol at the end. Perhaps I *would* have to rely on Ren if they tasted like that.

I placed the empty bottle away and cursed myself for letting them sneak up on us. There was no doubt these were three of the Players that Ren was trying to kill. That they had shown up right after I was done was a small blessing, rather than catching me in the—

The air changed as a superheated ball of fire surged across the clearing toward the tent next to me. It turned out that my moving while being out of sight was paying dividends—especially if they themselves remained rooted in place. Their missed attack also did something else. It gave me a good idea of where the Wizard was casting from.

I crouched at the back of this tent, smelling the burning fabrics and wood from beside me, hearing the crackle of consuming flame . . . but eyes always focused on where the fireball had originated from. A card bloomed up in front of me, and I almost growled in focusing my energy onto it. Forward, through the tent and out the front—across the clearing that I couldn't see. I told it to do nothing but go straight ahead.

Reward came with a yell—a pained cry to signal that my card had found a mark among them. Likely, my position was now compromised, but I wasn't about to stand around and find out.

"Max!" Ren yelled.

I moved immediately, going around the tent with a card in motion already to see what was happening.

The enemy Ranger was trying to shrug away the hound nipping at him, drawing a knife to better melee the wounded dog. Behind him, the Wizard was pale, blood soaking through his clutched chest. Now several strides away, the Knight had broken free of the entrapping vines and was approaching Ren. The elf lay back with an arrow through her thigh. Her bow appeared to be caught on part of the tent nearest to her.

It was time for the showstopping finale. I ran on tired legs, anger forcing my shaking hand to create a stronger card—and it was off. A wide arc that circled from their views before zooming in, taking the distracted Ranger through the neck and curving around to strike the mage in the actual heart this time.

The Knight turned to me as I continued running toward him. Crimson energy flared up around his body as he readied himself. His helmet only had the slit visor, with the mouthpiece just dozens of holes. It wouldn't look out of place with a feathered plume out of the top, and I briefly remembered using one as a prop.

"You cannot beat my defenses," he crooned.

As a card spun up over my hand, a radiant flare of light flashed across toward him as Ren used her arrow skill. The Knight raised his shield and deflected it, a flicker of crimson pooling from the armor as he did so.

I was about in melee range now, so I threw my projectile.

With a clang, he brought his shield up in front of his face and blocked it. "See?" He chuckled. "I told you . . ." As he lowered his shield he saw the Tusk falling to the ground.

Holding my card between bloodied fingers, I collided with the heavy man, jamming the glowing rectangle in one edge of his visor slot and swiping it to the other. He yelled and struck me with his sword. It was . . . unpleasant, but my closeness to him dampened some of the force of the blow.

Plus, my body was already aching with pain, my suit torn and soaked with blood. It was difficult to know what he did. I stumbled away as he swung wildly through the air, blinded by my attack.

"Do you need to question any of them?" I called, stepping to the side so as not to give my position away too obviously. The Knight stumbled toward where I had spoken from.

"No." A simple reply. Cold and businesslike.

I rolled my neck and watched the flailing man. For my next trick, the vanishing blade. Once he had swung and left himself open, I stepped forward, pushing the nose edge of his helmet and stabbing the dagger up through the small gap into his throat. I received a bash from the shield, numbing my left arm as he staggered backward. He slowly dropped to the ground, trying to clutch at the blood pouring from his neck.

My eyes closed for a second, and I wavered—enjoying the breeze as the heat of adrenaline started to wear off. I clicked my tongue and walked over to the Oathwarden as she pulled the arrow from her leg with a growl. She glared up at me.

I gave her a bow and a smile, extending my hand to help her up.

"And then there were five."

CHAPTER FIFTEEN

Backstage

It was important to have times where you did nothing. Not only to let your body recover, but to allow your mind to process and move past the trauma and descent into chaos. Mixing the Bandits with the Player ambush was a recipe that left a sickness deep within me for some time. My first dance with darkness. Not the last, and in time my footwork would improve, and I'd really put on a show once death extended a skeletal hand for my time at the ball once more.

We sat on chairs, although I did not remember where we got them. Before us was a crackling fire, set up within the woods some distance away from the Bandits. Even in the afternoon's light, beneath the canopy the light from our own camp illuminated both us and the nearby surroundings with an amber glow.

For a while, we just stared at the flames. I watched as they danced against the light breeze. The wood cracked and split from the heat, occasionally shifting the pile abruptly. The warmth enveloped me and brought comfort.

The ambush from the other Players had gifted me some actually useful armor. I seemed to have an affinity for spell-caster gear, so the Wizard had been a special little trove of clothing to increase my Mana and Intelligence. Just words to me, at this stage. Whoever designed the System would be annoyed that I preferred to play things by feel rather than quantify how the numbers worked. Ironic, given how I spent the idle processes of my mind. Enough food to last us a few days, but they carried little else of use. They must have a storeroom or safe house in their hideout. I worked my jaw in thought.

"Max, are you okay?"

I raised an eyebrow at the elf, who was frowning at the fire still. "Never better. I'm having the time of my life."

She chose to ignore the sarcasm. "I watched you. Figured you'd need rescuing or have to run off from the fight. You did well."

Part of it had felt natural to me. The taking of lives. Maybe it wasn't some hidden facet of myself, but just something inside that could separate the fact that they were real. In the sense of having . . . a soul? My brain was still behind the times and had no intention of catching up.

"Thank you," I eventually offered. My first proper show, successful to rave review. Audience of one, but that's how things had started out way back when I was a child.

"For what it's worth . . ." She trailed off before looking into the surrounding woods. "I'm sorry to put you through that. Both the Bandits and the Players."

"Forgiven." My frank response actually drew her glare, a brief surprise within the scowl. I smiled, while internally I screamed. All the turmoil would pass in time. I just had to soldier through it. Show must go on.

"Just like that, really?"

"Your methods of teaching me are rather harsh, but I understand it to some degree. You expect me to measure up to some standard to be of any worth to you and your cause." I tried to position myself more comfortably in the chair, but my body wasn't having it.

She glared at me, and I tried to read her bright eyes. Despite her brow, there wasn't really anger behind them, a lot of anguish maybe, some internal conflict I wasn't privy to.

From my Inventory, I pulled out a sweet cake for us each and passed one over.

"More?" She took it eagerly but eyed me with suspicion.

"Ration Boxes or something. Just the two though." I took a bite and slunk down in the wooden chair, closing my eyes in an attempt to relax.

Silence covered our small clearing, except for the occasional bite of cake and the crackling fire. It was peaceful, and any residual pain had started to become a numb ache across my battered body.

"I didn't come here alone . . ." Ren said quietly.

I turned my head toward her and opened my eyes back up, the glow of the fire illuminating an odd expression across her face.

"He . . . We were engaged. Planning to run away from my responsibilities to be together. Somehow we ended up here. And he . . . He died, as we tried to escape from the group that attacked us."

My tongue caught in my mouth. "I'm . . . really sorry." That's all I could manage. Barely had I been able to get over the loss of my mother in my previous life. I was in no position to advise on something so close to her heart. It pained me that her expression was no longer that of a grouch but of exhausted sadness.

Just as soon as it was there, she shook it away. "Well, you've killed four of the fuckers for me. That makes you alright in my book."

I stared back at the fire for a bit. "The other five will come for us now?"

"No, more likely they'll hole up in their hideout. They won't be so reckless now. I doubt they expected both of us to be here, and for you to be so . . . capable."

Capable was a word I wasn't sure I could affix to the action of being a proficient murderer. Although she had perhaps just meant the use of my new Abilities.

"I'm probably not supposed to bleed from the hands though." They looked fine now, and I brought them up to check. Some bruising, otherwise healed and fine.

"Looked like blood magic. I was worried you were going to explode or something." She tilted her head and narrowed her eyes at me.

I caught her look and smiled. "You were *worried*?"

"Don't be an asshole, trickster." She scowled at me. "I just opened up to you and everything."

"I figured that was more the sweet cake than anything I had done." I leaned back in my chair and smiled to myself, content enough to just hear her sigh in resignation. From my Inventory, I withdrew another cake and waved it toward her.

"So full of shit." She took it from me. "But thanks."

"Life is both full of shit and full of pleasant surprises, Ren." The smile faded from my face as I looked up at the canopy. "You need the ebb and flow to keep you going."

"Poet now, are we?" She shook her head and stood up, finishing the cake and wiping her fingers off. "If you want to grumble on or espouse romanticisms, we should at least walk while you do so. Your level up is soon."

"And then you'll take me a little more seriously?" I stood and watched the chairs collapse into her Inventory.

"You said I was forgiven," she said as she glared at me.

"You are. When you called for me, I came immediately to your aid. Like a proper Party member would." I crossed my arms and smiled, enjoying the last of the fire's warmth before it went out.

Ren looked down and away. I wondered if she felt shame for having to call for my help or embarrassed that I did so even after she had thrown me to the wolves. Her brow had softened, despite the glare cutting into the patch of dirt on the ground.

"Max, I don't . . ."

"I get it." I walked past her. "Don't trust easily. Have high expectations. Those feelings are rooted in your past and are valid. Just have a little faith in me. *Suspend your disbelief.*"

I carried on toward the objective marker, allowing her to get rid of the fire before catching up. The interesting thing about faking it till you make it was that sometimes it actually worked. Whether the System smoothed out the edges using

Deception was neither here nor there. Inside, I was full of panic and uncertainty. My hands were fine, but looking at them, I still saw the blood. I could hear the last dying breaths. Pulses of crimson, shocked eyes, the snapping of bone. *Escape* was gnawing at my insides.

Latching on to pepping Ren up was a shackle to keep me grounded. An act born from a scared truth given full bloom of life. I wasn't lying to her with what I said. It was just a thought that had been given center stage, buffed up by my best grandstanding.

Ren caught up, and we walked on in silence. This time, there was a bit of awkwardness in the air. At this stage, I honestly didn't know what to do. Conflict and close personal relationships were as foreign to me . . . no, more foreign to me than ending lives. My tongue rolled against my teeth as I tried to recall something.

"Hmm." I tilted my head. "When I started here, the System said something about soul duplication and merge."

At first, I wasn't sure if the elf would respond, but she eventually scrunched up her face. "Really? Shit."

"What do you think that means?" I looked off down the road. The little house should only be fifteen minutes or so, I reckoned.

She exhaled through her nose. "No idea. You have two souls in you but combined into one? I'm not sure how that could happen."

I didn't feel like any less of myself or any more of anyone else. Despite the weird feeling that I had a life I couldn't remember different from my *magician* past . . . I somehow knew it had still been me. Just a different me. My body shuddered at the thought. Also, my jacket had a few holes in it now that let the breeze through.

Magic was my normal life. Perhaps demons were my alternative life—hence the Class I now had. Questions beyond me, yet settled in for the long ride.

"We might have to push you a bit to get your level four." Ren tapped at a side pouch on her belt. "We'll want to strike while the iron is hot and get the five before they really fortify themselves in."

I glanced at the elfin woman. The burns she'd received from the Wizard earlier had all but cleared up. Tired, but her radiant hair and bright eyes didn't look any worse for wear. I wondered if scars were even possible here—I certainly still felt the toll on my body even if I wasn't outwardly injured.

"We can't see Classes or levels, right?"

Ren nodded. "There's a skill for that. It's called . . . Analyze, I think. There was one other before you here that had it."

It was my turn to frown at the Oathwarden. "By one other, do you mean you had a *friend*?"

"Someone who wasn't a giant asshole, yeah. Human named Fiona. Some kind of fighter Class."

"She didn't want to stick around and help you?"

Ren worked her jaw, perhaps unsure as to how talkative she really felt. "Everyone has their own ambitions, trickster. Hers took her to the mainland."

I smiled. "No objections to finding her and asking her to join our Party then?"

"I haven't said I'll . . ." She rolled her eyes. "One bridge at a time, Max."

Personally, I considered it a done deal. She may come off as cold and aloof, but now that I had shown myself as a dependable and *definitely* mentally stable person, she was bound to agree to Party together on the mainland.

As far as other Party members went, sure, that could be a bridge to cross or burn later. If everyone had to crawl through the dirt to catch up to us, then that'd slow us down and leave our options limited. But we would need someone we could trust with our lives.

My eyebrow raised as I looked off into the tree line. "I trust you with my life."

She deflated, clearly tired from my haphazard attempts at conversation. "What? Why say that now? Do you expect me to say it back?"

I shrugged. "Either you do or you don't."

"Fucking dickbag, Max." She scowled off toward the woods. "Yes, alright? I do."

Unfair of me to push her when she clearly wasn't the opening-up type. Maybe even hypocritical, if I let the thought sink too deep in my brain. Part of me did need the reassurance, though. If she wanted to grind me to dust to find out what I was worth—that was fair. But I needed to know there was something greater worth the suffering. Those who helped your performance didn't need to share your vision, but they needed to be competent and on the same page. That was the mirror we held up to each other.

The farmhouse loomed up on the road now, the old man still sitting and awaiting my triumphant return.

"After you level up, we'll go inside. Get washed up before the next Quest."

I nodded. He probably wouldn't mind, being stuck on the porch and having to give out Quests all day. He probably didn't get much use out of the place. "We can spare the time?"

"You smell like a morgue shat you out, and I have been roughing it for almost a week. *Yes*, we can spare the time."

There wasn't much anger in the statement but an edge of desperation for some creature comforts. After the death of her partner, I was sure she had gone through a lot—although perhaps not a good idea to get creative with more than she had let on. Every life has a shadow and all that.

"You return, adventurer!" The old man grinned, a sparkle in his eye that disarmed me. Easy to forget who they were—or weren't, as the case may be.

"Certainly, sir. One family heirloom and lots of bodily harm and trauma. Although I think I'll hold on to those!"

"Please do." His grin persisted as he held his hand out. The heirloom, some form of jug, touched his hands and then vanished.

"Feel accomplished yet?" Ren was leaning on the wall near the front door, a dull look on her face.

"Thank you, adventurer. I don't have much, but please accept these."

[Quest complete]
[Progress: 1/1 Heirlooms retrieved]
[Receive Reward?]

[Experience gained]
[50 Gold]
[Deployable Grill]
[Ration Box (3)]

[Level up—<3>]
[Stats increased]
[New Ability: <Demonic Pact>]
[New Passive: <Master Summoner>]
[New Passive: <Mana Extension>]

"Oh yes." I smiled and tipped my hat toward the elf. "I certainly do."

CHAPTER SIXTEEN

Clean Cut

With one of my feet usually halfway in the grave, the mud and grime of adventuring was like a friend. Not one you particularly cared for or spent much time around if you could help it . . . but, okay, more of an acquaintance then. Mental note to go back through these introspective musings at a later date and remove the terrible parts. Which seems to be most of it. If this text still remains, then either I died before I had the chance, or perhaps I finally learned to love all the minor imperfections in life and accept them for what they were. The former being more likely.

The couch in the otherwise relatively plain house was reasonably comfortable. At least, compared to the hole in the ground and the weapons of the Bandits. Other than the inert fireplace across from me, the table and chairs in the corner, and two doorways leading to other rooms, there wasn't a lot going on in here.

Ren stood at the bottom of the stairs, her arms folded. "I'm going first. I trust you can stay alive for ten minutes by yourself?"

"I'll set a timer," I said as I smiled before recoiling from her glare. "Oh, want to see a magic trick first?" Although her glare didn't fade, her continued presence told me that she was at least humoring the idea.

I withdrew a gold coin from my Inventory and held it in my right hand. The brief thought of how they ran an economy based solely on the singular denomination threatened my suspended beliefs, but I harried them away. It was cool to the touch and just the right size to make it comparable to what I was used to.

Not quite feeling myself, I didn't stand to perform the brief illusion. Instead, I reveled in the continued safety of the cushioned seat. I held it up to show her the normal coin, nothing untoward about the object. Placed it between my knuckles and flipped it over and over to the next—before, with a quick flourish, I revealed my empty palm to her. Something simple to get the ball rolling and enrapture my first potential fan.

A slow blink was my only reward. "You could have just put it in your Inventory. I'm going to have my bath." She turned and walked up the wooden steps.

I frowned as the coin dropped from the back of my hand, and I held it to feel the texture. Her footsteps could be heard moving above me, followed by the sound of running water. With a sigh, I put the coin back away.

A purple card appeared over my hand, and I idly spun it as it hovered a few inches in the air. Perhaps a good time to review my new Skills.

The <Master Summoner> one gave all my summons ten percent additional Health and Damage—which, I supposed, was *okay*. It was an upgrade at least. It was flat. Guaranteed. The sort of thing that contented me. Would have been nice if it increased *my* Damage as well, but I felt too fresh to the System to want to write a letter of complaint.

<Mana Extension> gave me a higher capacity for Mana storage. This one would be a massive boon, as I seemed to starve myself bloody of the stuff given half the chance. Hopefully, it meant more card tricks without them being such a drain.

The <Demonic Pact> Ability, however, was something else. I had already read it once and closed it away from my vision—thinking I maybe had read it incorrectly. On second glance, I had not. Why I had considered that my demonic Abilities would be limited to bringing about cute little temporary followers, I didn't know.

I could place the pact on a corpse—there were plenty of stipulations on what that encapsulated—and my demonic patron would inhabit the body for a short duration. It sounded a bit like possession-based necromancy. What interested me most, past the appalling visuals of the skill, was that it seemed like it would be the same demon every time. I didn't remember signing any pacts on arrival, but it looked to be something already dyed into my existence. The deck felt heavy in my pocket, pulling at my thoughts.

Brain totally overwhelmed, I breathed out my nose, shut down the blue boxes, and began throwing my card out—and then brought it back to catch it. Just to see how close I could get to the wooden wall opposite. The running water had stopped, so Ren must be bathing now. An inch or two closer to the wall, and then I caught it on the return. A small sliver of blood ran across one of my fingers. I'd put that to rest for now.

Relenting to accept what the elf had said, I sighed and brought down my tattered top hat to give it a try. Surprised it had even made it this far intact and remained on my head. I put one hand inside of it and pulled out the power token—from my Inventory, but for all intents and purposes it looked just as the magic trick would have if I had performed the trick manually. It was . . . saddening that it was that simple, yet also small waves of ideas began lapping at my barren shores.

While others two-finger tapped to mentally access their STARs, I could touch-type, and it felt more innate. Intriguing.

I held the odd stone up. It looked almost like a ruby, but opaquer, carved into a smooth diamond shape, with a thick frame of gold around it. Even holding it in my hand, I could feel the residual . . . *magic* within it. How odd. I brought up the information screen.

[Power Token: Use (1) to upgrade a basic Skill to advanced.
Use (10) to upgrade an advanced Skill to expert.]

Hmm. I hadn't known that Skills could be improved, but that was the fault of my own ignorance. Getting my feet wet with immediate violence and seemingly having bypassed the usual hand-holding the System usually dealt out. All my skills seemed to be basic level currently, and I wondered how rare these tokens were or how much they really improved the Skills. Which even would I choose to advance when I had so many to pick from?

I must have been pondering for longer than expected, as Ren started down the stairs. Her armor was pristine and undamaged, and she looked clean and radiant. Whatever sweat, grime, and vegetation she had accumulated as of late had been scoured away—I'd have even less of an issue imagining her as a princess in this state. Briefly, my tongue caught in my mouth.

"All free for you." She returned to crossing her arms across her chest.

"Look what I found—a power token." I held it up between my fingers, mostly stalling, as I didn't want to leave the couch even with the promise of a bath imminent.

"You found a . . . Can I have it?" She tilted her head.

I rolled my tongue across my teeth. Clearly, they had some rarity then. Still, it wouldn't go amiss to crawl further into her good books for now. "Sure." I flicked it across the room, and she caught it.

She held it up to the light to observe it and, after a few seconds, walked over to the couch. She chucked it back in my lap. "*Dickbag.*"

"What?" My surprised mouth was unable to formulate a full sentence past that.

"We'll have to beat that people-pleasing attitude out of you." She sat down on the couch next to me. "You'll get us killed otherwise."

I popped the token back into my Inventory for now, still taken aback from the very accurate point-blank skewer straight into my psyche. Plus, she called me a *dickbag* again, which didn't feel much like an elfin-princess thing to do. Based on my very limited knowledge of both of those things.

Before she could dig deeper into my inner workings, I decided now was a good time to get washed up, so I stood.

"Inventory, Other Options, Repair Cosmetics. You'll want to do it in private usually, unless you are an exhibitionist." She glared at me. "Which I wouldn't put it past you."

"I'm a showman, but that doesn't mean . . ." I rubbed at the bridge of my nose. She was riling me up on purpose. It was sometimes hard to discern the banter when she looked as though she wanted to bend both my elbows back the wrong way. Getting my suit fixed up sounded great though. "Thanks, Ren." I gave a brief bow out of habit and went for the stairs.

"Hey, Max . . ."

I turned my head to see her scowl had softened.

"Could you summon a Hellhound down here?"

"Of course." I smiled and brought the card into the air. I kept it hovering in front of me for a second, my brow furrowed. Instead of summoning close to me, I focused on keeping the card empowered—and threw it down beside the couch.

I continued up the stairs as I mentally commanded the pup to keep the elf company. He wouldn't last long, but perhaps if I kept the bathroom door cracked I could fling a card all the way down the stairs and . . . Did that count as people-pleasing? She would probably be content enough with the time she had. If only life were that simple in all things.

The bathroom was small, and the air was pleasantly warm from whatever residual steam had come from Ren's bath. The tub itself was simple, a circle of wood with a tap at one end. With the door closed behind me, I twisted the tap on and hummed to myself. My show tune again. I went through the menus to select the repair option, and my clothes vanished, aside from my underwear. That the System had surpassed me in magic already was humbling, but if anything, it would soon become a tool I could wield.

I took the rest off the old-fashioned way and sat in the filling tub. Already it was warm—the perfect temperature, in fact. The little progress bar in the air told me I had five minutes before my suit would be done—and I assumed it would pop straight back on to my bathing body. As much as I would like to spend hours in the comforting water, I relented to washing myself before that inevitability.

Bruised in places and some soft scars still healing, but no real damage despite what I had endured. Medical miracles. It would just be my mental capacity that would suffer under the constant turmoil of battle. Washed and still with some time to kill, I went through my Inventory and opened up the Rare Chance Box.

[Robe of the Caster: +2 INT, +10% Mana regeneration]

Straight on the little box where the basic leather armor from the thugs had been sitting. I wasn't really much for robes, but if I didn't need to show it then I could live with wearing whatever beneath my show suit. My brain needn't concern itself with how that worked.

With a sigh, I exited the warmth. Stood for a moment in the room just steaming from the damp heat. Ren had been right. We *did* have the time for this. It was only a sadness that it couldn't go on for longer. But I was now only a level behind her, and catching up would let us get her revenge and move on from the island. Was taking up her burden also people-pleasing?

My clothes popped back into existence upon my body. Thankfully, I was dry enough to not make it an uncomfortable experience. Pristine and perfect, just as Ren was. Her armor and outfit, I meant. In the small mirror at the side of the room, I gave myself the side-eye. Now that the bath was behind me, the drab future started to darken my spirit. Death and bloodshed—and apparently my demon patron possessing those that I slew. Briefly, I wondered if the old man was looking for permanent tenants.

I popped out a purple card as I walked toward the door, flipping and twirling it just above my hand. The more time I spent getting used to them, the more things I'd be able to do. It was like any normal deck of cards in that regard. Learn the texture, the shape, and the way they slid and cut against one another. Muscle memory needed forming. It was different now with actual magical power involved, but some of the core components were the same.

Down the stairs I came into the main room, where Ren was looking rather forlorn and staring at the floorboards.

"Penny for your thoughts?" I asked, flipping a gold coin into the air and having it vanish as it disappeared into my Inventory.

"I had a dog once." Her blunt reply was edged with enough of a story to paint a clear picture.

"Anytime you want, just let me know." I looked out of the side window, the quiet woods shifting slightly in the breeze. I didn't want to see her glare at me for that offer, but even more so, I didn't want to see anything but a glare.

"Let's get going, trickster." Some of the usual terseness was missing from her tone. "We have a bunch of goblins to slay."

I nodded, already halfway through my Skill list, ready to pick which Ability to upgrade. "Well then, we'd best get this show on the road."

CHAPTER SEVENTEEN

Stagehands

A whole new world of possibility before me, I had stumbled over some of the smaller blocks on the way. With aching hands I had tried to hold on to the things of my past, stuck in my old ways and unable to grow. Once I had been forced to adapt, I was then in free fall through almost infinite possibility. Getting to that point without all the blood and heartache would have been nicer, but wishes seldom came true.

Although I now had the power token burning a hole in my pocket, I was cautious to spend it so soon without knowing how rare they truly were. At worst, I would wait for my looming level-four abilities to have the full picture of what I had available before we started preparing for what lay ahead.

I stopped to let the elf go beneath some overhanging branches before I did. "I suppose most people are rather tight-lipped about their Classes and Abilities?"

"Most," she said as she nodded briefly before going ahead. "It's not like they can be stolen, but sometimes the threat of the unknown is enough to keep people wary of you."

"Sometimes," I agreed, following her through the foliage.

"If one of the thugs had escaped, they would be able to report back that you can summon demons and throw cards. They could prepare for that." She stood in the small clearing beyond the trees and crossed her arms.

"I can also turn a corpse into a demon." I grinned, my stomach sinking at how terrible that sounded.

She tilted her head. "Is this new demon also a dog?"

The skill description hadn't really mentioned, so I shrugged a response, not ready to commit either way.

"There are a few other Quests you usually do first, but we can skip ahead to this next one. It's quicker to get your next level up, and you only miss out on some junk items." She gestured her head to the side, and we continued walking.

"So you can't get to level five without being teleported?"

She scowled back at me as we resumed traveling between thick trees. "No idea. But I don't want to risk it."

"Didn't your friend, the fighter—"

"I pushed her away before she left."

We carried on in silence. Once again, unfair for me to fill in the blanks, but I could imagine a conflict where one wanted to stay and one wanted to leave. I didn't want to pry, mostly because conflict and I were often at odds. She would elaborate if and when ready.

After a few more minutes through the woods, a Quest popped up on the side of my vision.

"Kill *thirty* Goblins, really?" My shoulders already felt tense at the mere mention of the mass murder.

"It will go by quickly. They aren't as sturdy as the Bandits, but there are a lot more of them. It's a repeatable Quest."

"*Repeatable,*" I repeated, mostly due to not being able to help myself. "That means I'll be killing more than thirty."

She nodded slowly. "I'm glad you catch on quickly. They're just over this ridge."

I could see now that the tree line about forty feet off petered out, and the horizon was almost visible. Straining my senses, I could make out the slight sound of something, and the smell was different. Less clear vegetation and more . . . burning wood and leather. Perhaps that was placebo, and my brain was filling in the details it wanted.

Walking ahead, I tried stretching out my fingers to limber them up. Maybe I could go back and have another bath after this—that almost made the ordeal seem worth it. Reaching the edge of the trees, I knelt down and moved to peer closer to the edge, rising up slowly from a bush.

Below me was a small valley teeming with little green bodies milling around. Stout shacks of rough wood and leather roof coverings dotted the edges of the valley walls, while a well-worn dirt path stretched from one end to the other. The Goblins themselves were short—maybe three to four feet tall, by my estimation. Pointed ears and noses, grim mouths full of sharp teeth. Either equipped with some manner of tools, or at least having weapons stowed on their sides or backs. Their sharp features gave them a malevolent look, not helped much by their bright-yellow eyes and constant scowls.

"I take it you'll just be watching from a distance as usual?" I murmured as I focused on the little green skins.

At the back of my neck, I felt the pointed tip of something metallic press against me.

"What would you do in this situation?" she asked in a level tone.

An arrow to the back of my head, point-blank. I could now hear the slight flex of the bowstring. I worked my jaw. Although at this distance it wouldn't have the full force of a fired arrow, I still wouldn't want to see what the actual effect would be on my head holder. A confident smile sparked at the corner of my mouth.

"There's already a card behind you, and an Imp to your right holding a fireball."

"Hmm? No, there's—"

The card spun around back into my hand, and the arrowhead bounced down my back to the ground. "You're right. I lied. I just needed a moment to actually cast the card without you spotting it."

She relaxed the bow and crouched beside me to look down to the village. "Acceptable, but you can't always rely on tricks."

I smiled, knowing that was my whole thing. "What would you have had me do?"

The elf shrugged. "Wasn't my place to imagine a win condition."

Exhaling through my nose, I furrowed my brow at the Goblins. She could probably tell I wasn't much of a fighter in my previous life and was massaging my brain into thinking like someone whose life was on the line. Shouldn't be too difficult to pretend to be competent, although I had been pretty close to shaving off the back of my head or some of her fingers if I had rushed the card any further. Despite the test, I trusted her—just as she must have trusted me to actually have a way out of that situation without hurting either of us.

The slope before me seemed to be the best spot in the area to really breach the Goblin throng successfully without drawing too much attention. I stood and readied myself to go in hot—a group of three Goblins sat at a table right at my proposed landing spot.

"Hey, Max?"

I raised my eyebrow and looked down at the scowling elf.

"Don't die, okay? I've invested too much time into you already."

A smile crossed my face. "I can only promise to put on a good show." As I went to give her a bow, my footing slipped, and I began to slide down the loose gravel toward the Goblins. Something that would have been much more amusing had I not been living it and if I could stand any slapstick in my acts.

My card went out into the air, striking the first Goblin in the neck as I hit the dirt. I rolled forward to absorb the impact and brought my dagger out, stabbing it into the head of the closest one as the magic card zipped into the neck of the third and dissipated. That may have just saved my reputation.

I drew the dark card of <Demonic Pact>, the picture on it showing a similar rabbit to the one the deck box had upon it. I threw it at one of the dead Goblins.

Immediately, purple mist began to swirl around the body, and it slowly clambered back to its feet. The yellow eyes then popped fully out of their head onto the ground, to be replaced by burning circles of bright-purple light. From the top of the Goblin's head, two long ears of purple energy burst upward, shattering through the skull.

"Oh fuck! *I exist.* Who am I?" The demon's voice was tinny and harsh, and he clutched at the face of his new temporary abode.

The inhabited corpse turned to me with a look bordering on confused elation but to me was just abject horror to see the puppet body look so grim.

"Uh, you are Roger. It's time to kill Goblins." Bringing up names on the spot wasn't one of the tricks I held up my sleeves, but something about that seemed to fit. "I am Max."

"Okay, sure." Roger shrugged, and he picked up a discarded sword from the ground. "Straight to the action. I like that, boss."

I hadn't imagined I'd need to make rapport with a demon so soon in my journey and probably shouldn't have been surprised that he would be so intent on violence from the get-go. From the deck, I threw out an Imp and readied a card toward the next group of four Goblins.

The purple card sliced off the arm of the first before embedding into the chest of the second. Roger was already halfway over to them, running awkwardly as if he didn't quite know how the body should function, with sword raised.

With a flash of amber, the Imp's fireball shot across the two dozen feet to explode against two of the group just before my pact demon arrived. He waved the loosely held sword around wildly, doing a decent amount of damage while receiving a few choice stabs in return. This didn't seem to bother him at all, however.

I spun the next card around him, slashing at the backs and hands holding raised weapons before twisting through one of their necks. Roger cracked the skull of one of the pained Monsters and did a little dance of joy, his left arm being lopped off in the process.

There was a mania to it that I struggled to parse. My brain couldn't work its way around the macabre cartoon character having a blast using a corpse as a living host to enact further violence. Even standing here, severing Goblins to pieces myself, there was a slight dissociation that made me feel like a spectator.

Already the next fireball was on the way to a second group of Goblins as my card finished off the last of the first. Although I hadn't directed him overtly to pull more enemies, there was an unspoken acceptance that we were capable. Perhaps he could read my intent the same as the lesser demons. I gave the Imp a nod, which his little round head returned. My card twisted and cut into the leg of the closest Goblin, hobbling him to a knee so that Roger could run in and club him around the head.

"This is fun as fuck!" Roger yelled out, now starting to use the sword to attempt to block attacks.

From way in the back, I felt like a conductor. Moving my hands around and directing a card at a time so as to not force my Mana reserves too hard. I tried to imagine music to dull out the sounds of violence. The Imp tugged at my slacks, and I looked down to see him wave goodbye. So soon? He had done well, and I gave him a brief bow. Without realizing it, we had gotten through another two groups while my mind had been trying to block out the process.

I paused as my card finished off the last Goblin in the group. Let myself breathe so that I could summon another Imp. My pact demon paused and rested his good hand on his knees, as if out of breath.

"You okay, Roger?"

"Yeah, boss. Having the time of my fucking life over here." He stood up straight and worked the goblin body into grinning. I hated it.

We were now in the middle of the village and had cleared maybe a fifth of it. As I held the Imp card ready, I checked the Quest progress.

[Progress: 23/30 Goblins killed]

"How long are you with me, Roger?" With only two packs until completion, we could either push ahead to get it done or take a break if I needed to bring him back.

He tilted his head from side to side, his purple ears of energy flopping back and forth. "Time's almost up—but I can jump into one of these other bodies if you want me to stick around?"

"I'd love that." I smiled and nodded, despite thinking the opposite. I'm sure I would see worse in my time in this world, but today had been filled with death, and the taste of it was numbing my senses.

I watched as the mist pooled away from the body, the ears dissipating and eyes fading as if blown away in the breeze. The empty corpse dropped to the ground, and a different Goblin rose, his eyes bursting out as his skull cracked open to allow the ears.

"Either these guys are short as fuck, or you're a fucking giant, boss!" Roger stumbled his puppet body over to me and looked up, hands on his hips.

"It's the former." I managed to grin. "Try a different weapon. You need to get used to a variety if you'll be borrowing all the time."

He nodded way too violently and hopped over to the last pack we had killed, this time bringing an axe into his hands. "Let's go, boss. Chop-chop!" He mimed waving the weapon in the air.

I wondered if the System had a way to check my sanity. Doubtful. As Ren had become my mentor, I too had to teach my fledgling demon to become more effective.

Another Imp was summoned from a magic circle, the pudgy demon giving Roger a quizzical look before offering me a slight bow.

After returning the gesture, I brought up a card, spinning it over my hand. It turned out that killing was relatively straightforward, even *easy*. The smile faded from my face, as I could almost feel Ren's glare burning into the back of my head.

The part that was actually difficult was remembering to loot everything.

CHAPTER EIGHTEEN

Twisting Aces

I never really got the idea of experience—in terms of how the System decided you should progress. There were moments where I had suffered and learned a lot about life and my own strength that had no reward, and then other times I handed a box of cakes from one town to the next and received jubilant praise, lavished with gold and a few notches closer to a boost of power. At the end of the day, I was just a performing animal, jumping through hoops for the treat at the end without understanding the nuance of the show. Yet knowing this never stopped me.

Sweat ran down the side of my face, and I hunched over to catch my breath. Dark crimson marred the thighs of my suit, where I had wiped off some minor exertion blood from my hands. Mostly under control. Pacing myself. Looting had become tiresome, as most of the goblins only had meager gold and basic equipment on them. Leggings and bracers with +1 Dexterity had been the best prizes earned from the massacre.

Roger twisted a dagger around in a flourish, his current body covered in the insides of some other Goblin.

"This is fun, boss—we doin' this all day?"

The sun was now waning in the sky. We had been at this for hours. We were on the fourth repeat of the Quest. Each time a reward of gold, experience, and an Uncommon Chance Box. By the time we had cleared the area, the earlier sections had started to respawn. An odd visual of moving and living beings just fading into view, as if they were there all along—ghosts, now made real. We *could* do this all day, but I was exhausted.

[Progress: 16/30 Goblins killed]

"Fourteen more, Roger," I said with a smile, now partially used to his terrifying visage.

"Aw, then I'll have to go. Fuck! But you'll call on me again?"

Despite being bits of near-white light shaded by purple, there was an amount of earnest innocence in his eyes. *Innocence* perhaps being the wrong word, after seeing the joy in him as he slaughtered mass goblins—but he had simple desires and wants. My barren friend list wasn't too picky, at this stage.

"Of course." I tapped the side of my nose. "We have a pact, after all."

Did things work like that? I didn't really know, but it helped make the demon happy. Despite my apprehension, I realized I would probably be quite sad if my next attempt to summon him brought a different demon forth. For the simpler creatures, it was fine, but after spending quality time with . . .

Quality time? I must be losing my sanity.

"Alright, let's get this over with. I've had a long day." I drew a Hellhound card and threw it out at the next pack of Goblins.

Roger was getting used to the Goblin physiology now and ran toward the group with more efficiency. My card circled around the fray, cutting and interrupting to allow my summons the advantage in the melee.

I hadn't seen or heard from Ren during this time. It must be somewhat boring to see me so efficiently dispatching all the foes for hours on end—it wasn't a trial of fire like the Bandits. Roger acted as a distraction, and with him paired alongside the hound, I rarely needed to worry about a Goblin coming in my direction. Naturally, any armed with ranged weapons I took out first, and the times we'd draw two or three groups by accident, I could just exert my Mana for a more durable card.

My left hand held my right wrist, and I did just that. A blazing card hovered before zipping through the air, leaving a trail of energy behind it. Into a new group, neck, neck, neck. Like a surgeon with a scalpel, I expertly cut through all three Goblins before allowing the card to vanish. I flicked the blood from my hand onto the ground.

"Seven more." I grinned at Roger as he withdrew his blade slowly from a dead Goblin. The hound trotted over and sat by my feet, and I gave it a pat on the head. They may all be different, but word of mouth traveled fast. Assuming they had a way to communicate in hell and that hell was an actual thing.

"Do you give your card techniques different names, boss?" He slowly pushed the blade back into the body.

"No, should I?" I supposed all tricks had different names.

"It's a well-known fact that Skill names are fucking awesome!"

"Didn't you only start existing a few hours ago?"

"Well, I made up the fact, so it must be true." The puppet body frowned, and he shrugged.

I couldn't really fault that logic and didn't want to attempt to have it darken my thoughts for a moment longer than necessary. While card tricks had a variety of names, there weren't many for when you slit the throat of three mortals or punctured through someone's head.

"Let me think on that." I had already established I was bad at thinking up names on the spot—and if I was one thing, it was reliable. Mostly.

Remembering to loot these last few along the way, I gestured for my card to return to my hand as the last Goblin dropped to the dirt.

[Quest complete]
[Progress: 30/30 Goblins killed]
[Reward Received]

[Experience gained]
[80 Gold]
[Uncommon Chance Box]

"You have much time left?" I raised an eyebrow at Roger. "I'd like you to meet Ren. She's . . . a friend of sorts?"

"Couple minutes, boss." He shrugged, not having any frame of reference for what I could be referring to.

My STAR was glowing gold, which meant I had leveled up. It was exciting and nerve-racking at the same time—knowing there was more power to be had, yet also aware that we were soon to be fighting more Players. Plus, I didn't want to go through that right now until we were out of the Goblin village.

I narrowed my eyes to the place where I had fallen down here and watched as the end of a rope now mirrored my journey down, albeit more intentionally than I had. Roger faded away and came back into one of the nearest bodies to have a bit of extra time, and then we jogged over to the side of the valley.

With a last pat for the Hellhound as it faded away, I sighed and looked up at the rope. "I should have put more points in Strength." I grinned, hoping that was a thing that made sense. My pact-bound demon just stared at me blankly. Whether that was because he knew Stats were automatically assigned by the System, or because . . . Well, given how new to existing he was, I couldn't fault him for not getting the context. I barely allowed it to settle in my own mind.

Perhaps the most humbling task of the day—realizing how hard it was to pull myself up a short rope—was a battle both hard won and not worth the reward. As I rolled over the bushes and lay prone on the soft grass, Ren stood over me with her arms crossed and a scowl on her face. Still, after the hours of grinding out death with a corpse puppet, I *was* happy to see her and those disarming blue eyes.

"You could have done that a *little* faster." She tapped her foot.

Roger followed my example, tripping over my legs as he tried to power through the bushes and fell atop my back. "Ack! Oh fuck. That's a weird-looking Goblin. *Disgusting.*"

"That's Ren, Roger." I shuffled him off of me. "She's an elf."

"Then elves are disgusting." The demon rolled into a sitting position and crossed his arms.

I pushed myself to my feet, dusting down my suit. "She is not. Ren is very . . ." I caught her intense glare, and any compliment that tried to balloon into my mind was quick to burst and wither away under the heat. ". . . Pleasant?"

"Your new pet has a terrible mouth but seems useful."

I managed to nod slowly, now caught between the two who were giving each other the most intense glares I had thought possible. They would need to get along if this was going to be a long-term Party thing . . . but currently I didn't care to invoke any more of their ire onto myself.

"Oh, let me do my level up." I forced a wide smile to hopefully distract the pair from any brewing argument.

"Actually." Roger raised his hand. "Wake me when you need something killing, boss." The purple energy blew away in an invisible wind, and the Goblin corpse, now inert, fell back across the ground.

"*Pleasant*, Max?"

"You have a certain charm I find pleasant," I murmured, slowly turning away from her and focusing on the blue windows now appearing.

[Level up—<4>]
[Stats increased]
[New Ability: <Card Fan>]
[New Passive: <Soul Bind>]
[New Passive: <Hell Born>]

I rubbed my eyes. Now level four and twelve things I could use my power token on. "Is it always one Ability and two Passives per level?"

She didn't reply at first, and I turned back to her to make sure she hadn't vanished. But no, she was there, looking like she had something to say she had been chewing on. Whatever it was passed as her frown met my gaze.

"I've heard at five there are no Passives, but you get a core Ability—like a keystone Skill for your Class." She deflated and rubbed at her head.

Core Ability? I wondered what that could be for me—I could already summon demons, including one that was semipermanent. I couldn't imagine the System would give me another summoning ability so soon. Ren began walking, and I followed behind as I brought up my Ability window.

<Soul Bind> shared 5 percent of my stats with my summons, which didn't sound like much. It was a flat benefit though, and the stronger I became then the more they would reap the advantage. <Hell Born> just increased both my Fire and Demonic Resistances—which was a little abstract, but sure, I could go with the flow on that. Anything that kept me further from death's door was appreciated.

The active Abilities were always the interesting ones. <Card Fan> used three cards and created a brief wall in the direction I aimed that would absorb a certain amount of damage on a short cooldown. It didn't say whether I could use my magic cards through it or not, so some testing would have to be done. Currently, it seemed I could only cast one Ability at a time, so I'd need to temper some expectation, but a defensive skill for a supposed spellcaster was definitely a boon. Not every enemy would be a weak Goblin or distracted by my summons.

"Anything powerful that can save us a headache?" Ren asked, briefly looking over her shoulder at me.

"Tell me your Abilities first, and I'll tell you mine."

The look in her eyes grew tired, but she slowed down to walk beside me. "<Smite Shot> is the radiant shot you've seen. <Entangling Shot> is the one with the vines. My heal, <Nature's Blessing>, can also be imbued into an object."

I waited a second before it looked like she wasn't about to continue. "The fourth one I don't think you've used?"

"Correct," she said plainly, then looked up at me. "It helps me kill . . . demons."

I looked back at her, trying to read the expression she was attempting to give me behind the constant scowl. As an Oathwarden, it made sense to have abilities to help thwart whatever was threatening her . . . grove? I had started making things up now to justify my thought process. Being some manner of Paladin that could fight demons gave another layer to the constant disdain she tried to point my way.

"Nice. Mine are the magic card, the summoning of either Imp or Hound, Roger, and now I have a defensive wall I can bring up."

She didn't reply at first, maybe expecting more of a pushback on the reveal of her ability. If anything, I just felt bad that it wasn't more useful currently. Perhaps she thought I wouldn't trust her knowing that she could expel my fighting force easily.

"Sounds good," she eventually agreed. "Apart from *Roger*, but the defensive ability will help since we are both ranged."

I looked around the quickly darkening forest. "He's a demon, but he means well." Before she could argue the point, I continued. "You know, is it odd that we haven't seen any other Players?"

She followed my gaze around. "No, new Players are becoming uncommon . . . There seems to be some metric as to how they're added—maybe related to rarity? Word of mouth says there used to be a dozen or so a day at one point."

Interesting. My hand rubbed at my chin. "You think the thugs hanging about and not moving on could be a bottleneck, keeping new people from joining?"

"If so, we are about to do the System a favor." She looked off away from me. "We will rest tonight, unless you can see in the dark and have the energy for it?"

"Sleep sounds nice. Give me a chance to go through my Inventory and prepare. Tomorrow we will kill those that remain."

Ren looked back at me, her frown full of her determination to see the deed done. With a brief nod, we set off to find somewhere to camp.

I took the opportunity to open the four Chance Boxes, as much as I disliked the process.

[Gloves of the Sea: Minor Water Resistance]
[Shoulder Pads+: Increased Defense]
[Boots of Quickness: +1 AGI, +1 DEX]
[Sandals of the Wise: +2 INT]
[Dagger of Luck: +1 LUCK]

A sour expression crossed my face as I looked over at my Equipment boxes. The sandals were at least useful for my build, so I put them on. I was incredibly thankful that the System allowed me to keep my suit over the items rather than look like a clown with so much mismatching gear.

I'd hate to be a spectacle.

CHAPTER NINETEEN

Audience Participation

Judgment was a double-edged sword. Although the System had a dim view of Player-on-Player murder, it didn't really do much to prevent it. That a gang of those with bad intentions could hold part of the world almost at ransom with no recourse for punishment showed a serious flaw in the grand design. Perhaps I could let my ego have this one, think of myself as the solution brought into the world to carve such tumors from those more law-abiding. Although, that didn't allow me to feel any better about what I had become.

With our potential enemies holding down their fort, we elected to be more overt in our creature comforts for the evening ahead. One campfire, two tents. An uncontested night's rest. A multitude of boxes to sift through and equip whatever gear gave me an Intelligence or Dexterity bonus. The bigger question of what to use my power token on.

I was a man of simple flare. When you started from the beginning, you worked on the basics.

[Use Power Token on <Pick a Card>?]

While I had started growing quite the crop of interesting Skills and Abilities, it seemed pertinent to start with my bread and butter. Without a second way of dealing damage aside from my summons, it seemed as though the card throwing might be my long-term solution. A basic attack, if I allowed myself to make it sound so plain. An upgrade would remain effective no matter what.

Despite her inquisitive glares, I didn't allow Ren to be part of the selection process. It had to rest solely on my shoulders, and now I knew in part the reason she had given the token back. Not just that I had found it and should allow myself the share of my own spoils, but because a unique Class had more potential. I assumed anyway. A bit of late-night melodrama had put the sparkle in my eyes.

[<Pick a Card> is now advanced: Two cards may be summoned at once]

I sat outside my tent and grinned, earning her ire as I felt content with my choice. Not wanting to encourage her to move over and throttle the information out of me, I drew a purple card into the air, and then slid it to the side to reveal a second.

"More card tricks." A statement delivered impassively.

It was much harder to move them separately than together as a double card. I focused on trying to juggle them like a cartwheel. Possible, but without the finesse I was used to. More things to play with and learn.

"You're impossible. I'm going to sleep." Ren turned and entered her tent as I allowed the purple cards to vanish.

I looked down to see my hand was bloodied. At least it didn't hurt that time. Resigning to getting some proper rest, I entered my own tent and lay on the bedroll. Not quite as beautiful as seeing the stars, but a step above a hole in the ground. With the thin slit of the front of the tent open, I attempted to thread a card through it. Narrowed my eyes and cooled my breathing to focus. At first, successful as it zipped out into the night. Then, after putting a card-shaped hole in the side of the fabric after a near miss on the third repeat, I decided to call it a night. Closed my eyes and let the worries flood out with a deep breath.

A dreamless sleep hit me like a sack of bricks, and before long, the murmur of a voice barely roused me from my bedroll.

"Max? It's your turn to cook."

With a groan, I slid from my tent out into the dew-laden grass and bright light of early morning.

"It's murder day, trickster. We'll need our strength." She wasn't smiling, but there was an energy to her. Apprehension? Excitement? Hope that I had more sweet cakes stowed away?

I did, but that was beside the point. Murdering through the Goblin hordes had earned me enough boxes of food that we could have a banquet. As I groggily got to my feet, I stretched out and clocked that she had called it *murder day*. Not that I was capable of forgetting such a fact. Perhaps some kind of mistranslation.

With a deep breath, I picked my jacket up from the ground, not really remembering taking it off. I waved it through the air to reveal the grill now standing on the grass.

Ren rolled her eyes. "Are you always this insufferable?"

"Yes," I said with a grin. "Usually more so, I'm afraid."

"Even when you're alone?"

My mouth opened and closed while my brain tried to catch up. Internally, one of the boxes at the back of my mind was bulging, about to explode. "No?" I eventually offered to release some pressure.

"Then just act as though I'm not here. Although still make me food because I have quite the appetite this morning." She brought out a chair to sit on.

I considered that saying, "Yes, your highness" was liable to get me an arrow through the neck. Her bow lay against the front of her tent, just about within arm's reach. Still, that gave me a thought.

"Who do you think is faster out of us?" I asked, taking some meat from my Inventory.

"Hmm?" She raised one eyebrow, but the other doubled down on scowling.

"See that tree over, about sixty feet through the clearing? You reckon if I said, 'Go,' now, you could hit it before me?"

She looked over at the tree in question, then back to me, where I had tongs in one hand, a slab of raw meat in the other. "Say, 'Go,' and we'll find out."

I waited a few seconds to build the suspense. I could see her tensed up. The meat squished in my tightening grip, the grill sizzling beneath.

"Go."

I dropped the meat, and my card was the first out, slicing through the air in a tight arc just as she had rolled into a crouch—bow picked up and drawn with arrow at the ready. It took her a split second to aim, and then it was on the way, traveling much faster than my Skill.

And then, just as her projectile would pass mine, I split the card out into two and crisscrossed them quickly in the air. The diced parts of her arrow lost momentum and fell to the ground as my two cards slammed into the distant trunk.

She turned her scowl to me and sighed.

"Ta-da!" I announced as I took a bow. Blood immediately burst from my hand, spattering across the nearby grass.

"Well, you're burning the meat, trickster." She rolled her eyes and moved back to her chair. "If you injure yourself before the fight, I'll be pissed."

Her facial expression might say otherwise, but I could tell she was impressed.

"The leader is a woman called Lady in Red . . . *I know.*" Ren rolled her eyes in seeing the look on my face. "She's some kind of Wizard or similar. I only know her name because of her second-in-command, Grak. Huge Orc Barbarian, dual wields, and talks loudly in third person. He's the one who . . ." She trailed off.

I nodded. "The rest, any specific Classes?"

"Not exactly. It's been a while since I've been up-to-date on information." The elf put her forearm over her eyes to shield them from the sun as she thought. "A type of fighter and a healer, for sure. Not sure on the other—possibly something melee."

We had been making our way to their hideout—a small village in a cove by the shore—for several hours. Somehow, I had become calmer about the whole ordeal rather than more anxious. There was some finality to it, the last act before the curtains went down and I could relax. Possibly in a shallow grave.

I watched as Ren fired an arrow off, striking a deer through the chest and killing it outright. We walked over, and I summoned Roger through it. The same purple energy, bright eyes, and weird ears despite the corpse not being humanoid.

"Woah, this thing has weird fuckin' legs. Oh. Hey, boss!"

Definitely Roger still, not a different demon—which somewhat comforted me. "Just giving you a heads-up, the next time I summon you, you will be in a human like me, most likely, and I want you to do your best to kill anyone you see that isn't us two." I jerked my thumb between Ren and me.

"Of course, boss." He tilted his head to the side to glare at the elf standing behind me, who I assumed was glaring right back at him.

"It would mean a lot to us both if you could give it your all, and once you decide what kind of weapon you like, I'll try to get you something nice and rare to keep." I gave him a wide smile.

"Yeah? Okay, count on me then, boss. I'll go, if that's all—I don't think I can actually move without falling on my face."

I gave him a nod, and he vanished away, leaving the deer to collapse to the ground after giving the elf one last grimace. It was nice to know he could leave at his own discretion and wasn't forced to stick around, even if I forced him to join this plane of existence.

"Let's keep going." Ren walked off. "We'll be there within the hour."

We had chosen a path that would weave around the various Monster spawn points and anything that could interrupt our progress. While not as short of a journey as we would have liked, it did mean we arrived at the cove uninjured. We had the best gear we had found and enough healing supplies to carry us through, and I had secretly been holding on to two sweet cakes for our celebratory party.

The only ingredient left was murder—something I had become blissfully cozy with.

Ren stopped, and I did the same. The sound of waves lapping at the island could be heard clearly now. Something I hadn't heard in probably—

"Boost me." She gestured to the nearby tree.

"Huh? Oh, sure." I stood with my back to the tree and interlocked my hands so she could hop up to the nearest branch. As she clambered up, I shook the mud from my hands. "Your boots are filthy," I murmured.

She paused and looked down at me. "Do *you* want to climb the tree?"

I shook my head and wiped my hands across my sparkling purple trousers. They already had enough blood and who knows what else pasted across them. I really needed to get better adventuring clothes. Or be more diligent at repairing them when I had privacy.

After a minute or two, the elf climbed down, landing deftly on the ground. "They have two watchtowers near the road in. Our side is a steep hill like at the Goblin village. The other side is remarkably mountainous. Then at the back of the hideout is the sea, opposite the road in."

My brain tried to jumble the picture around to make sense. I tried to think of it as we were south, and the road in was from the east leading to the west where the sea was.

"Watchtowers don't look occupied, but we'll see." She was scowling off at the far distance, her eyes moving about as if trying to read the plans her mind was concocting.

I let her ruminate without interruption. This was her show, after all. While my life was on the line, and I had an important role to play, this had to go how she wanted things to. While the front of my head liked to think I was being altruistic, the back of my mind knew this had been an anchor for me. A purpose for a man in purple, lost within a dangerous world.

"You ready?" She turned to me, still frowning but blue eyes now searching me. Last chance to run and hide away, save my skin and escape the small pocket of terror she willfully inhabited. Just as others had done to her previously—I could read behind that expression all too well. Might not even blame me for losing heart and fleeing.

Unable to force myself to grandstand or come up with some heroic spiel to carry us forth, I just nodded, a grim expression on my face. "Ready."

No further words were spoken until we were on the ridge, prone and crawling to peek over. Time seemed to go fast when you had murder on your mind. It was a small village, with little huts dotting the sandy area, waves lapping at the shore only a weak stone's throw away. Idyllic, really—the sort of place you'd holiday to or maybe retire once all the magician debt had been paid off.

To our right, the two watchtowers flanked the road leading into the village. The farthest one seemed empty, but the closest had a figure leaned against the back wall, staring off at the road away from us. Even with the vegetative cover we had crawled through, I'd stick out like a sore and sparkly thumb if they were even barely proficient in their role.

Down between the houses, a pair of figures moved from one house to another—and knocked on the door. Two more figures stepped out. None of them looked to be particularly green or red—and including the watcher that would make the cove a little more populated than we had anticipated.

I raised my eyebrows to Ren, and she just worked her jaw as she glared back at me. Nothing needed to be said; evidently they had done a little recruiting since she last had a chance to check. Even being this close to her, seeing the vibrancy of her eyes and concern wrinkling her otherwise—

She leaned in and whispered in my ear. "Plan stays. Take the tower, burn them out into the open." She moved back away.

For a second, part of me short-circuited and took me out of the large scoops of belief I had managed to suspend so far. Being corralled by a beautiful elf almost-princess to murder a village of possibly real people to avenge her fallen lover, by summoning a host of demonic entities by manner of magic. Perhaps I had hit my head, and this *was* a fevered coma dream or the afterlife. No. I wasn't that lucky.

I nodded at her and gave her the best smile I could muster before turning to look at the watchtower.

A card of purple energy appeared over my hand and began to turn. I forced more energy into it, expending my Mana as it glowed brighter—ready for what I considered an empowered single shot.

With a brief prayer to whatever entity might be listening to my inner monologue, I sent the attack off.

CHAPTER TWENTY

Escape Artist

The beauty of the System was the flexibility it allowed. Even excluding the powers it gave us, the application of some of the options made us almost superheroes. Almost. For when faced with strength and the ability to punch down, many chose to be more of a villain. Although, perhaps not that dramatic—after slaughtering hundreds, it was hard for even the most benevolent of us all to not become numb and apathetic. And I was certainly not benevolent. Being harsh on myself, I might draw a line from the hard points in my life back to this day and how the ball was sent rolling far off course due to our actions and the resulting chase that ensued.

The card beamed across the gap, splitting at the last second to gouge both sides of the person's neck. I held them with a twist in the hope that I could cut through the windpipe if not the arteries, and then let them vanish. I wiped my bleeding hand on the grass idly as we both stared and awaited the outcome.

With a jolt, they clutched at their throat and turned wildly as if confused or trying to raise an alarm. Their eyes met our half-concealed shapes up on this ledge before they then slumped down out of view. I raised an eyebrow at Ren, and she nodded.

I threw a second card—an Imp one. Partly worried that I wouldn't have the range or skill to land it where I wanted. With a little pain through my hand, I was pleased to have it land just on the edge of the watchtower wall. The Imp rose up from a circle and wobbled a little, surprised to find itself on a precipice. After he stabilized himself against one of the wooden supports, he turned and gave me a little wave.

Start fireballing the houses, I thought toward him. I even tried gesturing with my head and eyes, for the little that I could move while remaining prone.

Regardless of which manner of communication he understood, a ball of fire began forming in his hands.

"Get ready," Ren muttered. "Maintain positional advantage until they force us out."

"Understood." This was what all the training and tough love had been for. Running our own ambush over the slight cliff gave us the height advantage and a means to escape if need be. The previous battles had put me through the wringer so that I didn't falter when I stepped onto the main stage and all eyes were upon me. There was slightly more on the line than a few bad reviews. We had faced death before, but this had the almost tangible weight of Ren's revenge labored upon it. I could almost feel her radiating anger.

The first ball of fire careened down from the tower and struck the wooden roof of a hut, catching it alight.

Silent tension thickened the air between us. No immediate response from the cove, where the figures had gone into various buildings before our assault. A second fireball went out and struck one of the larger buildings. The door flung open, and two figures stepped out, their raised voices catching the attention of two more that had been wandering over from the back where we couldn't see.

After some confused yelling, a fifth figure emerged from a different house, stepping out to where the others were gathered. A Wizard in white robes cast a spell to douse some of the flames, as the rest of them scoured the area for the culprit.

"*Up there!*" A Ranger pointed a finger toward my Imp before bringing his bow up. Other than a Wizard, it looked as though they had a medium-armored fighter with a shield, a lighter-armored fighter with an axe, and what might be a healer or other spellcaster.

Target the healer, I told my Imp. He switched targets and let the ball loose, just as the Ranger fired his arrow. As the projectile attack traveled a lot faster, my Imp took the attack straight to the forehead and dropped back into the watchtower, out of view. *Bastards.*

"*To me!*" the Wizard yelled.

They rushed together into a group, and just before the fireball struck, the spellcaster raised a dome-shaped shield that absorbed the burst of flame.

"Now," Ren hissed and leaped to her feet. I followed suit, in my . . . suit. *Stressful performance*, I apologized internally.

As the fire and shield faded out, Ren's entangling arrow immediately struck the Wizard through the chest, blood soaking through his white robes. Just as soon as the light had left his eyes and he slumped to his knees, my card then struck him. Pact demon. A difficult distance to throw Roger's card, but through bloodied hands I made the attack with enough precision, and purple light began to pool around the dead spellcaster. Entangling roots gripped at the group, holding them in place. Rookie move to group up.

"*Up there.*" The Ranger pointed unnecessarily at the two now very obvious figures on the ledge. Part of me wondered why Ren allowed me to continue to wear my garish suit, but I supposed that could be a question for a time less dangerous. As the opposing Ranger drew back a Skill, Roger lurched up at him, using the wand he was holding as a dagger and jamming it up into the underside of the man's jaw.

"Where the fuck are the main two?" Ren seethed as she drew back another arrow. We had been somewhat lucky in that these chumps had clumped up to avoid the fireball, which left them easy pickings. Punching down had clearly left them weak in other aspects. She was right though, something *was* off. Her arrow deflected from the warrior with the shield, and I feigned my card toward him before twisting it into two—one hitting the supposed healer in the face, the second severing fingers of the other fighter. Pain wracked my hands.

The entangles broke on the other two, the shield-bearing warrior now stuck between defending against our ranged attacks or helping against the demon possessing the dead Wizard. Roger leaped unhindered atop the blinded spellcaster and renewed his assault. Ren drew up her <Smite Shot> and held it, waiting for an opening. It went out and struck the shield bearer in the shoulder just above the metal object, rendering that arm weak and inert.

There was something in the air, and not just the smell of burning wood. Magic perhaps? A card spun over my hand as I paused, a noise distracting me from taking my next strike. Ren heard it too, and we turned around.

From within the forest, a large green figure burst out of the tree line toward us. Must have used a Skill to get close. Invisibility? Teleportation? With a large hammer in each hand, he roared in delight at getting the jump on us. His face was a mess of scars between yellow tusks and yellower eyes.

"Grak knew you were sneakin' about!" he bellowed with a grin, running at us full speed.

Ren drew an arrow—but he was quick. A red energy flickered around his body, some Ability giving him power. He swung both hammers down at us as she let off her arrow. I dropped my card to raise a <Card Fan> in front of us just in time.

They weren't enough, and the glowing cards shattered. The remaining force pushed us back . . . over the edge.

A brief slideshow of pain, brown dirt, gray rock, and then I was on the sandy road with a thud. Blood dripped onto the ground in front of me. *Naughty*, I hadn't allowed it to leave my body. My head rang as it tried to catch up with the distance traveled. Mentally, I made the note that I no longer liked heights. I broke the stick on my belt that held one of Ren's heals within it. My legs no longer felt numb, and I dropped a Hellhound card as I stood.

Vision still shaky, I raised my eyes to see Ren lying prone on the ground. Blood running from her mouth, and a leg looking like it forgot proper anatomy. Roger was rolling on the sand-covered road, grappling with the last of the group, and I'd help him right after sorting the elf. Ren healed her injury with a grunt, the bone cracking as it snapped back into place, and I stumbled over to offer my hand.

"Bad luck with that leg, huh?" I smiled as I helped her up, her eyes immediately shooting up.

"Move!"

We leaped apart, rolling across the ground as the Orc slammed down onto his feet in the middle of us. How he managed to crack the ground but not shatter his legs was a trick I'd probably not find out the answer to. Maybe he was just built differently.

"Aw, Grak wanted to crush little friends."

I stood back to my feet with a wobble, my hound standing in front of me and growling. Ren was not so eager to stand around and start a monologue to savor the moment—as soon as she was back to her feet, another radiant arrow pulsed into her bow, and she fired it from the short distance.

The arrow burned out and was deflected mere inches from the large Orc by a shield of crimson magic.

"*Now, now—who is this come to spoil our fun?*" A smooth female voice came from behind me, but I was hesitant to look away from the hulking barbarian in front.

"Lady in Red, I assume?" My hands were lowered, but a card spun in my right one. I tried to calm my nerves. Performing for a small crowd was always more stressful. All eyes on me.

"Correct. Are you looking for gainful employment, Bard?"

I winced. A change of outfit was definitely necessary. A figure stumbled back-to-back with me, and somehow I could tell it was Roger.

"She looks even more disgusting than the *elf*," he hissed through a mouth he wasn't used to. "Being a giant is fun, but I'm pretty ruined. Have three more bodies to transfer to."

"Thanks, Roger. Doing great." Why I was whispering to my demon during this standoff, I wasn't sure.

Ren fired another arrow at the Orc, which again was blocked. I could see the fury and frustration in her eyes. Months of buildup and she was driven to one thing only. That he was just ignoring her and her attacks were ineffective must be driving her mad.

"I guess not then . . ." the Lady continued, unconvinced by my silence. "Grak, show them out of this world."

The Orc tensed up and licked his lips. "Grak going to enjoy this. Will break man first . . . *again*."

"Can you hear me when I command things in my head?" I muttered to Roger, flexing my hands.

"Yes, boss."

Then he knew what to do. So did I, which was—not die. I didn't fancy my chances against the figure a good two feet taller and three times as wide as me. From my side, I drew my new dagger into my hand. Ren was focused on Grak. Grak was focused on me. Lady in Red was focused on . . .

"Good news, Grak. You'll be the first to die by my Dagger of Luck." I grinned and flipped it around. It only gave +1 Luck, whatever that did, but I needed all the help I could get.

He chuckled briefly. "Funny words for a pancake!" The Orc leaped forward, amber energy flaring up his body. He *was* fast.

Hellhound darted in with a growl. Roger moved away, screaming as he went. Ren drew back another shot, unbridled fury in her eyes. My card left my hand, a calm amount of acceptance across my face.

The hammers hit me, unopposed. Upper right arm, shattered. Left shoulder, dislocated and broken. I hit the ground like a sack of potatoes and rolled, skimming my head on the sand-swept stone. My ears rang, but I still heard the sound clearly.

"*No!*" a female voice screamed out.

Not Ren's though. Different. I twisted my head around on a complaining neck to see the Orc standing confused, an arrow lodged in the back of his neck. He pawed at it briefly before a second hit right next to it.

A flash of blue illuminated his face and any other surrounding objects my fading vision could see. My body dissociating from the pain. I had perhaps been more injured from the cliff fall than my hubris allowed me to believe.

Third arrow—then a fourth struck the back of the Barbarian. His arms were slung low now, as if his energy was being drained. An awkward plodding came over to me, and my vision was filled by the face of a corpse with purple eyes.

"Ugly bitch vanished, boss. You okay?"

He stood back up straight, allowing me to see the elf run up and stab the dying Orc over and over. I closed my eyes so I could pretend not to see her tears. My Hellhound came over and licked my face to make sure I didn't fall asleep.

"Good . . . job, guys," I managed to murmur out.

They had telegraphed their scheme too easily, and I saw through their trick with Ren's assistance. The Lady put some manner of shield over the Orc so that he couldn't be hit. He thought himself invincible and was overconfident. Ren was hell-bent on putting an arrow through his thick skull, so I had to work around that—take away the shield.

On my mark, both the hound and Roger had run straight for her. I had the demon scream so that I could approximate her location and send my card her way, split it to be sure. Forced the error. Overwhelmed by sudden threats, she had to save her own life rather than hold her protection up on Grak.

A gamble on my part. I couldn't aim the card at the same time as bring up the <Card Fan>. If I had been struck in the head, I would be dead. If I had been way off the mark on how her Abilities worked, I would be dead. For telling myself I was averse to risk-taking, I had taken a big gamble.

Still though. Some tricks you can only pull off once. It wasn't good magic but made for a good story. As long as there were people around to see it.

A burst of radiant energy flowed through me, the awkward crunch and pop of my limbs resetting grating at my senses. The heal was comforting and warming, for as long as the pulse lasted. I opened my eyes to see the whining hound paw at me.

"*Max?*"

I exhaled. The side of my face against the ground seemed to be wet with what I hoped was my own blood. "Yeah, Ren?"

She didn't reply. Which was partly concerning, but perhaps it wasn't right to address a sort-of princess while lying as a broken body on the ground. Arms aching but mostly functional, I managed to push myself to my knees and then to my feet, allowing myself a long groan as I rose.

The elf stood before me, a furrowed brow as usual but a face spent of emotion. Eyes red and tear tracks down her face, she had managed to compose herself *almost* to her normal state.

"Thank you."

I smiled and held my arms open, unsure what really to do with myself. Shocked that she actually came in for the hug. It was brief and awkward, but I managed to hold my own emotions in check.

"*Easy*," I said as she stepped back and observed the carnage we had wreaked.

"Just don't do dumb shit again. You're not *actually* expendable." She sighed and rubbed at her face.

Behind her, the Orc began to move and stood up straight again. Tension flooded through us, before the Barbarian's eyes popped out and ears burst from his head.

"Woah, this fucker is *ripped*!" Roger flexed the arms.

"That's half the job done, at least." Ren shook her head, a long sigh escaping her mouth as she lowered her bow.

"Half?" I narrowed my aching eyes across the village. For some reason, I expected another wave of bad guys to pop out of the rest of the huts. As if I hadn't courted death enough for one fight.

"Lady teleported to the mainland." She gave me a glum expression, almost too tired to keep her brow lowered.

I clicked my tongue. "You want to level up and go hunt her down, then?"

"Most sensible thing you've ever said." She nodded, and a bit of life returned to her eyes.

"One thing first though." I gave her a stern expression and raised a finger.

I brought down my blood-soaked top hat and twirled it around. Reaching a hand inside, I withdrew two sweet cakes and held them out.

"You are the *worst*." Ren shook her head with a sigh. She grabbed the cake, and a smile almost graced the very edges of her mouth. Not allowing me the satisfaction of seeing if anything further was about to bloom, she crouched down to pet at the Hellhound as she ate.

Giving the rest of the buildings in the cove a side-eye, I imagined the worst was yet to come.

CHAPTER TWENTY-ONE

A Bigger Stage

We had cut the green tumor out from New Forest and bought some manner of closure to what ailed Ren. The cancer still remained, and it would take more than one brief and desperate act of violence to truly scour those that sought to cause pain wherever they trod. What drove a person to have such little disregard for another's life was something I still didn't grasp, fully aware of the irony as I stood at the end of a bloodied path of those I had killed myself. Delusion was one of the greatest tricks I ever mastered.

I furrowed my brow as I concentrated. It seemed as though bandages just needed the act of being applied to the body for the healing effect to take hold. Arbitrary, sure—but something I could work with. Currently, I was focused on manipulating one with my left hand, trying to roll it around my fingers single-handedly. It'd take a bit of practice to get the muscle memory down pat, but with a glare of insistence, I was rewarded by the little progress bar—and then the warmth of healing.

After having a little too much fun with Grak's body, Roger departed as Ren and I split up to loot the cove. She hadn't been wrong about the System not being well equipped to deal with Player-on-Player violence. Defensive skills were one thing, but a sharp object to the neck or heart and you'd be good as gone. I was opposed to high-stakes gambles but had the feeling I'd be eating humble pie on that stance more than I'd be eating sweet cakes.

The dead Players offered me paltry loot for whatever their lives had been worth. The feeling there was that they hadn't gotten to level five, for whatever reason. Still, I gathered enough bandages to dress up as a mummy should there be a spookier-themed area and a few choice pieces of Equipment that looked useful. All their gold too.

[Wizard Hat of the Wise: +2 INT]
[Mana Belt: +5% Mana]
[Quick Bracers: +1 DEX]

I also took a couple of basic weapons to give Roger a selection next time I needed him. Everything else was either broken or unavailable or I didn't think I'd ever need it. We instead checked through all the houses, a time-consuming act but pragmatic before we left the area. Other than supplies, Ren had retrieved a sword and affixed it to her belt. The hilt was silver and engraved in a way that told me it was elfin. Her eyes told the rest of the story. Of whom it used to belong to.

For my efforts, I had found a book.

"What's in that?" she asked, raising an eyebrow.

I turned it over in my hands. "An attempt to burn it has been made, but . . . it's not recent. This was not in one of the huts that the Imp struck."

"Does it belong to the Lady? Why didn't she just hide it her Inventory?" Ren scowled but was eager to learn more.

It hadn't taken me long to get through what few pages remained visible. "Hard to say. It's like a diary . . . She wasn't too pleased about being portalled here. Thought that most new Players were easy to manipulate, that they all wanted the same thing."

Ren rolled her eyes and crossed her arms. "Willing to murder those that threatened the status quo of her little gang?"

I shrugged and put it away in my Inventory. Not enough to truly determine her exact motives without painting in the gaps ourselves. She wanted safety, perhaps, and saw being the overlord of the starter area being the simplest way of doing that. Whether through her charms or her Class, she had convinced others she held the key to happiness.

It had been pragmatic for them to kill, loot, or recruit new Players. Keep the equilibrium and maintain their control. At the end of the day, the only one surviving was Lady in Red—level five and abandoning her dead gang to avoid the same fate. Survival meant more to her than standing her ground. Although such callousness and self-serving interests didn't shock me, they still chilled my spine if I thought too hard on them.

She only saw them as a meat shield between her and the inevitable, not something to truly strengthen or enrich her time here.

I wiped the blood from my hands.

"That really isn't normal, you know?" Ren scowled at me as she fired off another arrow into the last Troll of the group.

"It's normal to me." I grinned and then wiped the sweat off my brow with the back of my arm, trying not to mix fluids. "Gives the whole demon summoning a dramatic flair."

She remained unconvinced.

I yawned and checked my log . . . Still eight Trolls to go. Now that Ren had relented to leveling alongside me, combat had been not only quicker but also less stressful on my Mana. Although we were both keen on getting to the mainland and tracking down the loose thread, the elf had seemed much calmer since killing the Orc.

Still just as grouchy, but there hadn't been the same amount of pressure for us to both excel. Combat remained relatively low stakes and brief. Perhaps that was a low-level thing and a reason why the gang had chosen to stick around.

My Imp gave a short bow before disappearing into mist. Their fire helped prevent the trolls from regenerating their Health, which allowed us to get through this Quest without too much stress. I had been giving Roger a break as he wasn't able to control the larger monsters very well—some limitations on his power. I dropped another Imp and sent out dual cards, circling each other through the air into the next target.

"One more Quest after this one," Ren reminded me. Third time so far.

Not that I didn't understand her anticipation—she had been stuck at level four for way too long. Being able to grow in power again must be nice. I was a bit apprehensive about my keystone ability. As if somehow it was part of a performance review and the System was going to decide on my career path.

Of course, I hadn't had much choice so far, so I shouldn't worry. My cards sliced upward on the pale flesh of the Monster, driving gashes across its chest. With the troll already starting to heal up, an arrow then struck it in the left, piercing a lung. A fireball blasted into it. The charred and injured creature lumbered toward us but didn't make it more than five feet before our second volley dropped it to the ground.

"Your cards are good at soft targets, but we'll have issues against armored targets."

I nodded, unsure whether to take that as a criticism or a plain statement. We did need someone to be the meat shield for us—as capable as we were at felling slow and brainless targets, we were bound to fall into trouble once on the mainland. Still, with only the recent agreement that Ren would Party with me when we got there, I wasn't about to rock the boat by suggesting finding a tank should be one of our first ports of call.

"We'll need to at least find someone to take aggro for us." She tilted her head as she scanned the hills for the next troll. "Perhaps make it one of our priorities."

"I suppose." I smiled to myself. Currently, I wasn't a huge fan of being almost snapped in half by anyone strong enough to throw about melee weapons bigger than me. The fact that the Orc had wanted to debilitate me before killing me outright was the only thing that prevented me from currently being a smear across the sand back at the cove.

"I would even say a rare Class, but chances are most will have a Party by now." She scowled out at the hills, as if they were part of the problem.

If people liked to keep their Class rarity secret, that would be quite the problem anyway. If the rarity had any effect on the power level of the individual, then it would put people like Ren and me in high demand—but might also draw unwanted attention. Better to not stand out in a world where murderers could get away with acting like warlords. My overtly dazzling suit glared back at me. *Better to not stand out*, I repeated.

Roger worked well for taking a hit, but he didn't exactly have any skills of his own—and certainly wasn't too careful with his own well-being. His sporadic appearances were a downside too, and I'd rather not have to drag corpses around with us in case of an ambush. We needed some kind of stability. An unfunny joke in the System so far.

"If the island starts getting more new Players seeing as we cleared it of the . . . supposed blockage, perhaps we might find someone around our level soon enough?"

"Maybe." The elf shrugged.

Despite the unspoken agreement we'd need a third, there was still apprehension in her for finding another person to trust, no matter how desperately we would need it going forward. Even my help had been a hard sell until I had shown my worth. Anyone with less patience for the arduous tasks—or an apparent numbness to grand violence—may have given up on her by now. Especially with the constant sour face she displayed. I never failed to win over a fan . . . although, I would also never refer to her as a fan to her face. But I *knew*.

"Is there a reason you're grinning to yourself and not helping with the Trolls?" She glared down at me from a dozen feet up the hill.

"Just thinking about . . ." My brain clicked a few notches, like the dial on a safe. ". . . The first big failure I had at a show."

"Mmm." She narrowed her eyes. "I feel like I will regret asking for more information."

She definitely would. "A tale for another time. Let's get these Trolls down. What was the Quest after this?"

"All the Troll Hearts we've been looting, we need to go take them back down near the coast. It's a long way but will get us to level five."

"All the Troll Hearts we've been looting," I repeated, nodding slowly as she clenched her jaw.

"Or . . . I'll be leaving the island, and you can stay here?"

My gaze moved gradually over to the last Monster we had killed. "How many hearts does a Troll have again?"

I yawned as we strode through the woods in the waning light of the early evening. Adventuring was tiring work, even more so than a weeklong show schedule.

Although magician work usually didn't involve so much of my own blood. Or the blood of others, I supposed.

We had been walking in comfortable silence for the better part of an hour. The day had been both a physical and emotional drain, with our social batteries both on their last legs.

"You know what I'm most looking forward to?" I raised my eyebrow at her. "A proper warm bed."

She nodded, validating my desire. "I hope to find a merchant that sells sweet cakes, and then I will spend all my gold there and eat until I die."

I smiled. "A good way to go. Do you not have . . . oaths you have to ward?"

"What drives you, trickster?"

The deflected question was clear, but her return caught me off guard. "Hmm?"

"I'd like to think you weren't just riding around on my coattails. I appreciate your help with my vendetta, but you don't exactly have a tie to the conflict." She paused and crossed her arms. "So, what are your ambitions?"

I stopped and furrowed my brow.

"You don't seem selfish enough for it to be about fame and fortune, even if you are self-absorbed."

My tongue rolled around my mouth in search of a concise answer. How far was I willing to stretch for some truth when something adjacent was much closer? "Performance is like . . . art. Growing in power will allow me more options and Skills to use. Plus, I like to see people happy."

"And you'll do that with tricks and illusions?"

"Probably a greater chance than with wholesale murder." I smiled.

With a roll of her eyes, Ren shrugged and deflated. She turned to continue our journey. "Latter worked with me," she murmured, just loud enough for me to question whether that was what I really heard.

I certainly hadn't made the group of thugs down at the cove very happy. It probably should revolt me more than it did, that I conflated them with the Goblins in how easily they'd died. Perhaps they *were* still low level, and the gang had recently recruited them but not allowed them to level up. No use working myself up over the past—I rolled my eyes at the irony of the statement—plus, I had almost died in one hit so shouldn't judge.

Ren had a point in that I had latched on to her own personal quest pretty easily, and there was perhaps nothing really forcing me to continue that path. We could split ways on the mainland. She was more than capable of hunting down the loose ends of the gang, and I could go and . . . be a magician for a few gold a night? Despite my constant drive to be a showman, part of me was working up the courage to convince the rest of me that combat could be a performance in and of itself. What would the System allow me to weave into my Class, to excel beyond simple themed wizardry?

Blend the two parts of me. Correct the evils of the world and bring a dazzling display to woo whatever local populace was under the darkened cloud of hardship. *Yes!* My mind started to roll with it, the momentum of what was so simple and yet ticked all boxes—I just couldn't keep it in.

"I . . . want to be a hero."

"A . . . hero?" The elf looked over her shoulder at me as we continued onward, her face a conflicted amount of interest and disdain. "You're certainly no gallant knight, Max. But you've . . . got the heart for it." Her eyebrow raised. "You'd think the portals would bring the heroic types in, but most people I've seen here are complete assholes. It's no wonder they fell in line with the Lady. At least you're . . . *pleasant.*" She turned back away to look ahead.

Not that I was seeking her approval or acceptance of my new dream, but it was nice to hear she was reluctantly on board. Already the images of posters and statues of me in heroic poses set in village squares had started to fill my mind. The Master Illusionist and Savior of Whatever Town. I could already do the hard part of killing Monsters and not dying in the process. All the rest was just public relations. Faux confidence was already waiting in my back pocket for a chance to spring forth.

Always had been, really. Ever since arriving in this world, I'd let any horror or disbelief slide right past my mind. *The show must go on.* Wherever I was, whatever I had to do. Keep going, keep learning, keep dazzling all I came across.

"We're here," Ren eventually said, as I realized I had been lost in my thoughts for a while.

We had reached the shoreline of the other side of the island from the cove. The twin moons reflecting across the pitch sea that seemed to stretch on forever— only the peaks of the waves close to shore picking up the pale light of the early night. Just to the side, against deep-gray rocks, was a small shack illuminated by a flickering amber light inside.

"Hand hearts in, level up . . . Teleport straightaway?" I raised my eyebrows at her. Apprehension filling us both, despite her frown.

She nodded slowly. "I don't want to spend another night here. We'll surely be able to find an inn or something on the other side."

"Ladies first then." I gestured with my hand, earning a scowl. It erased some of her nerves, however, and we walked down to the shack.

"*Hello,*" an old lady cooed from the doorway. "How can I help you, adventurer?"

"Troll Hearts for your illness," Ren replied bluntly, holding them out.

We hadn't accepted the Quest yet, but the elf had known about the requirements from word of mouth. Getting the items while we did the other Troll Quest was a smart move that saved us probably half a day's travel back and forth.

"Thank you, deary!"

"Same here." I leaned in to hold out the necessary hearts.

"Thank you, deary!"

"See you on the other side, trickster." Ren gave me a pensive nod. The mixture of relief and weight of the action illuminated by the amber glow of the fireplace in the shack.

With a flash of blue light, she vanished.

[Level up—<5>]
[Stats increased]
[Class Keystone: <Demonic Magician>]
[Teleport to mainland?]

I reached out a finger and pressed the Yes button, the physical act giving it more weight than doing it mentally.

CHAPTER TWENTY-TWO

The Rest

The world had opened up. Not just a bigger stage for me to be a spectacle on but a box full of more than I could have bargained for. Much like the handkerchief that never ends despite how much you pull it from your sleeve, conflict and desperation flowed out one after another before us. New Forest had dazzled me with the veneer of a pleasant and well-crafted world, but the fight against what was soon to be known as the Crimson Shadow was but a taste of what power-hungry sentients could bring to the corner of the playground—kicking sand in the faces of others as they laughed maniacally.

A wave of inertia struck my body, and everything became blue briefly. Like a waterslide, it felt like sinking through a tunnel—but was over in apparent seconds despite part of my body feeling like it stretched my core being out across infinity.

I stumbled onto wet sand, sinking to my knees to make sure my stomach didn't empty itself. Never much for adventurous rides but glad I didn't crack my head open on anything this time. My eyes scrunched closed as the vertigo swirled around my head, eventually diminishing. The dimming hum in my ears was the final reminder of the completed process.

Then, the sound of waves behind me, lapping at the shore. A cool breeze unhindered by terrain, briefly chilling my body. I opened my eyes to see the shaded darkness of night, the grains of sand briefly illuminated gray by the closest moon's reflection. There was a blue box too.

[Party request received. Accept?]

Looking up, I saw the extended hand of the Oathwarden, her face obscured by shadow. I just assumed it was a scowl under there, but I took the offered help and stood to my feet. Her hand was oddly warm, but the amount of damp sand now on my purple slacks distracted me from any further prodding at that thought. I brushed it off and checked the notification again.

[Party request accepted]

"Let's go be *heroes* then, trickster." She turned away, and I followed her gaze.

Cliffs rose up almost a hundred feet off, and a pathway led up between them. Over the horizon, there were darkened shapes illuminated by small dots of amber light. "A town," I whispered my conclusion out loud.

"More walking." Ren sighed but started to set off.

I joined her as I looked around us. In the darkness of night, there was little detail across the beach—and it didn't seem particularly large. More of a staging area to receive the fresh level fives and funnel them to the first point of civilization. Lady in Red would have had to come through here earlier in the day. Other than the cringeworthy name, there was something else unsettling about her. About her Abilities. Perhaps if I had actually seen her, or it had been a more protracted battle, then I'd know more.

With the potential different Classes, knowing what Skills the enemy had *was* invaluable. Now she knew mine. I was at a disadvantage.

Speaking of which, I brought up my skills to look at my keystone.

[<Demonic Magician>: Your successful Deceptions can now apply Dazzle to targets, and Damage is increased per stack of Dazzle debuff.]

My first thought was, what does *Dazzle* even mean? As a noun. My heart beat harder in my chest, something akin to wondrous excitement building in my stomach for the reveal. Dazzle was a key word that I could delve deeper into, to find out more.

"Oh, wow." I placed my hand on my chin and shuddered. Could this be real? I read it again to be sure.

"What is it?" Ren sounded concerned and looked me over as if I were about to explode or mutate.

"My keystone. It uh . . . There's . . . If I perform a trick or Ability that impresses or confuses an opponent, they get a stack of something called Dazzle—and then I am more effective against them."

The elf stared at me for a few seconds. "Are you bullshitting me again?"

"No!" It was difficult to hold back the wide grin from forming across my face. "The more prolific a magician I am, the more *powerful* I am!"

Ren groaned. "Great, like I need the System encouraging you as well."

I felt energized. Every foe was now my audience, and now the better a performer I was, the easier it would be to conquer them. It was as if the System had been setting up dominoes, knowing exactly how I needed them placed, and then knocked them all down. To raucous applause—mostly my own, *but still*. It was early days.

"What did you get?" I asked, trying not to make the show all about me just yet.

"Nothing so flashy or bizarre." She rolled her eyes. "You . . . ass. Defensive things so I can ward my oaths better."

"No need to be jealous." I grinned. "Rising tide raises all ships and all that."

"Drowns anyone who isn't a giant too."

"Then I guess you'll have to ride on my shoulders." In response, she muttered something that I didn't catch, but I smiled. I doubted she was actually annoyed at my Class being more powerful—more likely it was just the nerves of becoming part of the wider world.

I felt it too. As we walked up the stone slope and the buildings drew closer, there was a reality that was sinking in that we were both out-of-place outsiders. Given that she was an elf, I had assumed she had come from a more fantasy-based world—although that was just from my viewpoint of it, I supposed. While it was an unfamiliar setting to my previous lifestyle, Ren had also spent way too long on the small island. It was like we had just had a nice camping trip and now returned to a land foreign to us because we had run out of cell signal and sweet cakes.

The tension in my chest continued as we came to the outskirts of what appeared to be a small and rather quaint town. Dark wooden houses with thatched roofs were dotted around slim streets. A town square farther down the road looked to house a fountain and rows of flowers hiding away from the twilight. The brickwork building farther down looked to be an inert smithy, and a stable flanked the far end past the square before nature began once more.

Most important was the first building we came up to—it was only fitting that it should be the tavern of the town. Perhaps the largest structure too. Amber light pooled from the ground floor windows, while the ones above just had darkened recesses. A sign hung untouched by the breeze, the name written in golden foil—Driftwood Tavern.

Fitting, I supposed. But then again, I wasn't very good with names. I ascended the three short steps and pushed the door open, eager for rest.

Warmth flooded through my body, causing me to shiver. A roaring fireplace sat at the left end, near the staircase leading upward. Round tables, well-worn from use, seemed sporadically placed and had barely a tentative grip on where the chairs should be arranged—or how many each should have. Why I wanted to organize them, I had no idea. A glass window filled most of the right-hand wall, looking out to the ocean.

Across from us, the sole other figure in this downstairs area was a portly man with a thick mustache stood behind the bar. He rested his arms on a long counter of earthy-brown planks. In seeing our entrance on a slight delay, he nodded toward us as we gingerly entered the tavern. New ground for us both.

"Evening, adventurers. Late one?" His grin was wide but barely made it through his facial hair. There were currently no other patrons on the ground floor, System-created or otherwise, which seemed . . . concerning.

"Evening, sir." I gave him a bow before Ren jostled me forward. "How goes, uh, the business?" We approached the bar, and it seemed the elf was content enough with me being the face of the Party.

"Can't complain," he said as he smiled.

Probably because he was System-created, I mused behind my own smile.

"Can I get you two some ale?" His almost equally bushy eyebrows raised as he gestured to the stack of empty mugs lining the wall behind him.

"No, I don't drink." Both Ren and I said the same thing together.

We exchanged a brief glance before I returned to the barman. "What we could do with, however, is room for the night."

"Ah, not an issue, sir." He jerked a thumb back toward a small wooden board that had numbers and a single key affixed to it. "We have one room available tonight."

"Just the one?" I exhaled through my nose and grimaced at the elf. "I'm okay with bedroll on the floor?"

"Alright," she said with a nod, looking more exhausted than annoyed. "Barman, did a woman come through here today, maybe take a room? Bright-red dress and wide hat, dark-black hair."

He rubbed his chin in thought as I tried to paint a mental image of our current foe. A dress didn't seem like an advisable combat outfit, unless she was a spell-caster of some kind. The few scant details I had created the picture of a witch in my mind—still, she would be as easy to spot as I was.

"No, can't say I recall, miss."

"That'll be all then." The elf shrugged and looked back at the tavern door. It made sense that she wouldn't shack up in the first safe place if we may be hot on her heels.

I paid the man and received the key. A paltry five gold for the night. Again, I tried to not question how the economy worked in this world. I supposed the System side of things didn't need to make sense. The barman would be the bar-man no matter what he earned and presumably didn't need to scrape about for food or other necessities.

We ascended the stairs, a squeak resounding every other wooden plank. Well, at first every other—then nearer the top, it skipped to the third. Down the hall, more squeaks from the planks. Small paintings lined the wall opposite the doorways. Scenes of waves and boats, the shore in summer, and seashells. Not masterpieces, but it was clear time and effort had been put into them.

Door three relented to the turn of the key, and I stepped into the darkness. A beam of moonlight filtered in through the window and struck the plain linen on the bed. It was almost claustrophobic after spending a few days out in the open woods. A real building we'd spend more time than just a quick bath in. Ren lit a lantern by the side of the door, and the details of the room came into focus under the light.

A wide double bed was the key feature, with a cupboard, dresser, and small table with a chair arranged around the edges of the rest of the room. All made from the same wood, a simple and plain design that at least gave the impression they'd come from the same woodworker. Certainly wasn't the worst hotel I'd had to sleep at.

Ren moved around me to glare at the room herself, inspecting it for anything untoward. "You can take the bed. It was your desire, after all."

"Nonsense." I was already halfway through my Inventory to remove my bedroll. "You take it."

"Because I'm a woman, because you think I'm a princess, or because you put your suffering before others' as you can't stop people-pleasing?" She crossed her arms and glared at me.

I worked my jaw to chew on the answer. ". . . *Yes?*"

The elf sighed and rubbed her face. "There's enough room for us both. A hero that puts everyone else before them ends up a dead hero."

As much as I would have liked to argue further, I was actually exhausted, and an real bed would be divine. "I relent to your wisdom, Ren."

"Less relenting and more thinking for yourself. You prefer the right or left side?"

My brow furrowed. The times I had needed or allowed myself the luxury of a double bed had been scarce the last few years, but . . . "Right side?"

"Good answer." She went and placed the lantern on the nearby dresser.

I walked around to my side of the bed, and the room was plunged into darkness once more. Before my eyes had the chance to fully adjust to the gloom, I removed my hat, jacket, and shoes. Anything more than that would have been more comfortable, but I would wait until I had my own room to disrobe any further. Under the covers I went, facing the wall, and the bed shook as Ren repeated the same process on the other side.

As much as my brain was spent from the day, I relented to doing a little bedtime reading to soothe out my nerves before the darkness could take me. Although

I had nothing but begrudging disdain for my natural prowess being defined by numerical values, it would at least be a good idea to have a grasp on the inner workings so I had a base amount of knowledge to work from. Eyes narrowing to focus on my menus, I brought up my Stats. Seems they showed the total, and then in parentheses it was split between base and bonuses.

[Stats]
[Strength—5]
[Constitution—6]
[Agility—5]
[Dexterity—14 (11 + 3)]
[Intelligence—17 (11 + 6)]
[Wisdom—5]
[Luck—9 (8 + 1)]

My equipment was pulling some weight for my Intelligence. With my energy sapping away, it looked as though I received an average of 1.5 increase per level for Intelligence and Dexterity, 1 increase to Luck, and 0.5 for the rest. Enough to ballpark my progress; I shouldn't have to keep tabs on this every five minutes. Just pump my two main Stats and everything would be fine. Although, some more Health and Constitution would be nice for the times Luck couldn't save me from injury. With a sigh, I closed the windows down.

Despite the plain nature of the bed, I relaxed and sank into the softness of the mattress and melted from the warmth of the thick sheets covering my tired body. So much better than my bedroll in the tent. With my brain now accepting it needed to shut off, all the hardships of the day washed away like the distant sound of the shore from the open window. Almost immediately, I fell asleep.

Squeak.

My eyes fluttered open. The gloom of the wooden wall opposite me stared back impassively. *This was a common thing,* my mind reminded itself as confusion slunk away into the darkness. Sleeping in a new place was often difficult. Just a part of the brain that kept—

Squeak.

I held my breath as I regained control of my waking thoughts. Floorboards from outside the room. Light breathing from beside me—Ren was still asleep.

Squeak.

Every other step. Slowly approaching. My heartbeat raced. It was still dark out, the moon having left our room in near-complete darkness. Another squeak, ever closer, dried out my mouth.

Just another patron heading back to their room? The barman moving through an on-rails patrol route through the night?

A final squeak just outside our door. I turned in the bed slowly to glare at the open darkness gradually coming into some focus. The closed door told no tales, but my senses ached for a continuation of the movement. I needed to know either way whether my panic was justified or the days of slaughter were catching up to the sane part of my subconscious.

Silence.

My blood pulsed in my head, a rhythmic thumping that threatened to override any more important sounds that may arise. From beneath the covers, my hands withdrew, fingers flexing in anticipation.

With a brief crack of displaced air, our door opened an inch.

CHAPTER TWENTY-THREE

Room Service

Ever since my arrival in this world, I'd had a target on my back. Fame acted as a multiplier. As a magician, I had my share of fans who took things a little too far. Put me on a podium too high, thought of me as something greater than I really was, and wanted me to fulfill their odd delusions. None wanted my . . . death—even my detractors weren't so cold. So now, for the world to grow a crop of beings that wanted my existence erased, the only option was to fight back. Be greater than every new threat. One step ahead. The exercise was tiring, but I could do with the cardio.

As soon as I saw the silvered glimmer of something caught in the brief moonlight peeking through the gap of slowly widening pitch black, I brought <Card Fan> up in front of the bed. It flickered and dissipated as something struck it, and then I was up.

I leaped over Ren to the floor on the other side as the door burst open fully, a cloaked figure enveloped in shadow emerging and moving toward me. Darkness covered the room as something blocked the open window, and the growls of the Hellhound I had dropped on my side of the bed during my brief acrobatics caught the second would-be assassin before they could fully enter.

Why I had dived straight into the danger was beyond me. To protect the elf? As the first figure leaped toward me, hands both full of sharp steel, I reconsidered the bravado. I could hear the Oathwarden roll awake, standing atop the bed behind me.

My card went out, the bright-purple glow illuminating the room as it skirted past my assailant's head. He flinched slightly from the light but grinned wildly at my missed shot as the dagger in his right hand cut through the air toward me. I barely blocked it with my own Dagger of Luck, and my arm bucked from the force—which left my side open for his offhand swing.

"Oh, what's this behind your ear?" I hissed as my card made the return journey. Split in two, it came back past him, cutting through his hood and lopping both ears off before disappearing. The light of them briefly illuminated his shocked face as he went to clutch at his head. I turned to the side as Ren sprung from the bed over me, impaling the man with her sword and knocking them both to the floor.

Another card spun over my hand as I faced the struggling window-bound killer. My Hellhound had a grip on his leather trousers, not letting him abort the attempted murder. He was left stuck halfway through the opening, his hands clasped against the frame in trying to gain leverage. My magic projectile removed some of his fingers and turned the tide in favor of my canine glowing with crimson flame.

Ren stood from the corpse of our first attacker and moved over to flick the lantern back on. Her nightwear shirt was now soaked through with blood, clinging to her athletic form, but we had been one heavy sleep away from that being her own dead body lying on the floor. Her eyes burned with fury as the second of the men slumped heavily onto the floor, clutching at his injured hand.

I knelt down and pulled his hood back. A panicked man, sweaty and pale. His dark hair was cut short, and scars ran down one side of his face. I grabbed his ear and twisted it—not really intending to torture him but giving enough pain to get him to focus.

"This a hobby of yours, or someone put you up to it?" My voice was considerably calm, despite the circumstances.

"Can't say," he spluttered, wincing from my grasp.

"That means the latter then." I raised an eyebrow at Ren, who was now in her normal adventuring gear. Being woken up mid-sleep had done nothing to improve her usual mood.

"Lady in Red." The elf rolled her eyes. "She knew we'd likely be here soon."

"Can't say," the man repeated. The Hellhound moved closer to sniff at his face.

More fool us for wandering into the potential trap, but the tiring and emotional day had thrown a heavy blanket over our usual caution. It was such a nice sleep while it lasted too. The fact that I had awoken before Ren meant she had been a lot more spent than she gave away. I clicked my tongue and tried to gather the thoughts bouncing around inside my head. As the adrenaline wore off, I found out how tired I really was and how little I cared for this man attempting to murder us.

"There are some gloves with Action Speed and Luck on them here. Also, there's a letter."

I turned my gaze to see Ren looting the body of the first. "The gloves would be great. Dibs on the crossbow as well."

She exhaled and stood, showing the rectangle of sealed paper. It had a picture of a top hat with an arrow through it on one side.

"Our first fan mail." I grinned and turned back to the assassin to avoid any potential glare. "Hey, I don't usually do crowd work these days . . . but I bet we can find something to loosen that tongue, right?"

Ren cleared her throat as she folded out the letter. "If you are reading this, you have thwarted the hired goons I sent after you. I am not surprised if that is the case. If you desire to chase me down, I warn you that will be a fatal error. This is your one and only warning. Lady in Red."

"Ah." I shrugged. "I suppose we don't really need you after all." I released his ear and stood while he dropped to the floor. "All yours, boy."

The hound leaped atop him, tearing through his neck.

My right eye twitched as I turned back to the elf. A little heartless of me, but it was clear this was a dog-eat-dog world. Or dog-eat-assassin world. "I suppose we won't get our deposit back?" I grimaced at the amount of blood now soaked through the room.

"I saw you trying to tip the barman last night. Or . . . earlier this night?" Ren shook her head. "Things don't work like that here."

I flipped my dagger into the air and clicked my fingers, the weapon vanishing as it went into my Inventory. Unnecessary flourish, but it felt good. "Sorry to wake you."

"Asshole. I should be thankful you were awake." Her brow furrowed as she looked across the room. "You weren't doing anything weird, were you?"

"Light sleeper." I shrugged. "I'm often traveling, and new places disorient me." What I wouldn't give for a permanent place to settle down in, have a bed of my own to return to every night. She had a point though. I should have been up practicing some magic tricks.

"How are you even hiding items without touching them?"

My reluctance to give away trade secrets was quickly worn away by the glare of her bright-blue eyes. "Something to do with <Mana Manipulation> or <Sleight of Hand>, I assume. It allows me to extend my energy as if I was touching the object. Then it's just me focusing to bring up the Loot option as you would a held item."

She stared impassively at me for a couple of seconds as if she was trying to gauge my sincerity. With an eventual shrug, she changed the subject. "Thoughts on this, trickster?" She held up the opened letter.

I deflated and closed my tired eyes to think. We were being offered a potential out. Live a life less dangerous and more fruitful. Part of what Ren had said yesterday stuck out at me. How this wasn't really my battle. I had been along for the ride and needn't throw myself in front of danger just because she had an axe to grind.

"We should call her bluff." With a sigh, I opened my eyes again. "I don't trust her to leave us alone, nor would she have turned over a new leaf and not begun starting a new dangerous scheme already." While we weren't exactly vigilantes, let alone heroes, we had pushed the Lady onto the mainland, so I felt we bore some responsibility for anything untoward she wreaked upon it.

Ren shrugged. "Alright, if that is your plan, I agree to follow you."

I narrowed my eyes and paused for a second. "*Oh* . . . very clever. You made me choose for myself what I wanted to do. Do you agree with my conclusion though?"

"I would have let you know if not. If you had decided not to pursue her, then we would have parted ways." The elf yawned into the back of her arm. "*Fuckers* for disturbing our sleep."

"She deserves to die for that alone." I smiled wryly.

Her scowl was more tired than anything, and she relented to sitting at the edge of the bed. "I'm not expecting you to be the leader, just as you shouldn't expect me to be either."

A duo act. An interesting proposition that I hadn't fully considered. It was clear to me that Ren would be more than an assistant, and it was probably a fault of mine to want to shuffle my new contacts into the boxes of my old life. She didn't need the dramatic flair that I did to be a hero—there was the more pragmatic business sense that kept me on the rails.

"Point noted." I sat on the edge of the bed at the side closest to me. "An equal partnership then."

She didn't respond at first, and as the silence continued, I started to wonder if she had fallen asleep. Certainly, I felt like doing so myself. Something about the bloodied corpses in the room had me on edge, however. The hound whined at me, his time just about up. I gestured for him to go say goodbye to the elf and saw her pet him on the head before he went. Not asleep.

My eyes went to the window. The night sky had now taken on a deep-blue tone, the first sign that a new day may be soon starting. "Looks like a couple of hours till dawn. You able to get back to sleep?"

"Nope."

"Me neither. Want to get started on finding a Quest?"

She sighed. "Beats sitting around staring at dead bodies. I had hoped the first night on the mainland could have been . . ."

"Less stressful?"

"Mmm. There's . . . No, never mind." She stood up and scowled at the dead bodies. "You wanted this?" From her Inventory she brought forth a crossbow.

"Ah, yeah!" I stood and moved over to her, placing my hands on the weapon— but as I went to take it, she held a tight grip and stared me in the face.

"Why is it you can take a life so easily?"

As disarming as her bright eyes were, I didn't think my explanation of being two Max souls mixed together would earn me a reprieve from the perfectly reasonable questioning. I was just a showman, after all. An entertainer. Murder should leave me in a frazzled mess of sweat and vomit in the corner. "Would you have me any other way?"

Her eyes tried to read my face. A question to answer a question, and something not as dazzlingly annoying as I tended to be.

"As long as you don't lose sight of yourself." She relinquished the crossbow.

I stowed it away in my Inventory, making a mental note to work out how it functioned later on. "If I become a monster, Ren, then I would hope that you'd be the one to put an arrow through my neck."

"I will." She nodded, an impassive frown across her face. "And I hope you'd do the same for me."

"I promise."

We stood staring at each other awkwardly for a few seconds before I cleared my throat. "Ah, fresh air?"

She looked away at the floor and gestured toward the still-open doorway.

Having an intangible Inventory space to store everything certainly made checking out easier. With one last glance around the room, I led us out into the hallway and then down the stairs. My mind buzzed like a beehive. Some thoughts about Ren I'd need to arrange in their proper place when I was by myself, so she wasn't close enough to hear my inner monologue going full tilt.

The barman was still standing in the same place, which was remarkably creepy considering the time of day.

"Morning adventurers. I hope your stay was pleasant."

"It . . . Sorry, we were assailed by assassins in the night, and they left a mess in the room." From down here, he would have been able to hear the thuds on the floor and growling of my hound . . . That it hadn't prompted him into action made sense but left me with an uncomfortable feeling. My eyes narrowed at the board that held the room keys. All were present except for ours . . . Perplexing.

"Oh, I'm sorry to hear that." His brow furrowed. "There has been a lot of that lately."

"Assassinations in the tavern?" Ren asked with a scowl, stepping around to the front of the bar with me and jostling my thoughts from my head.

"Lots of bandits and thieves. There should be information on the Town Board."

I nodded slowly. There was an uncanny amount of understanding of our conversation mixed with reading prompts from a script. The hint that the town had some issues washed away the nature of our night's stay, and he had moved on quickly to telling us we should point our adventuring noses in the way of a noticeboard for Quests. It was all so . . . predictable?

"That'll be our first stop then." I sighed and raised an eye to Ren. "I'd rather gain a bit of power today than chase footsteps fading in the sand." The Lady was unlikely to be standing around nearby waiting to hear back on if her goons had done the job. We were a thorn in her side but not a blockade to her ambitions. Getting a few more levels under our belts would hopefully give us some advantage while we got the lay of the land.

"Agreed," she said with a nod, "but less poetic."

The barman leaned forward toward us. "If it's power you're after, rumor has it there is a Dungeon out in the Silent Forest that holds Power Tokens." He moved back to his default position and lifted a mug to clean out.

"A Dungeon," I echoed. "Sounds . . . *gloomy.*"

"We'll hit that if we get another Quest in that area. We need to be efficient about this."

Something about it drew me in. A subterranean lair built for sinister purposes and filled with all manner of devious traps and Monsters from the darkest shadows of existence. It was a place I needed to conquer—to survive. A badge to affix to my belt to show my achievements. There must be other Dungeons in the world, and I wondered if there were any sort of accolades for—

"*Max.*" Ren raised her voice from the front door. "Move already!"

CHAPTER TWENTY-FOUR

Board Already

Part of me always liked Quests. Something about a set process gelled well with me. Do this and then you get that as a Reward. No need to negotiate, work on time management, rehearse, budget, and all the other facets that got in the way of doing a show. It simplified life. When you had death knocking at your door and threatening to push you down the hill into the graveyard, having fewer complications allowed you to dodge his advances for a little longer. It was one of the few things enabling me to have a hold on my sanity.

Looks like three options then?" I tilted my head as if that would change the number of pages affixed to the Town Board. A number of planks painted white with notices nailed to them were as loose as they could get to the term *Town Board* without it just being an unfinished pile of debris. Still, the way the System STAR interfaced with it gave it some credence.

"Bandit Camp. Thief Hideout. Boss Monster Hunt." Ren confirmed the options.

None of them sparked any joy within me. If anything, I wanted to go back to sleep somewhere. Preferably somewhere with fewer hidden assassins . . . which might not be *anywhere,* if they were hidden. Now that the barest crack of sunlight had started to edge over the horizon, I doubted my chances of getting some shut-eye were anything more than slim. The slight amount of light illuminated Ren's blonde hair to glow almost more so than the lantern she held, which was interesting.

"What are you thinking?" she asked, glaring up at me.

"Pretty sick of Bandits, if I'm honest. Which I always am." She rolled her eyes as I continued. "But I'll go for whatever is either closest to our current position or has the best Reward."

"Pragmatic, trickster. In both those cases, the Bandits are the answer."

I groaned and rubbed at my forehead. At this time of the day, the town was still deserted. It was almost a shame we'd come and go without seeing it in full bloom. Like a shadow through the night, we had barely paid lip service to civilization and almost lost our lives for the brief benefit. Part of me wanted to hang about and see it come to life, but the majority of my soul felt on edge. Like there was pressure on us to keep moving and grab at any power offered.

Rather than let my feet continue to itch, I relented to her wisdom. "Do you have a preference?"

"We can accept three Quests now. Did you not get the pop-up? There's a route we can do all three and hit the Dungeon on the way back."

The map came up, and she sent through the coordinates and planned path we could take.

"After the second point, the Boss Monster Hunt, we should camp for the night, then hit the Dungeon and Bandits on the way back tomorrow."

I needed to bring Ren back to my world and replace Reggie. Logistics were a nightmare on the road. If you had someone with the brain for that, then . . . No, I was distracting myself again. Two days of adventuring was quite the plan, but it *was* efficient. Get all the Quests done and then circle back for more—assuming we didn't run into the Lady or any other potential trouble along the way. Rather than feel like I had just doomed us to that, I mentally jumped into gear with both feet.

"Brilliant, Ren." I grinned at her. With things planned out, I almost had an appetite for the inevitable danger we would be putting ourselves in. *Almost.*

"We'll need to keep an eye out for Lady in Red and whatever lackeys she has hired. If she is trying to level, there is a chance she is in the same area."

I was glad we were on the same page. With the map, I oriented myself and told the STAR to point in the direction of the first objective. "Alright then, the Thieves first. Kill on sight, no grandstanding." Probably ironic coming from me.

She again rolled her eyes at that statement. "Let's move on."

It wasn't long before the town slowly fell away behind us as we traveled slightly uphill toward a small woodland. Although our terrain being even more trees seemed a bit old hat now, I had a feeling Ren had more of an affinity for them than I. Instead, I just allowed the pleasant beauty of nature to soothe my tired senses. Pretend we weren't off to go kill things.

I looked back at the town as the tree line of the woodland began, now slightly populated by tiny moving figures half shrouded in darkness. It was a shame we couldn't make use of the amenities there or perhaps look for a third Party member. I understood it though. We had to be careful with our trust, especially around the town that we were almost murdered in. There was always the possibility the low-level Players there could be compromised. Even more fool us if we took on someone with ill intent in their heart, after everything we'd been through.

Ren stood waiting for me to catch up. "Apologies in advance, but I get really grumpy when I'm tired."

I maintained eye contact with her scowl and slowly nodded. It was hard to tell if that was a joke or not. Safer to err on the side of caution—her normal glares didn't usually reflect her actual mood, so a genuine grouchiness might be worthy of being wary of.

"That's okay," I eventually offered as I caught up beside her. "I get less annoying when I'm tired. We'll maintain our usual standing."

She rolled her eyes, doubting my statement could be factual. "Do women in your world find you too annoying?"

"Huh?" My eyebrows raised as the shadowed canopy of the trees enveloped us.

"You said you didn't have anyone close to you. For all your faults, you're . . ." She tapered off.

"My schedule made it hard to socialize. If I wasn't working, I was practicing. Any woman I met was usually a fan . . . and we both know how that is."

"Yeah, gross." She shook her head.

"We have hardly been apart since meeting, Ren." Ignoring the parts where I had been put through a trial of fire. "This is the most social I've been . . . in years. It's refreshing that you don't care who I am."

"You must have hit your head too hard yesterday." She sighed and brushed the hair from her face. "It's the opposite, Max. I don't care about who you pretend to be."

I wrinkled my face up. The Max I pretended to be was just the larger-than-life figure I was trying to grow into, surely? It wasn't a . . . Well, part of it *was* an act—but that was the point. I was left chewing on my thoughts as the elf continued.

"You're the one who doesn't care who *I* am, which makes you tolerable."

"Nicest thing you've ever said to me." I shot her a grin. Coming from a world that didn't have elves and never having met a sort-of princess before, Ren was both an odd novelty but something so plainly normal at the same time. With softer ears and less radiant beauty, there'd be little difference between her and a human—at least on the surface. A little less demon summoning and I'd be a normal human too, I supposed.

"Well, you'll probably have time to socialize here, without the baggage of your old world." She looked off into the deeper woods. "If you don't die, you will eventually find someone to break you out of that shell."

I slowed my pace with a frown across my brow. My internal organs seemed to want to continue at the same speed, and an odd churn within me grew uncomfortable—but I didn't know which part of her statement had caused such a reaction. By instinct, a smile went across my face, and I exhaled slowly from my nose.

Under the early-morning sunlight, the small, rocky hill before us looked otherwise unassuming. Actually, it was quite the opposite, the longer I looked. *Very assuming.*

"Definitely in there," I murmured.

A wooden door painted gray sat over a dark hole hewn through a similar gray stone. Not quite the same hue, but an effort had been made. The ground around the supposedly hidden entrance was scuffed and muddied.

"Terrible thief hideout," Ren agreed from beside me. "Based on the Quest, I'm assuming two dozen or fewer on the inside."

"Close range, maybe traps." I nodded. Although still a foreign world to me, I was starting to put the puzzle pieces together based on what tropes and brief knowledge I could pull from the back of my mind. Close range meant hound and Roger, fewer opportunities for Ren to use her bow.

"I'll switch to sword if I need to." She caught my raised eyebrow. "I've trained using them before, but my Stats are Dexterity and Wisdom based. Agility is my minor."

"Intelligence and Dexterity here, Luck minor."

"That's surprising." She tilted her head, and her bright eyes narrowed slightly.

I opened and closed my mouth, then narrowed my eyes in return. Definitely a jab about my smarts. Or that my luck seemed to involve barely surviving hitting my head on things. In fairness, I tried not to think too hard about that side of the System. I would increase the Stats it said benefited my abilities, but trying to tie the loose numbers against tangible existence seemed futile—or at least beyond my current tired brain.

"I'll go first then," I ventured, so that we weren't just glaring at each other all day. "Let me kill something to get Roger out, and then we'll go from there. I'll support you."

Ren placed her hand on my shoulder, oddly warm through even my suit jacket. "And I'll keep you safe." She nodded, which I assumed was in place of a reassuring smile.

I then stood from our hiding place—more of an awkward formality given my sparkling purple suit—and began walking toward the hidden entrance.

It was even less of a perfect disguise as I stood before it. The woodwork was so shoddy that I could see clearly into the dark cave beyond—the dull amber of a torch farther in. In fact, if I were a little slimmer, I could just slide in between the gaps in the planks. An exaggeration—so unlike me.

Now, if I were a Thief guild, I would probably have either a very well-hidden entrance, a tough lock to break, or some manner of trap or alarm that only guild members would know about. The latter option seemed the most plausible, given the circumstances. I moved my face up to the gaps and narrowed my eyes, peering around the inside and—ah!

"There's a small wire tied to the door." It looked like pulling the terrible covering open would pull on it and ring a bell hanging from the ceiling a bit farther back. Assuming it wasn't magic, cutting the tension beneath the bell should disable the trap.

I could feel Ren's presence behind me by a few feet without hearing her make any noise. Perhaps I had been too focused on the door, but she was remarkably quiet when she wanted to be. I needed to learn that. A card of purple magic filtered through a gap in the wood and quickly snipped through the cord attached to the bell.

Hands clenched tightly, I waited a few tense seconds. Nothing happened, and I relaxed. Shot a glance back to the Oathwarden, who nodded her readiness, her sword already drawn.

With one last deep breath of fresh air, I pulled the door open and stepped through. There was an expectation of a second trap, and my body was tensed, ready for something to suddenly pop out and cause me ruin. A lesson from the System to be diligent. But, after a few seconds of remaining unassailed, there was no second trap.

"Amateurs," I whispered back at the elf, who just shrugged in return. If I had been in charge of security, well—I could at least think up some better traps than a *bell*. Perhaps I should save that mustache twirling for later in the day. This was presumably still early-level stuff, if we came here straight after our starter-island landing.

I crept toward the light farther down the tunnel. It was pleasantly dry but dusty, and whoever had carved this place out had done a reasonable job. The tunnel twisted to the side, and the Hellhound card sat ready in my left hand to be thrown.

Murmured voices ahead. I peered around the corner to see another door. Just as badly fashioned, but this time they had forgone the gray paint. I gestured for Ren to look, and she held on to my suit as she leaned past me. Her eyesight was better and may be able to make out more from the gaps in the woodwork.

Eventually, she moved back and whispered in my ear.

"Four figures around a table, two farther in."

I shivered for some reason, then nodded. There were bound to be more—but knowing we'd have to deal with potentially a handful at once was good to know. System-created should be easily held at the choke point of the doorway, if we were smart. Which we *were*, on occasion.

As I moved across the hallway, I took the torch from the wall, putting it in my Inventory and plunging the tunnel into darkness. With held breath, I waited to see if I had been noticed. No, it didn't seem so. Only after the act did I wonder how the Thieves would react to the darkness, if it even affected them. There was one way to find out.

Keeping the hound card back for now, I instead drew dual cards, held together in my right hand. The tunnel illuminated in the dim glow of purple. With one eye closed, I focused on the gap in the door—the darkness now showing the slits filled with the amber glow of the light beyond. A difficult angle against targets I could hardly see but free damage and a chance to tip the scales in our favor.

I smiled and set them both free.

CHAPTER TWENTY-FIVE

Secret Compartment

Sometimes I tried to look back and find the point where my real-world illusion mixed with the magical Abilities that I now had. I had treated the deck of cards just like any other, fiddling, moving them around, and trying to extend my capabilities any chance I had. It was perhaps one of the things that smoothed over the jolt of joining the System. Something similar but slightly off. The answer I could never pinpoint. As soon as I had recovered from my head injury and sent the first card off—it was a natural part of me that grew in strength alongside me.

With practiced precision, the cards spun off into the room through the slim gap in the wood, and I split them out of view toward the seated bandits. I made a mental note to try for thinner gaps when we had downtime. If we had downtime.

"Ow, the fuck?"

"Who was that?"

Ren exhaled from behind me. "Didn't kill them?"

Footsteps thudded toward the door, and I shook my head. It wasn't just the near-blind attack that dampened my first blow, but they also hadn't been as fragile as the Bandits we had fought on the starter island. I'd hate to think my card damage was falling off already . . . Perhaps I should have better gear at this point— we did skip some Quests to get here quicker.

"Hold this and duck." The elf pushed her sword into my hand as I threw down the Hellhound card out to summon a demon before the door. It was surprisingly light, even compared to the other swords I had held in my brief time here. The handle was slightly warm too—but that could just be from her holding it. Overthinking. I needed to focus.

With a hefty kick, the door burst open and revealed the first Thief. A slender man with tied-back brown hair and a nasty-looking slice across his face, courtesy of my magic deck. The arrow fired from behind me into his eye socket did little to improve his appearance. He levied no complaints, however. As he dropped, blocking the way of the second Thief, I threw out the pact card to allow Roger to inhabit him.

Ren awkwardly drew a second arrow in the confined space, my squirming blocking some of her movements. The dark passageway burst into light from the radiant glow of her <Smite Shot> as she aimed it toward the room.

The first Thief regained his footing as purple ears burst from his skull. Without turning to us, Roger leaped at the portlier second enemy and knocked them to the ground, his arms flailing wildly at his target.

"I'm a fuckin' *giant* again," the demon growled with joy, trying to choke out the prone figure.

Under my command, the Hellhound ran into the room as the other occupants readied their weapons toward us. The radiant arrow was let loose and arced over my canine to slam into the chest of a Thief near the back.

"Go now." She quickly slung the bow and took back her sword from my grip.

I stood back up straight after avoiding her shot to the back of my head and threw out a purple card, splitting it in the air over Roger and embedding both into the raised arm of a Thief trying to cudgel the demon off his comrade. His attack faltered as he grimaced from the pained arm, saving my demon from having his brains knocked out. Well, not *his* brains.

Another two cards went out and struck the same man as I stepped closer, but he didn't drop. My right eye twitched at the System pop-up.

[New Monster: Thief <7>]

Ah, that might be why. I hadn't checked the intended targets of the Quests as we accepted them, assuming that Ren would have bought it up if it was going to be any issue. It wouldn't be, I was sure . . . Just a little more of a slog than I had hoped.

"At last, a worthy audience," I boomed, slightly distracting those not currently being throttled to death. My hat dropped from my head, and I reached inside to withdraw a sword twice as long as the hat was deep. I then flipped the hat back up onto my head perfectly. That one was a hard-coded skill from months of practice. Nice of the System to give me the hat I was so used to wearing.

The sword felt awkward to wield, just from the length rather than the weight. Nothing as easy to hold or as warm as Ren's sword. But with some effort, I swung it around in a wide arc at the Thief with a cudgel. He raised his weapon in an attempt to block—and then my sword vanished. Instead, one highly powered card zipped from my grip. He didn't have the time to react from this short distance, and it went below his raised weapon and into his throat.

"He's dead, Roger." I sighed and put <Card Fan> up by reflex to block a crossbow bolt.

The Hellhound whined and withdrew as he became outnumbered, sporting a gash down his right flank. Ren leaped over the dead body as my pact demon rolled up to his feet, her sword glowing a light blue as she swung it through the air.

My eyes blinked as I could see a little hovering box depicting Dazzle Stacks by each of the remaining two Thieves for the first time. Little white squares with sparkling stars in deep gray. Wait, two Thieves? No . . . There should be three? My eyes darted around the room as a card spun in my hand. Ren had engaged the crossbow Thief, and the hound was harrying the other to keep it from gaining the advantage against the elf. There was a closed doorway out of here, but . . .

I spun the card out and split it, causing them both to circle around me in orbit, with a slowly increasing diameter. My hand started to bleed, but then—*there.*

One of them struck something in midair to my left, and a muscled man appeared in view again. My fist flashed out, and I punched him in the chest. Which did nothing.

He chuckled. "Weak!"

I threw out another punch, hitting him ineffectively. His grin widened, and he raised his weapon. As I readied another punch, he had all the confidence in the world that he wouldn't need to block it. I had set the precedent, of course. At the last moment, my dagger appeared in my hand, stabbing straight between his ribs before he could bring his own weapon down. He twitched away with a growl and swung wildly at me. My <Card Fan> shimmered out and burst from the blow, with the remaining force sending me stumbling backward.

Roger and the Hellhound had taken the other Thief down, the demon continuing to strike the inert figure with something heavy as Ren withdrew her sword from the guts of the last. She kicked the female Thief to the rough floor and finished her off by slitting the throat of the wounded System-created.

Not too shabby. Being able to see the Dazzle Stacks just incentivized me to go for racking those up. It was probably a fool's errand to chase down more dopamine in the process of murder, but my mind had already bolted from the stable and hungrily rooted around for ideas among the fertile ground. *Magic.* I turned my attention to our surroundings, a gleam in my eye.

Ren furrowed her brow further and wiped her sword off on the dead body. "You're really looting all that junk?"

The Thieves had been gambling, and the table had an assortment of interesting little things. Poker chips, small trays, and even some dice. But by far the most important thing was a pack of loose cards. Not a full deck, for some reason, but it was a start. "Yeah, trust me, it'll be worth it. Oh, I'll have that crossbow too, if you don't want it?"

"Sure." She shrugged, retrieving it from the ground for me.

I flipped one on the poker chips into the air. Once it spun back into my hand, I flipped it again—only now it was a gold coin. As the coin touched my hand, a purple card repeated the same process.

"You're . . . exceptionally quick at switching through Inventory items." Ren tilted her head as she handed over the weapon.

Was that a compliment? I'd take it. "Mmm, it's just remembering where everything is, mostly. Like sleight of hand but for my brain." The actual *sleight of hand*, not just the System-granted skill of the same name. Although both seemed to tick the right boxes.

"So just thinking quickly then." She rolled her eyes.

Roger stood up from the body and dropped the rock he had been carrying. "Being a giant is *powerful*," he hissed.

"You're normal size. It was the Goblins that were . . ." I paused as his form dissolved into mist as he transferred to a body he hadn't beaten to a pulp. "Never mind."

Ren tutted as she watched the new puppet stand. "I know he is a demon, but you shouldn't let him maim dead bodies."

I opened my mouth to disagree, but she had a point. It wasn't as though he was a *child*, but I was still responsible for how he interacted with the world. He stood up in the body of the crossbow Thief, his ears bursting from her skull. I winced, but it didn't move the needle much.

"Roger, don't play with dead bodies. Kill the target and then move on." I wasn't used to being stern, but being bound by a pact should at least carry some of the weight of my request.

"Right, boss." He looked down at the mashed head of the dead Thief but didn't have anything further to say.

Ren kicked one of the bodies. "This one has boots with Mana bonus on them and a power token. Rest is junk. We'll split gold at some point?"

"No rush. Flat bonus or percentage for the Mana? What are you using the token on?"

"Flat. My heal." She looked as though she was already on the way to doing it.

"Pass then. Good choice. I'm sure I'll need pulling from the fire often enough." I gave her a grin, which she dismissed with the wave of her hand as if I were a System notification.

"It's best if we both stay alive. It has increased the heal percentage, and I can have two Charms now. One each."

I nodded and looked around the room. It would be rather greedy for me to take both; she couldn't heal if she was dead, of course. I relented to looting the corpses beside me, hoping to find something useful.

[32 Gold]
[Metal Bar (Scrap)]
[Soap]
[Oranges (3)]

I pulled a face at the loot disparity between what Ren had found and . . . whatever you could call that. There wasn't much else in the room aside from some spare furniture that looked like it had been exclusively used to store dust. The exit door was considerably better made than the two prior and looked rather secure. Oddly so. Roger caught my gaze and went over to it.

"No, don't." I raised my hand and furrowed my brow.

Ren loosened up her sword arm. "Trapped?"

It wasn't even that. "Most definitely, but there's something else." My brain did a quick rewind and checked around the room again. "There's a body missing—we saw six at first, right?"

The elf petted the Hellhound on the head as it sank from this realm. "They probably went through the door then, unless they're invisible too?"

I rubbed my face, briefly distracted by the fact that I found I couldn't put corpses in my Inventory. Probably not living things either. Made sense, but somewhat disappointing. Some of the furniture on the other hand . . . "*Ah*, no, I think we would have seen or heard it. I think that is a fake door."

Roger leaned forward and sniffed it. An awkward motion for the body he was puppeteering. "Looks real to me, boss."

"It's too perfect." I shook my head. "It's the first thing I've seen in here that is well-made and in good condition."

Ren tilted her head. "So what are you thinking then, trickster?"

A poker chip appeared in my hand, and I turned to the wall behind me. The only one not cluttered with aged wooden furniture and debris. I flicked it to the left, and after spinning through the air, it bounced from the wall and rolled across the stone floor. Then a second one more toward the middle. Bounce. Then at the far end, the chip sank straight through, the slight sound of it rolling across stone dissipating beyond.

"An *illusion*." I grinned, congratulating myself for not also saying, "*Ta-da!*"

"You'll send Roger in first then?" The Oathwarden rolled her eyes. "I'd hate to go through and find there are thugs on the other side waiting to break my skull open."

"Might be an improvement," the demon murmured.

If she heard it, she made no sign of it—which was either an extraordinary poker face or something to do with the pact.

The demon walked over to the part of the wall I had designated and felt around for the upper edge of the secret passage. Part of me expected him to go full speed into it and knock himself over—perhaps that was just me hoping for some levity rather than wishing slapstick injury on him. Just above waist level—crouching but not crawling. He slunk down and then was gone.

After the demon had fully disappeared down into the hidden passage, Ren sighed. She caught my slightly raised eyebrow. "I have what you might call holy energy. That's why he finds me so distasteful."

"That makes some sense." I nodded. Demonic and holy energy . . . or *magic* . . . seemed opposite to each other, and somehow that explanation was more palatable than just the idea that he didn't think she was pleasant on the eye. He was strange but surely not that crazy. I briefly took her in before looking back to where he had gotten to.

I tilted my head, trying to hear his progress. As much as I had wanted to send cards through, attacking blindly when I didn't know the depth of the passage was futile. "I feel *somewhat* guilty for sending him to test for traps."

"Better him than us. At least he can come back with another summon." She shrugged and walked over next to me.

If he ran out of time, then it was simple enough to throw another card at a corpse. If he actually died in combat, then it wasn't so straightforward—there was a much longer cooldown. At this stage, I wasn't sure if it would then bring me a different demon or if he would need to reform back in hell before coming back. Either way, I'd be down a pact demon for a while.

"Feeling okay, Max?"

I looked at her; her glare was no less menacing than usual. "Better than ever," I responded, actually with a healthy handful of truth to it this time. Not only was I getting a better hold of my magical abilities, but fireworks of inspiration for new tricks were in constant bloom in the darkened reaches of my mind. My eyebrow raised. "Why do you ask?"

"There's just furniture missing from this room now." Her impassive stare gave no hint at her actual concern or perhaps amusement. "Odd that you pale at the idea of looting beneficial items but want to fill your Inventory with junk."

With faux surprise on my face, I glanced around as if I had only just realized the room was half as cluttered as it previously was.

Her bright-blue eyes narrowed in anticipation, already knowing me well enough to see that I was about to earn myself a renewed glare.

"Couldn't have been me . . ." As I tipped my hat with a nod, I barely hid my grin. "Must have been *magic*."

CHAPTER TWENTY-SIX

Prop Work

One of the most concerning things about the System was how it broke its own rules. You could encounter a Monster that acted a certain way—simple, routine, and barely a hindrance—then suddenly there would be one who broke the mold. This was even before the consideration that some enemies had elite or champion designations that improved their Abilities and intelligence. We were talking about normal foes who would one day decide to ruin your life just for the amusement of it, as if some childish god was sitting behind the switch, gleefully watching you flounder.

As we stood and waited for my demon to report back on the secret passage, there was an odd sound of . . . ripping? I didn't want to add any more visceral clarifiers to what my mind tried to imagine was the cause.

"Clear, boss." Roger's voice came from inside the secret passage. Not dead, then.

I sighed as I couched down, feeling around for the height again so that I didn't knock my top hat off. It might offer my vulnerable skull a little protection, for all that was worth. My face went through the illusion, and beyond was a rough, dark tunnel that went on for a dozen feet before turning to the left. The bright-purple pits of light that were Roger's eyes glared at me from the other end.

A smell then hit me. Blood and other worse, damp things.

His face contorted in the dim light. "Well, there *was* a trap, but I think my legs jammed it up."

Now, with my eyes adjusting to the darkness, I could see some kind of saw or spike trap had extended out halfway through the tunnel. The corpse he had been puppeteering had been caught on them, splitting the legs from the rest of the body and leaving a trail of internal organs down the last of the passage. Even the trap had been surprised at the process and was now gummed up and stuck with gore and other things my mind tried to ignore.

"*Oh joy,*" I muttered. Trying not to breathe in most of the smell, I leaned back out of the passage and grimaced at the elf. "Roger has been cut in half. We'll have to crawl over the parts, but the trap looks to be inert."

Her expression dulled, which wasn't saying much, but she nodded.

"Boss, there's a dark room to my side here. It's empty, but I can hear voices. Whispering voices. They beckon me to the light . . ."

"Roger?" I watched as the purple faded away and the spent corpse went limp. From checking my Ability, it looked like he had self-dispersed rather than died—but clearly had to add a little bit of melodrama on the way out . . . because this whole encounter wasn't stressful enough, apparently.

I crawled through and held my breath, trying to ignore the squelches and fluids soaking into my suit. Squeezing past the torso of the woman he had been piloting, I pushed into the dark room he had mentioned. In the dim light, I could see boxes to the right and left walls, a rather normal and worn door ahead of me. My breath escaped, and relatively clear air entered my lungs. The System truly didn't pull any punches, and I wondered if the lack of Players encountered so far on the mainland was due to the more naive and carefree being turned into mulch by the harsh world. A far cry from the cute Slimes.

A small amount of grunting behind me, and Ren came through next. I offered a hand down to help her up, which she took.

"Hate that demon," she grumbled, looking back toward the remains of the spent body.

I wasn't a fan of how we had to crawl through the remains of the body he had possessed but couldn't fault him for disabling the trap. Much rather him than us, as she had said. I was sure she still held the same view but was also unhappy about getting gore soaked through her outfit. That or the whole holy-demon thing went both ways. I'd better not dwell on that.

She crept toward the door ahead of us and moved her long ear closer to it, while I squinted around the room for anything of interest. It looked like it was used as a storeroom, although all the crates had lids on them. It would be too noisy to open them right now with potential enemies just through the threshold. Somehow I doubted they had much useful to loot anyway.

Ren moved back from the door quietly and put her mouth near my ear. "At least five in there," she whispered, causing a shiver to run up my spine. "Ready when you are."

I brought a card into my hand, putting it away and drawing it again. Purple light flickered through the room. My right eye twitched, and a short pain ran down my fingers as I split the card into one magic and one Hellhound. I wasn't sure the System was meant to allow me to do this, but I saw no reason why it shouldn't be possible. It just *hurt.*

Dagger of Luck came up in my other hand, and I nodded to the elf. She had drawn her bow, and the green energy that swirled with strands of gold began to rotate around the arrow.

Assuming they didn't all have ranged weapons, pinning them in place would allow us to pick a couple off and raise Roger again with little danger to ourselves. Hoping I didn't make a fool of myself, I stepped forward and kicked the door. Thankfully, it swung open, relenting to my show of force. As I immediately drew the attention of all within, I then ducked and threw my cards out at the nearest figure.

Six Thieves in the room—two by a closed doorway to the right, two around a table in the middle, two farther back on a slightly raised area with some wooden boxes. None of them looking too happy to see us appear in their hidden room. Perhaps we should have brought a gift . . . Oh—*I did*, but they probably wouldn't like it.

I curved my pair of cards around in the air, pain radiating from my wrist as the System fought the use of my summoning card this way. With a final flick, I sent the magic card into one of the Thieves by the doorway, the canine card striking the wall beside him. As it was a *summon* card, I couldn't use it to attack. Seemed arbitrary, but I'd play by the rules as long as I could keep bending them.

Ren's arrow flew over my head straight after, striking an opponent near the table. Vines spiraled out from the rock floor and held the four in that direction, the two by the door either out of range or resisting the effect. My Hellhound spawned from an arcane circle on the wall and set upon the legs of the Thief I had struck.

"Go," Ren commanded, a statement to let me know she wasn't about to put an arrow through the back of my head accidentally rather than through her impatience.

I *did* go, vaguely unsure as to why I was approaching the danger but still know-ing I had to erase it from my view. As I stepped into the room, the two at the back started to draw Crossbows.

One at the table growled, unable to come at me with a rather wicked-looking curved sword. "Shouldn't have come h—" he began.

My card found his open mouth wanting, and just as it reached his maw, I split it in two to slice through both cheeks on the way to his throat. His eyes flashed wide, and he dropped the sword to the ground to clutch at his face. The sound of an arrow zipped past my ear and slammed through his hands and into his head.

<Card Fan> flashed up in front of me, absorbing one crossbow bolt while the second was dulled but still struck me in the shoulder. Painful but superficial, hardly worth worrying about. I pulled the bolt out and threw it at the second table Thief—but switched it for a dagger at the last second. Expecting a harmless stick, the gruff man instead raised his arm to be pierced by the sharp blade.

I dropped the pact demon summon on the first corpse as radiant light illuminated Ren's bow.

The sudden rush of air beside me had me stumbling backward by instinct, the slash of a blade cutting through my left arm as a seventh Thief appeared from invisibility. I clutched at the wound as it burned. Some kind of poison? As he stepped toward me, I moved backward again, and he stumbled against a chair that was suddenly in front of his feet. While brief confusion flared across his bearded face, I hopped atop the chair and brought both hands down—the metal cooking grill appearing in my grip, which I slammed down onto his head. I hopped down after him and spun with a flourish, both objects vanishing behind my flared jacket as I stood straight with a click of my heels.

Dazzle icons popped up on all the Thieves paying me attention. With a quick twirl, I popped the cork from an antidote and downed it. Almost as gross as the healing one.

A flash of golden light came from the door where Ren stood as she shot one of the Thieves with her smite arrow. The figure stumbled backward, their plain tunic soaking through with blood. Next to them, a sweaty woman scowled at the hound, her arm and leg shredded from his attacks.

Roger flipped the table over as his ears burst from the top of his skull, pinning the other Thief behind it. He took two crossbow bolts to the torso and stumbled slightly, the arrow Ren had fired also still sticking from the head of his puppet. The demon then flopped atop the trapped enemy, clawing at the man's face and trying to gouge his eyes while his own bloody maw hung open, drooling blood.

Purple cards flew from my hand, splitting through the air and coming down on the two at the back—but not aimed for them exactly. Their weapons jostled as I cut through the taut cables of their Crossbows, rendering them loose and inert.

After a brief look of confusion, they dropped the weapons. One of them drew a sword and broke free of the entanglement to come straight for me. An arrow zipped toward the door pair. A crunch came from the table where Roger lay prone. I grinned and drew two cards, tense in anticipation for the imminent melee with the sword-wielding Thief.

As he reached me, I held out my empty left hand toward him—the lit torch from earlier then appearing from my Inventory, blinding him and waylaying his sword swing. My cards went out straight into the forearm of his weapon hand. The pain made him let go of it, and blue System boxes flickered quickly in the side of my vision. The commands activating at speed, I pushed in toward him, and the weapon vanished, now in my possession as I looted it from the air. I spun, the flame of the torch circling behind me and then emerging from the other side as my dagger instead, stabbing straight into his wounded arm as he tried to block it.

His other hand punched into my stomach. Not exactly damaging but winding. As I stepped backward, a blur of blue enveloped his foot, and he stepped forward to trip me. The whole hideout shifted, and the stone floor hit me hard, knocking the hat from my head as my skull earned a new bruise. Neither of these events I really appreciated—even less so when the wounded Thief landed on top of me, knocking the air from my lungs and then wrapping his rough hands around my neck.

I needn't have even bothered panicking, really. I was in a room full of allies, and despite the dark spots flickering through my vision, it was only a matter of time before one of them—Oh, there it was.

The horror show that was the possessed corpse loomed over the thief. With his jaw open wide and running with blood, Roger's eyes of deep purple pits stared down at me before the hands that had been punctured by Ren's arrow wrapped around the chin and neck of my assailant.

Having the life choked out of me wasn't exactly fun, but watching my demon slowly snap the man's neck backward while my vision dimmed wasn't adding to the experience either. At last, the hands relented, and I took a big gasp of air—only to be rewarded with a hideous crack of bones as the man's struggling muscles were overcome. Roger pushed the body from me and helped me up with his bloodied hand.

"You okay, boss?"

I was still panting and regaining my vision, but I gave him a nod and a smile—just before a hammer cracked his head in two. He dropped to the ground with the last spasms of life, the purple mist fading away to reveal the assailant. The last Thief from the back, an arrow in his chest and his face contorted from pain. The Hellhound leaped from the side and took his arm, disarming him as a second arrow struck him in the forehead.

Silence now filled the chamber, except for the growled gnashing of the hound and my own heart and lungs screaming out, the noise echoing inside my head.

"Sorry about Roger," Ren said, stepping over.

Either I had hit my head too hard in the fall, or that was genuine sympathy for my bloodthirsty pact demon. "Oh? He'll be okay. He gets a little holiday now, I suppose." I turned to the elf, and she handed me my top hat. I twirled it up to its rightful place.

"You're not a brawler, Max. Stop getting so friendly with death." She sighed and rubbed her face. "As good as I am, I can't risk firing arrows into melee with you."

"Sorry, I did get a little carried away." That was putting it lightly. I ran up and hit someone with a cooking appliance.

"I don't want to say anything that might encourage you, but you seem to be able to do a lot with *bullshittery*." She glared at me, hoping I didn't take it as permission to flirt with danger. "From what I've seen, people aren't normally able to interact with the Inventory that quickly, especially to switch things mid-combat."

I likened it to typing. While most people could plod along using one or two fingers, my words per minute were bordering on showing off. Naturally, that was just par for the course for the world's greatest magician. Open, select the intangible grid square, select Hold or Drop. A process that I seemed to take to like a duck to water.

My mouth turned up into a wide grin. "I feel like I am just getting started. I'm practically salivating for another power token."

"Next one is yours, trickster. Just don't waste it by dying immediately after." She raised an eyebrow, knowing she was inviting destiny to muddy my plans.

I smiled and nodded though. There was no intent to die just yet.

In fact, if I got good enough, we'd never had to worry about dying ever again. We'd be infamous.

CHAPTER TWENTY-SEVEN

Luck of the Draw

From that day onward, any time that I almost died, I would make a mark on the ace of diamonds card I had acquired from the thieves. Of course, at some point in my journey I had lost it, or it had become damaged beyond recognition. At first, it bothered me that I could no longer tally up the truly lucky days. After a short while, I realized the lucky days were the ones where I was in no danger and could just enjoy living. The fewer and further apart they became, the harder I pushed to bring them back.

Ren sighed and rolled her neck. "Pretty disappointing in terms of loot."

[68 Gold]
[Deft Leggings: +1 AGI]
[Crossbows (Broken) (2)]

She was correct. Other than gold and the random assortment of odd items I had been filling my Inventory with, there wasn't anything spectacular in this room. The leggings gave a single point of Agility, which wasn't really necessary for my build but was better than the default gear I still had on. The other Equipment with Stats was even less useful.

Nothing to fit the slots I already had filled. "Lots of Strength gear. Shame we didn't have a warrior or something in the Party." I drummed my fingertips on the boxes at the end of the room I had rifled through. Mostly things that even *I* couldn't see the value in, which was saying a lot.

The elf walked around the room, scowling at everything as if it may reveal another hidden passageway. "I'm not sure what you'll do with half of what you pick up. I'm surprised you didn't take the table."

"It wouldn't let me," I said with a shrug. She was looking away, but I could almost hear her eyes rolling. Empty bottles, a large tarp-like sheet, a jeweler's hammer, a pencil, and a handful of plain marbles. Sure, it was no Archmage's Slippers or Axe of World Ending, but some of the most functional of items could bring great form to a show. You never knew when a situation would require a specific, odd item.

"As long as you aren't too focused on tricks to be effective in combat. It sounds like I'm admonishing you, but . . ." She rubbed her face and turned to me. "Big balls are no good if they're easy to cut off."

My brow furrowed, and I leaned back against the crate. "Is that an elfin expression?"

She shrugged. "Maybe. We are speaking . . . the same language?"

It stood to reason that if portals pulled people from all manner of worlds, the system would have to utilize some kind of translation between Players. "Probably something the System smooths over. You just mean being overconfident is a long step toward a sharp blade."

"Is that a human expression?"

I smiled and shrugged.

[Progress: 12/16 Thieves killed]

"Only four of these useless Thieves left." I yawned. The lack of sleep was starting to catch up. "You'd think they'd have better loot being a whole hideout of them. What have they even been stealing?" Of course, being System-created, they would be stuck here doing whatever routine they were destined to repeat. More of a failure on the System then.

"Shitty Thieves," she muttered as she shook her head at one of the mangled bodies on the ground.

The Hellhound had gone already, and I couldn't call Roger for a while. While it was nice to assume the rest of the Thieves were sitting patiently in the next room, it would be careless to start making assumptions at this stage. Even with my brain wanting to hit the Snooze button. For the most part, I was annoyed that we wouldn't be able to nap anywhere without one eye open. One little assassination attempt and now I was paranoid that death was just waiting for my eyes to close for long enough to make a move. I shook that thought away and focused on the present task.

"These doors are probably combustible, right?" I hopped down from the raised area, being careful not to slip on the slick blood slowly congealing on the rocky floor.

"I suppose." She immediately turned to go stand in the farthest corner.

Although I still hadn't decided if creating a barricade of burning wood between us and the next room was a good idea or not, now that she had made the decision to move out of the way . . . I felt like I had to do it. You couldn't create the expectation and then squander it.

I dropped the Imp summon beside me and gave the plump creature a nod. Part of me wanted to know how the whole summoning thing worked. Were they just created when I cast the Skill? I had felt that the wounded Hellhound would be okay on the starter island when I sent him away—but if there *was* an actual hell, did that mean there was a pool of potential demons I was drawing from? What were the chances I could pull the same one twice?

With a shake of my head, I let the thoughts drift away for now. As much as I didn't like not knowing, I was sure to not like the Thieves respawning atop us as I was busy even more. Lost in my own head, I needed to sharpen my thoughts. Like their swords would be otherwise—sharp and in my head. I gestured toward the door, and the Imp began to form a fireball.

A purple card twisted over my hand, and Ren had drawn an arrow ready. It was not our fault if the System-created had a blind spot when it came to *different rooms*. If we could get the jump on them due to this, then that was one less bruise for the next morning.

The fireball zipped across the chamber, illuminating the dead and debris we had left scattered around, then struck the door. I watched it catch alight and start to burn. Not exactly the explosive result I had expected—so now we just had a door on fire in our way. I narrowed my eyes at it, willing it to collapse.

"I'll admit to being a bit underwhelmed." Ren relaxed the tensed bowstring. "It's not like you to disappoint."

Her expression was hard to read, but the words prodded the soft part of my brain that needed to perform to be accepted. I smiled. The fail-safe option. "Have a little more faith, Ren, for the real trick is—"

The door burst open toward us, wafting heated air and smoke our way. A large figure silhouetted against the hallway beyond.

"Enemies!" he growled and gestured to whoever was behind him, his angered face sandwiched between two thick sideburns that put most people's normal head hair to shame.

"*Ta-da*," I muttered at the sudden appearance of our foe. A little coincidence could be twisted to my credit. Another notification appeared in my vision.

[New Monster: Head Thief <7 E>]

Briefly I wondered if that meant he stole heads, but then again—if given the chance—I'm sure that was part of his intention. The *E* next to his level must mean elite—nice to have something written in plain text to let you know you were about to meet the blunt end of a heavy lesson.

With the arrow out and card not far behind, the large man flared up in a brief sphere of gray, the attacks striking but doing no damage to him. He stumbled forward, raising a thick cudgel in one hand and a long knife in the other. Behind him, at least three other Thieves were readying weapons.

The Imp's fireball did strike him, and his leg burst into flame. It was quickly extinguished but left his clothing smoldering around the burn on his flesh. Ren quick drew another arrow that was again blocked by his gray shield as it zipped across the room.

Hmm. It was a neat trick, but I had worked it out already. Unless I was wrong and my brains were about to decorate the back wall, it was simple. He was too close for repeated failed attempts, so it was time to see if this Intelligence Stat was correctly named or not.

The elf started to draw her sword as I whipped my hand around and threw a poker chip at him, anger flaring in my eyes.

Gray shield.

Then, my imbued card struck him through the side of the neck. An imperfect strike as he moved away from it at the last second—but he dropped his knife to hold the wound with a thick hand. One weapon down was better than—

<Card Fan> came up as he swiped at me, my damage doing little to stop his charge. The shield shattered and sent me back against the wall—air once again knocked from my lungs. I wasn't a fan of that. The Imp scrabbled out of the way as Ren fired her entangling arrow into the other room, rooting the rest of the Thieves in place so they couldn't assist their boss.

As the leader stepped toward me, I threw my hat at him. The gray shield flickered around him as he knocked it out of the way—the second of the two cards I threw along behind it biting into his chest.

Every third hit would go through his shield.

I rolled to the ground as his cudgel slammed into the rock wall where my head had been. As I stumbled back to my feet, I watched him pause and shift uneasily across the marbles I had dropped along the way.

"Duck."

I did without hesitation as a flare of radiant light bloomed behind me. The elite looked pretty confident as his shield of gray started to wash over him. It flickered twice, as my split cards hit right before the arrow imbued with smite shot struck him through the mouth and out of the back of his neck.

A blaze of orange flashed from within the next room as my Imp sent a fireball into the restrained Thieves, setting them alight and charring their exposed skin. It was over. A quick pair of cards and an arrow or two, and they were dead with nowhere to escape to. The smell of burning was heavy on my lungs, and I looked forward to getting some fresh air.

I leaned over to grab my discarded top hat and then rested my hands on my knees. Closed my eyes for a moment and allowed the exhaustion to take hold as the adrenaline and heat of battle wore off.

"Good job, trickster." Ren gave me a pat on the back. "I wouldn't have been able to get past the shield alone."

"Teamwork makes the dream work," I murmured, smiling but not looking up at her.

"If your dreams are like this . . ." She trailed off, little more else needing to be said. How far we had come from killing cute Slimes and Boars. Combat now felt gritty and high stakes, as if the System couldn't decide how to pace or theme the areas.

"Right now, the dream is a soft bed and safety. Again." I stood and stretched my bruised back out before taking a moment to bandage my minor injuries, practicing my one-handed approach. "Maybe a round of applause?"

"I can agree on the first two. After seeing how terrible combat is and how eager you are to hop into an early grave, we'd best temper our expectations."

I exhaled and flexed the fingers of my free hand. "We'll be fine. The System tried a bit too hard here, but we're leaving with barely a scratch."

She looked rather unimpressed beneath her scowl, but she turned to continue to loot the other bodies.

[Quest complete]
[Return to town for Reward]

Exhaustion wanted to take the reins back now that everything in the hideout was dealt with; the show was over, but we'd be moving on soon enough. No chance of slumping over in one of these rooms and decompressing for the rest of the day. We wouldn't even be back in town for a couple of days, which was a shame . . . but at least it gave us something to look forward to if we survived that long.

I looted the leader, expecting nothing worthy of our efforts.

[85 Gold]
[Unfinished Letter]
[Power Tokens (2)]
[Knife of the Trickster]
[Sausages (3)]

Other than the blue border around the dagger and the shining tokens, everything else was unimportant. I stowed away the food and letter for later, and I left behind other less important things.

"I found a rare dagger." I grinned. "You're going to love it." *I* sure did. It gave a two-Intelligence and one-Dexterity boost.

She raised an eyebrow and stood from the body she was investigating. "Oh? How so?"

"It's called Knife of the Trickster." My smile widened.

"Match made in heaven." She rolled her eyes. "Nothing much on these aside from gold, unless you need more random junk?"

"No, not right now." Although, I could do with picking up all those marbles again. "I have a power token for you, however."

"Shit, really? Next one is yours, though?" She stepped back over the corpses and over to me.

"Found two." I grinned and withdrew one to hand over to her. "I wonder if we are meant to have upgraded a handful of skills before attempting more dangerous Quests like these."

"Thank you." She shrugged. "Probably, we skipped most of the town Quests to do the challenge board."

"Challenge board? I thought that these were just normal Quests?"

Ren actually paused and crossed her arms, her normal permanent scowl almost breaking. "Max, please. You want to haul around bolts of linen for village folk and herd sheep for five gold and a loose handshake? We are doing the hard-mode questline. Don't you read anything?"

"I try to interface with the System as little as possible."

Her eyes narrowed further. "You literally . . . You know what? Never mind. *Token*, please."

As she reached over to take it from my clasped fingers, I clicked them together and instead it became a card—the ace of diamonds. "Is this your card?" I grinned.

Her eyes slowly went from the card to my own. "If I chose to kill you in your sleep, I wouldn't make any creaking noises to wake you."

"Good." I raised an eyebrow, clicking my fingers again to change it back to the token. "At least I'd still get some good rest then."

I turned from the elf as my STAR menus spun up. Spoiled for choice, I tried to decide which Ability to upgrade.

CHAPTER TWENTY-EIGHT

The Fool

There seems to be some parts of my notes missing here. Somewhere between "Thieves are terrible" and "Bandits are terrible," there's a gap. Not by itself a cause of concern, but as my memory is fragmented by so much now, sometimes the minutiae of the day-to-day got lost. Usually a gap meant either something happened that drew me away from the routine of note-taking—for better or for worse.

I breathed in the fresh open air of the outside world and sighed in contentedness. Quest complete and we had escaped the odd burrow almost unscathed. I turned to the elf as she stepped out from the darkness just after me, her eyes focused on System windows.

"I went with one of my Passive Abilities, to increase my attack speed." Ren blinked and frowned as she became awash in the daylight. Her blonde hair was practically glowing with radiance as the light struck it, and it took me an extra second to parse what she had said.

"That's . . . valid." I nodded and rubbed at my chin. "It might not be as flashy as your active Abilities but aids your overall effectiveness."

She rolled her eyes as she pushed past me. "Thanks for the approval." She exhaled and waved her hand. "Sorry, that's the tiredness talking. What did you decide to pick?"

"I'm struggling between two Passives." I stretched out. Although there was plenty of headroom in the Thief cave, being in the outdoors again was remarkably freeing. An amusing thing for a man who spent too much time in his home studio or up on stage rather than enjoying nature. "<Mana Manipulation> or <Sleight of Hand>. To be better with the cards or with the—"

"The bullshit?" She tilted her head. "I couldn't tell you which is best. Just decide before the next stage of our dance with death."

I gave her a brief bow, and we set off northward toward the Bandit encampment. We had altered the original plan and had put the Boss Monster Hunt after the Bandits. Less travel for ever-tiring legs. After the dim hideout, the warmth and color of the surrounding woodlands was calming and just made me feel even more like I needed a good sleep. The aching muscles and bruises didn't help either.

Ren could see it in me, and even her immutable brilliance beneath her normal scowl had lost some of its luster. "Maybe we shouldn't burn out on the first day." She grimaced and looked up into the treetops. "Some form of hammock might be reasonably safe."

I shrugged and gave her a tired smile. "It sounds preferable to death from exhaustion."

"We'll go a bit farther from the caves and find somewhere suitable."

We went on for a while longer, although the scenery didn't change much. I occasionally stumbled on thick chunks of grass or tree roots attempting to trip me. The token still hung unused as I deliberated on which was better to pick. <Mana Manipulation> would give me better control over my cards, but <Sleight of Hand> should increase the speed at which I could access and swap things from my Inventory. I *could* already do that pretty quickly though . . . so I chose <Mana Manipulation>.

[<Mana Manipulation> is now advanced: You have greater control over your Mana reserves]

Another slice of vagueness from the System. There wasn't even a numerical figure for how much Mana I had, nor a bar that would decrease or regenerate. It was just innate—something I could feel. That it was a specific Ability that my Class had been given could mean that most other spellcasters weren't so flexible in their magic usage. This was all new ground for me, and some things were harder to learn than others.

"You know, you don't always have to be *fine*?"

I raised my eyebrows and looked over at the elf as she took me from my thoughts. "Hmm?"

She stopped to lean against a tree and rubbed at her eye sockets. "You're always *fine* or smiling or needing to push forward. You can be more open with how you really feel."

"This coming from someone who is permanently scowling?" I crossed my arms, subconsciously trying to hold the snappy retorts back. Well, not so subconscious, I supposed.

"I have a lot to be angry and sad about, trickster." Her impassive eyes looked up at me. "Don't you?"

My jaw was clenched, but I wasn't sure why. Things *were* fine. I took a second to breathe deeply in and out, twice. "The show must go on," I eventually said with a grin, even if my heart wasn't fully behind it.

"Why? What happens if it doesn't?"

I opened my mouth, but my mind was blank. Some knot had formed in my stomach, and I stared at the elf to see what she was trying to get at. Other than clearly being tired, she was both remarkably hard to read and stubbornly not accepting my silence as an answer.

"I'm"—I licked my lips—"unsure as to what response you are trying to elicit. Am I not trying hard enough?"

She tilted her head, but her expression didn't change. "I just want you to actually be fine, not just say it. If you *are*, then that's okay. Forgive me for twisting the screws."

I felt remarkably warm. A purple suit was not the best clothing to be wearing on a hike through the woods, it turned out. I removed my top hat and wiped my brow on the back of my arm. "Wow, and I thought the Thieves were tough."

"If you can deflect crossbow bolts as well as you do my questions, then you'll be twice as useful." She stood and nodded through the forest. "A little bit more and we'll stop for food."

I smiled, but it faded from my face as soon as her back was turned. Not that I was even annoyed at Ren exactly or that I blamed her for the weird cramping inside me. I was just tired and hungry and wasn't prepared for thinking about it any more than that. So much killing, not enough downtime, perhaps? I pushed any further thoughts from my mind.

Instead, I drew a card. Held it in my hand and let it hover above it as I tried to feel for any difference. Nothing major. I threw it out a dozen feet and split it in two.

There it was. I brought one back alone, the other hanging in the air as I walked. I put energy back into the first as I sent it back and withdrew the second, repeating the process. Better control over the split cards. I could now juggle them. With my fingers relaxing, I let them dissipate. No blood on my hands.

Well, none of my own.

I looked out into the woods and deflated somewhat. For some reason, I didn't feel much like practicing, even though I was *fine*. It was at least a small blessing that the route we had traveled had not been dense with wild Monsters—or crawling with Players wanting to literally pick our brains. They'd have to try extrahard to get something worthwhile inside my cranium at present.

"Here should be fine." Ren stopped and put her hands above her eyes as she looked up. "Canopy is dense enough. We should be near invisible if we go high up."

My eyes followed her gaze, and whatever joy I had left in me sank out to be lost in the thick grass. I was suspicious of heights after the thing with the Orc and preferred not to tempt fate. That said, I'd court death for a decent nap. "I have . . . some sheets and rope?"

"Perfect. Finally, a good use for your kleptomania." She stepped forward and held her hands out.

"I'm not a . . ." My brain replayed the scenes of me looting every odd and end from the Thieves' hideout. "It's no different from . . ." I sighed and gave up the point. Two sheets and a couple of bundles appeared in my arms, and I handed them over.

"I'm sure you are excellent at tying knots." She continued to impassively stare at me. "But I'd feel better about our safety if I made the hammocks."

"As you wish, your highness." I gave a bow but couldn't manage a signature smile.

She turned and flipped me off as she walked away. Not an especially elfin hand signal, but then maybe some things were universal. The exhaustion was eroding my sensibilities. Usually a tough tour run would burn me out, but I could at least be solitary and lie in bed all day. Watching videos on new tricks, of course, but it was still resting.

I kept an eye on our surroundings as Ren did her work. Even sat on the soft grass for a little and enjoyed nature for what it was. There was a small clearing just beyond our trees after a short slope. Any wandering adventurers should be too focused on their footwork to be gazing up at the canopy where we would be dozing. Even the thought of it was lifting my mood. *Sleep.*

Ren descended, dropping to the grass near silently. "That's yours done, trickster. I'll put mine up a little farther away but still within arrow distance."

Presumably she meant for assisting if trouble found us rather than potentially assassinating me if I snored too loudly. She walked behind me as I stood to my feet, her shadow passing over me as the sun lit her hair.

"Hey, Ren. I'm sorry for being an asshole sometimes."

She nodded and gave me a pat on the shoulder as she continued to her chosen tree. "It's fine. You can't help it."

Regardless of whatever expression she had as she walked away from me, it did give me a little smile. That was until I turned to my tree and grimaced at the prospect of having to climb.

And it *was* agony. One branch at a time and trying not to think of the distance. I wondered if she put it higher than needed just to spite me, but that was unfair to her. Maybe. Eventually, I reached the proposed sleeping arrangement. It looked like a death trap, with two ends attached to thick branches with a further tether to the trunk. With trepidation, I sat into it, the linens absorbing my body as my internal organs panicked.

I didn't immediately die, which is all I had wished for—and after a few minutes of being fully tense, I relaxed into it. If I closed my eyes, it was easy to imagine I was a lot closer to the ground.

But I didn't want to sink into the darkness just yet. Hunger still gripped my insides. I opened my eyes again to check through my Inventory. It slightly amused me how certain items stored inside the intangible space. The torch had remained lit. An inkwell didn't tip or spill. I withdrew it, alongside a journal I had nabbed from one of the rooms, as well as a fountain pen. While I had intended to use it to stab someone in the eye eventually, it might make do to start keeping a diary of some kind. As I opened the book onto my lap, I withdrew some food into my left hand to chew on.

The first couple of pages of the tome I would need to remove, as they had already been used briefly by one of the Thieves. Nothing interesting. The next page, blank, stared back at me as I thought. After tapping my chin for a minute, I eventually wrote down, "Thieves are terrible." I'd fill in the earlier stuff when my brain wasn't so exhausted—oh, but that reminded me the leader had a note on him.

I tried to adjust my position and panicked briefly as I forgot where I was, rocking the hammock. The motion was . . . slightly relaxing once my muscles gave up the ghost. The piece of paper snapped into my hand from my Inventory, and I read it. Something about an important shipment of something, stopped just off the road a little ways off. It looked as though there was going to be a further piece of information, but it hadn't been finished. Probably a warning. I stowed it away and marked the location on my Map. Food downed, it was time for the final curtain call.

Exhaling slowly, I closed my eyes. Putting the trials endured so far today behind me, it didn't take sleep long to blanket my tired mind.

In this hard-earned darkness, a weird dream took me. Being chased through a shallow pool of crimson. I couldn't turn around to see what was after me, and only darkness surrounded me. The splash of footsteps behind me, keeping pace. Somehow, just hearing it was even worse than knowing what was trying to track me down. An echo calling my name hummed in my ears as I felt constricted and trapped. My limbs felt numb and unresponsive as I struggled and fought against the invisible restraints, desperate to break free. I reached out as far as I could.

And then, with a sudden jolt of vertigo, I *was* free. My eyes shot open, and the light of day hit me just as quickly as a thick branch did. Warmth flooded through my head and cooled instantly from the rush of air as I dropped.

Pain lit up my face as twigs and leaves scraped past me. It happened so fast, but I must have hit at least another three main branches before bouncing on the ground and sliding down the brief incline to the clearing beyond.

[Health Report]
[Nose injury (Broken)]
[Left wrist injury (Heavy fracture)]
[Rib injuries (Light fractures) (3)]

"*Fuck you*, System," I hissed through the pain, blood running down my face. Unfair. I had brought up the information by instinct—although it didn't take a genius to see the odd angle that my hand currently faced as I clutched it to know that it was broken. "*Fuck you*, trees," I added, my eyes blurring.

The sound of Ren quickly descending her tree came from over behind me, and she slid down the incline.

"*Asshole*, Max—I even made it so that it was more difficult to fall out." She put her hand on my shoulder, and I could see the concern breaking through the admonishing scowl. "Are you alright?"

"I'm . . . *fine*." I grinned through a face that felt like it was bruising already. A pulse of radiant energy flowed through me, warming and soothing my injuries. Still, my head throbbed even as my wrist clicked and I regained the uncomfortable use of my left hand.

"Stupid shit, you can't even be honest when you—" She paused and looked up, the slight worry in her face immediately washed away by a stoic frown.

Blinking away the pained tears, I followed her gaze out to the other side of the clearing.

Stalking through the tree line was a large creature. Bright amber eyes that were set among thick brown fur. It was *massive*.

As it stepped out of the shadowed canopy and into the light of the late afternoon, the grizzly bear's sharp fangs glimmered with saliva. He growled and moved toward us.

CHAPTER TWENTY-NINE

An Odd Dance

There was a time where sanity felt like an actual skill I could write off on my list of character traits. Went through hell and back but still sane. Gradually, I wondered whether my definition of insanity just changed over time. Plenty of things you had to just accept and move on if you wanted to survive in this world. Some of it was beyond my understanding, but you couldn't let that shape you. Allow yourself a little ignorance if you hoped to be even slightly happy.

I had never seen a bear in person before. Well, no, I had seen one in a zoo once. A dejected and bored-looking beast. This one was almost twice that size and looked full of ambition. Mostly a desire to make a meal out of us—but for a wild animal that was as good a reason as any, no matter if I had any disagreements about it.

"That's a *bear*," Ren whispered. Her eyes were focused on it as her hand slowly went for her bow.

Perhaps she thought my world didn't have bears or maybe assumed I had made scrambled eggs of my brain on my greatest-hits tour of the tree branches. There was another quip in there somewhere, but I was too preoccupied with the hulking creature slowly approaching us to really draw it out through my mouth.

"I can fight," I weakly muttered. I'm not sure how the System divided up healing between my broken parts. The nicest assumption would be that it prioritized the lifesaving stuff rather than share around equally. Ribs were still tender, but my left hand could now move—even if it hated the process.

"Might need to entangle and run." Her voice was calm despite the clear danger.

I stood to my feet slowly, rising with her. Somehow, my hat was still on my head. True magic. My legs could probably run, given the alternative. Where to wouldn't really matter. System-created must have some kind of aggro drop at a certain distance.

"Ugly packaging for a boring meal," the bear growled at me, drool running from his open jaws.

"What?" I wrinkled my face up. "You can talk?" Also, my suit *wasn't* ugly, but that seemed like a point to make when so many teeth weren't being bared.

"Irrelevant." He stepped another large paw forward.

Ren had an arrow at the ready but hadn't nocked it yet. Thoughts clattered down through my brain like I had through the tree.

"Are you a Player?" I asked, slowly removing my hat.

He paused. "That sounds like something the boxes said. Do you control the boxes?"

I shook my head and grinned. With my good hand, I reached into the awkwardly held top hat and brought out a slab of meat. I could also audibly hear Ren's eyes roll. "No, but I'll trade food for conversation."

"Give me the hat." The bear licked his lips, but his body language relaxed slightly.

"*No*," I repeated. "But as a show of good faith . . ." I lobbed the meat across the clearing, which the bear grabbed and devoured.

"I feel as though this is a dangerous game you are playing, trickster." The elf had now lowered her weapon and was prepared to cross her arms for added effect. Lecturing me clearly worth risking being a second slower if we were attacked.

"What? You never wanted a pet familiar? Seems cliché, I know, but—"

"I would *much* prefer a wolf." She shrugged and stared at the bear impassively.

The large creature licked the last of the meal from his lips and sat down, his amber eyes no less full of fury. "I will talk, food giver."

"My name is Max, and this is Ren. What's yours?"

His nose twitched, looking between my held hat and the elf. ". . . *Wolf*," he eventually decided.

Ren's brow lowered further. "Your name is *Wolf*. As a bear."

"I like it." My eyes dazzled. A stage show set in my mind, the magnificent magician and the talking bear that could do tricks. The elf assistant in a shimmering blue dress with a wide smile on her—Oh. No, that broke the illusion.

"Could you think any louder?" She glared at me as I refocused. "One-track mind, Max."

"I wasn't thinking of a—of whatever you're saying I was thinking." I ran the risk of becoming too predictable. That or I had spoken some of my daydream out loud but didn't realize it due to my head injury.

She rolled her eyes. "Red is not my color. Plus, I don't wear dresses."

I clicked my tongue. "It was blue, actually."

"See! I knew it." She shook her head, exasperated. "*One-track mind.*"

Plus, I didn't really work with animals as much as I could help it. If Wolf could consent and was intelligent enough to understand, then that was different. I turned to give him a resigned shrug, and he looked mostly perplexed.

"Are you going to attack me or give me more food?" He tilted his head, looking as though those were the only two options he was used to.

I tapped the rim of my hat. "Answer me three questions and you can have three more pieces of meat."

"I'll answer ten questions." He licked his lips.

A smile crossed my lips but faltered slightly in seeing that he was injured. His flank on one side, mostly obscured by his thick foreleg, was matted with dark crimson. I turned to Ren and raised an eyebrow, and she gave a nod.

"My good friend here is going to heal your wounds too. Is that okay?"

Wolf looked at the slowly approaching elf and sniffed at the air. "I accept."

"First question then. Do you remember coming from a world prior to this one?"

He tilted his head in thought, then turned to sniff at his wound as it closed up. The radiant warmth of the Oathwarden seemed to comfort, if slightly confuse him—but he allowed the elf to place her hand on his broad shoulder.

"Yes. It was different to here, like a dream where I couldn't talk. There was something new near my home . . . I remember pink?" He chewed at the air as if continuing to process the words after the sentence had finished.

Ren continued to brush at his fur. It was hard to tell if she was secretly enamored with the animal or was just plying a bit of kindness to keep him calm. The bear dwarfed her and could easily bite her head clean off if given half the chance. He had already answered my intended second question in regard to the potential portal . . .

"Second question. How did you get to this forest? Did you not start on a smaller island?"

He raised a large paw to scratch at his chin. "No, I've been here for a few weeks. Sometimes people attack me, sometimes I attack them. Nothing else."

How interesting. I was starting to put some of the puzzle pieces together, even if the picture didn't make any sort of sense. These portals could appear over different worlds or . . . realities—that part wasn't clear. Anyone unlucky enough to enter was transported to this world. Even if they were an animal, it seemed.

"Do you know how to work with the boxes?" Ren asked softly. "See what they say?"

"I . . ." Wolf looked at her. "They were overwhelming, so I try to pretend they don't exist."

"Could you though? For me?"

I almost opened mine up by instinct. Partially I wondered if the bear was keeping track of all the questions the elf was also asking and would expect payment. Part of me hoped that he did, if only to show his Intelligence was up to snuff.

The grizzly furrowed his brow in focus. "What did you need to know?"

"Class. Highest Stats. Level." Despite her softer tone with the animal, she hadn't been able to shift her default expression—a testament, if anything, to the times that she did.

"Forest Guardian, rare. Constitution and Strength are highest, then Intelligence. I am level five."

She nodded at each of the nuggets of information. "And how are you doing emotionally?"

The bear looked down at the ground, no longer having to read from his System interface. "I miss the simplicity of my home. Everything here seems to drive me into conflict."

The elf tilted her head toward me and gestured with her hand.

I shrugged, not sure what she was getting at. Animals had feelings. I already knew this. It was part of why I began a discourse with the large and threatening bear. Did System-created have feelings? Perhaps best to unravel that morality question another time.

Another rare Class though; that was something. The System must have filled out his Stats as best as it could imagine, putting him here among other bears, maybe in confusion, before layering on the Player parts of whatever ran this world.

"I realize you just said you didn't like conflict . . ." I stepped toward him now and suddenly remembered how much pain my body was still in once it had to do more than exist. "But would you like to join up with us?"

"If you can handle a little fighting," Ren added. "There is a lot of food in it for you."

Wolf looked between my hat, me, Ren, and then back at the hat. "I'll help you kill food, and I get a portion of it?"

"Probably most of it." I rubbed my chin. "I imagine our diets are different enough where we can all have plenty?"

Ren nodded and stood next to me, turning to face the bear. "Max is annoying, but he is strong."

I held a poker face, which was difficult due to how bruised it felt. "Ren is also *very* strong and very *pleasant*." Her glare burned into the side of my head. *Pleasantly.*

Wolf looked back out to the forest. A totally different animal than the feral beast that was previously stalking us. He now looked thoughtful. I wondered if we had judged him too simply to consider that he would be swayed onto our path of destruction just with the prospect of eating the spoils.

"Alright, I will join you," he said as he nodded. "You still owe me the question meat though."

"Of course." I bowed before him, only a tiny part of my brain considering he might crush it. What was left still unbroken after my fall anyway. "There are some ground rules though. First, we share all loot equally. Second, do not eat us—ever. That's probably the most important rule, really." I withdrew some meat from my hat and placed it on his open paws. "Thirdly, do not flirt with Ren."

She glared at me and looked as though she was considering escalating to physically admonishing me, before she saw the amount of damage gravity had wreaked upon me. "And I was hoping the tree knocked some sense into you." She shook her head. "Really, Max. How did you even fall out? You could have *died*. And then I would too, of secondhand embarrassment."

"I suppose that I was having a bad dream doesn't make it any better." I handed more meat to the bear, feeling a little lightheaded.

"Bad dream as in a premonition of things that may come, or a shadow of the trauma and emotions you have been suppressing?"

"Hopefully the former," I replied, watching Wolf and not looking at her. "How far are we from the Bandits?"

[Wolf has joined the Party]

"About two hours." She sighed and rubbed at her eyes. "It looks like we slept for about three hours before you decided to leave the nest like a baby bird."

Wolf nodded, his tongue lapping around his lips as he finished off the meat. I intended to give him the ten pieces, which seemed reasonable considering he could easily eat us if he wanted to. "You do look tenderized under that offensive wrapper."

I handed him more with a tired frown. "It's a *suit*." Sure, it was garish. It was part of the act—I had to stand out and be larger than life. There was a plan in the back of my mind to swap to the gear that I had equipped for Stats. Just as soon as it wouldn't make me look like a drunken wizard at a Renaissance rave rooting through lost property for a costume.

"It makes my eyes sad," the bear added, his paws out to receive more of his reward.

"He even sleeps in it." Ren crossed her arms.

It turned out that I missed being surrounded by fans. While criticism was valid, being under constant scrutiny just made me want to . . . *double down*. I grinned and gave them both a short bow. "A true showman never quits."

The elf exhaled through her nose, clearly not having slept enough for more of my bullshit. "Do you need any more healing, showman? You look like you're about to throw up your own brain."

"Dibs," Wolf interjected.

"I'm fi—" I stopped myself. "I'll use a couple of bandages. You should save your power. I will need another charm, though."

Her brow furrowed further. "You used it already? When?"

I pointed back up to the tree about a third of the way up. "About there, when my skull actually split open."

CHAPTER THIRTY

Filling Seats

The System would keep you alive, if you let it. Not that it cared whether you died or not, but it liked it when you played by the rules. Healing magic or items could bring you back from the brink, as staying alive was the core desire of such Abilities. It couldn't mend your soul or mental health and was content enough to leave you bruised and achy—but broken bones and split organs could be mended in a flash. If you were quick enough.

I sat on the grass as the elf slowly circled me, inspecting my hatless head for any signs of damage. The System message was quite clear that I had a healed skull fracture, although there was little current evidence for the claim.

"There's definitely some bruising. A bit of blood dried in your hair. No other signs of trauma." She stopped in front of me and knelt down. "Focus straight ahead."

My eyes stared off toward the horizon while she loomed in closer to make sure my pupils were the right size or something. I wasn't entirely sure, but after two bandages I was feeling back to normal—aside from some soreness. My right eye twitched as she moved her face even closer. Could almost feel the warmth of her body heat.

"This is a medical examination, Max. I can get Wolf to do it if this makes you uncomfortable."

The bear moved his wet snout down to sniff at the other side of my head. It was a sensory overload, and I found myself unprepared for . . . pretty much everything that was happening. Bring on the near-death experiences instead.

"I smell nothing wrong with him. It's just the suit, I think." Wolf moved away to sneeze across the grass.

Ren sighed and stood back up, patting me on the head. "Alright, trickster. Don't exert yourself too hard. We don't need your head bleeding all the time too."

"Agreed," I said, allowing myself a few seconds to relax and adjust before I stood up. Top hat back on and I felt complete. My decrepit social life in the old world hadn't prepared me to be assaulted by the constant presence of . . . these two. "We should head out."

There were no disagreements, so with one last look at the Map, we began our journey. It was actually nice having a third in the Party, as now the pair of them could make small talk and I didn't feel like I had to speak as much. Not that I didn't enjoy having all eyes on me, but I was still trying to settle my jumbled thoughts. Not least of all because most of them had just tried to tangibly paint the surroundings. Whether that dream had meant anything or not . . . I put aside. I was content enough to keep to myself and observe nature. All the trees and grass, some more trees. It was . . . nice.

The temperature cooled as the sun headed across the sky. We'd arrive at the Bandit encampment a little before dusk, so light shouldn't be a problem. Assuming they were easy enough to murder, then we'd be out and safe before night fell. With Wolf on our side, we could up the pace and the danger. Roger was a good demon, if you could stretch the definition of *good*, but he couldn't be our main threat absorption. His cooldown was clear now, so he could come help us with the Bandits. Oddly enough, I was looking forward to seeing him again. Abrasive in his own way, but weren't we all? He at least didn't ask pointed questions about my emotional competency.

Idly, I brought up a magic card and moved it through the air. I could slow them down a little now, not that it seemed helpful on the surface. After it returned, I caught it and allowed it to vanish. My brow furrowed in thought, and then I opened up my Inventory.

"Hey, Ren?"

She turned and caught the apple I threw to her. "Yeah?"

"Throw that back, please."

She shrugged but did so. I held out my hand, and it vanished instead of landing into my grip. With a flourish, I brought it back out into my hand. The gears were still turning in my head.

"I can see where this is going, Max. *No.*" Ren shook her head.

Interestingly, Wolf had a Dazzle debuff on him. Ren did not, and I had not seen one over her in the fights against the Thieves. I put a bookmark on those thoughts for later.

"That's probably sensible." I grinned. "How about just throwing the apple *at* me?"

She rolled her eyes but caught it deftly as I returned it. She bared her teeth and wound back, pitching at me as hard as she was able.

The apple thudded off of my chest, and then vanished. "Ow," I complained, rubbing at the spot where my next bruise would form. "But thank you."

Another tick box filled with details on how the System worked. I could loot items from the air if they were nearby, but not if they were *attacks*. Probably a good thing we didn't immediately jump to testing it with an arrow as I had first imagined. The showmanship of plucking ranged projectiles out of the air clouding my sensible desire not to be a pincushion.

Wolf just looked perplexed, his amber eyes wide.

"Max uses magic and tricks," Ren tried to explain as they continued walking. "He can manipulate things in and out of his Inventory."

"So he doesn't have lots of meat in his hat?"

She shook her head, but that seemed to make the bear appear more impressed rather than disappointed.

I was too busy inside my own head to capitalize on that. My mental footwork was stepping on crunchy gravel, new ideas underfoot and underway. The more questions I could answer, the more I would be able to accomplish. Answers would just have to hurry up. I was impatient.

"I'm a visual learner," the bear said with a blank expression, clearly now interested as to where the food actually came from. "Can you show me an example?"

Ren didn't look too enthused about it but raised an arm to me. Enter stage left. Or right?

I shrugged. A smile crossed my face, and I gave a bow as the bear turned fully to face me. I brought down my top hat and pulled a set of meaty ribs out from within. Dazzle icon. I drew my arm back and went to throw it to Wolf—his eyes lighting up and maw opening. Just as the meat left my hand, I had it swapped, and instead of the tasty morsel a handful of red flowers flew out and landed limply on the grass. Second Dazzle icon and a rather sad bear's face.

"Do not fret, young . . . sir." I walked up to him. "As—what is *this* behind your ear?"

I cupped his furred ear and then withdrew my hand, now holding the ribs once more. Third Dazzle icon. "All yours." I smiled and placed it into his wanting maw.

"I think the best part of the trick was the faux charisma." Ren stood with arms crossed and no Dazzle icons.

I shrugged. "I've had my fair share of hecklers who looked like they would *still* be unimpressed if I tore my own heart out onstage." It was hard to gauge how much of this was just friendly banter with how she scowled at me all the time. Perhaps there was something cultural I was missing.

"Probably the only . . ." She stopped herself and shook her head. "We're almost there. Let's save our energy for the Quest."

"I liked the bit where the meat came back," Wolf murmured.

We continued onward again, and Ren filled the bear in on all the details. About not eating the little demons that I summoned. Lady in Red and a potential gang on the rise that might be after us. Everything important that had happened in New Forest. Some of what being a Player and leveling up in the world meant. I didn't really listen in too intently.

My mind was mostly elsewhere. A headache loomed that made me wish I had some normal human painkillers to take. The fact that I could Dazzle my allies was odd and stuck out like a sore thumb. The most straightforward answer I could come to would be that I may get an Ability that could buff or assist my Party in some way in the future. That'd be a tough sell, considering Ren hadn't been fooled by a single trick yet.

Perhaps that just meant I needed to try harder. Nothing too simple or easy to wave away as being Inventory tricks. Something for a clearer mind. Mine was fast becoming foggy, and I needed any wits about me for the Bandits.

Ren slowed down to walk beside me. "You seem off. Did I go too far?"

"No, just feeling a bit rough. Sometimes you need a harsh critic to sharpen your tools." I gave her a smile but could already see her glare cutting through the attempt to downplay my status.

"Don't be afraid to call me out. I'm only your harshest critic because I believe the show could be better. I'm . . . invested in your successful performances." She pulled a face at herself. "*Gross.* How can you use all that terminology without cringing?"

"Many years of gaslighting myself into believing that I was some kind of visionary."

"Careful, trickster." She shook her head as she sped back up to join Wolf. "Some cracks starting to show there."

Yeah, right down the middle of my head. Or at least, that's how it felt. It was only by a miracle of my <Sleight of Hand> bonus that I'd had the foresight to grab at the healing charm as I fell. A second or two later, and my brain would have decorated the ground beneath the tree. I could still remember the brief flash of pain, the instant my skull split before the radiant magic sealed it back up. As much as I hated knowing, my idle thoughts brought up my current Status.

[Health Report]
[Mild trauma]

Nothing specifically broken or wounded in a way the System cared for or could assist with. My physical body disagreed. Chest and arm, bruised and sensitive. Left wrist aching and stiff. Nose tender, and my head still felt like it wanted to continue the job and open up like a walnut. *Mild trauma.*

Once upon a time, I was doing a show that involved some ladder work. I had put the wrong shoes on and slipped halfway up, fracturing my ankle as I landed awkwardly. Still put on shows through the recovery—but I had to change up tricks. Less movement and a more static experience but still with the same flair. The restriction had made me a better magician—shuffled me down a path to thinking outside the box I had been comfortable in. That's what I told myself anyway.

Did my current pain now do that? No, I'd much rather find a real bed some-where and hibernate. Fighting had forced my current improvements though—I couldn't deny that. Figuring out how to win a fight or ply the tools that I had at my disposal was . . .

My mind drifted off as a small patch of flowers caught my eye. A beautiful sky blue. As much as it was a shame to pick them, I was sure the System could find more. A select handful made it into my Inventory to replace the roses I had thrown to impress Wolf.

Kleptomaniac she had called me. A little on the harsh side, even if she was pulling at threads to annoy me. As adventurers, we spent plenty of time looting and taking whatever things that we wanted. I just had a broader definition of what was valuable or useful. I brought up my Inventory again and started to arrange items. It looked as though the display only showed a six-by-five grid at once, which was reasonable for now. Small objects to be thrown in the top row. Heavy items to drop in the middle. Healing and other useful consumables in the bottom row.

For a moment, as we walked, I read over each item a few times to remember their placement. Then I messed around with changing tabs and different menus options, trying to see if I could speed up the process. The throb of pain down the middle of my head made it less of an optimal practice, and eventually I gave it a rest. Part of me wanted to split the assortment of cards up in a way that made it easier to grab an ace or a specific suit . . . but currently there was no benefit. I wasn't doing *actual* tricks.

Nevertheless, my brain still buzzed with how many slots such an arrangement of cards would take up and how best to organize them—for when I did. Apparently, traveling around a new world with a radiant elf trying to pry open my bottled emotions with a crowbar and a talking bear who . . . well, that required no more qualifiers—all of this had become too mundane. I had barely even registered that the pair had now stopped in front of me.

I stepped up between them and narrowed my eyes over the bushes just before us. If the Bandit camp in New Forest had been a town, then what lay ahead was a city. A miniature fortress made of cut logs blocked the view of how many Bandits lay within. At each corner, a watchtower sprung up, two figures sitting in each.

Two small groups patrolled close to the walls in a clockwise direction. Two groups much farther apart circled wider in a counterclockwise direction. Some amount of noise could be heard even from this distance. The murmur of talking, clang of metal, and occasional jeer or humored laugh.

"Wow," I murmured, "what an audience we have tonight."

CHAPTER THIRTY-ONE

Uninvited Guest

Repeat Quests were an interesting oddity. In the traditional sense, a Quest was to achieve an objective, and you were rewarded for completing the task. "Kill thirty Bandits" sometimes had a tangible victim or town guard where you could trace the line between action and motivation. Sometimes the System would just praise you for completing the Quest fully detached from any sort of reasoning. And then you could do it again, and again. If anything, it cemented the fact that the System held no compassion for the beings it created. It would look you in the eye and shake your hand the same whether you had killed the minimum thirty or had been on a rampage for a week straight and erased thousands. Here's your gold and dopamine, Player.

The ensnaring arrow lit up the path in front of us as it struck the closest patrol group. Four Bandits, with better leather armor and mismatched weaponry than the ones from the small island. The bulkier of them now sported the projectile from his side as they glanced our way, weapons drawn. Shock spread across their faces as if we had appeared out of nowhere, despite our obvious presence.

My split cards struck those surprised eyes of the one raising a crossbow, blinding him. With their ranged Damage neutered, the rampaging bear then closed in under less threat of injury. With heavy feet that thundered across the earth, Wolf roared as he leaped at the group.

One of them tried to block the swipe of a giant paw with a buckler, but Wolf's overpowering strength still knocked the Bandit to the ground, even if the man wasn't shredded in the process. The ensnare that had been wrapped around his lower legs broke as he slid away from the remaining trio. With panic, he tried to stumble back to his feet until an arrow struck him in the thigh, and then my empowered card cut across his exposed throat.

A Bandit still entangled lashed out with a sword, stabbing into Wolf's dark fur. In return, the bear hopped forward with a bite, catching the attacker on the collarbone and neck. The crack of bones followed as he crunched down onto their torso before tossing the Bandit away like a rag doll. My <Demonic Pact> card flew out to the first one that had been felled, a pain radiating up the center of my head as I controlled it to its destination.

Ren lowered her bow, unable to get a clear shot now that the large form of our third Party member was fully intent on thrashing through the remaining two. A small wave of vertigo made me step forward as I watched Wolf crush one before disemboweling the last. Despite his otherwise pleasant demeanor, once in combat, he was feral and unrelenting—something that put even Roger's enthusiasm to shame.

"Even more effective than I'd hoped," the elf said as she tilted her head. "This might change our plans?"

"How so?" I winced, more due to the cracking headache forming again than our schedule being adjusted. Although . . .

"This is repeatable. We farm this out as much as possible, sleep nearby. We can get our next level here before moving on."

I nodded. With Wolf, our combat effectiveness jumped a substantial amount, and we wouldn't struggle as much to get through the Quest. If we could do this three times quicker than without the bear, then it made sense to make use of the resources. We had somehow stumbled into a reasonably trustworthy tank for our little group, as if the System had thrown us a bone after hearing our grumblings.

"Oh, fuck me!" Roger jogged over to us, his eyes and ears having pierced through the head of the fallen Bandit. "You got a much bigger dog now, boss."

"Bear, called Wolf." I deflated slightly at how useless that explanation might be to the demon. "He is our new Party member."

Roger turned to watch as the bear tore the face off of one of the dead Bandits and chewed on it. My rabbit demon whistled, which came out strangely from his puppet. "I fuckin' love *everything* about him."

"He gets in the way of my arrows." Ren tapped the end of her bow against the side of her boot. "We'll have to find a solution to that." Her voice caused my demon to convulse, as if he hadn't acknowledged her presence until she spoke.

"If he can circle around targets so that he is at the side of them and can knock some back from the fray, that should help." I tilted my head and felt like my brain was about to find the emergency-exit door by accident. Almost put my hand to my ear to make sure it wasn't successful, but I didn't fancy getting my hand blood on my face.

We caught up to the bear, and I tried not to stare at the half-eaten corpses. While death and dismemberment hadn't chilled me as much as they should, there was still something uncomfortable about seeing someone's insides on display. They were meant to be private, and I was happy to keep the knowledge of how bodies actually worked a secret. At least the bear was eating well.

"Good job, Wolf." I gestured a hand to my demon. "This is Roger. He is a temporary friend."

"Is that how you feel, boss?" The demon stared at me impassively.

"No, not like that. I—" I exhaled and rubbed my forehead, getting myself bloody anyway. A grumpy elf was one thing, but the manic demon and talking bear made me wonder if hitting my head adjusted some dial that made my life weirder. Not a theory I was keen to do some testing on.

"Looks like dead meat still." Wolf sneezed out a brief spray of gore and then shook his head.

Ren knelt down beside him and put her hand against his wounded foreleg. "How hurt did you get? Do you have any Skills to absorb Damage or regenerate Health?"

"At first I was angry because the meat was spiky, but then I felt better."

She narrowed her eyes. "That doesn't really answer my questions, Wolf."

"So . . . no meat reward?"

I sighed and turned away. "You can eat your fill of the bodies once Ren is done looting them. I'll get ready for the next group." My head was pounding, and the oddball antics felt like someone was pulling a bloodied zipper down my forehead. While I was normally averse to looting even when in a good mood, the prospect now made me want to empty my stomach out. Possibly my eyes and anything else that could be contributing to the pain in my skull too.

Roger padded up to me as I strode away from the carnage. "You alright, boss?"

[Health Report]
[Mild trauma]

"Doc says clean bill, so I'm peachy." I gave him a grin, which probably came out as more of a grimace.

"I know some of those words," he said with a nod. "Just point me in the direction of what needs murderin'."

I flicked through my Inventory, but it wouldn't even allow me to apply a bandage. This world couldn't be so advanced and yet have no way of pain killing? My eyes closed for a moment so I could refocus. No need to worry. A little headache never killed anyone. We were doing a lot worse to the Bandits—if I just pushed through it we could get this over and done with and I'd probably feel better. I'd feel *fine*. Not something worth complaining about.

A Hellhound popped up beside me, and I gave it a brief pet on the head. The second of the wide arc patrol groups was now coming around to our position. Another four Bandits. Being able to fight from range again was nice, and having Wolf deal with all the problems made my life easier. No need to pull odd tricks from my sleeve just to survive.

Partly, I missed that. Maybe at present it was more of a blessing due to my brain being only partially functioning. I felt tired, and my core being ached, despite the nap having energized me. Falling from the tree clearly knocked something loose that would take a little longer to recover from. I shook it from my head and held up my hand. "Oh, Roger. Can I give you a weapon?"

"Sure, boss." He shrugged, fully content to run in and attempt to beat the Bandits to death with his fists.

I wasn't sure how his level or power scaled, and as capable as he had been, we were nearing the point where running in blindly would get him banished from my control near instantly. "It's not much, but if you like it, I'll keep it safe for you." And if he didn't, I'd find something different. He deserved some comfort while he was doing my bidding.

From within my Inventory, I withdrew a mace. Uncommon, with an enchantment that gave two Constitution. Dark metal, leather-wrapped handle, and the bulbous head had tiny silver spikes. It wasn't the best that I had found, but it felt like it fit his nature.

"Fuck! Boss, that's gorgeous!" He took it and gave the air a few test swings. He was still awkward and sloppy with his movements, but I couldn't blame him when it wasn't his body. There was enough force in his swings that he'd do damage no matter how amateur the strikes—as long as he hit.

"Keep up the good work and I'll see what else I can get you." I gave him a smile despite my brain burning up. For a violent psychopath, he was at least loyal and friendly enough. Every show needed someone to grind away at the unpleasant jobs, and his enthusiasm was almost catching. "But for now . . ."

I raised my hand up, drawing a card and filling it with Mana. It glowed brightly, and for a moment, I was enthralled by the light. Roger and the Hellhound tensed up, ready to sprint toward the approaching patrol. But . . . I almost didn't want to let it go. Was there a limit on how powerful I could make it? Certainly. Had I reached it yet?

My arm shook slightly, and my fingers twitched. Why couldn't I let go? My hand was illuminated in pale-purple light. A beauty that warmed me as my eyes rose back up to the Bandits. Or it could just be the tracks of blood forming on my tensed hand. Right before it became untenable, I gave in.

It was gone. The light scoring the air as it traveled and my demons sprang forth. I saw the brief surprise on the face of the crossbow Bandit as the glow of my magic attack reached them. Their brains exited the back of their skull with a wet pop through the thin slit I gouged straight through their head, and I let the card vanish.

I wiped the blood running from my nose with the back of my shaking forearm. Either I had achieved a new flavor, or I had just tasted the hint of greater power.

Ren fired off an arrow from just behind me, as the thundering paws of Wolf vibrated through my boots and he charged past.

For a moment, I just stood there and watched. My fingers tapped my side as if trying to remind me to draw another card. The bear barreled through the group, knocking them to the ground or out of the way, and then positioned himself to the left. Out of the way of our ranged attacks—and although this would normally leave an opening for enemies to come at me or Ren, my demons distracted and prevented any from leaving the range of the powerful beast.

"Roger probably wouldn't mind if you accidentally shot him." I worked my jaw, watching the three in the melee pound and tear the remaining Bandits into mush.

"Would you?" She stepped up beside me.

"If you shot me or Roger?" The marble inside my head rolled around the track slowly.

Ren gave me a look over, her brow furrowed. "You're supposed to be taking it easier now we have Wolf, not pushing yourself harder."

"I'm f—"

"You're *fine*. I get it. We have a lot of Bandits to get through. If you're spent on the second pack, then you may as well leave the Party now and save us the headache."

Before I had the chance to respond, she had stormed off. Not that I was even sure what I was going to say. It was just a headache, and whatever mild trauma was. *Mild* wouldn't stop me from doing anything. I just needed to pep myself up a little and not ruin the show. The Quest. *Whatever.*

We took the next two patrols down with little issue. Roger switched corpses with each, which slightly confused Wolf and made him less inclined to gorge on the bodies of the dead. I let Ren do the looting, and so far nothing exciting had dropped. I tempered my Ability and didn't go over the top again. Every time I pushed a little too far, my nose would bleed—which felt a lot worse than when my hand usually did. My headache didn't get any better, but trying to play it safe kept it from getting worse. I found some balance.

"Watchtowers might aggro too much of the camp." She held her hand over her eyes to stare at the closest one.

"Ignore them and stay out of range until we've cleared some of the camp?" We were in parallel to the gates now and could see clearly inside.

Maybe three dozen tents in total. Perhaps a dozen more that we couldn't see. No, that couldn't be right—unless they stacked the Bandits three to a tent. There were at least five groups of between three and five enemies just in the area we could see by the gate.

"I'd rather pull three groups than seven," she agreed.

I couldn't draw much comparison to what this was like. A game where the prize was violent combat. We were just playing for how potentially deadly it could be. "The stage is all yours." I gave her a bow and stepped back away from her narrowed eyes.

Roger was leaning against Wolf and trying to wipe the blood off his mace on the leather trousers of the body he was in. Or maybe trying to paint them. It was hard to tell, given that it wasn't very effective either way. The bear himself had eaten his fill of Bandit but had a sharpness to him still. Fighting for the fight. I was glad to see it.

Ren exhaled and drew an arrow, getting ready to aim it for the closest group through the gate. Bowstring held back. She paused and slowly released the tension. Her eyes went to me. "Can you hear that?"

I'd had a slight hum in my ears for the last hour, so I shook my head slowly. Wolf sniffed at the ground and tried to flatten his ear to the dried dirt.

"Vibration," he grunted. "Something approaches."

We looked back at the Bandit camp. It was gradual now, but I could . . . almost sense it in the air. Looming danger. The gathered figures inside the walls turned to see something farther within. Ren and I exchanged a glance and readied our weapons.

And then a figure burst out through the wall of Bandits—someone on horseback. Black hair flowed behind his head. On his wild face was a bloodied handprint. His armor was a dark-ebony-and-crimson mix, contrasting with the light-brown horse he rode on.

Behind him, the entire campground full of Bandits chased, waving their weapons and firing Crossbows that didn't hit. He was riding straight for us.

"Lady in Red sends her regards!" he yelled, a wide grin across his face.

Ren drew her arrow and fired—just as the man and his mount vanished in a blur of blue light. Teleportation?

Dozens of pairs of eyes now switched to us as the ire of the entire angered Bandit camp focused our way.

CHAPTER THIRTY-TWO

Crowd Work

Griefing was something I wasn't particularly familiar with when I came to this world. I could understand it when people were assholes, even in malicious ways—but the ways in which Players could exploit the nature of the System to ruin the days of others was surprising to me. I learned later that the method employed at the Bandit camp was called a mob train where a Player would draw all the aggro in an area and then dump it on someone unsuspecting. Why you'd want to do this rather than just kill your victim yourself I didn't quite understand. The direct route was often quickest.

F uck!" Ren hissed. "We should run. Should *try* to run."

We were about in crossbow range, maybe a handful of seconds before the melee was inevitable. I didn't particularly trust my cardio level to believe it could take me far enough away to keep me from danger before the Bandits got bored. Didn't even know how long they would chase us before giving up. They were an audience primed for my gradually slipping sanity. My legs had already made the decision for me.

"I'm fighting." I drew a card, split it, and sent it out into the throng.

"*Max.*" She worked her jaw. "You don't have to."

"Can't let the fans down," I murmured, a smile curling up at the side of my mouth. The biggest show yet needed an airtight performance. A true test of what I had learned so far.

My cards cut into the forearms of one Bandit, disarming him. I twisted them downward into the figure running behind, in the knees and bringing them to the ground. Let them vanish as a twinge of pain ran down my hand, and instead I drew the Imp card, throwing it off to my side.

The vines of Ren's <Entangling Shot> burst out among the first group almost at our position, causing some of those running too close behind to collide and trip to the ground. Wolf jumped in, slashing down with his weight and crushing them into the dirt.

"Roger, stay by Ren and keep her safe."

"Yes, boss."

Ren glared at us both. "I don't need your—"

I flipped her off, then withdrew my finger and brought up a card in it instead. Not especially something that was like me, but we only had time for killing and staying alive. What remained of my sensibilities had worn thin. I could rise above the mountain of dead Bandits and keep them all safe and look fucking *good* doing it.

Wolf would draw the most aggro, so supporting him in staying alive was the most important thing. Ren would be able to deal with that if she was allowed to act unhindered. The bear wouldn't be able to handle them all, of course, and some of the System-created would go for the softer targets. Roger had a clear directive, and I'd have to trust him on that if I was able to focus on my role in this. The Imp would pelt the approaching horde as often as it could. A little firework display as we went painfully into the night.

A burst of amber surrounded the bear, and at first I thought he had been struck by some manner of spell—but it pulsed through him and empowered him. He finally found a Skill to activate.

The first fireball illuminated the Bandit targeting me as it flew past into a more distant group. Purple card up. It went out and split into two, the cards circling each other as I curved them through the right arm of my target. He stumbled to clutch at the wound, and I brought both cards back, embedding into the back of his head.

In my peripheral, I could see two had run past Wolf to attack the elf. She put an arrow straight into the forehead of one, while Roger jumped on the other. The crack of bone as he struck out with his mace enough of a tell that they were fine.

Another opponent was already by me. Either things were moving faster now, or my brain couldn't process the second-to-second detail. No matter. Attack the weak points. I sidestepped the swing of their hammer, drew a card out into their hand, holding it there until it cut through their thumb and the weapon dropped. Kicked them in the knee and brought my dagger around, the weapon appearing in my hand as they stumbled.

Reached inside my jacket pocket and withdrew a crossbow, firing it off to the milling crowd. Spun it around and replaced it with the second crossbow, letting off the bolt immediately—then the weapon turned into shredded paper to drift away to the ground.

The Dazzle icons racked up across dozens of enemies. Some hadn't been paying attention—and they'd pay for that—but *this was it!* A receptive crowd where you could tangibly see how amazed by the performance they were. My overcooked brain felt great. Sure, by now it was just a skull-shaped bowl of custard, but this new revelation put sprinkles atop it.

A grin that almost drew me into laughter painted my face as my card bloomed ready. Powered it up, despite the reservations from the nerves in my hand. Wide arcs through the air as if I was trying to draw my name, I carved gashes through two handfuls of banditry, letting go of it only when my fingers started to cramp.

The radiant light of Ren's <Smite Shot> pierced through the neck of a Bandit. Roger rose from a new corpse, caked in gore. Wolf was a dervish of slaughter, amassing small wounds of his own until a heal came in from the elf. This drew some aggro from the less mortally wounded Bandits—until a fireball struck a trio of them, their burning bodies dropping to the ground.

"Hand the Quest in. We're on a roll!" I jumped up and landed on two chairs that I dropped from my Inventory one after the other in quick succession, a foot on each like a miniature stage.

I spun around twin cards like a halo behind my head. If only I had some explosives to send off confetti or—

<Card Fan> came up a split second too late, a bolt sinking into my chest while a second was deflected. I didn't need the System to tell me my lung had been punctured. The first awkward breath from reflex burned, and that was enough. I dropped to the dirt as the chairs vanished and bowed to dodge two further projectiles headed my way.

A fireball slammed into my assailants as another came for me in melee range. I stepped backward, withdrawing a blanket from my sleeve to use to obscure my actions. With a swirl, I left a chair in my wake to stagger the Bandit, giving myself a brief moment to swig a Health Potion. *Disgusting* but necessary. The bolt fell from my chest as my respiratory organ healed up. Didn't do much for my splitting headache still, *asshole System*.

The Dazzle icons were still stacked up, although much of my potential audience was being chewed up by the bear. As the Bandit caught up and swung for me, I caught the weapon with the blanket and wrapped it around, pinning his arm from making any further attacks. Left me with no hands to use magic, however.

An arrow struck him in the side of the head, and he slumped over as I whisked back the fabric and his sword into my Inventory.

"Quit showboating," Ren growled. She had a few small wounds of her own, but most of the blood didn't look to be hers.

I shrugged. This was just how I worked, although . . . I think there was a wedge of mania trying to pry my head apart. A recklessness that I should know better to avoid. If the chest shot had struck me in the heart or head, it might have been a different story. The Imp gave me a wave to signal his departure, and I nodded my thanks. Time for a new assistant to take the stage.

Numbers were thinning, but I seemed to have drawn the attention of two more Bandits. The man dressed in bright purple, wavering like he was drunk and seemingly mostly attacking with household items probably seemed like a safer bet to engage than the giant form of the thrashing bear.

Into my hand, a poker chip. With a flick, I flung it high into the air over the approaching opponents. It didn't distract them, which was fine. I was beyond simple tricks. Stepping back, I threw a card out, too high to hit them. It struck the poker chip instead, and a magic rune circle appeared in the air above the first Bandit—a Hellhound immediately bursting out and landing atop them.

The Dazzle counter went up by one on the next Bandit, unsure if they should stop to help their System-created ally or just run straight toward me. They chose the latter. I held my hand out, my card immediately splitting and zipping off in a staggered manner. As soon as the first bit into the opponent, I brought it back and sent the other. Only doing light Damage, but as they stumbled closer, the intervals became shorter until they had to stop to take cover, their face cut to ribbons.

Both cards vanished, and I flicked the running blood from my hand, strode up to them, and jammed the stolen sword into their back between their ribs. The hound finished off the other, tearing their throat out—and I sent him over to assist Roger. The demon had a limp left arm and a couple of bolts in his current body but was still swinging away with the mace, like he was just having a fun day at the park.

Ren looked actually annoyed. I'd be sure to apologize for my part in this as soon as we—

I hit the ground. It wasn't intentional but an aftereffect of whatever had just hit *me*. Adrenaline didn't care where or how bad; there was pain somewhere, but I was more disoriented than anything. I turned to my back to see a figure above me about to bring down a two-handed axe. To split me in half, like a . . . Oh, no time for that.

The appearance of a wooden chair took the brunt of the swing, the blade wedged almost completely through. He growled in pain as an arrow struck him in the side, and as he tried to dislodge his weapon, I spun up an empowered card like a miniature circular saw. His axe came free, and he stumbled back from the ruined furniture. Then I flicked my card toward him. Ran it up his leg and into his groin. Held it until my hand twitched it away and a second arrow struck him in the side of the skull.

I pushed the remains of the chair away from me, the broken wood no longer having a home in my Inventory. As I rose to my feet, vertigo told me to stay down. But I wouldn't. Sounds came across echoed and distant, probably an aftereffect of something. It was hard to put my thoughts together. The sun was setting, and the last of the Bandits were being mopped up. I knew that much. Couldn't decide if I was cold or warm.

Most of my energy went into focusing on breathing, and I was sure I had it down to perfection. The oxygen went in, circled around my blood. I breathed out the rest in the hope of more. My body loved it. It kept me going.

"Boss? *Boss*, you okay?"

I turned my head slowly in case it fell off. It was hard to say that my pact demon looked concerned, as his face, hiding behind the corpse of another, looked more terrifying than any other emotion he might be putting on. Still, he *was* asking.

"I'm fine." I smiled, with way too much blood coming out of my mouth alongside those few words to make it seem genuine.

A hand placed on my back, and I felt a warmth radiating throughout me. Expecting some sharp words to be plunged between my shoulder blades, I was shocked and maybe disappointed to hear the soft voice behind me instead.

"Let's not do that again."

She moved away, and I shivered from her absence, as if she had taken my body heat along with her. Wolf came over. He was panting heavily, the whole front half of his body completely soaked through with blood and gore. He said nothing at first, a thousand-yard stare in his amber eyes, before finally he looked up at me.

"That was *actually* traumatic."

Roger scratched his back with his mace. "You get used to it." He then held out the weapon for me to take into my Inventory. "I'd like to use that again next time, boss."

I nodded as he faded away, leaving the empty body to slump to the ground.

"It's not usually that . . . intense." My apology to the bear tugged at my insides, and I felt like we may have dragged him into something more than he bargained for.

He slowly nodded at me. "I don't like to rush my meals. I will have a stomach upset tomorrow."

"Hmm." I blinked my eyes slowly, trying to not take in the carnage or acknowledge any of my injuries. "That went from bad to worse pretty quickly. Nice of the Lady to have someone nearby to help us power level though."

With a deep sigh, I leaned against the bear and held my head for a minute. Just to make sure it was still there and would remain so. The sounds of Ren looting through everything became a dull tone, low and numb to my ears, as if they were underwater. She said something I didn't understand and then was gone. I groaned and tugged at my lobes, the popping feeling bringing normal hearing back into my brain. "Did I just get rightfully admonished for not helping to gather loot? Or for being a giant asshole?"

Wolf pawed at his nose before shaking his head, spattering the area in droplets of crimson. "Ren said something about knowing the horsemeat man."

"Oh?" I turned around, my eyebrow raised, to see where she had wandered off to.

CHAPTER THIRTY-THREE

Truth Behind the Illusion

When cracks form in something, it is often impossible to fully repair it. Even with the right filler or adhesive, once the weakness is introduced, it can never get better. Keep ignoring the problem for too long and the cracks grow, threatening the stability of whatever metaphorical object you are imagining. Yes, this is an indirect shot at my emotional openness. Or lack of. The greatest trick had been convincing myself there wasn't even a crack in the first place.

I sat on the wooden chair, staring at the fire. Whatever ills had ailed me were now healed, aside from the apparent trauma. The elf had gone to find us a place to make camp just out of range and view of the Bandit camp and was in the sort of mood where I didn't want to prod her with any questions. She was now at the right side of the fire from me, sitting up against the sleeping bear. Staring at the fire just as I was.

My tongue felt around the inside of my teeth, a last idle act before I gave in and was the first to speak. I felt like it was my line, given I had taken the lead in committing to the combat. "I'm sorry for making us fight."

She tilted her head to the side and looked at me with tired eyes. "You called me your friend earlier."

I nodded briefly, some slight confusion on my face. An odd change in conversation that didn't make me feel like I had been forgiven for enduring the Bandit swarm. She patted the ground beside her, and as much as my body protested the movement I stood to go sit next to her. I sank briefly into the bear and was surprised at how comfortable he was.

"I think that we are," I ventured. "We're a little above being business partners . . ."

We stared into the fire. The crackling light was comforting, despite the potential dangers around us. The amber light melted away at the stress that had been building up within me. Something natural and archaic about it that spoke to the back of my brain.

"Friends share information about themselves," she stated, turning her face to me. "I'll begin. The reason I don't like dresses is because my mother would make me wear them on all the boring formal occasions. You were right though; blue *is* my color."

"Brings out your eyes."

"That's what my mother would say too." She sighed and looked up at the night sky. "Do you know how long I was on the island?"

I shook my head. "No, you were pretty vague."

"Three months. The first month, I was a wreck. I hid away and cried for everything that I'd lost or left behind. Flynn, my parents, my sister, and the responsibilities I was bound to inherit."

That was a long time to be stuck there, compared to how long it took me to get up to level five. At some point, I was envious of all that she had in her old existence compared to my . . . work-only lifestyle, but she probably envied me for having less heartache and loss over my past life.

"I didn't really spend too much time around other Players . . . until Hadrian. That was the guy on the horse."

"Oh." I wasn't sure what else to add at this juncture.

"He started off as the gallant-knight type. Rugged, strong, determined, and capable. After he tried to make a move on me, I told him I wasn't looking for that. I gave him the whole story of Flynn and Lady in Red. Gave me his word he'd help me find justice."

I nodded along. "But he didn't."

"No. The next night, he tried making a move again. I think out of everything, knowing that I had just lost the love of my life . . . still trying it hurt me the most. I kicked him in his stupid balls and stormed away. Never saw him again." She exhaled and deflated.

"And now he is working for the Lady too."

"*Fucker.* Can't wait to tear his miserable head off and stick it up his betraying ass." She looked over at me again. "This is one part of the reason I was so tough on you, and I'm sorry."

"It's understandable." I gave her a glum smile. "I'm sorry that you were treated that way."

Her face softened slightly, and I almost thought the scowl would disappear. The barest of frowns remained, which I took to be as close to a smile as I'd get.

"I think the point I'm leading to Max is . . . you can be annoying, and I'll tolerate it. You can flirt, and I'll tell you to fuck off. If you get us into shit, I'll forgive you. I don't actually expect you to be perfect or get everything right. That's just me projecting based on my own faults." She raised an eyebrow. "You don't need to impress me, okay?"

I looked into her tired eyes as she tried to read my face for my reaction. There were words inside me somewhere, but in all honesty, I was stunned. I wavered as if I might burst before allowing my rolling inside to calm. "That frankness means a lot to me, Ren."

From inside my jacket, I withdrew the small bouquet of blue flowers.

"Dickbag." She snorted, taking them from me. "But thank you. Were you keeping these for me or for one of your tricks?"

"Fifty-fifty." I shrugged. There was an odd feeling within me, of being grounded, exposed, and yet so far away, as if I were watching myself from a distance.

Ren rolled her eyes. "Well, just to prove my point, I'm not going to pressure you to give me information about yourself in return." She ran a finger around one of the closed flowers, almost as if she was trying to remember something.

I leaned back into the thick fur of the warm bear and looked up at the dark sky. There were stars. Two moons, one of which hid behind the other. *Mostly* there was the heavy weight of something in my gut that was worming its way up.

"Imagine this," I began as I closed my eyes, my heart louder than it needed to be. "A young Max, about to go on to do the most important show of his career. Some of the top critics, talent scouts, booking agents, and a full house in the largest venue I had been to yet. I had practiced for months to get it all perfect."

I turned my head to her to see that she was listening intently, and she nodded politely for me to continue. My eyes went to the dancing flames of the campfire.

"Almost a year's work in total, here and there, to get it flawless. The best tricks I had, a dazzling show—my chance to get my foot in the door. I was in my changing room the day of, getting prepared. An hour . . . maybe two before the curtains went up. Then my phone rang."

My jaw worked, and I paused for a moment, the vivid memories I had tried to store away making themselves known.

"It was my dad. I thought he was going to wish me good luck, but . . . but he was crying." I exhaled through my nose, closed my eyes, and looked down to try to keep myself in check. The sounds flooded back in, each uncharacteristic sob that he had taken twisting the knife in my heart once again, even after all these years.

A hand rested softly on my shoulder. I couldn't open my eyes to see her face. Not when I hadn't even said the line that threatened to break the dam yet. I took a deep breath.

"It was my mother . . . An accident."

"I'm so sorry, Max."

Compassion just made it worse somehow. As if it was a reminder that it was something actually valid that I should be more emotional over. Made it real when other people accepted it . . . Maybe because I hadn't.

Long-overdue tears rolled down my cheeks, my energy too spent to feign the smiling-showman facade any longer. "I wanted to go see her one last time . . . but my dad said to do the show. My manager said to do the show. *The show must go on.*"

"And you did the show?"

I nodded, flinging the quiet drops of age-old sadness onto my lap. "Gave it my all. Did it for her, I told myself. Heart and soul . . . And I *aced* it. Then . . . I just didn't stop. Somehow, I thought I could work past it if I kept on running, kept on being a better magician."

Ren gave my shoulder a squeeze and withdrew her hand. "My dad had a saying: 'You can't fill a hole by building a tower over it.' Eventually, the hole will get bigger, and the tower will come crumbling down."

"I'm feeling pretty crumbly now." I deflated, somehow even more exhausted despite resting.

"At least you've now addressed the problem. Only you can fill that hole in though." She handed me a single flower back. "Thank you for sharing, Max. I know it wasn't easy."

"I never imagined *you'd* be my therapist." I grinned, looking over the blue petals.

"If you want to do *adventuring* long term, we'll need to be that for each other. It's not only about killing things and . . . doing better tricks. It's difficult and draining."

My body ached, and I felt like I had been fully tenderized inside and out. "I'm . . . Thank you, Ren. I feel like I don't deserve the effort or perseverance."

She shook her head. "Don't be an ass, Max. It's not wholly selfless. I need someone I can trust to keep me sane too. Help stop me from building towers."

"I'll try." I smiled. We fell into a tired silence, our emotions as spent as our physical bodies, and the fire became our focus again. She unclasped her boots and took them off, wiggling her toes toward the heat.

I did the same and made the mental note to find some boots that matched my outfit that I could replace my dress shoes with. The equipment I had on currently was a pair of sandals that gave Intelligence—and I was smart enough not to show them to anyone.

"You think we're safe here with the fire?" I asked, shuffling into the soft wall of bear behind me.

"No. I don't think we'll be safe anywhere." She closed her eyes and crossed her arms. "We can't live in fear though. If we die, we die."

"Would be pretty miserable having this emotional revelation and then getting gutted in the night, huh?"

There was no response from her. I stared out among the darkened trees surrounding us, the lower branches illuminated by the glow of our lowering fire. The Lady already had a new gang, it seemed, and was poking at us to see how soft we were. Hadrian had found us somehow. It wouldn't have been too difficult for him to return a few hours later and come find our fire, if he cared to. If that was their intent.

But *did* they want to? It depended on her actual goals—we might just be a bonus side quest because Hadrian was in the area at the time. Maybe Ren was right. There was no solution to sleep easily until they were dead. They had the advantage in this situation, and I hated that. I *needed* the control.

I looked over at the elf, who had fallen asleep. Something ached in my chest to see her face relaxed without the tension of a scowl or frown. We were both posturing outwardly nonstop but remained fragile on the inside. Cold to the process of murdering for power in the hope that we could carve out a new life that fit us right in this world. Would the System even allow it? If this world was in constant conflict, willing to hold a knife to our throats just for existing, then we'd need to be strong to rise above it. Be above those threats.

My fingers held on to the single flower she had returned to me, and I placed it back in my Inventory. Dragged it to one of the grid squares where I wouldn't accidentally draw it into the world in the middle of combat. I wasn't even sure what significance it held to me yet. It just felt . . . symbolic of something.

Perhaps I was just too tired. We had completed the Bandit Quest twice over, and a third repeat in the morning would get us to the next level. The spark of excitement lit up inside me even as our campfire waned. What new tricks would the System allow me? How powerful would I be this time tomorrow? I tried to remind myself to temper my expectations and not push myself to the limit so often.

A quick glance over at the elf just cemented the fact that, if anything, I needed to take this more seriously. Not to be as reckless with my health and sanity . . . but the limits did need to be tested. We all needed safety—even Wolf too. Naturally, only through crashing through the greatest of dangers would we find the path to what we required. So I needed to be strong. Unmatched.

Learning only half a lesson, I closed my eyes and let the darkness take me.

CHAPTER THIRTY-FOUR

Back on the Road

Once you let go of things, you could feel weightless. There was the temptation to push the rest of whatever was holding you back off a cliff and dust off your hands. Pure freedom. You'd soon find that you needed the baggage to keep you grounded, otherwise your ego could inflate like a balloon and carry you off into the great beyond. Striking the balance that allowed you to walk tall while still having your feet firmly placed on the ground was a lesson learned slowly, through mistakes.

Max?"

A sharp pain in my leg woke me. My eyes fluttered open to early-morning sunshine and a brief panic that maybe the bear had seen me as a light snack. No, I had been lying against him, and yet now I was flat on the ground. My suit was damp, not with blood, but with dew. It was morning, and I was alive.

The shadowed figure of the Oathwarden loomed over me. "Morning, trickster. I'm cooking up sausages."

"Mrff." My tongue lagged behind my brain as my mouth was dry. "Uh—sounds perfect."

I sat up and rubbed my eyes. There was a dull ache across my head, but it paled in comparison to the pain of the previous day. A light mist permeated the surrounding area, and I made a face at Wolf being missing.

Ren caught my gaze. "We thought you'd wake up when he moved, but you've been dead to the world. Wolf is out in the woods."

My mouth opened to ask what he was doing, but I could probably guess based on context clues. Instead, I stood up and put my feet back in my shoes. Bones clicked along my back as I stretched out, which paired well with a groan. "How did you sleep?"

"Best sleep in a while, if I'm honest." She tilted her head as she shuffled the sausages on the grill. There was a frown there, but it looked as though it was more from constant habit than anything bugging her.

"Lots of combat." I nodded. "And Wolf makes a great pillow."

She narrowed her eyes and pointed the cooking utensil at me. "And . . . ?"

"And your hair looks radiant this morning." I snatched one of the sausages from the grill and vanished it into my Inventory, withdrawing a plate from behind me and having the cooked meat slide out from my sleeve onto it.

"You . . . ass, Max. I suppose that is on me for expecting an overnight change." She rolled her eyes and got her own plate ready.

"Hey, I complimented your hair—that's different." I smiled, waiting for her to be annoyed at herself for allowing me to be imperfect.

"It'd be nice if I give it a proper wash again." She sighed and scowled at the grill. "Funny thing is, I always used to be so jealous of my sister. She had such beautiful silver hair that would almost glow in the moonlight."

"Where yours almost glows in the sunlight?"

She nodded and took a bite of the sausage. "And *she* was jealous of that."

"There's a story like that in my world." I looked around us, the slight mist obscuring my vision from peering too far into the woodland. "About the moon and the sun." Wolf must have been gone for a little while. I wondered if he was okay. Surely the smell of cooking meat would draw him back.

". . . And you're not going to regale me with the tale, just leave me in suspense?" She withdrew a wooden chair to sit on from her Inventory.

I clicked my tongue and sat down on my own chair. "It may surprise you that I'm not much of a storyteller. The sun was a blazing extrovert and the moon a shy introvert. They swapped places somehow because people could stare at the moon but not the sun."

Ren slowly nodded. "You were right. You *are* a shitty storyteller."

"I know my weaknesses," I said and winced as she narrowed her eyes at the statement. "Strong-willed elves being one of them."

"Fuck off." She shook her head. "You'd follow a goat off a cliff if you thought you could enrapture it with one of your tricks."

"A goat wouldn't call me such foul names all the time." I waved my fork in the air in admonishment. "And you're supposed to be a princess."

"A princess shouldn't have to pull your ass from the fire when you try to fist fight gangs with no combat experience." She tapped her plate. "Or when you fall out of a tree."

"That tree was very powerful," I murmured to myself as I looked out into the mist to see the large form of Wolf return.

"I'm done shitting," he announced as he lumbered up to the inert campfire.

It was good timing, as I wasn't too sure where the back-and-forth with the elf was leading to. This was all new ground, and I didn't know where was safe to tread. We had ascended a step in our friendship that seemed to be filled with giving each other shit. I took her talk last night in earnest. The number of people I had opened up to about my mother were . . . Well, I wouldn't need my whole hand to count them. Which was convenient, with how violent our adventures were getting—I was liable to lose it at any hour. Maybe due to my own hubris.

"Morning, Wolf. Hungry for more Bandits?" I asked.

"I actually found the whole ordeal emotionally draining, and I am apprehensive about getting into such a big battle again." He sat and scratched at his stomach. "But also, *yes.*"

I caught the eye of the elf and nodded toward the bear. "It certainly didn't help my mild trauma, so I mirror your feelings of apprehension." Not so much on the wanting to eat the Bandits, however, but I wouldn't discount it if my sanity took another dive or two.

"Shit," Ren interjected. "The fight gave you the mild trauma Status? Has it gone now?" Concern furrowed her brow.

"Yeah, it's gone. And no, I had it before."

"Before? What is wrong with you?" She covered her eyes and sighed. "That means you *need* to rest. Like a proper day off. I'm going to beat your brains in with a rock one of these days."

"That would probably also give me mild trauma." I nodded with a smile as she growled at me. It probably helped loosen my tight lips over the past day. It certainly loosened something up in my head, but the Health Report was actually all clear this morning, so I had survived whatever it had been.

Wolf sniffed the air. "If you kill him, can I eat him?"

She shook her head, and he got the hint. Ren stood and packed away all the items. I'd like to think that there might be some manner of resurrection magic in this world and that I'd prefer to keep my corpse intact just in case Ren had it in her heart and the capability to bring me back.

I hopped up on the chair and stood tall. With a short spin, the chair vanished, and I dropped to the ground, turning on the spot as my hands were also free of plate and cutlery. Instead, I held a chunk of Boar meat, which I flung toward Wolf. He grabbed it from the air, and I grinned at the Dazzle icon over him.

My eyebrow raised toward Ren, but it looked as though she was waiting for me to look at her, to roll her eyes.

"You are relentless." She shook her head again.

"I'll get you with one of my tricks eventually." I crossed my arms. Maybe it was more than her cynicism that made her such a killjoy. Her elfin eyesight might be too good—paired with her knowledge of how the System and Inventory worked . . . I'd have to go for something really out of the box.

"Flattered as always, trickster. Perhaps use your skills for more than trying to impress me." She crossed her arms too, and we stared at each other with narrowed eyes.

I knew a challenge when I saw one. She didn't think that I *could* do it. It had to be inevitable. There must be a point where I could catch her off guard or her disbelief would have to be suspended, even for a moment.

Wolf looked between us. "Is this some kind of mating ritual?"

"No!" we both said in unison.

Rubbing her eyes with the back of her forearm, the elf gave me a renewed glare. "You didn't care to loot much. You want your share now?"

"Keep the gold for now, but did you find any gear I could use?" We hadn't had a great need for money so far in the world, aside from the pittance for the room at the tavern. I was sure she wouldn't withhold funds if there was anything important we needed when it came to it.

"You don't have anything on bracers, right? I have some with one Intelligence. Also . . . about three belts you could use?"

"Pretty sure I can only wear one at a time." I grinned as she rolled her eyes again. "What Stats?"

"I'll just give you them all, and you can sort it." She took each out one at a time into her hand, and I was intrigued at how long it took her compared to if I had done the same action.

[Lucky Belt: +2 Luck]
[Cat's Belt: +1 AGI, +1 DEX]
[Choice Belt: +1 INT, +1 Luck]
[Smooth Bracers: +1 INT]

I wrinkled up my face in having to choose. My current belt gave +5% Mana, which was potentially useful, although without the numbers behind it, I couldn't say for sure. Still, Intelligence increased the damage of my cards, and I could certainly use more Luck so that I would stop cracking my head open on things . . . So I went with the Choice Belt. Most of the rest of the loot must have been mundane or not the right Stats for me. I trusted her judgment.

The two belts I didn't care to equip, I held up in one hand. In the other, I took my hat down and inserted them. Turned my hat upside down and gave the top a tap—and a thick rope slid out of it onto the grass.

"Looks familiar," Wolf said, although a Dazzle icon did appear above him.

Ren sighed. "Let's just go kill some Bandits and level up?"

I nodded and gestured for her to lead the way. Hat back on and rope already scooped away. We should be able to get away with killing the patrols and maybe a couple of other small groups. Then level six, and we'd make our way to completing the Boss Monster Hunt Quest. Probably get into trouble along the way. It was quite the distance, and I doubted the way ahead would be devoid of anything other than our objectives.

"I still feel bad about putting us in danger. I may have been a bit too wrapped up in . . ."

"Showing off while your brain leaked out of your ears? Two brain injuries in one day isn't healthy, trickster."

I rubbed the side of my head, which felt perfectly intact and normal. "Two?"

"The guy with the big axe. You must have been pretty out of it." She tilted her head. "My heal must have allowed you to recover before some sense was knocked into you."

"Shame." I furrowed my brow. The injury must have been worse than I remembered. There was the shock and numb feeling, but adrenaline pasted over the gaps of what had been done to me. Nothing I hadn't survived though.

I turned to our bear companion as we rounded the hill and the Bandit camp came into view. "How was your first day as an adventurer, Wolf?"

"I ate more than I should have and made two friends that will drag me into more senseless murder for the pursuit of something beyond my understanding."

"So . . . good then?" I grimaced and raised my eyebrows.

"Our paths align, and I am content."

That was good enough for me. He had already proven his worth and had done most of the heavy lifting in the fight last night. There was still some manner of weirdness at having a talking bear following us around that my brain was trying not to have to process. I may have died during my escape from the tree, and this was the waning memories of a mind struggling to accept defeat. That, and the more cordial openness with Ren, painted this day in an odd light.

"This Hadrian then. Kill on sight?" I changed tact to something a lot saner. Murder.

"Yeah. *Especially* now." Ren fired her entangling arrow off at the closest patrol group as they rounded their route.

My card was already out and close behind her attack so that I could take out the one with the crossbow. "Good." Wolf thundered past us toward the enemy at an angle to not block our view. "Because he tried to kill us and is allied with our target. Not because he was a jerk toward you."

"Of course."

After having survived through half the Bandit camp the previous evening, taking out the smaller packs was a breeze in comparison. No need for theatrics or pushing myself too far with <Mana Manipulation>. It was almost relaxing, if you could ignore the whole violence of it. I let Roger have a rest and only used the occasional Imp to soften up the packs before Wolf tore them to shreds.

I tilted my head to the elf as she let off another shot. "You don't run out of arrows, correct?"

She nodded but didn't take her gaze away from the battle. "Replenishing Quiver. The arrows vanish after a while though. So no long-term shenanigans."

Some short-term ones might be possible though . . . although I didn't care much for having to wear a long quiver on my back just for the occasional trick. Maybe there was a crossbow equivalent that could fit on my belt; the smaller bolts might—

"That's it, trickster. Quest complete. Revel in your level up."

That went much quicker than I had anticipated. Perhaps not having my skull splitting in half slowly made things seem more mundane. I moved away from my pondering and looked up to see the bear returning over to us, his fur matted with blood. Ren stared off into the horizon as she worked with her System messages.

[Progress: 30/30 Bandits killed]

As soon as I had accepted it, my STAR illuminated gold. With the weight of anticipating what new Skills the System could labor me with, I brought up the information to become level six, slowly nodding to myself as I read the descriptions.

CHAPTER THIRTY-FIVE

With Wings

I often wondered who made the System. Although there were plenty of things I could perhaps believe came into existence naturally—if you stretched the meaning of the word—there were also a lot of things that had too much purpose of thought behind them to come about just by luck. How did the System decide what Class you were and which Skills pertained to certain levels? There was a design to it that seemed both flawed yet beyond the scope of mortal thought at the same time. More than once, I believed us to be in some manner of game conjured up by a bored and sadistic entity. But then, anything was possible when you believed in magic.

[Level up—<6>]
[Stats increased]
[New Ability: <Finale>]
[New Passive: <Star of the Show>]
[New Passive: <Summon Demon: Ember Bird>]

Even without checking any of the descriptions, I knew what the new summon would be. I turned to my Party and removed my top hat. Placing the card inside, I took hold of the creature that spawned within and brought it out in my hand. A superfluous flourish, or actually *no*—it couldn't have happened any other way. Not for the debut.

A dove—although a patchy gray-purple color with bright orbs of amber for eyes. I released it, and it fluttered about before settling on my shoulder.

Wolf had a Dazzle icon, but Ren just had her arms crossed. Early days. The bird might not be the most combat oriented of my summons, but it would find some use and was practically free as a Passive Skill. Not that there was any opportunity cost when I had zero choice in what I received.

<Star of the Show> was something I had expected to show up eventually. The first skill to mention Dazzling my own allies. For every stack I had on a Party member, it would increase the chances of getting one on enemies. After all, if my closest friends could suspend their disbelief, then why shouldn't the unwashed masses? I narrowed my eyes at Ren as she did something with her own menus.

<Finale> paired with my keystone and the subsequent Dazzle focus the System was shoveling toward me. It had a long cooldown but, when used, would take the total number of Dazzle icons in the area and do a wide attack that may have extra effects at certain thresholds. What extra effects were it wasn't so clear—but reading between the lines, it sounded like the skill leveled a stun on my afflicted opponents.

Anything that took away the capacity to act was powerful, given how easy it was to inflict mortal damage at this current level. Especially on other Players. Although, if I had received this a day sooner, we could have had a much easier time with the whole Bandit camp last night.

"Dare I ask?" The elf already looked tired with my potential answer.

"The System is keen on me to keep on performing tricks, I'm afraid. An area stun depending on how wowed the audience is."

She nodded, and I seemed to get away with using show terminology without admonishment. It just came naturally, an inside joke that never left the thick walls of my skull. "How about you?"

"Defensive shield that I can cast on one of you two, and my heals now also do a portion extra healing as regeneration over time."

"Nice." I smiled, glad that at least one of us was getting something more stable and normal. My eyebrows raised at the bear, who had been staring at my demon dove. "What about you, Wolf?"

"I got . . . hungry." His eyes switched to look at me and then at the elf. "I'm not sure."

He seemed to have issue in using the System, which made a great deal of sense considering he was presumably a normal bear in his previous world. If only there was a way that I could see his STAR menus to help assist him. "You used a Skill last evening though. Did that just come about innately?"

The bear tilted his head from side to side in thought. "I suppose. It's like discovering a new food growing somewhere and already knowing if it is edible."

"So you just have to dig around mentally to find the tasty treats and get a lick of them?" I rubbed at my chin as the talking animal nodded.

Ren held out her arm, and I willed the dove to fly over and sit on it as I mulled my thoughts over. She brought the demon closer to her face to give it a proper look over. Wolf not knowing his Skills but being able to activate them in certain circumstances that just felt right wasn't ideal . . . but it was better than not having any Skills at all. If anything, it was a bit of a balance—he was naturally powerful already. Went hand in hand with how the System didn't really know how to process making a grizzly bear a Player. Not that I had any brighter ideas.

I settled for giving him a pat on his large shoulder. "We should get moving then?"

The elf looked up at me from the bird and nodded, extending her arm again to usher it back to me. I dismissed the demon, mentally giving it my thanks, just as it reached my hand to give the illusion it had just vanished into mist. Which it had, of course. It was enough to give Wolf a Dazzle icon—my number one fan, it seemed.

"You might find some use for these, trickster." As we began to circle around the outside of the encampment, she reached out to hand me a pair of glass bottles. "Oil."

"Thank you." I stowed them away with a smile, my eyes already running through a list of possible scenarios that I could use them. There must be other bottled substances or magical potions that I could use in my act—maybe even explosives if I dared—

I wavered as I almost walked straight into the stopped elf. "Oh, sorry."

"Don't be." She sighed. "Just give your brain a break for a change. Help me keep an eye out on the journey?"

As much as I considered both of them to be much better suited to keeping watch in the woods, I nodded. We needed to look out for Lady in Red's goons and hopefully find some information about them to get the upper hand.

With the morning starting to wear on, the mist in the woods had faded away. A brisk breeze had settled in, and the rustling of the canopy overhead had a somewhat calming effect on me. Perhaps my mind did actually need a little rest. As we walked, I let my brain attempt to take a break from work and dabble in some other lines of questioning.

"If Oathwarden is a rare Class, does that mean there are others?" I was apparently unique, which seemed more self-explanatory.

She shrugged. "Never met one if there are. My understanding may be flawed, as it's just from the people I have been able to talk to, but the rarity seems to be more based on your power in your previous life."

"I see. So it might not be that there are only a few Oathwardens, but the Abilities that you are granted few may have?"

Ren tilted her head as if letting the prospect sink in. "Or my Abilities might not be rare, but the combination or order in which I am granted them to maintain my prior power would be considered beyond the norm?"

I nodded slowly. "I was not powerful in my old life, but perhaps the other soul of a different Max was—and I'm unique due to that." He was certainly more used to death and violence, so it might give credence to that thought.

She stopped to put her hands on her hips and furrowed her brow. Wolf went over to sniff some trees as she thought. "There was an old man back on the island.

Used to be a farmer. He found the portal beneath a sinkhole in his field or something. Common class. Hadrian was apparently a soldier of some kind. His was a rare class."

"So there's a disparity. Common for no skills, uncommon for some, rare for experienced. Unique for whatever it doesn't understand."

"I can accept that until we know for certain." She shrugged and started walking again.

Although that all seemed reasonable, there wasn't an exact way for us to find out, and I doubted the System would be keen to fill in the gap of knowledge. I worked my jaw in trying to chew some sense out of this world. Maybe we had missed some important exposition between our odd takes on the leveling process. Then again, things did seem a little unmanaged and out of control once you got past the initial prospect of simple Quests.

"What happened to the old man?" Wolf asked lazily as he caught us up.

"Found him dead. Looked like he tried to solo the Bandit camp."

Despite not knowing anything about the man other than that he existed, I felt bad that he had met that fate. It had been rough for me, and I had a comparatively well-rounded set of Skills compared to what he may have had. Whether through overconfidence or a lack of friends and understanding, he had met his demise on something the System had led him to with the promise of greater power and riches.

I snapped my fingers as my brain remembered a nugget of information. Without saying anything, I brought up my Map and shared the coordinates with Ren.

"Treasure cache? You got this from the Thieves?" She bit her lip in consideration. "Alright, sure. It's not too far off our course."

"And it might have something worthwhile." I grinned. At some point between the top of the tree and the ground below, it had slipped out of my mind.

"Like meat!" Wolf added, although his blank expression gave a hint he wasn't sure what we were talking about.

Ren nodded. "More likely it will be things that Max won't even bother to loot."

My mouth opened and closed, but any excuse was dead before it left my lips. I let the silent ghost of my argument lead us on toward our target.

An hour and a half of meandering through the woods, and we arrived at the location to find that at least one of us was correct.

"I guess we now know why the shipment was abandoned," Ren murmured as she narrowed her eyes through the foliage.

Conversely, I said nothing. While fighting Boars and Bandits had some semblance of normality, and the talking bear I let slide, what stood ahead of us tugged at my brain in uncomfortable ways. As if I couldn't already take a poke at it, the System was keen to fill in the details for me.

[New Monster: Cyclops <8 E>]

The Cyclops had tough flesh, tanned by years spent with only a leather loincloth to hide his modesty. His large singular eye gazed lazily around the small clearing, a vacant look as if he was waiting for his braincells to collide. A large club that looked like it was just an uprooted tree trunk sat in his hand. Fifteen feet tall, perhaps, and built like a barn. By his feet, a handful of containers sat beside the remnants of what was probably a horse-drawn cart. The remnants of said horse were also on display. More likely set dressing than something natural, but it sold the experience pretty well.

"Eight elite," I eventually whispered. "That's easy enough, right?"

"There's a *chance* our basic attacks might not even break his skin. He has high absorption, very sturdy." She caught my inquisitive gaze. "One of my Passives lets me see some Monster information."

I nodded. That was really nice, in fact. She just needed to be able to tell me what manner of tricks each creature preferred and that would make my life a lot easier. It would perhaps be unfair to expect Wolf to run in without a say, given that he might be the one taking hits from that club.

"They can talk, right?" I raised an eyebrow. "Maybe I could go talk to him, impress him with a little—"

"Run that scenario through your head twice. Best possible and worst possible outcome." Although she was glaring at me, she seemed to be earnest in trying to temper my whims rather than outwardly shutting me down. "If the worst version is too dangerous, then we don't do it."

As much as best-version Max was having a laugh, impressing and coercing the Cyclops into giving us the goods, worst-version Max was a miserable paste on the grass. "Alright," I ventured. "Let's play it safe."

Perhaps a bit too soon to call it character growth. In fact, I was already thinking of tricks I could pull off even if we didn't go the charismatic route. There were Dazzle icons to earn, of course, a reminder of my successes. They gave me a Damage boost too—so it wasn't solely for the act of it. I tried to remember to bring that up next time I was chastised for my over-the-top manner of fighting.

Wolf looked eager to go and hadn't moved his eyes from staring at the large humanoid since we got here. He just needed the word to be set loose. No muscle in his body was hesitant to launch himself into the fight. It was easier when you were a giant beast and could take the damage, I supposed. Part of me was apprehensive for him, but I trusted his instinct. Better him than me.

A swing from that club when I wasn't prepared would easily break bone, if not worse. Still, with potential treasure only a stone's throw away, we would take our best shot. As I raised my left arm slightly, ready to prepare a card or two, Ren put her hand on it.

"Hey, trickster. Do you have any cloth left over?" A small twinkle of something mischievous blazed in the back of her blue eyes.

CHAPTER THIRTY-SIX

All Eye on Me

When your world could apparently draw on people or creatures from across a multi-verse, you eventually gathered some odd characters. Why you would force such unknown factors together in the hope that they could dance to your intended tune on a functional level was beyond me. Would I ever find an answer that satisfied me in this regard? Doubtful, for many reasons. You just had to take everything in stride, unless you wanted to trip on the small details and crack your head open on something untenable . . . something I had become all too experienced in.

My hell dove flew out into the opening and fluttered around the head of the Cyclops. At first, he showed nothing but brief annoyance. With a grunt, he stared down the flapping bird as his anger level almost visibly increased. His patience hit the breaking point, and he lashed out with his empty hand and grabbed my summoned demon from the air. A brief crunch, and he held his fist up over his head to drop the remnants of his caught prize into his open maw.

Only, there wasn't the crushed corpse of a bird to drop out. Instead, a wisp of dark smoke floated away as broken glass and a clear liquid splashed down his front. The confusion in his one eye was almost childlike, which made the arrow also doused in burning oil seem rather cruel.

Out from the bushes where we remained hidden, the projectile struck his chest. Down his arm and across his torso, where the majority of the payload had been dropped, flames immediately burst from his skin. The thought of whether oil actually did that was quickly wiped from my mind. It clearly *did* in this world. The Cyclops stumbled around, trying to put it out. Probably wouldn't be enough to kill him, so we still had to act. Now we just had the advantage of the distraction.

My card swung out in the clearing and narrowly missed his eye, driving a cut along the side of his head as he tried to pat out the flames. I was disappointed that our ploy hadn't been enough to earn me a Dazzle icon, but given that the Monster hadn't seen me, it felt somewhat fair. The real bonus was having Ren come up with the idea and be willing to do a little scheming. Something to dazzle my own mind with when we were in less danger.

The Cyclops turned his large blue eye toward us, managing to pick out our attacks just as a radiant arrow slammed into his chest. "Tiny cowards, come fight fair!" he bellowed out and made to run toward us. Despite my bright suit, it didn't seem as though he had actually seen us—just where our attacks had emerged from.

Wolf burst out of the bushes slightly away from us and growled at the Monster, his deep tone shaking throughout the trees. The large humanoid immediately turned to him and stomped heavily across the worn dirt to bring his club around.

Some kind of taunt, I imagined. Or perhaps the bear was just that loud. It was hard to judge. Ren held her palm forward beside me, and a radiant shield appeared around our tank, orbiting him like a golden moon. That'd be her new Skill then.

The club came down toward Wolf and struck him hard. He dropped to the dirt onto his stomach, and the radiant shield broke and faded away. Panic flooded through us both at seeing the bear fall from a single blow. He didn't look bloodied though. It must have been some kind of stun.

"Shit!" The elf cursed and began to cast her heal.

The Cyclops chuckled to himself and brought the trunk back up over his head for a follow-up smash on the prone and dazed bear. Small flames still lapped at his burned chest, although they were now mostly extinguished.

"Ren, *I trust you.*" I gave her a smile, which did nothing but confuse her, before I turned back to the fight. "Hey, big guy!" I called out, stepping through the bush into the clearing. "Want to see a magic trick?"

I could hear the Oathwarden grumbling as her heal went through to the bear, but I'd rather Wolf didn't receive an unprotected strike from the weighty weapon of the Cyclops. It was my job to receive the head trauma on the regular. While the bear might be tough and hardy, he had little actual avoidance from strikes—which was a big deal when it came to being out of our depths. We would need to come up with something for that, assuming I wasn't about to get my head eaten off.

"What trick?" The Cyclops turned and stepped toward me, his brow furrowed. Despite being engaged in a fight, he was surprisingly receptive to my offer. Might just be boredom or how great my suit looked in the sunlight.

Top hat in my hands, I reached inside and drew a handful of meat. Some kind of pork chop, as if I had properly butchered it at some point. Dazzle icon. I passed my hat over the front of it, and now I was holding a jug. Two icons.

"Bring meat back." He frowned at me as he leaned in closer. Close enough for me to smell his burnt flesh and stale breath.

"Hold out your hand then and I'll change it back. You'll never see a trick like it again, I promise you." Not a lie but a bending of the truth.

He was enamored, drawn by the lure of potential food and the mysticism of the little human that could conjure it out of thin air. I too felt enraptured by this audience member, so besotted by the simple trick. Almost made the final reveal such a shame . . .

His empty hand extended before me. The thick fingers intimidating. He could effortlessly crush my head just as easily as he had the demon bird. I placed the jug upon it.

"Now, watch *very* . . . carefully . . ."

The Cyclops was bent over, his head getting closer to his hand as his bright eye widened in anticipation. Drool fell from his mouth and onto the muddied ground in front of me.

Slowly, I lowered my hat over the jug until it was now sitting on his palm. My heart was pounding in my chest as he stared in the hope of a tasty snack soon to appear. A whistle of displaced air went somewhere between my shoulder and ear as an arrow barely missed me and struck the Monster straight in the eye.

He roared in pain, and I leaped backward, diving across the grass to roll away from him as his club swung through the air wildly. With a growl of his own, a patient Wolf jumped up from his prone position and bit into the back of the Cyclops's thigh, ripping into the thick skin and muscle.

I threw another dove card at the nearby tree, and the bird flew out from a brief magical circle. Sent it to harass the head of the Monster. It wouldn't do any Damage, and he was already blinded—but if we could confuse his hearing and make him believe something was right above him constantly, it'd draw the focus away from us. Well, mostly me.

It was one situation where we didn't want to use the <Entangling Shot>. As he swung in an attempt to dislodge the bear and escape the dove, he was walking blindly about. One of his errant attacks struck a tree, and the combined shock mixed with the cluttered branches held the weapon caught. A magic card sliced across his stomach before embedding in his outstretched forearm. Damage but not much. At the base level, my cards were having a tough time getting through his skin to do anything substantial.

He let go of the club and turned to grapple at the bear. Wolf saw the attempt and bit into one of the encroaching hands, slashing out with his paw at the other arm. An arrow embedded into the back of the Monster's neck. Lethargy was beginning to overtake him from all the wounds he was sustaining.

"Not fair," he huffed, dropping to bloodied knees. "Man make trick on me."

He slumped over to the ground, either the pain or eventual blood loss overtaking his desire for violence. With a tearing sound, Wolf bit through his neck and put the creature out of his misery.

I walked over and picked my hat from the dry dirt. Dusted it off and turned to the approaching elf. "*Are* my tricks unfair?"

"I'd say *overdone* more than unfair. He was just too ignorant to understand them." She shrugged.

Now it was my turn to roll my eyes. "Please. Try to tell me you didn't have fun getting him with the oil trick."

"It wasn't a trick." She wrinkled up her face and frowned at me. "I admit *nothing*."

Wolf walked over to us, licking his maw. "My head hurts."

"You alright?" I moved over to him and rifled my fingers through his fur to check for any serious damage. It was matted with blood, but I couldn't see any wounds, so it might have belonged to the Cyclops. I turned back to the elf, who had her head tilted to the side.

Wolf looked up and rubbed the side of his face against my arm. "I'm happy that you saved me, Max."

I grimaced at the slobber soaking through my jacket but turned it into a warm smile. Genuine, despite the situation. "I wouldn't say that I saved you . . . It's just part of what we do, right, Ren?" I raised my eyebrows at her.

"Something like that." Her face softened. "We keep each other alive. That's just being part of being a fam—A Party." With a nod to us, she looked away, back over to the crates that the Monster had been guarding.

"Let's see what we got here then." I agreed with her unspoken gesture. My hand gave Wolf another pat on the head before I could consider if that was con-descending or not, but he didn't seem to mind it.

I hummed to myself. All things said, that went a little better than I had expected. Certainly, I had put a bit of pressure on Ren to fire past my shoulder without impaling the back of my head. That brought a smile to my face. Imagine dying of *that* and flopping my corpse atop the Cyclops's open hand as the end reveal to the trick? *Ta-da!* Here's the meat, just like magic. The meat was me. Although the other two might not have seen the humor in it.

"Should I be worried that you are smiling while looting?" Ren looked up from the first box as I checked from the other end of the pile.

"If I said no, would you still be?" I scooped through what the meager items were in this container. Everything else was junk.

[18 Gold]
[Candles (4)]

"Probably," she said with a shrug. "This was good practice for fighting large enemies though."

"Definitely room for improvement." I looked over to Wolf, who was sniffing around the dead body of the Cyclops. I'd have to remember to loot the corpse if Ren didn't get there first.

"That's where you excel, trickster. Improvisation."

I turned back to her and raised an eyebrow. She perhaps had a point, but I hadn't seen it that way. Each trick or Ability I had was just a part of the process—like matching dominoes. I just had to see what the enemy had going on and pair it with the numbers I held. Usually these things were planned out well in advance rather than on the fly. That said, I would definitely hold on to that compliment and cherish it for longer than was healthy to.

"Oh." She tilted her head. "That's unexpected."

I gave up on trying to decide if I wanted to take the set of cutlery from the second box or not. *I did*, and I did. She had moved over to the Cyclops while I had been deep in thought.

"*Four* Power Tokens." She looked half ready to express her excitement but decided against it. "There's a spear with a point of Luck and a couple pieces of Strength gear. Wolf?"

"I'm not sure how to put clothes on. Or if I want to." The bear tilted his head and managed to look disgusted with the notion.

"I'll keep them until you see sense then." She rolled her eyes. "Spear, trickster?"

"Please." I held out my hands as she passed me the weapon and two tokens. It might not be immediately useful, but seeing as I could only withdraw items into my hands or onto the ground within my reach, having something with a bit of distance to it could be beneficial.

"I'll look after Wolf's for now, if that's alright?" She looked down at the beast with a wrinkled-up nose. Our tank was seemingly no longer interested in this necessary part of adventuring.

I smiled and nodded. "Of course." It wasn't even a matter of trust. She didn't seem too power hungry despite how much of a boost the items could be. Wolf definitely needed his own when he could understand how to work the STAR properly. Perhaps I'd save one of these so that he could have two when ready and catch up to us quicker. I was amazed that he was this strong without playing to the System rules, but that only meant we needed to get him on board with the rest of it to make the best use of his capabilities.

The bear growled as Ren put the tokens back away in her own Inventory.

"Easy, bud." I raised my hands. "It's just temporary."

He wasn't looking at us, but past me and out to the woodlands.

"Someone is nearby." He continued to glare off at the trees and bushes.

There was no reason for me to doubt that his senses were good enough to tell, even if now I could not hear the approach of anyone. To be fair, Ren was almost silent when moving sometimes, so I couldn't really be the best judge. Already the elf had an arrow to her bow.

A purple card appeared in my hand as my mouth dried. Standing in this clearing, I suddenly felt exposed, expecting an arrow or spell to find itself in my neck from one of the shadowed bushes. Without consciously doing it, I was pooling more Mana into the card than I needed, causing it to glow brighter as I held it.

From within the bushes, a dark shape sauntered into view.

CHAPTER THIRTY-SEVEN

Changing Shapes

Knowledge equaling power was a common saying, probably across all the realities that Players came from. It could be a key to open a doorway that hindered your progress. Just as easily, that door could have been preventing something untoward darkening your porch, and the knowledge had instead just drawn you closer to your doom. Perhaps I should draw some smiley faces next to my notes to make them feel less drab. :) No. That just seems disingenuous.

We tensed up as a black cat walked into the sparse light of the canopy swaying in the breeze. With the shimmer of a dark mist, the small creature rose up into the figure of a woman. Her adventuring gear was various shades of black and dark-gray, a slight bagginess to them that signaled to me she possibly wasn't much of a melee fighter.

Her bright-green eyes were a contrast to her dark skin and black hair—but perhaps the second and third most striking things about her were the cat's ears atop her head and the tail that waved behind her as she leaned lazily against a tree.

My fingers gripped my card too tightly, drawing blood from my own hand. "Who are you? Do you work for Lady in Red?" My voice came out a lot sterner than I was used to, my usual flare washed away by the stress of potential antagonists.

"Me? No . . . I do not." She grinned widely, seemingly amused at the attacks readied toward her. "I'm perhaps one of the few that do not work for the Crimson Shadow now."

"*Crimson Shadow?*" I asked, still not convinced this woman was worth trusting.

"I see you are lacking in knowledge. Allow me to introduce myself." She bowed, her tail flicking side to side behind her, before she leaned back against the shadowed tree. "My name is Hannah. Perhaps we can trade?"

I shot a side glance toward Ren, and the elf just shrugged in response. Wolf was still on edge, possibly slightly confused that the cat had turned into a person. That could just be me projecting. I had seen enough oddities to know when to suspend my disbelief, but the regularity was almost unpalatable.

"Oh!" Hannah narrowed her eyes. "Is your bear a shape-shifter too or a pet?"

"I'm just a Player," he grunted in response.

She nodded slowly. "Fascinating. This System really is something, huh? So how about the trade?"

I exhaled through my nose and allowed my card to fade away, flexing some comfort back into my fingers. Ren kept her arrow drawn, which was fine. I could be a little careless if she had my back. "What did you want, and what are we trading for?"

She sucked her teeth. "Well. That depends. Are you after information on the Lady and her new gang? She's quite the up-and-comer around here."

"And what in return?" I worked my jaw. This information could be worth its weight in gold, and perhaps the shape-shifter knew this. We were currently stumbling around in the dark when it came down to the Lady and the goons she had gathered. If we could get the upper hand, then perhaps we could sleep a little easier at night.

"I may have overheard you received a couple of Power Tokens. You're new here, so I'll even make you a deal. I'll give you the information first, and you give me a token once I'm done."

Ren huffed. "What's stopping us from taking the information and not paying up?"

"Well . . ." Hannah grinned widely. "The Crimson Shadow might pay me well for *your* location."

"So what's stopping you from telling them even if we do pay you?" I was already growing tired of the games. It was easier when someone was a friend or foe from the outset. Despite my usual charms, I was slowly starting to accept that I didn't need to wow everyone into being a fan. Just most people.

She shrugged. "I suppose you'd need to trust me."

Ren and I exchanged glances. Still a scowl there, but I reckoned we were on the same page. I adjusted my hat and stood up straight. "Very well, we accept."

"Purrfect." She grinned again. "That's a little cat joke. You have no idea how it tickles me to annoy people with it."

"I can imagine," Ren said plainly, ignoring my questioning glare.

"So, this Lady in Red." Hannah rubbed at her face. "She came over and almost immediately herded all the black sheep of the area. No idea how. She must have some kind of Ability for it, right?"

I nodded. "She was running a criminal group in New Forest before we forced her out."

"So we have you to thank." She rolled her green eyes. "Good information, *thanks*. Anyway, she formed a group called Crimson Shadow—which is as cringeworthy as your costume." She waved a finger at me. "But they are all business. Player killing, theft, trying to exploit the System. The System always had bad apples, but they were usually self-serving, or at least stuck to the usual rules of society. Now they're all on the same page and willing to do whatever she wants."

"Which seems to be 'be more murderous.'" I grimaced. How had she managed that so fast? We were barely a day behind her, and she had roused a mercenary group to do her bidding in the time it took us to beat up some thieves and fall out of a tree.

"Yeah, no kidding. There was a Party of five that liked to hang around this area to help low levels that came through. Crimson Shadow poison bombed them in their sleep while they were camping and then peppered them with arrows as they stumbled around disoriented."

I could feel the tension in our group rise. Whether that was because of the cruelty against our fellow Players or because that could have easily been us last night, it didn't matter. We couldn't be safe while they still roamed the area.

Hannah sighed and pushed away from the tree. "Honestly, part of the reason I'm giving you this up front is because it sickens me. Not that I expect you three to do anything about it. But you are at least *warned*. You know what's out there." Her eyes unfocused a little as she stared off at the side. Accessing her STAR. "Honestly, there aren't many good apples left; things are moving fast. Apocalyptic almost."

"Are there any places the Crimson Shadow stays on the regular?" I asked.

The shape-shifter tilted her head toward me. "Heroic type, eh?" She looked at Ren and then back at me. "If you know what you're doing, there's a small camp due east of here, but I stay as far as I can from it. Some horse-riding nob and a gaggle of jerk offs. No Lady though. She moves around a lot."

"Hadrian," Ren muttered, perhaps just tasting the name to make her hate more concrete.

I popped the Map up on the side and checked potential places. It'd be out of the way from the Boss Monster Hunt. But in a way, it was toward a greater one.

"That's about all I have time for, I'm afraid." Her smile returned to her face, and she held a hand out. "Worthy of a payment?"

With a sigh, I went through my Inventory as I took a few steps closer to her. "We'll see you again?"

"Doubt it." She shrugged. "By choice, of course, not that I intend to fall foul of the Shadow."

With a brief smile, I flipped the small object through the air, straight toward her rather than in an arc. She caught it deftly and immediately pocketed it. She gave a brief bow.

"Best of luck to you." With a twist of brief smoke, she shrank into cat form and padded off nearly silently into the woods.

I watched the Dazzle icon fade from view and then turned to see Ren with arms crossed, a Dazzle icon also over Wolf.

"What?" I shrugged, grinning. "Do you think that was a mistake?"

"I feel like it will become a problem for us in the future," the elf said as she deflated. "But I appreciate you not giving away some of our power."

"I'm surprised she didn't check it before leaving. More fool her." I smiled off at the woods. A simple trick that shouldn't have worked—perhaps my bonus to Deception paying off?

Ren gave the bear a pat on the side before walking over to me. "Is that why you were dicking around in the Thief hideout so much? I think we are done here. We should move."

I nodded to both parts of her sentence. "I had hoped to get some gold paint at some point, but splitting that metal bar up into fragments was worth the effort." It was too good to pass up—almost the right shape and thickness to pass as a faux token. One from each end of the bar I had looted. I figured they'd become useful eventually.

"Not a lot of good meat there," Wolf grumbled as we headed back into the woods.

"Afraid not." I gave him a smile. "But I'm sure a better meal awaits us right over the next horizon."

He lifted his head up and glared at the mass of trees before us. "Seems a bit far."

Ren said nothing and just looked out into the surrounding as we continued on. After a few minutes of silence, the tension was too much, and I had to say something.

"Still letting the information sink in?"

She nodded. "Yeah. It's . . . bugging me that they're *there*, and we *know* they're there . . . but I don't know if we should . . ."

"Surprise attack their camp and kill them all?" I raised an eyebrow.

"Exactly." She sighed.

"It would be nice to strike while the iron is hot, but we should get a little more powerful first. Be more prepared before jumping into danger."

Ren gave me a nod but didn't continue the conversation, once again looking off to the side through the trees. I could understand her frustrations. A known threat should be dealt with as soon as possible before they became more of a problem, but I was equally keen not to have our plan backfire and cause us injury. First time for everything.

Instead of worrying over that, I turned my attention to my Inventory and activated the power token. While we were getting more skills than tokens currently,

I assumed that they would level out eventually if we had to gather ten per Ability after the first upgrade. There was the temptation to start stockpiling, maybe get something important powered up early . . . but I had already spent this one in my mind. The other I was keeping safe for when Wolf could use them. As desperate as I was for further power, we each deserved to rise together.

<Sleight of Hand>. While not something that overtly strengthened my fighting capacity, it had become the linchpin of my fighting style. There must have been some manner of intention in the System for that to be the case, otherwise it wouldn't be rewarding the actions with Dazzle icons and powers that worked together. There must be an element of procedural development to guide the progression of Players.

[<Sleight of Hand> is now advanced: Your Deception success chance increases with both INT and DEX]

The skill upgraded, although the description didn't change. Not even a change to the vague *increases* to show that my token hadn't been spent for naught. Only the border of the Skill window changing to a silver color denoted that the upgrade had been successful. A small plus symbol beside it when viewed.

I furrowed my brow. Maybe I'd just have to try it. Mentally, I went through the menus and brought my Inventory up. No real increase in speed there. Perhaps there was a hard limit? A knot in my stomach started forming, thinking I'd made a mistake. I took a deep breath and went to retrieve an orange from my Inventory— to find it was already there in my hand.

It swapped to my dagger, and I flipped it into the air before it vanished.

"Everything okay, trickster?"

Ren was looking at me with a tilted head, and Wolf was mostly oblivious but had a Dazzle icon over his face.

"I seem to be able to access certain items innately without having to go through the process of quickly going through the STAR options." My furrowed brow continued as we stepped through the thick grass beneath the shadowed canopy.

"Sounds like more bullshit then. Just Inventory?"

I nodded. There wasn't a way I could swap Equipment that quickly. Quicker than most, perhaps—but the Inventory system was where my abilities really shone. From my head, I took down my top hat and held it in my right hand. From my left, I pulled the orange out from behind my ear and dropped it into my open headwear. I then tipped the hat upside down, and after a couple of seconds of nothing, the spear began to slowly slide out onto the ground.

Wolf had a couple of extra Dazzles, but Ren was unimpressed as usual.

"Can you turn the orange into meat next time?" the bear asked with wide eyes.

"What do you mean?" I grinned. As I leaned over to retrieve the spear, putting my hat back on with a flourish, I brought it up to reveal it was now a linked chain of sausages.

He gasped as his icon increased by one, and I threw him the meat to consume. It felt smoother to do the switching, like I had more control over the speed or where and how things came into my hands. Barely registered the screens in my vision, actually—it was almost like I was doing it by thought alone.

"I can't tell if you're getting better, or I'm just tolerating it more." Ren tilted her head, and her frown relaxed slightly.

I gave her a brief bow and a warm smile. "I'll accept either at this stage. What did you end up choosing?"

"<Entangling Shot>. Slightly wider area, stronger entangle. It's one of the few crowd-control skills we have and helps us all out." She shrugged.

"Pragmatic. You really do pull most of the weight for us. Sure, Wolf can take a hit." I gave him a pat on the side as he finished lapping up the meat. "And I have my good looks and charm, but you're keeping us alive."

Ren just rolled her eyes. "I'm not sure if you're trying to flatter me or yourself with that statement. Enough trickery for now. We have a Monster to hunt."

I grinned as we started back out, pausing briefly to glance around the terrain behind us. There was an eerie stillness to it that I couldn't quite shake. Something telling me to be wary.

Quite frankly, I felt like there were plenty of Monsters hunting *us*.

CHAPTER THIRTY-EIGHT

Similar Pages

I recall a time I had sprained my ankle on one of our many travels through the wilderness. It was an amusing abstraction where we had all this power and magical ability, yet a slippery step could humble you just as easily. Apparently it wasn't dire enough for the System to consider it an injury. I had just hobbled along in the hope that everything would be okay. Poignant.

Wolf stopped to scratch himself up against a tree. The branches shook and a few leaves fell down from the force jostling them about.

My mind felt reasonably blank. The walk through the woods was as pleasant and tiring as always, but it felt like . . . not *quite* like we were being watched. More that we were being judged. We had the location of some of the Crimson Shadow, yet we were walking over to some Monster that would probably beat the stuffing from us.

All for Quest experience and gold, presumably. It felt disingenuous. We were out filling in surveys instead of saving the cat from the burning barn. Leveling up was important. Neither of us could deny that, but combat between Players had been so brief and visceral that we fancied our chances. Of course, the deadliness of it was one of the reasons we should get more powerful.

Ren must be feeling the same way, as her expression had been . . . Well, I could just tell. Mostly because she had been ignoring the tricks I had been practicing along the way rather than feigning disdain or admonishing me for it. Wolf had seemed interested at first, but gradually his focus had faded, and I was rewarded with no Dazzle icons. I wondered if that was some form of diminishing returns, or he just stopped caring.

Either reason made me a little sad.

"You going to say it, or should I?" I stopped to watch the bear continue to scratch himself.

Ren paused and tilted her head, looking like she was tired of the conversation already. "You'll have to be more specific than that, Max."

Hmm. My mind started to race over all the possibilities that she might be expecting me to fill. I stuck to my guns. "That this is a poor use of our time when we could be killing people." I wrinkled up my nose. "That sounded better in my head."

"We can't have it both ways." She relaxed and rubbed at her eyes. "Either we Quest to get more powerful, or we hunt down the Crimson Shadow in the hope of getting a lead on the Lady."

"It's just a thorn in our side. Any other situation and I'd gladly get my teeth punched in by whatever Monster we're hunting down. But now that we have information . . ."

"That we don't know if we can trust. It might be a trap." She raised a hand to stop me from speaking. "And are you saying you haven't read the Quest objective yet?"

I closed my mouth and shook my head.

She rolled her eyes. "Is that some kind of executive-dysfunction thing? Where you can't do everything because you're so hyperfocused on your tricks?"

As much as my brain wanted to try to imagine an executive elf, that was probably some kind of translation from the System that smoothed over the difference in languages. In the end, I just shrugged.

"I'm not . . ." She gestured for us to continue moving. "If you're like that, it's fine—I just need to know so that I can plan around it."

"You'd think I'd be all in the details." I began walking with her as Wolf joined us. "Although my show sets were very tight and structured, they usually started off with me just going to the feel—or the flow of the act. If that doesn't sound too weird."

"No, it doesn't. I imagine it's like painting without a sketch. Once the idea takes form, it has a proper shape that you can work from . . . but before that—"

"It's messy, yeah." I smiled. Her take on the process was a lot more generous than my own.

She brushed some of her hair from her face and looked between me and the bear. "I'll take on the heavy lifting when it comes to reading then, but that means I have more control over which Quests we end up doing."

I gestured to Wolf, who shrugged his large shoulders. "Sure." I nodded. "I trust your judgment without question."

"Perfect," she said with a deep sigh. "Then we are going to kill the Monster, which is a big owl."

My tongue rolled across my teeth. A *big owl* was probably not an accurate descriptor if it was a Monster worthy of a Quest being generated for it. I wondered if that was a permanent fixture on the board back in town and if the creature just respawned after a certain amount of time. If the System could procedurally generate Classes and Skill sets, then it could probably make up Quests or make new Monsters. Some questions for a different time.

I brought up the Quest Log to avoid annoying the elf further. While my charming personality was slowly eroding at her default disdain, being that our new vocation was prone to violence, I didn't want to rock the boat too much.

[Defeat Ghostgust, Ethereal Owl Sovereign]

A big owl . . . that was also a ghost and could probably use wind attacks, if the name was anything to go by. Now that I had actually read the briefing, my brain went into overdrive thinking about the possibilities. Could we even damage a ghost? Ren had a radiant attack, and I assumed my magic would be able to, but that would be reducing our effective Damage output a lot.

If they were an elite or worse, my cards wouldn't be that effective—aside from cutting off a few ethereal feathers. Expecting Wolf to tank something he couldn't hurt, that was possibly as damaging as the Cyclops, seemed unfair too. Ren had seemed pretty dead set on fighting the Monster, and it was experience and Rewards, assuming we survived.

A war raged within me. The cold knife of my survival instinct met the warm softness of wanting to people please. How could I win my Party over if I didn't support them in their choices? I'd be even worse off in that regard if we were dead, however. My heartbeat was unnecessarily loud and muddied my thoughts. In the end, the lump of pensive energy blurted forth and out of my mouth.

"I don't think we should fight the Monster."

Ren stopped and turned to face me. She crossed her arms and stared at me blankly. "You would like us to abandon and fail the Quest?"

The words stabbed into my ego, and I physically winced. My mouth opened in instinct, ready to walk back my outburst. I closed it again and waited for the swirling panic to calm. "After reading the Quest, it feels as though we are underprepared for the encounter."

She didn't change her expression in the slightest. "Is that your decision?"

My muscles tensed as if trying to stop me from making the motion, as if it went against all that I had been building up. I nodded.

"You'll have to convince Wolf too."

I raised an eyebrow at the bear, who looked tired of the words back and forth. "The Monster is a ghost and would have no meat."

"Gross." He shook his head as he stuck his tongue out. I had expected a *little* more pushback.

Ren rolled her eyes. "Alright, you've convinced us. Now what?"

I brought up the Map and narrowed my eyes. We were almost at the farthest point from the town and would need to circle back now to avoid whatever was beyond the woodlands. We had only taken up the challenging Quests from the town, but if there were some basic floating ones we could hit on the route back . . .

"We'll go around toward the Dungeon, avoiding the middle part where we think the Shadow is. Pick up any minor Quests we are offered along the way. Hit the town safe and in one piece to hand in the Thief Quest and get some rest."

She nodded and gestured off to the side. "Lead on then, trickster."

I did, and we started back down through the forest at an angle. There was still a pit in my stomach where I felt that I had forced the issue and changed our course. Had I made the right decision? Perhaps this was another point the elf was trying to force out of me. My brow furrowed, and I tilted my head at her.

"Was this a test to see if I could override my need to people please? Or to be more of a leader?" I rubbed at my chin in thought.

"Perhaps I just wanted to make sure you could actually read." She didn't meet my gaze, but she seemed calm enough beneath the usual scowl.

"After you said you'd deal with the Questing stuff." I clicked my tongue.

She turned to me now and narrowed her eyes. "If you want to follow blindly, I could gouge your eyes out now."

I glanced at the bear, perhaps the biggest third wheel on this side of the continent. Whatever his thoughts on the matter, it seemed he was content enough to let us work our way through the problem first. In honesty, I wasn't sure where I stood on the matter or what Ren's actual complaint was. With a shrug, I gave her a glum smile.

Ren sighed deeply and rubbed at her forehead. "I'm . . . sorry, Max. Not everything should be a test. I'm not sure why I have to keep trying to squeeze change out of you." She looked away from us, out into the woods, and stopped walking. "Growing up, I had so many expectations forced on me. I feel like I'm just lost to the wind in this world. Trying to build something I am more used to, as if it could make me . . ."

Some of the pieces clicked together in my mind. I imagined that aside from the loss of her family and groom-to-be, the pair of them were being shaped into being leaders of their enclave or whatever elves had. A community needed certain skills to keep it afloat. Without them and her equal, she felt adrift and was trying to see if the boots fit me in some manner. Meet up to her expectations, but I had missed the whole presentation on what she was really looking for.

I sighed and gave Wolf a pat on the side. "Party meeting, huddle up."

Conflict was something I tried to avoid in my own life. Even when some of the stagehands were sloppy or someone had failed to take direction as was their role . . . I maintained good standing and tried to guide them with a smile on my face. Often forced and giving them more leniency than deserved. Reggie was usually better at that sort of thing. It didn't really feel like my place. I was no prima donna, despite my flare for seeking fame. A rousing speech to rally the troops? I'd done one or two before, and perhaps that was what we needed to maintain course.

Ren turned back around with her arms crossed, and Wolf circled so that we were in a loose triangle.

"Right. We've been running like a rudderless boat recently." I looked between them, trying out my stern expression for a change. "And as much as you are both equals in my eyes, without each of us performing as expected, the show will be a flop." My right eye twitched.

Ren opened her mouth to speak, but I raised my hand up to stop her. "If you want me to lead or be more decisive, you need to approach it in good faith rather than trying to break me down with tests." I put my hand on her shoulder, a pang of panic rising within me in expectation of how long it would take for me to regret it. "I can't bend to the shape you expect me to be, but we can meet halfway?"

Her mouth opened and closed a couple of times before she relented to nodding and looking down at the ground.

"Wolf." I put my other hand on his shoulder. "Your voice is no less valuable, even if your needs are simpler. You will often suffer the brunt of our decisions, so do not be afraid to weigh in."

The bear wrinkled back his nose. "I think you both have more issues than I'm qualified to engage with."

I nodded with a wide grin. "To conclude, although I may take center stage, a good performance is only the sum of its parts—I'm just the pretty face at the front, but without your support and guidance I'd just be . . . a bloodied mess in the dirt." The metaphor started to fall flat once I realized that I couldn't get away with copying my prior speeches wholesale. A lot less murder in my usual acts.

My hands withdrew from them as the enigmatic fervor faded away and I had to continue to talk to my peers instead of abscond to my backstage hideaway.

"Almost convincing." Ren tilted her head. Wolf sniffed at the air and started to wander away. Something inside me was burning, a flickering flame that was unfamiliar.

I turned to face her and pressed my index finger on her shoulder. My eyes met her renewed scowl. "We *can* lead this together. I will do my part in my own way. If you think you can handle that and will support me."

As much as her brow was knitted together, the tension around her eyes softened, and her eyes shone brighter.

In comparison, my face tensed up, more due to self-inflicted shame than anything. "So no more tests. I need you, and you need me. Can you accept that?"

She nodded, but her tongue appeared too caught up to give any more of a lucid response.

"I accept it too," the bear murmured, continuing to sniff at the air as he wandered farther away.

"*Good*." I smiled. "Then let's go level up."

I turned from the stunned elf and walked away, mostly to hide both the panic and grimace on my face. My insides were a turbulent sea. It felt like briefly I had let something out. My own demon. I tried to think of the last time I hit my head . . . Did I really emerge unscathed from the Cyclops fight? I hadn't walked away in a particularly useful direction. I just moved, and my eyes stared unfocused while my brain flashed warning lights.

Eventually, I blinked them away to see that the bear had stopped dead. I cautiously approached him, unsure if he was just answering a call of the wild.

Wolf had his eyes narrowed ahead over an outcropping, his large form squashing the bushes between two trees. He turned his head as I approached, my thoughts a whirl of false bravado and unabashed panic.

"Trouble ahead," he growled as a Quest notification popped up on the STAR.

[Available Quests: 3]
[Rescue Villagers from Orc Convoy]
[Progress: 0/3 Villagers rescued]

CHAPTER THIRTY-NINE

Blinding Lights

Finding my place turned out to be more than just adjusting to the new world. I had to juggle new friendships and social entanglements amid all the potential death and strife. Being the showman, there was an expectation that I could be a one-man powerhouse, when often I just felt no better than a performing animal. Repeating the same basic motions while those with bigger vision created the show worth watching. Turn off the lights and remove the glitz and glitter, and I was just a small man struggling for attention and validation. At least in this world . . . I could kill my critics in cold blood.

Standing alongside the bear, I narrowed my eyes at the valley. It looked like three groups of figures escorting a prisoner each. System-created Orcs that looked larger than a normal humanoid but not as hulking as Grak had been.

Ren came up beside us. She didn't look visibly flustered but seemed a little out of sorts compared to her usual grumpy fare. There had obviously been a lot of gears spinning in her mind after my odd outburst, just as there had been in mine. I even had to double-check my memory to make sure it *had* been me. Walking across the knife's edge, I pressed my point and tried to slide into being something we both needed.

"Three groups of Orcs, hostage rescue. Thoughts?" I raised my eyebrow.

"Reward is poor, but it's still experience. Combat should be medium threat." She nodded to me, her intent that we should accept this Quest. Why not, when it had been provided to us so conveniently?

"Wolf?" I nudged the bear, who hadn't moved his gaze from the troupe since I'd knelt beside him.

"Yeah, I could eat. Can I have puppy friend?"

"Of course." Hellhound seemed to be a firm favorite among my peers, assuming he meant to assist him, rather than to eat. I accepted the Quest.

We slid down from the outcropping and started to work our way down the slope of the valley to the dirt road they were leading their captives down.

"Six normal Orcs each group, with what looks like an elite in the front group." Ren withdrew her bow as she scoured their formation. "Focus to reduce their numbers and draw the rest up the hill."

"Understood." Roger's mace appeared in one hand as I drew the Hellhound card.

She paused to ready her aim and fired the upgraded <Entangling Shot> into the air in a high arc. As the blazing green arrow flew toward her target, she drew a second to empower with radiant energy and leveled it more directly at the back group of Orcs.

I split the card so that one was of purple energy, with only a slight pain in my hand. The three groups were almost out of sight now as they traveled through the more wooded area—but then Ren's first shot struck.

Larger vines sprung up around the now-confused Orcs, just as her <Smite Shot> struck one through the chest. Wolf powered forward, his large paws thudding against the grass. I felt the vibration of his charge through my shoes as my cards circled over his head.

The middle group turned and looked our way, angered shouts ringing out as they ran in our direction. Group one at the front was slower on the uptake but had now seen something was wrong. All too late for the back six.

My card struck the face of one, the Hellhound hitting the ground and jumping out of the magic circle to bite out at the unprepared foes.

[New Monster: Orc <6>]

Only level six; that brought me some amount of calm. Wolf thrashed through the remaining opponents, tearing the arm off one with his sharp jaws and mauling a second to disembowel them. I may have the unique Class and a whole host of things to work with, but the simple power of the bear was something to behold. From a *distance* and as an *ally*.

The other two groups wanted nothing to do with that torrent of violence and were using the space <Entangling Shot> had wreaked between their troupe to ignore the bear and run up the hill toward us. Not exactly ideal, but after my speech, my ego was still at the top of the roller coaster before the inevitable drop.

Ren planted an arrow in the forehead of one just before my pact-demon card hit it, and Roger burst out of his new puppet. Too far for me to pass him his mace, so I pocketed it for now. Wolf had finished with his group and would need to catch up to lure some of the ten remaining away from us. Time to see what this old dog had learned.

I picked up a stone from among the sparse grass and went to throw it at an Orc with a small buckler. He didn't seem too bothered, raising it slightly in preparation for the weak attack—before the stone left my hand as the Spear of Luck. It was a terrible throw, and my lack of Strength did me a disservice—but the surprise attack caused the Orc to impale himself on the sharp point as the blunt end hit the soft ground first and friction gave me the assist.

After the throw, I continued the inertia of my movement, spinning in a circle as I drew my hat from my head. I threw it in the air, and a blanket of dark fabric dropped from inside, obscuring me from the onrushing assailants. Two cards burst from the middle of it, splitting the fabric and arcing wildly to strike a pair of Orcs. I clapped my hands, and the blanket vanished, leaving my hat to twirl back into my grip.

An arrow pierced the heart of another, but there were still too many. My grin was widening at seeing the Dazzle icons among those approaching. Ren had stepped backward, about to draw her sword. Wolf would join a couple of seconds after we were engaged in melee. Roger was down the hill and looked to be trying to wrestle with the elite. Hellhound was just behind the bear and gaining just as quickly but still too slow to save us the hassle.

"You're all so eager to see more," I boomed, my best stage smile illuminating my face. "Shame this is the <Finale>."

Bright lights flooded the area as small explosions popped one after the other behind me in a row. The Orcs stopped, blinded and briefly shocked—no— *enraptured* by my performance. It had been a short show but unlike anything they had ever seen. Briefly, for the two seconds that it lasted, I basked in the adoration. The acceptance and validation. I put my inner demon back away as the dopamine took the reins. I gave them a deep bow—my sincerest thanks.

Just as quickly as it had appeared, the luster and pomp vanished, as if sucked from the air itself. The Orcs shook their heads, regaining their senses, just before Wolf plowed into them.

I watched one get crushed immediately, broken spine, before the bear's claws tore the face off of a second one. Once again, I was thankful we had him on our side. Radiant light pulsed briefly as Ren shot one of the nearby enemies, who looked as though they were beginning to waver.

There were now only four remaining, undecided whether to engage the two ranged targets or turn to face the bear chewing through their peers. In the end, they chose to try to escape. I cut the ankle tendons of two as Ren dropped the third. The padding of paws through grass followed as the Hellhound leaped up to the last and dragged him to the ground. Wolf stomped up to the injured ones and finished them off with the wet crunch of broken bones.

"What the fuck was that?" Ren scowled at me, slightly taken aback at the sudden loud noises and bright lights. No Dazzle on her, still.

"*That* is how you end a show." I grinned, but she didn't seem impressed with that answer. She already had some idea, but I waved my hand as I went to catch up to my pact demon. "My area stun." I tried to mentally remember how many Dazzle icons were in play—I needed to do better next time to see how *extra* it could get.

Roger and the elite were still rolling around the grass, grappling and trying to overpower each other. Any weaponry had been discarded down the hill slightly farther away.

"Hey, boss," he gasped as his throat was being constricted by the thick hands of the green Orc. "How's *things*?"

"Up and down. Trying to strengthen the Party under the constant threat of an organized crime group." I watched them tumble about a bit. "You need help?"

"Fuckin' . . . *Nah* . . . Just about . . . got him, boss."

The Orc leader was a good head taller than me and as muscular as they came. The fact that Roger had managed to get this far was a testament to either his Strength or lack of common sense. Wolf came to stand beside me, licking his lips. Out the side of my peripheral, I saw Ren petting the Hellhound.

"Who's your bet on?" the bear asked, watching the two figures scrabble about.

"Roger." Although the odds should be against him, I was getting used to being able to punch above our weight. Plus, he could hear me—I wanted to support his efforts and give him the drive to succeed even if he was outmatched.

"Isn't this a bit cruel?" Ren now joined us with her arms crossed.

I raised an eyebrow. "For the demon or the System-created bad guy?"

"To the prisoners." With a nod, she gestured down the hill to the road where the three that needed saving had just stopped in place, awaiting release. The one at the back had apparently been in spray distance of the massacre Wolf had committed and was drenched in Orc viscera.

Fair point; we had experience to claim. "Finish it up, Roger. Show's over."

"Yes, boss." His hiss turned into a gradual pained growl before the rough cracking of the Orc's neck vibrated through my ears and the figure beneath him lay still. The rabbit demon stood up and gasped for air, hunched over in his muscled puppet.

"Top marks for taking down an elite bare-handed." I shot him a finger gun as we started to walk down to the dirt road.

"It wasn't me," Wolf disagreed.

"You did great too though, Wolf." I patted his side, getting blood on my hand. "You as well, Ren."

"It could have been more efficient. We should have attacked from the back to draw them *through* Wolf or used the entangle on the second group to relieve the pressure on us." She scowled back up at the corpses.

"We got through it without injury. That is a success. But I am open to your tactical changes next time."

She turned to me and nodded, her eyes lingering on mine for longer than I was used to. I smiled and looked over at the prisoners as a way to escape the glare of the piercing blue eyes. The Villagers seemed to be System-created too, which I found to be a good thing in the grand scheme of it all. After we removed their bindings, they ran off toward wherever they felt was safe, without much in terms of thanks.

The third one, however, paused and scratched at his rough brown beard. "Thank you, adventurers. There's an outpost you can rest and resupply at nearby. Let me mark it on your Map."

He leaned forward and made some pen-like motion in the air before turning and running off like his fellow detainees had. I raised an eyebrow at Ren, who shrugged in return. Opening up the Map, there was indeed a new location marked, not too far off from here.

[Quest complete]
[Progress: 3/3 Villagers rescued]
[Reward Received]

[50 Gold]
[Bandages (3)]
[Common Chance Box]

Not really worth the price of admission, but at least it was something. Even the experience of combat was worth the effort even if the experience gained was minimal. Grimacing as I opened up the Chance Box, my mind turned toward what the freed Villager had said.

[Crossbow]

"I wonder if they have proper beds," I thought aloud. From my Inventory, I dropped the two broken Crossbows to replace with this whole one, silently cursing myself for not making a trick out of the process.

"And nice meats," Wolf added.

"There's enough distance where if we take a slightly scenic route, we can possibly pick up another location Quest or two and arrive there by dusk." The elf was frowning at her own Map with her eyes unfocused.

"Perfect." I grinned. "Let's loot these bodies and get moving." Oh, maybe I *had* turned over a new leaf?

Roger gave me a brief salute, which I returned with a nod as he went away and the body fell to the ground. The Hellhound had already gone, and I hoped Ren told him that he did a good job.

Picking the battlefield for spoils was one of my least favorite parts of this new existence. It was different if treasure was found from a chest or delivered unceremoniously by the System itself, but looking through the corpse menu to see how much a life was worth was . . . It felt like learning the secret to a trick you saw someone else do. Once you had the formula and motions down, saw it for what it really was, it took some of the luster away.

"Anything good?" I asked the elf as we finished looking.

"Not much. A couple of things I'm saving for Wolf. You have any rings on? I have a basic Mana-increase one you could have."

"Oh, I don't—that'd be great." Despite the odd paper doll of me with boxes in my Equipment screen clearly having ring slots, it hadn't crossed my mind before. My search through the bodies hadn't revealed anything more than gold and basic weaponry. Most damaged or paled in comparison to what I already had. I had been on a bit of an unlucky streak with looting lately, and I hoped it was just in preparation for the System giving me something worthwhile.

She flicked the ring through the air, and I caught it in my hand, opening it back up to reveal an orange now in my palm instead.

[Ring of Mana: +10% Mana]

Ren rolled her eyes—but no Dazzle icon.

"Aw, I missed the trick." Wolf came and sat down to watch to see if I would continue.

Well, I couldn't let an eager audience down, could I? "I'm not *much* for juggling, but . . ."

My left hand went into my trouser pocket, and I withdrew two more oranges. I relaxed my shoulders and exhaled as I began juggling the three of them. Wolf already seemed completely sold and was grinning with his mouth open wide. Ren was less impressed, but I still held her attention. Sometimes that was enough.

On one of the rotations, I changed an orange to a dagger and continued. A few rotations later and the second orange became another knife—and then soon after a third, and I was now juggling three blades. Wolf clapped his paws together.

With a flourish, I threw each of them high into the air as they reached my right hand, and then I held my palm out. As the first knife went to pierce through my hand, it turned back into an orange. The second struck atop it as an orange too, with the third remaining a dagger and piercing through them both, holding them together.

I took my hat off and dropped the offending items into it before taking a bow to the raucous chuckling of the bear.

"Now turn it into *meat*," he suggested.

With a smile, I pulled out a pork chop from my hat and threw it to him.

Although I rarely did requests, I felt we needed all the levity we could get before the inevitable shadow of something terrible smothered us. We each had different things we desired . . . It was only right I did what I could to make us all happy. Not exactly people-pleasing, but . . . I caught some awkward eye contact with the elf.

Well, people deserved happiness. Even me sometimes.

CHAPTER FORTY

Burning Within

We had wreaked our fair share of evil onto the world—although that word per-haps needed a qualifying asterisk. Even the adventurers who tried to be model heroes had their fair share of blood on their hands, and we were a couple of rungs lower than that. Rather than allow the gloomy clouds prevent us from climbing higher, we held strong and acted as a barrier to those far below, lurking in the filth with bloodied claws and gnashing teeth. Certainly, at several points we could have fallen and become one with them, but our true strength lied in the balance of not deluding ourselves that we could be any better, while having disdain for any who were worse.

I rolled out my right shoulder. "That doesn't really seem like something that should be a Quest."

Ren pulled a face and shrugged. "It's experience without risk."

Other than the risk of carpal tunnel, I presumed. I leaned back to look up at the tree, bringing the Quest back up to make sure I wasn't missing anything.

[Available Quests: 3]
[Cut Through the Tree Blocking the Path]
[Progress: 0/1 Tree cut]

This was *clearly* the tree. We had made sure of it. The fact that it seemed to be twice as wide as all the others nearby and a slightly different hue gave our deci-sion credence. There was hardly a path for it to block, but Ren was right. Cutting a tree down *should* be murder free, and I did suggest we look for Quests to find. Perhaps it might fall on my head, in an odd twist of fate. I didn't think the System had that good a sense of humor, however.

"Not scared of a little physical labor, are you, trickster?"

"Only one thing scares me, Ren." I sighed and started to remove my jacket. The freedom of movement would help, although I didn't really know what I was doing.

"Failure? Lack of attention? Emotional vulnerability?"

I narrowed my eyes and glared at her.

"Me?" Her eyebrows raised in a rare holiday from her usual grumpy expression.

"Maybe at least two of those things. Do you have an axe?" I worked my jaw and rolled up my shirt sleeves. They had long been dirtied from blood and sweat soaking through them. It was about time I gave them a repair.

"For the tree, I hope?" Her eyebrows lowered again, and she looked through her Inventory. "You should have looted some from the Orcs."

I turned my dull glare toward the bear, who shrugged. *Sure*, the Orcs had some, and it would have made sense to keep a couple around, but I was hoping for something smaller—hand axes that I could juggle or throw with greater ease. The spear that I owned had suited my need for a long weapon, but perhaps I should start diversifying.

"I'm surprised you haven't tried using your magic first, before trying to impress me with your muscles." She handed over a heavy two-handed axe.

Despite looking smart in a suit, I was pretty lean of build—even without the System needing to quantify how low my Strength and Constitution really were. "Probably more chance of that than with my tricks," I murmured louder than inside my head.

I closed my eyes and stepped toward the offending tree, peddling from one embarrassing situation to the next. The plan was to weaken it enough to where Wolf could then push it over, or something. I felt very out of place and yet was unable to stop myself from continuing the charade. I had *accepted* the Quest, after all. The call to action.

Clenching my jaw, I gripped the axe tightly, hefting it backward before making the first cut into the thick trunk. A sharp thud echoed out around us from the impact. Then, a crack vibrated throughout the full four-foot diameter of the tree and with a grinding snap it began to topple over away from me. My brain was relieved it wouldn't have to dodge away from it.

I turned and gave the pair a bow, flourishing the axe with a twirl as it turned into my jacket to hang over my shoulder. "Impressed yet?"

Wolf had a grin across his face and a Dazzle icon over his head, continuing the trend of being my longest living fan. Ren looked rather impassive, which I took to be a sign of her surprise.

[Quest complete]
[Progress: 1/1 Tree cut]
[Reward Received]

[10 Gold]
[Wooden Planks (5)]

"Didn't move the needle much experience wise, but we got a little show, and it took no effort," the elf said with a shrug. "Let's keep going."

I put my jacket back on, trying to gauge which show she was talking about. Not wanting to look a gift horse in the mouth, I also wondered *why* that had been so easy. Something to do with my <Sleight of Hand>? A bug in the System? Perhaps it was even intended that way, as bizarre and immersion breaking as it was. Wooden planks though. *Score.*

"You doing okay, Wolf?" I gave him a pat on the flank as I caught up. "You've been quiet lately."

"I'm okay." He lifted his head to look at me. "There's only so many thoughts in my head, and I am not yet used to talking so much. If anything, it amazes me how you two manage to talk near constantly."

"Such is the burden of a busy mind," I said as I smiled at him.

"All I know is when I'm with you two, I enjoy the rush of combat and the taste of meat even more. Although you two do not mate, I consider you part of my sleuth."

I winced, then tilted my head. If Ren heard, which she most definitely did, she made no sign of turning or commenting on his statement. "A sleuth is what you call a group of bears? Like a family?"

He nodded. "Family. I like that word."

It was kind of strange, but I did too. For whatever existence I now had to eke out in this world, my current two companions were some of the best I could have hoped for. Ren might be prickly, but there was an earnestness in her heart and a drive to push me to be better. Wolf was a simple brute, but he was loyal and was always impressed with my tricks. That's why he was my *favorite*. I narrowed my eyes at the back of the constantly unimpressed elf.

She turned her head and gave me the same look, perhaps assuming I had been ogling her rather than knowing I was plotting to Dazzle her, eventually.

"Something to say, trickster?"

"Yeah . . ." I narrowed my eyes further to emphasize the point was something valid. "Is Ren short for something?"

"Renesara. It's only used on formal occasions though. I dislike it." She turned away to look ahead but slowed down so that we were walking together.

There was some comparison there to my own. "I only use my full name for the stage. It's so gaudy otherwise." I smiled at her. "Did anyone used to call you—"

"Little wren? Yeah, Flynn did." She exhaled through her nose and looked out to the horizon.

"My dad would say, 'I didn't name you Minimum,' whenever he thought I wasn't putting in enough effort." I tried to turn the wheel to skirt around the sad point of the deceased elf, more because I didn't want to feel like a dickbag rather than thinking I could course correct that easily from something so important to her.

"He should have seen you cut down that tree." Ren whistled and turned her eyes to me. There was something in them I couldn't quite pinpoint but certainly more emotion than I was used to seeing from her—despite the soft frown still being present.

"Well, I know what my vocation will be if this adventuring thing doesn't pan out."

Wolf sniffed into the air, raising his head. "Hmm. Burned wood. Death."

Any budding rapport quickly cooled at his words. "Which way?" I frowned and scoured the surroundings as if we might have just been oblivious to something untoward in our midst.

The bear stood up tall on his hind legs, possibly the first time he had done so in my presence. It was humbling, as he was nearly twice my height. It was no wonder he shredded through most of the humanoid opponents.

"That way." He pointed a paw up before settling down back to being on all fours.

Ren already had her Map up, and her face turned into a grimace. "That's the direction of the outpost."

Part of me had known it as soon as Wolf had said *death*. Our scenic route hadn't dragged up many potential Quests, and we were close to circling back around to the intended resting place for the night.

I nodded, and we set off at a slightly quicker pace. Apprehension caused a knot in my stomach, and I was too focused on the possibilities of what we might find to be fiddling with tricks or talking with the others. Ten minutes later, as we drew closer, I could smell it now too.

The harsh, smoky tones of burned wood were unmistakable. Nothing as soft as a campfire put to rest. This had the odor of unwanted property damage written all over it. While I couldn't pick out whatever *death* the bear had been able to smell, there was definitely something wrong that prickled at the back of my neck.

Another five minutes, and the sun was clearly sinking toward dusk. I was thankful now that our journey had been mostly uneventful and we'd arrived here while daylight still graced us rather than stumbling into the unknown at dark.

We came across a pathway that led to our destination, and with weapons now drawn, we followed it until its conclusion.

The outpost.

Or perhaps, what was now left of it. The log wall smoldered and had been completely burned away or destroyed in parts. The watchtower was little more than a weak ladder leading to a sheet of charcoal. Various shacks and small tents had been set alight, and only the charred skeletons of their previous structures remained.

We stepped slowly into the area, eyes looking around for potential saboteurs.

"It looks like a dragon hit it," I murmured, unsure how likely that was in this world.

"Not a dragon. Look." Ren gestured with a nod.

To our side, upon part of the wooden wall that hadn't been scarred by the flames, was a handprint of crimson blood.

"Macabre coincidence?" I worked my jaw and looked around. As much as I . . . hoped for that to be the case, part of me knew it couldn't be anything but what it clearly looked like.

"Same as what Hadrian had on him." She exhaled, echoing my thoughts.

There were other places around the destroyed outpost that had similar prints. Some had been half burned away or dried and flaked off in parts, but it was now clearly a deliberate act. A warning to anyone who came here that the Crimson Shadow was around and in charge.

"Over there." Wolf sniffed around the dirt and led us to circle one of the husks of the prior buildings.

There were the bodies.

Ren grimaced and averted her eyes, but I could not. I stepped forward and knelt, drawing a cloth from my Inventory to cover my mouth. There were maybe a dozen or so corpses stacked into a corner like refuse. Each had been terribly burned to the point of being little more than shriveled flesh and charred skeletons. Dark red and black, it reminded me of hell for some reason.

I blinked away the thoughts of memories I didn't understand. There wasn't much I could tell from looking at them. As much as I had hoped to be able to chalk it up as them being all System-created, something told me it wasn't that easy. The truth would be closer to the worst-case scenario than I could imagine.

"Why would they do such a thing?" I stood, my mouth still covered. So destroyed were the figures that the System hadn't even prompted me to loot them. They were inert.

There was violence, and then there was . . . *this*. Slaughter, sacking, and the absolute disdain for life. It was abhorrent.

Ren said nothing, but her eyes were practically alight with blue-flamed fury. She stepped away to look around more of the ruins, and I nudged the bear to follow suit. System-created should respawn, or so I believed. What if the destruction of the area had turned it into a zone where the System wouldn't bother to bring things anew? Seemed futile to destroy something if it would pop back into existence at some point. Unless the outpost was just collateral, and Player-murder was the true goal.

The bear continued sniffing across the ground. It was marred with different hues of ash and mud, so I wouldn't have been able to pick out any tracks if I tried.

"Lots of blood," he muttered.

"The hope is that the cremation was postmortem then." I exhaled, not particularly comforted by that thought. How long had it been since the act was carried out? I knew little about that sort of thing. Not that we could have stopped it. We should be owl feed around now.

"Fuckers." Ren deflated, and her arm holding her bow sagged.

"I guess this settles it then." I rolled my neck around, but it didn't loosen the tension. "Killing Crimson Shadow is going to be our priority."

"You thought I wouldn't find you—"

Ren swiveled at the sound of the voice, her radiant arrow streaking through the ruined outpost even as I still drew my card up.

A blur of shadow went to move but was too slow. The pained yelp following the voice was familiar, and I held my card as they came into view.

"*Assholes!* What the . . ." Hannah growled, looking at the end of her tail, part of it severed from the rest by the arrow and stuck to the wall behind her.

Her pained anger turned to confusion as her wide cat eyes took in the surroundings. ". . . *Fuck?*"

CHAPTER FORTY-ONE

Contracted

The scene had been set. Murderers. Vigilantes in a way, trying to wipe the filthy stains of those intent on ruining the System in this world. Some of these stains were more stubborn than others. A little bit of elbow grease, in the form of personal hardship. It was an acceptable price to pay if we could ever complete our goal. Even after all this time, the visual of those poor souls at the outpost had stuck with me. Not the last horror to hang its coat up on the rack inside my mind, but one of the first to truly weigh on me.

Ren rose her bow back up at the woman, arrow readied. "Stand perfectly still, otherwise the next one goes through your skull."

The shape-shifter narrowed her eyes but stayed put, only wrapping her injured tail around herself so she could hold and nurse it. Whatever her combat abilities may be, she didn't fancy her chances of dodging a second arrow.

"What are you doing here?" I asked as I crossed my arms.

The reason was clear enough by the scowl on her face. "*Somebody* plied me with a fake token, so I came to leverage a real one from them." Her green eyes looked around the outpost. "What about you?"

"We came here to use the outpost but found it burned to the ground by the Crimson Shadow." I gestured with my hand, and she looked over to see their marking. Her expression sank, but I still had to ask the next question. "Did you tell them about us once you realized we had tricked you?"

"No." She shook her head. "You called my bluff. *Congratulations.* You're still assholes though."

I bowed. "Guilty. That was all me though, so aim your ire here. We're pretty on edge right now, so what will it take to smooth this over?"

"Two tokens."

Impassively, I turned to Ren. Her arrow was raring to go, and currently, to my lagging mind, that seemed like an easy solution to our current problem. I didn't want to be like the Shadow, despite the call of the void. We needed to be . . . pragmatic, sure. Cautious, even. But we shouldn't chase them down the dark path, lest we lose the actual warmth worth fighting for among cold hearts. Still, I wasn't eager to give up the power we had bled for. Earned.

"How about your life?" I grinned.

"You wouldn't."

My grin persisted. "Did you want to call *our* bluff?"

She looked at the three of us and sighed. "Fine. No use having information if everyone wants me dead. I was just going to guilt trip you into paying up."

I stepped over close to Ren and leaned over to whisper in her pointed ear, perhaps a lot closer than I had originally intended. Told her my intentions, and she gave me a brief nod of acceptance. Wolf . . . I figured he would be indifferent, so I broke protocol and didn't ask his opinion.

"Hannah, how would you like to help us fight against the Crimson Shadow?"

She pulled a face and stuck her tongue out in faux disgust. "I'm not much of a fighter, so I'd rather not sign my own death warrant, thanks."

"Not as a fighter but as a scout. We can always use information, and we'd actually pay you for the efforts." I had told Ren that the tokens would come out of my share if necessary, but good information could keep us alive. She knew that we were still mostly blind in this area—knowing how bad the threat was and *where* could keep us out of harm's way until we were ready.

She swirled her shorter tail around. "You want to . . . employ me?"

I shrugged and let her word it how she wanted. Currently, we held all the cards. There was also the feeling that my senses had been overworked from the overbearing smells around us and had numbed. It wasn't the nicest of places to hold negotiations.

Hannah worked her jaw and bared her teeth—sharper than a normal human's. "*Fine.* If you are going to unfuck the woods, then I'd rather help than get in the way."

"Perfect!" I beamed, and with a glance, Ren lowered her bow. I brought down my hat and pulled a power token from it.

All eyes on me, I flipped it into the air straight vertically, then reached back into my hat again. The hell dove flew up from my hand as I withdrew it, catching the token in midair. The bird then flew it over to the shape-shifter, who caught it as the small object was dropped.

Ren was glaring at me in my peripheral. "You are ceaseless," she murmured.

I was. Part of it was my compulsion to constantly be a showman, regardless of my own feelings or wants. It was expected of me. The other part of me reveled in it, perhaps in the same way gamblers chased the high of a win. I too now sought the dopamine of seeing the Dazzle icons pop up.

"Anything else we should investigate before we leave?" I turned to her properly now, addressing her as the Party leader rather than the over-the-top magician.

The elf shook her head. "Nothing more to see here."

Hannah was still eyeing up the power token to ensure it was real and not one of my other tricks. Consuming it would be the easiest test, but I didn't want to seem overbearing so soon into our working relationship to pressure her into validating it. We had nothing to prove.

"Let's head back into the woods to discuss?" I gestured off to the side toward the entrance. Now that she had what she wanted, there was the possibility she could run and never return, but I had a feeling she wouldn't be satisfied if there was the possibility of gaining more left on the table.

She nodded, and I patted Wolf on the side to get him to follow along. He may have an even dimmer view of death and destruction than us being so disjointed from humanity, but he looked like the smells of the place had become oppressive, and his eyes were unfocused. Perhaps he was trying to work his System, which would also explain the sour expression on his face.

Without ceremony, we left the place behind. At least, physically. I'm not sure my brain truly accepted or processed what we had seen. Now I just ached for vengeance, or some manner of justice. A couple of minutes later, our feet had taken us away from the remains of the outpost, and we stood among some trees in the waning light of the evening. It was cooler, and the fresher air was a relief, even if it made me feel more tired.

"So, what are the terms?" the shape-shifter asked.

Understandably, she was a little put off at having to stand before us three. Wolf was imposing enough on his own, without the glare of the elf and . . . whatever I had going on. I rubbed my chin and looked at Ren. "I'd say the most important thing is don't die?"

The elf nodded and narrowed her eyes at the cat woman. "A dead scout is a worthless scout."

"Secondly," I continued. "We mostly need information on their campgrounds, any bases, and their movements. If you can work out Classes or levels then you get a smiley face on your end-of-quarter peer review."

She rolled her eyes at this. "So just somehow find you every so often, give you coordinates and anything else I can safely get?"

"I can't promise you a token every time you return, but we'll find some way to compensate you fairly." After all, the power was best kept in-house. The odd token here or there for information that could keep us alive would be worth the cost in the long run, now that she seemed more trustworthy, at least.

Ren tilted her head and shot a glance at me before looking at Hannah. "If you could find out their actual motives, that'd be nice too."

Of course. Evil for the sake of it usually only happened in fairy tales. On the small scale, burning down an outpost or killing a group of Players could easily be the actions of someone sadistic or malicious—but there had to be an end goal of the group as a whole. What did the Lady want, and why did it involve so much wholesale violence?

"Sure." Hannah exhaled. "I'll see what they like for breakfast too if it helps?"

I nodded slowly. She was being sarcastic, but I was sure I could do something with poisoning or switching out ingredients. "*Anything* you can get will be useful."

"Alright. Other than the camp I told you about, I know of two other groups. There's a small one that moves about a lot. Like their own scouts but more violent. There's also a larger one down south past the town to the west. Lots of activity there in the past couple of days. I'll probably head there soon to see what they're doing." She turned to leave. "I'm still pissed about my tail, but I'm glad it wasn't my head."

Ren worked her jaw. "For what it's worth, I am sorry."

Hannah waved her off as she departed. "You can owe me an ale. Meet you back at the town if you're not dead by then."

After two dozen steps, she turned into a cat and vanished into the bushes beyond our vision. A few moments of silence followed before the elf turned to me.

"You think we can trust her?"

"For now." I took a deep breath and then gave her a smile. "She doesn't look to have a Party, so she is perhaps just a lost soul in this world as we were." Partly I wondered if we should consider offering her a Party invite. She wasn't so eager to engage in violence as we were, however. We couldn't provide the safety she needed in the direct sense either. While flexibility could be a strength, consolidating the three of us was working out well.

She narrowed her eyes at me but gave me a nod, turning once more to look past the sparse canopy. "It'll be dark soon."

The statement didn't seem to have a follow-up coming, which I took to mean she was waiting for my lead for our next steps. I gave Wolf a pat on his side. "No point getting our brains bashed out wandering around in the dark. Camp tonight, Dungeon tomorrow, then head back to town where Hannah will hopefully have the actual location of the Shadow." With all things going well, the Dungeon would give us some power worth the effort too.

"No campfire tonight then." Ren glanced backward at the outpost. "We also don't want to draw any attention to ourselves."

I agreed. There was something comforting about the warmth and light of a fire, but after seeing the burned-out ruins, I was less inclined to put myself beside the destructive force and invite whoever was in the area to join us.

With little else to say, we ventured away from the site. Anger still rolled around inside me, but it needed to cool. Riding our emotions into battle would sharpen the edges of our blades but also just as easily get us in over our heads. Currently, I was hoping to keep mine on my shoulders, even if the System was keen for me to dash it upon every hard surface in my vicinity.

As the light darkened across the sky and the twin moons began to show themselves, we eventually found a suitable enough spot to hole up for the night. A shallow cave set into an outcropping of rocks where there was just enough room for Wolf to curl up and blend into the shadows and obscure our presence. We could squeeze in beside him and be hidden from the outside world, to a degree.

"Pretty cozy," I murmured, shuffling in after Ren, between the bear and the cold rock wall.

"Reminds me of the dirt hole I used to hide in." Ren had sat up against the warm body of our other Party member, facing the side. "Not exactly a fond memory though."

I sat down almost right beside her. "Here, it's pretty chilly." From my Inventory, I withdrew a blanket to share across us. From within this nook, only the barest amount of moonlight shone through.

"What a fucking day." She sighed, sinking into what warmth she could.

With a smile, I looked up at the low ceiling. "Yeah. Plenty worse to come, I'm sure."

"Sounds like it's been bad enough to erode your positive attitude, trickster."

The mental images of the charred corpses threw themselves in front of my mind before I turned my head to her. She looked as exhausted as I felt. In the light, she put on a good show of being cold and stoic, but the trials of the day wore on her the same as they did me. Honestly, right now I could barely conjure up a true smile, let alone put on a performance up to my normal standards.

"Can't all be fun and games," I eventually relented. Straightened my head and closed my eyes, only the briefest difference in darkness compared to having them open—yet still, it was relaxing.

"Not all, sure. Some of it has been."

"Hard to tell with you." I smiled, hoping she could see it in the low light to know I was just trying to rile her up. There was silence for a moment before she spoke again.

"There was one guy who said I'd look a lot prettier if I smiled more."

"Did you kill him?"

"What? No, that's a bit extreme, Max." I heard her sigh.

Sleep was trying to get me to hurry up, the exhaustion and emotional turmoil of the day finally allowing my brain to turn into mush and rest. "I would have killed him for you," I murmured.

I didn't hear her response, as the darkness took me just as soon as the thought had slunk from my mouth.

Actual rest didn't come easily though. Between all-too-vivid dreams, I found myself waking in a brief panic every hour or two at any sound or imagined movement. Heart beating and tired eyes trying to focus on the darkness to see if something untoward was nearby. Nothing. One time was because Ren had slid over and her head was resting on my shoulder. The next time I awoke, she was back in her normal position, so I was unsure if that really happened or my half-lucid dream state was running roughshod over my grip on reality.

How I wished for my own bed. A proper thing of comfort and peace. Even the worst of the hotels over the years were a step above a hole in the ground with a giant animal to rest upon. A life without demons and murder, where everyone showered my efforts with praise and didn't call me a dickbag.

"Hey, Max? Time to get up."

My eyes cracked open like eggshells as I turned to the elf, who was trying to prod me out of the way.

"Shit, you look like garbage. Get out of the way and I'll fix you up."

I groaned and leveraged myself from the shallow indent, body aching and stiff. Hopefully, by fixing me up, she meant she was just going to break my neck and put me out of my misery. The morning sunlight burned at my retinas, and I grasped at my eye sockets in the hope my brain wasn't about to rupture itself out and escape.

"See, the trick is not to tense your muscles."

My glare escaped from between my fingers as I watched her clamber out too. Her hair burst into radiant gold as soon as she stepped into the light, and despite her soft scowl, she seemed all too glad to be existing. It was almost enough to melt away at my thorns, but not quite.

She brought out her grill, which was motivation for the bear to pop up to his paws in expectation, amber eyes wide.

"This is not really my sort of thing, but you look like you could use it." From her Inventory, she withdrew a glass bottle and handed it over.

Cyanide, maybe? A sleep potion? Some manner of healing miracle?

No, something even more valuable and magical.

Coffee.

CHAPTER FORTY-TWO

On Tour

Some days blurred into one another, especially ones that involved nothing more than travel and light skirmishes. Others stood out like streetlamps, painting the surroundings with their distinctive hue. While I often loved to stand in the limelight, some of the lanterns along the path were too bright and hurt my eyes. Others just a color that would be more warranted being displayed at a horror show. Still, anything was better than the darkness. Anything.

The first part of the morning was a brisk and picturesque scene of joy. Perhaps it was the coffee, but the illumination of the bright morning sun made everything feel vibrant and put the dark images of the previous day far back in my mind. The rich browns of Wolf's fur paired with his affable spirit, Ren's elegant poise and canny wit, the radiant gold of Ren's hair, and the piercing blue of Ren's eyes. The trees and shit were nice too. I did *not* do well with lack of sleep.

I lent a hand to help the elf up a ledge, which she took without complaint.

"If I had known coffee made you less insufferable, I'd have gotten it out sooner." She rolled her eyes but gave me a nod of thanks.

In truth, I felt off-kilter still. Between the lack of sleep and the odd caffeine, a mania had set in—good-natured but slightly weird. It wasn't necessarily stronger than what I was used to in my own world, but there was something odd about it. A *magic*, if I dared use the term unironically. I looked down at the bear, who was waiting to see if I'd lend him a hand of help next.

"All the good intention in the world, and I would sooner end down there than you up here, my friend." I grinned and stepped back to allow him to clamber up himself. He looked a little more morose than before but accepted the reality of the situation. Unfortunately, I couldn't work miracles yet.

But in the future? Certainly. I was sure of it even if I currently wasn't too sure of myself. There were limitations of the Inventory that I needed to try to override. Objects being too large to store being one of them. Items only being withdrawn into my hand or dropped to the floor was another. I could briefly adjust their exact position and place to some degree, but it was still within the reach of my wingspan.

Some things I'd just have to wait for the System to allow me with further Skills. I was already a stenographer in a world of two-finger typists. Whenever Ren used her Inventory, I could see the motions made with her eyes or slight posture changes—it required a certain amount of concentrated effort to work around, and she wasn't exactly slow of mind. Whereas I was close to just thinking things into existence. Almost a magic unto itself.

"Do you think it is some degree of force or the intent that prevents me from snatching arrows from the air?" I asked the surrounding forest, my internal monologue too loud to contain.

"I doubt the System can read intent." Ren narrowed her eyes at me. "More likely that it has a way of calculating potential Damage that would meet an attack threshold."

Now it was my turn to furrow my brow at her. It wasn't like her to delve into the gritty side of things, especially if it came to my trick-adjacent musings.

"What? I can't have been thinking of these things too?" She looked behind to wait for Wolf to catch up.

She had a point, however. Things must have some manner of measurement when it came to the physics and Damage that could be dealt. Intent just wouldn't track unless the System was constantly subjected to my inner monologue. Even if we could trick the System into thinking she was just passing me an arrow at high speed in a *friendly* way, it was unlikely I could convince our enemies to play the same game.

"So then . . ." I tapped at my lips in thought. "It would depend on when the calculation is made—when the attack is released or when it strikes."

"You'd need to either reduce their Damage or increase your defenses?" She bit her lip and wrinkled up her face.

"Thinking about me in a suit of armor? Yeah, me too." Despite wearing my cosmetic suit over my actual armor, the thought of clunking around in full plate seemed too restrictive. Too slapstick.

"It would ruin your aesthetic, trickster." She gestured with her head and began walking.

It certainly would. Sleep had seemingly given a boost to the elf's mood too. She seemed less prickly than usual and more radiant. *Perhaps* that was my own perception. There were a handful of reasons why that may be, but I chose not to overanalyze it. I'd live for the day while it was good. No doubt it wouldn't last.

"Any luck with your menus, Wolf?" I turned and walked backward a little as he came up between us.

"No." His amber eyes looked between us. "I tried, but I'm not sure what I am doing, so it's just a lot of windows and words in my eyes that make me mad and confused."

"Hmm, I wish I could see your STAR information and help you." I swiveled as he matched our pace so that I could see where I was going. "Do you think there's a Skill for that, Ren, like Analyze?"

She shrugged. "It wouldn't surprise me. Whether either of us would get it is another thing though."

True enough. There would probably be Classes that got them early on, but we seemed to be built for combat. Or doing magic tricks. I rubbed my chin in thought. Maybe I was thinking about it the wrong way—did I *need* to see it?

"Hang on, Wolf. Let's try something." The bear stopped in place as I circled around to his left side, just behind his head. I knelt down beside him as the elf leaned against a tree in impassive interest. "The boxes appear on this side, right?"

He nodded.

I clicked my tongue and squished up a bit closer to him. In my hand, a sausage appeared. "Don't eat this yet. What screen do you have up now, the text at the top?"

"Says Map." His eyes darted between the held meat and the intangible screen.

"Okay." I closed my left eye and brought up my Map. "This might not work, but I want you to follow the sausage with your eyes and then focus on the end when I stop."

He gave another nod, the prospect of food enrapturing him.

I lifted the sausage up and moved it in the air, up and then to the left. Mimicking the motions along my own menu. After I paused, Wolf narrowed his eyes and licked his lips.

"Did the menu change?"

"Map is gone. Now says Inventory."

A grin widened across my face, and I looked up at Ren. She seemed amused, for all that she didn't show it. "Alright, there should be a grid. You'll need to tell me what is in the first box, and we'll go from there."

Gradually, we went through the items that he had managed to loot despite his awkward grasp on the System, and with some trial and error, he equipped what he could. Mentally, it was exhausting—but it was time well spent. Eventually we'd need to work out how to trade the tokens and other things we had been keeping safe for him.

"Great job, bud." I flipped the sausage into the air for him to snatch and consume. Dusted my slacks off and noticed that Ren's clothes were clean and prepared. Did she do that while we were sleeping? More the fool me for not doing the same. Although my sensibilities were worn and soft today, I wasn't quite at the point where I could walk around in my underwear for five minutes without dying of embarrassment, so it'd have to wait.

"You ever work with kids?" Ren asked, an eyebrow raised.

"Huh? Oh, not really. Couple of kids' shows, birthday parties, and the like when I was starting out."

She pushed away from the tree and started walking off again. "How old did you say you were again?"

I rubbed my chin. "Don't think I did but twenty-eight."

"Twenty-five."

Wolf licked at his chops. "Eighteen, I think."

Both answers seemed reasonable, although I half expected the elf to be three hundred or something else outrageous and fantastical. "That's rather old for a bear, isn't it? No offense."

"Perhaps. It wasn't something I used to consider."

That stood to reason. There were a lot of things any of us hadn't considered before we'd landed in this world. Personally, murder was one of those things. Although . . . it *had* come easily to me, so who really knew who the demon lurking within me truly was? Perhaps I shouldn't personify them lest they get any smart ideas. Especially when lack of sleep thinned the veil.

Gradually, the colors around me dimmed, and I grew tired of walking through the woods. No surprise, as it was now twenty minutes later, and the coffee had worn off.

"Is it odd we haven't come across many Players?" I wrinkled up my face as I looked through the woods, fully aware I asked this question almost every day.

"The disparity between free agents and Crimson Shadow is worrying." Ren stood up beside me as if she could assist in my directionless glare. "I can't imagine it's meant to be this . . . sparse."

I nodded but had little to add that wouldn't sound melodramatic. It felt as though the world was against us, with any allies few and far between. Well, just Hannah at this point, although the barkeep had been amiable. Didn't seem too bothered about the assassination attempt, but he had a solid customer-service voice. If the island hadn't been sending new Players across, then that might be part of the equation. If it only took a couple of weeks to level out of this area, then perhaps that was painting a more plausible picture.

"I took a chance in aiming to go only for the toughest Quests to level quicker." She looked up at me. "There's probably a lot of exposition we missed out on."

It wasn't her fault, and I offered a warm smile as a consolation prize. "It's fine. If I wanted an easy life, I wouldn't be here with you two."

"*Dickbag.*" She exhaled through her nose. "You sure about this Dungeon?"

"I'm sure it'll be dangerous, but it's guaranteed experience, right? Walking around hoping to run into random Quests and avoid the Shadow will just get us tired and killed. You have reservations?"

Ren paused for a second, then shook her head. "It's the smart choice."

Something was going unsaid there, but I didn't push her further. My brain felt like a handful of broken stone rather than something solid I could wield around. I needed my wits to pull together if we were going to get through whatever the Dungeon could offer. It *would* be my greatest show yet.

I wondered how many times I could tell myself that before even I grew tired of the cliché. At least *once* more, I hoped.

Another hour later and my feet were aching from my poor choice in footwear. I had been enduring it for a while, but my ability to smile and carry on was a few cards short of a full deck after my terrible sleep. I leaned against a tree to try to stretch them out.

"Ren, I don't suppose you have any good boots I could wear?"

She stopped and raised an eyebrow, waiting to hear the reason first—in case I had a trick or something in mind, maybe.

"You know how I love to suffer, so this *is* a true cry for help." I doubted the System would care about trying to heal up some blisters, and I didn't want any more agony in the Dungeon than it was already offering.

"I have some basic boots with no stats. Can't you switch to your equipped gear?"

Slowly, I shook my head with a wince. "My equipped footwear . . . is a pair of sandals. I may have foolishly discarded the other boots I had found."

"Sandals," she repeated, a blank expression on her face as she passed over the black boots.

There was no question that she knew what those were but was clearly trying to imagine me clopping about the woods with my bare feet barely gripping to them. Even worse than my dress shoes—but the Stats were important.

"I'll just stick these in my Cosmetic and store the dress shoes for a more appropriate time."

Wolf came to the side and sat down as he watched me swap footwear around.

Ren tilted her head. "Like a funeral?"

"They *were* murder on my heels," I said as I grinned at her. "So . . . eventually." I lifted one of the offending shoes into the air and made the motion of pushing it into my mouth, instead placing it in my Inventory.

Ignoring the rolling eyes of the elf, I hopped back onto my freshly booted feet. A new lease on life granting me a few minutes of contentedness before I found something else to rain on my parade.

Actual rain, now approaching, would be most likely culprit. As if my thoughts could twist the ear of narrative intent, gloomy clouds filtered over the sky as we progressed. Once the gray blanket had obscured the previously bright sky, a light rainfall started to patter among the leaves.

"Hate rain," Wolf grumbled, eyeing up the surroundings in the hope of finding more cover.

"I like it." Ren held her hand over her brow to look up toward the canopy, the drab weather almost sapping away some of her own drabness.

I found the middle ground between the two opinions. "It's nice to watch, but I don't want to get ill being out in it too long."

"You're in luck then, trickster." Ren pointed out ahead of us, slightly to the right. "We are here."

Between the gaps in the tree line, a mound of wrapped vines and aged bark sat shadowed under the gloom of the day.

The Dungeon.

CHAPTER FORTY-THREE

Wooden Response

Dungeons were an oddity in the System. While most of the world had degrees of procedural randomness to mimic a normal world, Dungeons were a construct more akin to a puzzle. Something for me to try to solve. In the times I had the energy and inclination to repeat one, it became obvious that they were set pieces. Same Monsters and same traps. Combat was more fluid and affected success more than anything else once you knew the rooms. This never helped the first attempt, of course, which was the crux of why they were so deadly.

[Dungeon: Fallen Grove]
[Open—Expected difficulty: Medium]

I pulled a face. "Nice of the System to forewarn us." I looked at the portal entrance. A swirling vortex of pale green and brown enshrined in the thick vines covering the area. *"Medium difficulty."*

"I wouldn't trust that." Ren glared at the shimmering doorway. "Something tells me that the System has a skewed view on what is difficult."

Another reasonable take. When an arrow to the neck could end our adventuring careers early, any trap worth its weight should be taken as being above medium difficulty. "Probably just means the Monster levels." I scrunched my tired eyes up to try to bring some life into them. Maybe the Dungeon would have lodgings with soft beds—even a little café and gift shop to make the whole process pleasant and pedestrian. Now I really was losing my sanity.

"I'm ready." Wolf pushed up against me, eager to get out of the rain.

"Lead on, trickster."

With a sigh, I straightened out my jacket and walked toward the portal. Half expecting to be tossed into a spiked pit immediately, I was almost disappointed that after a brief moment of wavy vertigo I stepped into an empty chamber.

Constructed of rough gray stone, it looked long abandoned. Vines and spent leaves covered most of the walls and some parts of the floor. Lanterns sat in small alcoves cut into the walls sporadically, spreading a light glow across the room toward the single exit—an open doorway to a corridor that went to the left immediately.

I stepped to the side as Ren and then the bear walked through behind me.

"Initial impressions?" My eyebrows raised, and I crossed my arms.

"I'm glad the hallways look wide enough for Wolf." She gave him a pat on his flank. "How did you want to approach this?"

Not being able to take our big pal through with us would have been detrimental to our success. While I didn't want to just push him forward to absorb all the danger, he at least needed to be present to assist when things got dicey.

I spun on my heels, the spear now in my hand when I came back to face them. "We'll have to do this old-school. I'll go first, and we'll take it slowly." I tapped the blunt end on the stone floor for added effect.

Ren didn't respond at first, as if processing something, before she blinked and an eyebrow raised. "Old-school?"

"Yeah," I nodded. "I had a . . . friend?" Now the word seemed awkward, but at the time it was true, to a degree. "Back at school, he was into the whole role-playing thing and was relentless with filling my head with information. First, you need a large pole."

"Can we start over?" She shook her head. "I think I lost you about three times there."

"It was the friend bit, right?" I grinned and held the spear up. "To poke around the floor for traps, I guess."

Ren rolled her eyes. "This room doesn't look like it needs assailing. Shall we take a minute to prepare?"

I narrowed my eyes. "If you make me another coffee, I would be greatly indebted to you."

"How indebted?" She put her hands on her hips. Wolf shuffled uncomfortably.

My tongue rolled across my teeth. I *really* needed that coffee, and there was almost a tangible feeling of my inner self starting to unravel. I'd rather not see what lurked within the core. "Name your price."

"Alright, you'll owe me a favor."

Before I had the chance to process or agree, she already had the grill and kettle out. I shrugged at the apprehensive bear. How bad could owing her a favor be? "Hungry, Wolf?" I withdrew some steak and lobbed it to him as he nodded, snapping it out of the air. We'd need to gather some more supplies at some point. Some of my meat reserves were getting low.

Not a sentence I expected my brain to ever have to think.

"Here." Ren passed me the steaming mug. "Hope it'll be worth it."

"I'd walk into the maw of a dragon for a strong brew on a bad day." I lifted it up to take in the smell. Bliss.

"Noted." She went into her Inventory to get her own food out.

It was perhaps the most mundane start to a Dungeon possible, but with the addition of a pair of chairs, we had ourselves a small picnic. There was a gloomy dampness to the chamber, but after walking all morning, it was heavenly just to rest and recuperate for a handful of minutes. In a way, I felt safer in here between these unknown walls. If I closed my eyes, it almost reminded me of some backstage areas. The feeling grounded me, just as the caffeine soaked back into my bones.

"I feel like I could destroy giants." I grinned as I stretched out, our late breakfast now all packed away.

"You never want an ego big enough that you'd die falling from it." Ren tapped at one of her side pouches. "Although I'm sure you could pull it off doing some of your usual bullshit."

I gave her a bow. "Your faith in me is almost as uplifting as the coffee was." Perhaps I needed to tone it down a bit. While the warm liquid had filled in the cracks of my psyche to give it the appearance of an unblemished surface, if anything, it was just adding fuel to the fire that had been growing from embers since I'd arrived in this world.

Wolf stretched out and was ready, so with spear in hand, I walked toward the exit of the first chamber. I paused at the threshold and observed the frame. More fool me to make it one step and get eviscerated because the Dungeon constructor was especially devious.

Nothing looked untoward, so I stepped forth. Immediately, I was completely whelmed. To the left, a short staircase that led to a closed stone door. Although there was a lantern by me and one down by the door, the stairs themselves were partially obscured by the gloom.

Without needing to say anything, Ren went and brought one of the lanterns from the chamber. I placed the spear tip through the curved handle to extend it over the darkened area. Our caution was soon rewarded, as among the littering of leaves and aged vegetation clawing at the edges of the staircase, there was a step that looked *off*.

"Pressure plate, I think." Ren pointed it out, her eyes better than mine.

I crouched down and surveyed the surroundings. "The ceiling looks different to the rest, like it's intentionally obscured. I imagine there's something that swings down from there."

"There's also a trip wire near the door." Ren crouched down beside me. "Can't see what it does from here."

"Devious." I smiled at her. How her eyes remained so bright and energized in this . . . I shook the thoughts mentally. "Right." I stood back to my feet. "Watch me mess this up and turn into bloodied mist."

Neither of them tried to stop me or said any last words of encouragement . . . *that it was nice to have known me.* My feet took me cautiously down each step, my eyes switching between the pressure plate that definitely needed avoiding and the ceiling full of death. I made it to the bottom unhindered and shot a thumbs-up to the others. "Let me check the wire first."

The last thing I needed was the bear stumbling down after us, crushing our bodies into the door and setting both traps off. They nodded their agreements, so I turned and knelt down by it. A tense cord ran from one wall to the other, around ankle level, about a foot and a half from the door. With my finger, I traced the path into the wall, trying to imagine where it could lead. There was part of my understanding of magic that helped fill in some of the gaps with rough assumptions.

A purple card spun into my hand, and I cut through the cord. I could hear the two up the stairs physically tense up, whereas I didn't move a muscle. Frozen, I waited for the hint of a sound or slight movement. Nothing. "Interesting," I muttered and gestured for them to descend. Some kind of door lock or alarm, to alert the inhabitants of our arrival or keep us out. Such a simple thing that would set a Party on the back foot through the whole encounter. Nice of the two traps I'd come across to be tension related and easily solved by cutting.

I placed my hand softly on the door as the other two carefully made it down to shuffle in behind me. Enough room for Wolf but he couldn't exactly move to the front. If there were traps, it would be better for me to continue leading anyway. My eyebrow raised as I turned to them, my words caught in my mouth as Ren put her hand against my upper arm.

"Are you alright, Max?"

My brain spun around briefly. Odd time to have some emotional exposition, and physically the traps hadn't maimed me. "I believe so. Why?"

"There's . . . It's probably nothing. Just a bad feeling." Her hand withdrew, leaving me somewhat perplexed. There was concern in her glare.

I blinked, trying mentally to parse that situation. "I'm expecting combat beyond the door. After I enter, I'll swing to the right to make space for Wolf."

The bear nodded, and so did the elf after a brief moment of consideration. I wasn't sure how troubled I should be that she worried for me but didn't know why. I hated premonitions almost as much as I hated having my head split open. Which was *a lot.*

Fingers tucked into the handle indentation, I opened it to the side as quickly as my strength would allow. The stone doorway slid into the wall on one side with a deep grinding noise.

I stepped into the square chamber, to the tune of six pairs of eyes turning to me in surprise. Four figures sitting at a table on the top left, playing . . . *cards*. Two more standing to my direct right in the corner, discussing something over a held book.

[New Monster: Treant <6>]

While the System filled in the specifics, the treelike Monsters were something else to behold. Seemingly made of wooden trunks and thick roots themselves, their shoulders and heads covered in dense mosslike foliage. Their humanoid faces looked sinister as their deep-set eyes were cold yellow light among shadowed recesses. They also didn't appear to appreciate my unwelcome entrance. Needed more fanfare, surely.

Two cards already left my hand toward the pair on the right as I strode toward them. The purple card embedding and severing some of the first Treant's thick arm, where the Hellhound card struck the book, my canine friend leaped out of a magic circle to cling to the opponent. The second Monster lurched to swipe out at me.

Ren's <Entangling Shot> blasted through the room and pinned the table-bound four as they tried to rise against us, right before the large form of Wolf burst through the doorway after the elf and charged the short distance toward them.

<Card Fan> blocked the slashing tips of the vegetative fingers, and as the Monster rose back to follow up, I withdrew the lit torch into my left hand. The Treant shirked away from the sudden appearance of fire and allowed me to press the advantage as my right hand now swung in, holding my dagger. Embedded straight into the pit of their left eye, and they screeched. Arrow struck the side of their head as they stepped back. They went for one last-ditch attempt to grab at me, and I moved away, a sheet of cloth suddenly obscuring their vision. Empowered single card straight into their chest, destroying what I assumed was their heart.

The cloth fluttered to the floor, revealing my showman's bow as the light faded from their eyes. Carnage was being wreaked in my peripheral as Wolf disassembled Treant and furniture alike in a fury of heavy paws. Splinters and shards of wood clattered and slid across the stone floor as he tore through everything. My Hellhound had caused some damage to the one remaining by me but wasn't really built for breaking through their tough bark-like skin.

Weapons gone, I flipped my hat to the floor, turning as I drew one crossbow to fire the loaded bolt into the side of the Treant's head. I dropped it to my hat as I drew the second with a turn to repeat the process. As they hit my upturned top hat, they vanished as if they had fallen inside. The Treant stumbled away with two bolts lodged in their head, the lights in their eyes dimming. My boot stomped to the floor, and the spear ejected out of my hat into my grip. With a short flourish, I jammed it through the wooden neck with a fatal crack.

I turned, spinning the spear further to see if my assistance was required. Wolf had finished off the other four already and now was just chewing and cracking their remaining pieces. Perhaps it was good for his dental health. With the tip of the spear, I flipped my hat back up off of the floor and onto my head. Shot Ren a grin. "I know. You can say it." I was insufferable.

She sighed. "Frankly, it's stunning both that you do that intuitively and that it actually works most of the time."

Stunning. That was a new one. I hadn't even paid any attention to the Dazzle icons this time around, but I was sure she wouldn't have had one. Things had just seemed to flow, like my exhausted brain allowed things to happen on autopilot. Smoothing over the gaps where I might usually overthink.

Why my autopilot defaulted to near-slapstick violence was something I would think about later.

I knelt down and pulled a face as I went to loot the Monsters. Not only did they not drop gold, but a lot of their loot was . . . assorted tree parts? Not even planks, just vines or bark. My brow furrowed harder at them, as if that would reveal some secret items they were holding back from me.

"You seem unimpressed, Max." Ren tilted her head as she watched me rifle through the bodies a second time.

With a shrug, I stood. "I was hoping for more of a show . . ." A wry grin formed at the side of my mouth. "But their performance was rather . . . *wooden.*"

CHAPTER FORTY-FOUR

Polished Woodwork

The world was created for us. Although that sounded egotistical, there could be no other explanation than there was some thought given to the fact that we were intended to experience what it had to offer. The levels of Monsters in certain areas, the dangers in Dungeons, Quests that took you through conflict for the chance of Reward—all were made with the intent that you should grow at a certain pace. It wouldn't be easy, and you could die along the way, but there was a route to follow. We often found ourselves taking shortcuts, having our own ideas for what we wanted. Taking the offerings piecemeal and leaving the suggested paths to gather dust.

It took a few minutes before Ren would even talk to me again after the bad pun. Still worth it though. I rolled out my shoulders. "There's a necklace here. Increase to radiant Damage?"

"Definitely need." Ren flexed her hand out in anticipation to grab the loot from me.

Nothing much worthwhile for me, so far. I handed it over and rubbed at my eye sockets. It was now three rooms since the first, and whatever energy I had was quickly wearing off. There wasn't much appetite to stop again so that I could refuel—which was probably a good thing. If I got reliant on the caffeine to get by, then we'd run into problems once it ran out.

I yawned. "Just to forewarn you, I'm liable to get grumpy soon. I apologize if I snap."

They exchanged glances.

"*You*, trickster? You'd wish your own murderer a good day as they plunged the knife into your heart."

I rubbed the back of my neck and shuddered. "Why would you put that out into the world?" I wasn't that bad, was I?

Wolf wasn't looking too sharp either. After another dozen Treants, he was getting pretty bored with wooden Monsters that weren't very edible. He had tried, of course, and the vomited regrets lay in one of the prior rooms. You could only have so much of a good thing. Bad things too.

With a sigh, I shuffled part of the latest inert corpse away from my feet. "Say, Ren . . . This isn't, like . . . against your beliefs or anything?"

She furrowed her brow at first. "Oh? No, not really. I have an affinity for the woodlands, but I'm not a 'wood elf' as you might understand it."

Watching her do the air quotes was amusing and perhaps a reminder that this wasn't a world based on my own pop-culture references. "For some reason, Oathwarden sounded like something where—"

"Where I had promised to protect the forest, nature, or life? Something cliché like that?" She tilted her head.

I nodded. "Although maybe that's closer to what Wolf has then?"

"I like to eat meat," he complained, only halfway between the conversation and his own rumbling thoughts.

With a grin, I looked over at the next doorway. The inside of the Dungeon proper hadn't really had traps—with the Treants presumably living here, that would make it inefficient. Still, I kept my eyes out as best as I could. I trusted the System to betray my complacency, so I would try not to give it the satisfaction. "So, what is your oath to protect?"

"It's complicated." She avoided my inquisitive gaze. "A longer story for an easier day."

That was fair enough. All things in time, and it wasn't exactly important information right now. I looked at my hands. A little blood, but nothing terrible. I had been managing my Mana a lot better and not exerting so much. Using my Inventory tricks often allowed enough time to regenerate a sufficient amount of the magical power to not constantly burn out. Having Wolf about to manhandle more than his fair share of combatants also made things less stressful on me. Once again, I was thankful for our third Party member.

I placed my hand against the cold stone of the door, wondering who did all the masonry, seeing as the Treants lived here. Perhaps it was something prior? Or maybe the System didn't think too hard about that kind of thing. Was *I* thinking too hard about this kind of thing? My tired eyes idly went back around the room. There might even be lore among all these books and containers. Neither of the other two had seemed concerned about doing a little learning in here.

As they nodded their readiness, I pushed through into the next chamber. This one was different. No enemies, and one side was curved instead of squared off. A recessed part on the right was filled with water like a shallow pool, and said water had an almost unnatural blue hue to it.

Wolf went to push past.

"Nope." I held my arm outstretched to keep him in place—a fool's errand given his massive size and strength, but he did stop.

He pouted and looked up at me with bright amber eyes, reflecting the light from the water. "But I'm thirsty from all the wood."

Ren tried to push through too. "It's not normal water. Probably some sort of Treant juice."

Exactly my thoughts, as amusing as her choice of phrasing was. Perhaps a translation hiccup. With no way of properly detecting magic or what the effects might be, I wasn't about to risk getting ill or cursed from it. "Best we just pass it?"

The bear looked a little forlorn at the prospect of missing out but relented to our caution. Ren nodded to agree with me, her blue eyes even more dazzling in this chamber. It would still be here if it turned out to be useful for the Dungeon progress—I imagined some places might have puzzles . . .

I stopped and knelt down beside the pool, feeling the sudden glare of the elf on the side of my head. Perhaps it would be useful . . . Like, maybe a magical fire covering a doorway that could only be put out with this water. Or it was used to regrow part of a root that blocked our route. It surely wouldn't hurt to scoop a little up—I had an empty potion bottle in my Inventory, after all.

But then . . . I could just use my hands too. I stared at the surface, as it shimmered with light movement. It looked so inviting. I bet it was really cool and calming. After all, I was tired and definitely deserved a rest more than my companions. So selfish of them to deny me this. *The fucks.*

Yet, I didn't move. My eyes blinked away a blur that had covered them, and I stood up. "Huh," I said and stepped over toward the door. Ren had a look of concern across her face again, but all I did was look at the pool of water for a bit, just in case. Then, with a warm feeling in my chest like a flickering flame, I stopped looking at it. Simple and nothing to worry about.

"You haven't summoned Roger yet, not that I'm complaining."

I turned my head back to look at Ren. "True, I wasn't sure how much he'd like to be a wood person." There was another reason, but I couldn't grasp what. Maybe I was just tired enough already and didn't need his crazed antics grating on me. That'll do for now—I pushed that excuse into the void to fill the gap so I didn't have to think about it further. For some reason, the exhaustion gave me less patience for who I was or what I could do.

The next room was longer than the rest and slightly wider, with a tall ceiling. Roots and vines ran up the walls to host a large bulb in the middle of the roof. Green and blue hues shimmered across the chamber as a podium illuminated within and filled with water stood in the center. There was little else inside other than something that looked like a long treasure chest on the opposite wall but was more likely a carved bench.

I narrowed my eyes up at the large bulb as Ren stood next to me. Easily a dozen feet in diameter in the shade of dull red, I imagined it either held a beautiful flower or something macabre that was going to try to eat us. Despite having a moderate Luck stat, I was erring toward the latter option.

"If this is the boss room," I ventured, "I'd rather not find out what that does the hard way."

"There is a doorway out of here, so it may not be." She gestured with the tip of her bow to the side wall, where an exit was overgrown with vines and vegetation.

"Can I drink *that* water?" Wolf pressed his large head in between us to look at the raised area.

"Unlikely, friend." I made the mental note to start storing more liquids when I had the chance. Maybe a large dog bowl—although that seemed condescending. Thinking about it, a few large glass containers filled with water—or worse—could be a nice addition to my repertoire. Especially if I started messing around with fire, which seemed like an inevitability.

"I could just shoot the bulb from here." Ren tilted her head. "If you think it'll attack us."

What *didn't* want to kill us? At this point, it felt like steam was coming off of my brain. This was some manner of puzzle to access the boss room, I was almost sure of it—as if part of me could just read between the lines of the Dungeon. One last trap or encounter to wear us down before we headed into the true danger. My normally astute mind was lagging behind. With only the barest notion of what I was meant to do, I started to gather fragments of a plan together.

"It's a puzzle." I yawned and rubbed at my eyes. "Let me go look and then if it eats me, you can shoot it."

I stepped forward, not waiting for the confirmation, and put my hands in my pockets as I made my way around the outside walls. Although I wasn't immediately assailed by anything, there was an uncomfortable feeling the closer I walked over to the raised podium with the water atop it. My nose wrinkled up as I looked between it and the plant looming above me. Following the roots that ran down from around it, they all seemed to stop at points along the stone floor.

Air exhaled from my nose. The ticking of a watch inside my head as gears worked around. The podium of water, the trough atop it about a foot square, didn't seem to have any markings or places that could move or indent. Ren watched me from the entrance still, an interest in her face to see what I would conclude. While disassembling a puzzle or trap wasn't entirely similar to working out how a trick was performed, there was a familiar thread of deductive reasoning. Not that I had the hubris or mental energy to pat myself on the back any harder for my supposed Intelligence for realizing that.

Wolf had checked out long ago and looked to be trying to get something out from underneath one of his claws. Wood pulp, most likely.

"The bulb appears to be parched. Judging from the slight lines on the floor where the light moss has been disturbed, I assume that it drinks from this offering pool to rejuvenate."

Ren nodded slowly. "The bowl is full, yet it does not feed?"

I glanced back up at the large bulb. Perhaps a particular spell or phrase woke it up? Had our disdain for the written word left us with a missing answer? It was probably a simple thing. I shouldn't get ahead of myself when my brain was already rattling around. Too many sharp edges in here that I might trip and strike my battered skull on.

In my Equipment, I swapped my gloves to being shown—and now some rather gaudy light-brown gloves appeared on my hands. They were nice enough for their purpose. Useful. I clapped them together, and then an empty glass bottle was between them as they parted. Cautiously, I stepped up to the water and scooped a portion out, not wanting to look into whatever was illuminating it.

Once contained, it looked relatively normal except for the slight blue hue to it that remained. I still *wanted* to drink it. Delicious and refreshing, undoubtedly. My lips felt dry, so I licked them. I gradually raised the bottle toward my mouth, eagerness dancing in my eyes.

"*Max!*"

And then it was gone, as I put it in my Inventory. I shot the Oathwarden a sheepish grin and no longer felt the need to drink it. If my brain had been sharper, I would have done that immediately. Whatever effect the tainted water had didn't seem to work when stored away, as evidenced by my lack of desire to withdraw it even though it took little more than a conscious thought to do so.

I stepped over to the largest of the partially withered roots that led up to the bulb and gestured for them to be ready. Ren drew an arrow, and Wolf hunkered down, ready to pounce. Partially, I wanted to pause my action for a bit to draw out the tension but wasn't so keen to test my arrow-catching abilities on the fly.

Into my gloved hand, the glass bottle. As soon as I could grasp it, I poured it out atop the root. It splashed, dampening the vegetative appendages as well as the floor around it. Nothing immediately happened, as if it was waiting for me to make a note of such out loud so it could surprise us. I held up a hand to keep the others silent, and I called the bulb's bluff. I wouldn't be beaten at my own game.

Eventually, with a begrudging creak, the petals slowly opened as the roots slithered across the stone to the podium. The reds and ambers within the bulb as it bloomed were much more vibrant than the outside, and it pulsed with a rose glow. No giant teeth or barbed vines to assail us with.

The roots went up into the stone basin and drank from the odd water. Why it was already full was beyond me, but it seemed to give the plant life—and as it pulsed and brightened, the vegetative coverings over the door began to crack and shift away.

"Not the strangest lock I've seen." Ren shrugged and relaxed her bow.

At her word, a brighter pulse came from the flower. Tiny motes of pollen burst down around us, saturating the air before we had a chance to cover our mouths. I winced, and we ran for the exit, pushing it open and closing it right behind us.

I took a gasp of air to find that I felt . . . reasonably fine.

"It's a curse." Ren deflated. "Nothing dire, but you can see it on your Status window."

[Curse: Fallen Grove Pollen—Exhaustion, Mana burn, reduced Stats for (1) day]

The joke was on the System—I was *already* exhausted. I hadn't seen Mana burn before, so I brought up the description. Magic Skills were twice as effective but used three times as much Mana. That almost seemed like a buff in the short term. Living for a whole day causing agony to my hands might make me change my tune on that.

I rose my eyes to see the room that we had gotten ourselves into. Our short walkway was more of a bridge that led to a circular stone platform. Around this area was a moat of water. The walls were thick trunks and vines intertwined that rose up to a high domed ceiling. Blue light flooded the chamber from a large glowing crystal at the apex.

Due straight ahead of us was a large tree in the moat. Deep brown and aged wood, thick verdant leaves. It was a beautiful specimen, if you liked that sort of thing. Also very out of place, considering. With a nod, we started off down the bridge, and I wondered if either of them had noticed me swiping another bottle full of that liquid before we walked in. Not that I intended to deceive my Party members, but sometimes a good trick took a little calculated risk—and they may not appreciate that stance. I just had to prevent myself from drinking it.

As we stepped into the middle of the circular chamber, ripples in the water emanated from the trunk as two large arms rose out of the shallow pool. It wasn't just a tree, after all. Large eyes of bright yellow opened up as a crooked maw split in the middle of the trunk to grin at us. Although it went without saying that this had to be the boss of the dungeon, I had the—

[New Monster: Treant Elder <8 B>]

Oh. Thanks, System.

CHAPTER FORTY-FIVE

Root of the Issue

I never got tired of the taste of victory. Whether it was for gold and magical items or just to sleep a little better the next day. When you saw how much this world could wear you down, you clung to the good times. Finishing a Dungeon was an accomplishment, even if it left you feeling as though you had been pushed through a grinder. Sometimes they weren't as rewarding as doing Quests, but they were contained. You could complete them without worrying about outside interference . . . :)

Throughout the Dungeon, Treants hadn't seemed to be too impressed with my magical tricks. I wasn't sure whether it was something to do with their culture, perhaps, or their minds just didn't work the same way. Maybe they could just see through it, like Ren could. Either way, I didn't fancy my chances with dazzling the large one now emerging from the surrounding pools. Which was a shame, as it always felt good to win over a critic.

Wolf slid across the stone, already snarling with a pulse of amber energy flowing over his fur. I dropped an Imp to the floor beside me and started spinning up a purple card. Ren let off a radiant arrow to strike into the boss. The tree was slow; we shouldn't have had trouble keeping at range from it—especially with the bear constantly on it.

The <Smite Shot> struck the Monster, but the flare of light didn't seem to do much to dissuade him from continuing toward us, closer to dry land. In my peripheral, I saw movement.

"Ren, look out!" I shouted, throwing my card toward her. She dove to the floor as a barbed root lunged for her. I twisted my magical attack and sliced it lengthwise, the appendage shuddering and shrinking away. It was long, reaching from the moat and across the circular platform to grab at her. Undoubtedly to try to drag her toward the foul waters.

The elf was already up into a crouch and leveling an arrow toward me. Well, past me—I hoped—at another vine. I turned as she let it loose to see the thick vegetative tentacle raise up and be impaled by the shot. From my hand, a card went out to sever the tip and then return like a boomerang.

Around the room were several more that weren't an immediate threat, but I seemed the best equipped to deal with them. They didn't seem to care for Wolf but waved in the air as if to signal they were happy to become a problem for us at the back.

"Focus on the boss," I assured her. "I've got the vines."

From beside me, my Imp threw out his fireball, striking the Treant Elder in his dense canopy and igniting some of the leaves. The Monster seemed a lot less impressed with this show.

Wolf jumped away from the large fist of the boss, swiping and biting into the outstretched arm. An upswing from the other arm knocked him back slightly as a radiant shield absorbed some of the impact.

While the bear kept the large tree occupied, Ren started filling it with more arrows. I spun a card out around the room, circling the perimeter to zoom in to the closest vine, severing it. I held the card in motion, a slight pain in my hand. Second vine sliced and then I had to let it go. Wiped the blood from my fingers.

The curse was doing more damage; I was certain of it. Could almost feel the exact power I was putting into the cards—even with the minimum amount of effort, they were stronger and more durable than normal. I almost didn't want to split them as I could feel my Mana draining incredibly quickly. Even after throwing a handful out, my hands had bled from the exertion. Drips of crimson splattered against the gray stone beneath me. Currently uninjured, but that didn't stop me from risking doing worse to myself.

Ren hit the boss with an <Entangling Shot> as Wolf backed away so that she could heal him. Although he was holding up well, he had a nasty gash that ran from his shoulder down to his head.

Another fireball illuminated the chamber as it burst on the Treant, more flames coursing over his body.

A green light began to orbit around the tree Monster before a pulse of energy rocked the platform we were standing on. The floor began to glow with pale-green runes, and my eyes darted around to see where to escape to. Nowhere. The whole stone circle was awash with the light. Back to the bridge? It would take too long.

Vines burst up around each of us, almost in mimicry of Ren's skill. Except these were barbed. Sharp thorns dug into my right leg as I protected my left with a quickly drawn plank of wood. The others were pained, and my Imp faded away under the damage wreaked to his small, round body.

Magic card flew out to shred the vines away from the plank so I could step out of them. Wolf had burst from his, another glow of orange around his body. It looked like Ren had healed him so that he was prepared to engage the boss again. The elf seemed to be stuck among the vines, blood staining her leggings.

My right eye twitched, and my heart lurched to see her in pain even if it was minimal. I let another card go and threaded it between her calves, cutting through half of the vines so that she could use her sword on the rest. I carried the card on through to sever another creeping probe that was coming from the water on her side before letting it vanish. Imp card to the bridge behind us so that he had some high ground. My forearms ached from the constant casting.

More vines were on my side as another radiant arrow slammed into the boss in my peripheral. Fingers twitching, I dealt with the encroaching problems before they became anything more. I could almost feel the heat of the fireball as it went across the chamber, my Imp summons had been gunning hard for promotion with how well they were taking to this encounter. Effective Damage.

The Treant roared, plumes of water shooting up like jets around the circular area. With a loud hiss, the flames across his canopy were extinguished. His bark cracked and shed, revealing a darker ash-gray body, and his eyes swiveled to a red hue.

He looked angrier. *Even less likely to be Dazzled,* I sighed to myself. My wrists and hands ached to a degree that set my jaw clenched. Part of me wished for a chance to use all my tricks again instead of pure casting—although I shouldn't invite malady onto myself. Too late to take it back.

No corpses for Roger, which was a shame. As I watched Wolf gouge a chunk of wood from the tree, part of me felt bad for not inviting him on this adventure. Maybe I felt guilty that I only drew him to this world to enact violence in my name. Or maybe the fact that he was a demonic entity who only craved violence made me uncomfortable. Or too comfortable. I hadn't decided which.

The Treant began sucking in air, even as his new torso became peppered with arrows. He then leaned forward, pointing his half-burned branches toward us. His canopy changed hue slightly, as if the leaves were becoming thicker, or—

"Defend!" I yelled out, right before the burst happened.

As if mimicking a cannon blast, the boss blew all the leaves out right after they hardened, like scores of throwing stars. A wide cone that covered most of the chamber.

<Card Fan> protected me from the initial blast, only a few sharp leaves making it through to shred at my suit. Ren stood, bloody lines across her skin fading away as one hand held an emptying Health Potion, her other hand held out toward Wolf—her healing spell keeping the point-blank bear on his feet.

Even with that, long tracks of his fur had been scoured off but were now growing back. Wolf had even leaped closer to the boss immediately after the attack and clattered through the thinner branches, snapping them as he bit into the main body of the Treant. His claws tried to find purchase and dug through the eye sockets of the tree.

With some minor struggle, the boss faltered and fell to the ground. The bear tore a large chunk from him and went to town on crushing and ripping as much of the remaining body as he could.

I stretched out my bloody fingers. "Ah, well, that wasn't too bad for our first Dungeon boss, right?" My Imp sat down and played with his little pitchfork, awaiting his time to go. I let him vanish with a wave and dismissal.

Ren was breathing heavily and didn't look too pleased, but she nodded her agreement.

"Next one needs to be made of meat." Wolf sat glumly and began licking at his paws.

[Dungeon complete]
[Reward received]
[360 Gold]
[Mana Stones (2)]
[Antidote]
[Cloak of the Forest]

Ren grumbled as she looked at the body of the fallen tree. "Two tokens, after all of *that*."

"Anything else?" I wrinkled up my face in the hope those were not the only spoils.

She clicked her tongue. "Agility hat, Strength boots, a staff with Wisdom and Luck, and then gold and the usual stuff."

"Pass then." Who needed Wisdom when I had a cool *trickster* dagger?

A little pain and suffering for some medium reward. I'd still count it as a win. I equipped the cloak, which hung over my left shoulder and covered that arm. Exceptionally useful for obscuring that hand when bringing things out of nothing. I was enamored immediately. It even gave a small amount of Dexterity.

[Cloak of the Forest: +2 DEX]

The antidote removed curses, and I watched as Ren and Wolf both drank one, the latter struggling a little until the elf helped. Slightly unsure why, I feigned curing it with an empty bottle as she turned back. Something at the back of my mind liking the surge of new power, despite the cost. Well, the antidote was still there for after I had my fun—or had been admonished. Mana Stones appeared to be something to put in gear sockets, but I was yet to have anything of the sort. Still, I could swoosh the cape around, and it added a certain flare that seemed to immediately tire Ren's patience.

Just as I was finished flourishing it around, our gazes were drawn away as a portal opened up across the foot of the bridge back into the Dungeon. Similar in appearance to the one we had first entered by.

"And they just let us out like that. No need to backtrack?" I pulled a face and gestured toward it. Almost seemed *too* kind.

Ren sighed and stretched out her back. "Perhaps the System likes us after all."

Would be one of a few so far that did. I smiled to myself as I took in the scenery, now that it was calmer. The curse *was* annoying and felt like it was tugging at the edges of my patience—at the sensible me weary for a good sleep. But there was something beautiful about the place. Perhaps it was just wildly different from what I was used to. The bright lights of the stage, ruddy tones of hell, the plain brickwork of my dressing rooms, and bland hotel rooms. Hmm. Something wasn't right there, and my brain danced around the misunderstanding of the odd one out.

"Ready to go, trickster?"

Her voice took me out of probing further. "Sure. You ready, Wolf?" He nodded in response.

We gathered our wits and strength and made toward the portal.

"You know, I was thinking we should head to the town already—get some actual rest?"

The portal shimmered as I stepped back out into the light rainfall and cool air of the day. I turned to walk backward as my eyesight adjusted so that I could continue talking as Ren walked through behind me.

"Yeah? You could do with a bath," she said, some softness around her eyes.

Then they immediately sharpened.

Warm pain flooded my back as I was struck by something, and I spun to face four figures of shadow before us. The lowering bow one of them held painted the picture clear as day that my panicked muscles hadn't processed yet. Was my lung pierced? I held my breath and tried to focus.

Wolf burst out from between us, knocking me to the side before stumbling and dropping to the floor, unmoving. A spellcaster in the opposing group held a shape in his hands, some manner of enchantment or channeled spell. Not dead but down for the count.

A clatter sounded on the stone behind me as Ren dropped her bow, and I turned my head to see a fifth member had grappled her from behind. The burly man with a short goatee held a knife up to her throat.

"Well, well, well . . ."

My glare turned back to the group as a figure stepped forward. Each of them wore dark clothing and had a red handprint on their face. Crimson Shadow. My insides burned just at the sight of them. I was beyond exhausted now, the fire within me stoking something red-hot and eager for violence.

The ragged man, who looked like he had dropped his sanity down a well long ago and bathed himself in the suffering of others, continued toward us. Black hair and beard, slick with oil, and a wild look in cold eyes. A *dangerous* look, someone who killed even more freely than us. "Looks like Hadrian was right. You did survive the Bandits."

"What do you want?" I seethed. My heartbeat thundered in my chest. It was both a general question as well as one pointed to his current plans. My left hand beneath my cloak was tensed as if I could squeeze the life out of him from here. He was some sort of fighter, and they had a Ranger, two spellcasters, and the one with Ren was probably a Thief type. Not great odds. I wasn't a gambling man . . .

"It's always difficult to decide whether to kill the guy or girl first." He tutted and withdrew a shortsword made from a dark obsidian-colored metal, giving his group a leering glance. "I can see that look in your eyes though. You'll fight harder if you think you've got a chance of saving her . . . and luckily for you, my sword is itching for a little combat."

We couldn't have foreseen this. Not without living in constant paranoia that the enemy was around any corner. I clenched my jaw.

Still, I felt foolish to have been caught off guard. It could have been over so easily, our corpses a testament to our complacency. Still could be the end. Normally, I wasn't an angry person. But currently I was furious, shaking with rage. Something inside of me burned and fought for an escape. My incensed eyes turned back toward Ren and the man restraining her.

I trust you, she mouthed.

CHAPTER FORTY-SIX

Snap Shot

Life was fragile and fleeting in this world. Well, it was in my previous world too— but at that time it had been filled with significantly less violence and conflict. There was me and my job. Stress, sure, but I got by. Now I had murder on the mind and blood on my hands. A heart full of care for others that could just as easily fall and cease to exist. It was maddening, and all I could do was gnash my teeth together in rage and become stronger to keep them safe.

The grizzled man spat on the damp ground as he flourished his sword. "Here are the rules. You try to help the pretty little elf, Garren there will cut her throat open. You try to help the animal, and Henikk will put an arrow through his skull. This is just mano a mano."

Adrenaline and anger shook within me, a dangerous cocktail that had me drunk on bravado. He was full of it too. Considered himself something of a duelist or just liked toying with his prey.

"What if I kill you?"

His crooked smile widened. "Then you can kiss my ass in hell, as you three will be there soon after."

What a bind we found ourselves in. My breathing was slow despite the rage, and my back ached from where I had been shot. Thankfully, I had been able to activate a bandage in my hidden hand without them knowing. Still, even being back to full Health didn't exactly put me at even odds with someone built for melee fighting.

It wasn't like I had any other option but to perform my best. They had set the stage, and I knew what role I had to play. Already exhausted and drained from the day, I was in danger of slipping further past my autopilot and into something my subconscious was trying to hide away from. The part of the other Max. They intended to kill all of us either way, so I needed to think beyond the scope of just saving my own skin.

"Whenever you're ready then, asshole." My opponent flourished his sword again and got into a stance ready to attack.

"Prepare to be amazed." I grinned, mania grasping at the insides of my brain, trying to push through. "As this will be the finale for one of us."

My dagger spun into my right hand as I ran toward him. His confidence briefly shook as my attack from too far away with the short blade suddenly switched into the large two-handed axe. Sparks flew out as he blocked it, one of his defensive Abilities kicking in to enable him to weather the surprise strike.

"Smart fuck, are you?"

He slashed outward at my exposed torso, but the axe I held turned into the spear in a vertical position. I was knocked back from the force, but the wooden shaft took the brunt of the attack. It spun as I flourished it to create distance, then I went to throw it at him. He dove to the side, and the spear vanished. Instead a chair appeared in front of my boot already lashing out—kicking the furniture into him as he rolled back. Not really doing a great deal of damage, but the Dazzle icons were starting to rack up.

There was some amount of chuckling going on within his ranks that his death glare silenced as he stood back to his feet. Shame I couldn't see humiliation stacks—although the amount of increasing rage in his eyes did almost a good enough job.

"Some kind of object-creating Wizard, very fancy. I'm surprised Lady in Red didn't try to recruit you."

"Do you always monologue right before you die?" I seethed back at him. My eyes were wide, and blood ran from my right hand. It wouldn't take much for me to be cut down.

He growled, and his sword burst into green flames before he launched himself back at me. I drew a sword to block the first strike, another for the second. Being able to conjure things directly into my hand gave me better dexterity than trying to wield a single weapon into the right places to defend. Especially with my lack of actual melee proficiency. Weapons thudded onto the damp grass as I didn't have the time to properly swap, only draw anew and then release. Leave nothing to chance. Always using my right hand.

A cut across my right shoulder that drew blood. Then a near miss across my stomach that ripped my shirt but left my skin mostly unharmed. We circled as his attacks seemed unending. Anger in his eyes blazing away at failing to fell me and in being made to look foolish in front of his underlings. While my opponent was relentless, his mood was making his moves sloppy. More desperate to end me and gain back his standing. I didn't care. My ego was the only one here intending to be stroked. An ill task for a bloodied hand but a necessity all the same.

Plank of wood went up and split in half as I tried to stop one of his combat Abilities reaching me—the tip of his blade still pierced near my collarbone, causing me to twitch in pain. The follow-up was blocked by a second plank, which I vanished to then grab at his wrist. Whipped my head forward to headbutt him. I received a weak slash in return, my hat dropping to the ground as a line of warmth throbbed across the side of my head.

He stumbled backward, clutching at a broken nose. While I didn't have the Strength to do much Damage, I had at least wounded him with the surprise act. As much as I was tiring and slowly weakening due to only using one hand, the mental Damage I was causing to him gave rise to some odd elation within me. Bullshitting my way away from what should have been an easy kill for him.

"You're bloodied." I grinned. "Making *me* the victor."

"Fuckin' idiot." He spat on the grass. "You look like you're about to pass out from blood loss."

I raised my right fist to see that it was soaked in blood. My blood. I clenched it closed, causing drops to fall onto the grass. My right eye twitched from the constant pain. I had been ignoring it, but it had gotten to the point where the reveal was long overdue. Nothing more to gain except further cuts and potential death. It was time for me to take control of the performance.

"You'll have to forgive me," I said in a hushed, shaky tone, an uncomfortable feeling rising in my core. "A lot of this set I've never tried before. It might not be perfect."

"What are you . . . ?" His brow furrowed, voice cut off as I revealed my left hand.

Equally dripping with my own blood—but much more impressive was the card I held within it. Bright white, as if cut from the sun itself. The purple energy around it was all but scoured away by how much Mana I put into this. Not just all my Mana but more beyond that. Using the Treant curse I had poured and poured everything I could muster until the agony almost became enjoyable. Couldn't cast any other spells while holding it, so I had relied on my Inventory to bide time. A little twist to turn the tide and subvert expectations.

I was riding a high that was about to hit its peak, like a firework. Max was about to explode, and whatever was left would shock and awe . . . I only hoped what was left after was more than a spent casing when the dust had settled.

"Nice trick, but—"

The bloodied finger of my right hand rose to my lips, telling him to be quiet. I was shaking. Grinning from ear to ear. Manic. "This next part isn't suitable for all audiences."

I turned, and the card was gone. It cracked through the air like a lightning bolt, a near-instant transmission of energy from my grasp to the intended end point. There wasn't much option; there was *no* real option. I hoped I could be forgiven as my spent hands hung low. The afterimage of the power hung in the air between Ren and me. Surprise in both our eyes. I wasn't a gambling man, the thought once again sank from my slowly eroding mind. Yet with that one action, all our lives were on the line.

"Fuckin' dick," her restrainer growled, "now I'll slit her—"

He paused, confusion furrowing his brow as he could not move his arm. A line of crimson ran around his forearm by his elbow like a lit fuse. He jostled to try to get some feeling back into the limb, but with a slick slurping sound, the hand holding the knife lowered as his arm separated at the joint to drop to the ground.

My hands raised in the air. <Finale>. Shock radiated throughout the group as they stood, stunned. Lights painted the area, and I felt on top of the world. My greatest trick so far, perhaps—yet the show was not over. The blood loss made me lightheaded, and even with the dopamine coursing through my system, the anger had not abated. What they had tried to do to Ren. How they intended to kill Wolf and even me. Unexpected. Unpalatable. Unforgivable.

Ren stamped on the Thief's foot and flung her head back into his face to knock him away.

I turned my head toward the ringleader—or was that a circus thing? Purple electricity danced around my body as I smiled calmly. The demon dove I had dropped immediately after sending off the magic card swooped up from the shadows and into the spellcaster's face, trying to peck at his eyes. It was enough to disrupt the sleeping enchantment that had persisted through the brief stun, and Wolf began to stir.

Ren rolled forward to pick up her bow, leaping into the air in the same motion to draw her <Smite Shot> back at the stumbling Thief. Too quick for him, the radiant shot blew straight through his neck.

Their Ranger let loose an arrow toward the bear, but my <Card Fan> appeared in front of him to block the shot. Agony through my hands at the first time I had used the shield away from my own body. Wolf stood and roared, two different Skills activating and pulsing around his body, painting the drab area in bright lights. Beautiful in its own way.

For my efforts in protecting him, I received the sharp end of the dark sword straight into my side. It was uncomfortable in the way it sliced through skin and muscle and jabbed around in my precious internal organs. I was disjointed from the pain now. Distant, dissociating. Too heavy a day for the part of me that was still soft. But part of me lived for *this*. Heavenly, among the hellish scene.

Lazily, I turned my head to him. "I'm sorry. Max is not home right now."

The crossbow in my hidden left hand fired a bolt into his thigh, and he stumbled back as I dropped the ranged weapon to switch to the second loaded one, firing a bolt into his other thigh. He lashed out at me and tore a gash through my cloak and left arm.

I brought my right arm around with a plank of wood, numbing his arm and causing his grip to falter. He dropped the blade, and then it was mine. I brought it out as he dropped to his knees, his legs weakening. Held it to his neck.

"Are you the ones that destroyed the outpost?" I crackled with energy. My face loomed up close to his as the tip of the sword drew blood.

"Eat shit."

"I don't have any. But I have this." My left fist swung around and smashed him in the face, the glass I held breaking and covering us both in the contents. He sputtered and choked, a mouth open but spewing no apologies or regrets. I filled it with the hot end of the torch, igniting the spilled oil.

Their healer attempted to cast something on him as I rose to face them. An arrow struck his knee, and the spell faltered. I was already upon him, even though I barely registered moving. Just a blur of purple and anger. I heard the rip and tear of muscle and sinew as Wolf broke the screaming Wizard into more digestible pieces in the background. The Ranger lay dead already, an arrow in the head not the most becoming fashion trend, but he wore it well.

"You're going to talk," I hissed and pulled the man closer to me. "Or I'm going to open up your skull and retrieve the information with a fucking spoon." Into my hand, a spoon emerged. A very real threat.

He was faltering. Face pale, the sudden shock of the bullies getting their just desserts making him doubt every decision that led him to this point. His watery blue eyes tried to search me. I'm not sure what for. Did I feel different? Maybe it was the blood loss.

"Where is Lady in Red?" I pressed my bloodied forehead against his so I could stare into his eyes, draw the information that I craved. I could always take the eyes out if he didn't want them. Feed them to him, make him see that his tongue wasn't offering up the goods.

"S-she's across the river now, past the Golden F-Fields." His mouth trembled.

Purple cards burst over my hands and spun like saws, cutting through his neck and spraying me with arterial blood. Comforting. I dropped the limp body and stood, contented. The rain was loud now, combat having abated, as if I hadn't even noticed the inclement weather until now. My heartbeat thudded in my head as I idly twisted a bandage around in my left hand. I stared off into the horizon, trying to ignore . . . all of this. Show was done; I was spent. Max must go on. *They had to suffer.*

"*Max?*"

I turned my gaze to the side to see Ren with an arrow leveled at me. An interesting white energy circled the arrow in a slow spiral. She lowered it, no scowl upon her face, but worry.

"Everything okay?" I asked. As soon as I spoke the words, agony immediately rushed over me like a switch had been flipped. I stumbled and held my hands up.

Both pure red, my left one also embedded with glass. My suit was soaked through in several places, especially my side, where it felt as if someone had thrown a match inside me to cook my organs from within.

"Your eyes . . . They . . . Here—" She held her hand out, and her radiant healing flooded through me. Oddly uncomfortable at first but then soothing and warm.

I groaned and sat back, a chair appearing underneath me. My eyes burned, that was for certain. Across from us, the leader of the group lay aflame like a bonfire, flickering against the light rain. Wolf was eating his fill of the others behind.

Catching her eye, I placed a second chair beside me, and she sat. Not even the heat from the fire warmed me. I felt cold and empty.

"The Wizard had this on him. You think it was used to track you? Since we keep getting ambushed?"

I turned my eyes over to a page she held. It looked like a child's drawing, a crayon approximation of a man in a purple suit with magic runes plastered on the rest of the paper. For all that I could muster, I just shrugged and groaned.

The elf ripped it in half and then into further pieces that fluttered away in the air.

"I didn't take my antidote," I admitted, the empty feeling allowing some truths to slide out.

She shuffled in her chair. "Figured. Why didn't you say? To avoid the argument, or some things just have to be a surprise?"

My face screwed up as I couldn't take my eyes away from the burning corpse. "Closer to the latter. I'm not trying to hide things from you both . . . I just . . ." I shuddered as my aching body tried to relax against the wounds I had accumulated. "Part of it is the need to grandstand. Have all these little tricks and options only known to me. It's not something done with malicious intent."

"Okay," she replied. "Secrets aren't good, but you don't have to tell me everything. As long as you're acting in good faith for the Party."

I managed to look toward her tired blue eyes. "Always. I promise, and I'm sorry."

With a nod, we both sank back into the morose silence. Listening to the rain. Being alive and drawing breath for another day.

"I think I'd like to go to the town now," she eventually ventured, when we had been doused with enough of the light rainfall to make this untenable any longer.

"I could definitely use a bath." I stared out blankly at the far distance. Idly, I worked through another bandage or two to try to repair whatever the System thought was dire enough. I tried not to look at the Health Report to see what was exactly wrong. Too much, for certain. But it wouldn't list what really mattered.

The shards of glass dropped from my hand as I raised it, the healing ejecting the painful objects to fall to the grass.

The demonic dove fluttered over and sat on my numb hand, tilting its bloodied beak to observe me. I wasn't sure if I could spare the energy to thank it out loud, so mentally I commended it for its service.

"Max . . ." Ren began, staring out at the corpse crackling from the heat of the burning oil as she stood. "Do you think your Class is more . . . literal?"

"*Demonic Magician*," I murmured, savoring a taste I didn't yet understand.

CHAPTER FORTY-SEVEN

Beyond the Shadows

A magician that summoned demons. It seemed simple on the surface. Even from day one, I seemed like an odd mix of capabilities. Summoning demons was one thing, but to have a classical magician slant to it was another. The real question mark was my ability to manipulate my Inventory to move things around at will. That almost seemed like a potential Class of its own, yet the System had accidentally slid me something more powerful than intended. Of course, the real trick was that this was all a distraction from what I really was. What I could really become.

We had looted the remains of the Crimson Shadow and left the area as quickly as we could. Some small equipment upgrades, but no information. Other than the Lady not being here.

[546 Gold]
[Shoulder Pads of the Wise: +2 INT]
[Bracers of Hope: +1 DEX, +1 INT, +1 Luck]
[Forest Leggings: +2 DEX]
[Blade of Shadow: +2 STR]

More bandages, a few Health Potions that I put away with a grimace. Ren and Wolf had their pick of other items. If you ignored the hardship and stress of the attack, it had been a truly efficient way of increasing our own power. Still, what I craved even more was an end to this. I had opened the Map maybe a dozen times as we were walking to see where the river was. The distance we had to cover to find her.

Even beyond the dampness from the persistent drizzle, I felt cold. Completely drained of any strength and emotion. Short scenes played in my mind. Snapshots of the battle still aching in my muscles. Most of them were of Ren. Her pained panic when she had been grabbed. The calm and determined glare when she told me she trusted me. The uncertainty in her eyes as she held the demon-killing arrow aimed toward me.

She hadn't said that's what it was, but I could read between the lines. We had been dripping the paint for a while, and the resulting picture should have been no surprise. The vague mention of the Ability. The promise to end each other should we fall into darkness. How ironic for her radiant powers to fight alongside my demonic ones. I wasn't a demon myself though. Felt like one, for the low I had sunk to craving satiety through violence.

There were several other realities, or splits in time, where we'd all died there. Where I'd failed or the plan had gone awry. Our lives gone in an instant. I tried to clench my jaw and will the what-ifs away. We were here *now*, and we had survived. There was no elation about it though. It hadn't been a fairly fought duel where the noble victor had just been the better combatant. I had risked it all. Everything. If I hadn't practiced my aim so much with the cards or had overdone the power and gone through the both of them . . .

"Don't beat yourself up so much."

I startled slightly at Ren's soft voice beside me, so lost in my own head I hadn't been concentrating on much else.

"It's what I do best." I grinned, but my heart wasn't in it.

She didn't seem to want to jostle me from my pity party, which was fair. But they hadn't brought the cake out yet, and I wanted to snuff out those candles that burned deep inside me. Until then, I would stay a mirror of the gloomy skies that continued to pelt us with light precipitation.

Did I become a demon? It was the elephant in the room that my mind was keen to ignore. Ren had said there was something different about my eyes briefly before the battle abated. And during it I . . . If I were honest, I felt like I was acting like Roger. Sure, I'd used my tricks and Inventory manipulation to kill people in pragmatic and uncaring ways before . . . but I'd never showered myself in the fresh lifeblood of an enemy. Perhaps I was just having a bad day. Needed more coffee.

I kept telling myself the Crimson Shadow deserved worse. *They did*. The images of the outpost flashed through my mind, and I knew it twice over. Did I intend to lose myself and become worse than they were? It was due to my Mana exhaustion, I was mostly sure—along with my physical exhaustion. It weakened the barriers to whatever lurked within. Unabated and uncaring. Willing to be the worst to save those close to me. Could I guarantee I could bounce back after the fact, every time? That was the crux of it.

"I'm sorry," I said out loud, unsure if that was to myself or not.

"We're alive because of you. What you can become is a problem, but we can work through it if you trust us." Ren wasn't even glaring at me, her expression neutral.

Wolf turned his head and nodded. "We need to be stronger. Less sleepy."

If I trusted *them*? My understanding was they should have to trust me for this to proceed. The tired marbles clacked around inside my head as I tried to make sense of everything.

"We're at the town," the bear noted.

Immediately, I felt some relaxation hit my bones, to be near something normal and not in the depths of the wilderness. Would have run toward it, even, were my legs capable of that currently.

Despite the gloom, there were plenty of System-created wandering around and facilitating the function of the small town. There was the temptation to try talking to some of them, but sleep was calling for me. I looked at Ren, and she had the same look. We scoured the surroundings for any hint of either Crimson Shadow or any unaffiliated Players. None.

Surprisingly, Wolf got no odd looks, despite being a giant bear. Even as he struggled to squeeze into the tavern behind us, he was greeted by the barkeep the same as any other Player would be.

"I'll just sleep down here by the fire," the bear grumbled after one glance at the stairs. There were a few System-created patrons in and drinking, but he shuffled them out of the way to collapse beside the crackling fireplace.

I scrunched up my eyes a few times before addressing the man behind the bar. "Ah, do you have any rooms to rent?"

"Yes, indeed. All rooms are vacant at the moment."

With a nod, I readied to bring out my gold. "Sure, we'll have two—"

"Just the one, if that's okay?" Ren interrupted, working her jaw as she stared at me. "Safety, after last time . . ."

"Of course, one room—with a bathroom?" Pragmatic of her. I had expected she maybe wanted more space, but with potential assassins about perhaps it was safer.

"That'll be room one then, sir." He placed the key down, and I paid him. The en suite was apparently an extra two gold, but I would literally murder for a hot bath—so it was a good deal all around. I imagined the gold came from the stash looted from the Crimson Shadow, for petty reasons.

I gave Wolf a pat on the head. "Any trouble and I'll send a dove down to you? If you get any trouble . . . just roar and break everything."

"Don't tempt me," he muttered, keeping his eyes closed.

Ren and I went up the stairs, and I locked the door behind us. The room looked practically similar to the one we had previously slept in, except for the door presumably leading to the en suite. With narrowed eyes, I slowly pushed it open to reveal a plain tub—not unlike the one from the old man's house in New Forest. Nothing lurking in shadows.

"You go for it first." I gestured toward it and slunk back into the room.

"Sure?" she asked but was already halfway through the door, closing it before I had the chance to answer.

I grinned and palmed at my eye sockets. It couldn't be that late in the day, but I was fully spent. Even some of the rougher tour weeks didn't shatter me this badly. Then again, I didn't often have a sword jammed through my side or have to avoid being crushed by living trees. The sound of running water was comforting, and I exhaled, sitting on the edge of the bed. As much as I wanted to lie down, I didn't want to dirty up the bed with my soaked clothes. It would be nice to get them fixed up.

Interestingly, as my STAR menus came up, I saw I was able to hand in the Thief Hideout Quest from where I was sitting.

[Quest complete]
[Progress: 16/16 Thieves killed]
[Reward Received]

[120 Gold]
[Uncommon Chance Boxes (3)]

My soul felt like I had done enough gambling for one day. Well, at least this kind didn't threaten death over my head . . . so I relented to giving in to the System's demands. I'd never hear the end of it otherwise. They'd just be there, waiting for me, every time I opened up my Inventory.

[Ring of Regeneration: +10% Mana regeneration]
[Ranger's Gloves: +1 AGI, +2 DEX]
[Boots of the Brave: +1 STR, +1 CON]

Not as terrible as I thought it would be. The ring went into the second slot. Apparently I could only receive the Stats from two at a time, despite the physical limitations not being so restrictive. I'd ask Ren about the gloves, and the boots might fit Wolf . . . which was an amusing thing to think about. I sighed and closed down that menu.

The experience received from the turn-in was enough to push me over the edge, and the STAR glowed a bright gold.

[Level up—<7>]
[Stats increased]
[New Ability: <Vanishing Act>]
[New Passive: <Bloodletting>]
[New Passive: <Stacked Deck>]

I closed the windows without even looking at the descriptions. Too tired for whatever the System wanted to labor me with right now. My palms hid my eyes again before I relented to covering the window with one of the blankets from my Inventory. Despite the overcast sky, there was enough daylight left to burn away inside my skull. Soon, I promised myself.

Time must have flown while I existed in agony, as Ren opened the door and stepped out. Radiant once more, her clothing and hair pristine. Still the worries of the day playing in her eyes. But if a simple bath could wash away the horrors we endured, then this world would be that much more palatable.

"Better?" I asked with a grin.

"Heavenly. I could have stayed in there for hours, but I didn't want to be rude."

I tilted my head and paused as my legs willed me toward the bathroom. "I just realized your Cosmetic outfit is what you'd have worn in your old world too, right?" The muted shades of browns and greens of her leather-and-linen outfit just seemed to make sense for a Ranger-adjacent Class.

"Hmm? Oh. Yeah, it's not exactly battle gear, but it's what I wore when out . . . It was an expected look. A uniform, in a way."

"Certainly more appropriate for adventuring than this." I gestured to my purple suit, realizing that it was torn to shreds and soaked with dark reds and browns.

"You make it work," she said, averting her gaze. "Thanks for covering the window."

Too late to continue that conversation, I was already in the bathroom and closing the door. Hit the taps to allow the spray of water to start filling the tub. Stripped the old-fashioned way.

There was a mirror in here, and I allowed myself a glance. Despite the healing, a lot of my body was bruised or had bright-red lines of fresh scars. I had taken a beating and wasn't sure how I had survived the blow to my side. That place was especially sore and unhappy looking. Taps off and I stepped into the water.

I clasped a hand to my mouth to avoid groaning out loud. Heavenly was putting it lightly—Ren had really undersold it. There was a chance I might melt and become part of a Max soup. The screaming of my healing wounds just made it a little bit more exciting and stopped me from falling asleep. It was a slippery slope to start tempering my mood with pain, but I allowed it in this instance. I deserved it.

In fact, sleep was probably an actual concern, as I felt my eyelids sag even despite the protesting wounds. Instead of being bested by the tub, I gave myself a quick scrub down. Stepped out of the beckoning warmth to sit, steaming, on the edge of the bath. Clothed myself and set it to repair, returning to my underwear. Had a dig around and finally found my Sleepwear slot of Equipment and changed to that. A simple beige linen top and trousers. Modest, comfortable, and other descriptive words my lagging mind couldn't parse.

With one last longing look to the emptying bath, I exited back into the bedroom. Ren was already under the covers, the light of the lantern low.

Funny how earlier I had risked it all to keep my life, but at this scene, I would gladly slip into the abyss. Around my side of the bed, I lifted the covers and slipped in. Yes—between these soft covers, completely relaxed and clean—sleep could take me forever. I'd allow it. No regrets.

"Heavenly," I noted, grinning at the plain wall at my side. There were a few moments of silence, where I considered she may have fallen asleep already—I could hardly blame her when I was in danger of drifting away almost immediately myself.

"Max?"

I turned onto my back. She was on her side facing away but had turned her head to talk. "Yeah?"

"I . . . I'd like to call in that favor you owe me now."

Not so relaxed now, was I? "Of course. What is it?"

"Could you put your arm around me?" I could see her jaw working. "This isn't an invitation to—"

"I know," I interrupted. "And sure."

I shuffled a little closer to her and put my arm over her in the most platonically appropriate way I could muster. She leaned toward the side table and turned the lantern off before settling down.

"I just . . . need to feel like everything will be *okay*." Her voice was soft, sad almost. One bad decision away from having her throat slit, I understood her feeling a little vulnerable.

"It will be." I honestly didn't know that it would be for certain, but it seemed like the best thing to say. She had lost so much, a lot more than I had. Yet we were both struggling to keep hold of our past normality. Both showboating in front of our more fragile selves, just in different ways. Even the brief impasse where we butted heads felt years ago after the more traumatic afternoon that we had just endured.

She had wanted me to fit the gap that her previous life had been left expecting. A strong and decisive warrior, disciplined. I wanted her to be an adoring and encouraging equal, bringing her radiance to my constant need to perform. We had agreed to meet in the middle and both be better for it. It was a weird juxtaposition to go from having almost nobody to baring my heart, killing and risking my life, for someone I had only recently met. I didn't *dislike* it, however.

After ten minutes, it seemed as though she had fallen asleep. I waited another ten to be sure, then slowly rolled away to the other side. Took a deep breath of air that wasn't thick with hair and tension.

Perhaps looking at my Stats sheet will help clear my mind of thoughts I wasn't sure I wanted to dwell over.

[Stats]
[Strength—6]
[Constitution—7]
[Agility—6]
[Dexterity—17 (14 + 3)]
[Intelligence—24 (14 + 10)]
[Wisdom—6]
[Luck—12 (10 + 2)]

Yeah, that helped. It didn't count the stats from any of my weapons while I was in my Sleepwear, which made some sense. I now had +20 percent Mana regeneration, which seemed useful, given my apparent disregard for how to properly use that. Satisfied with the numbers for now, I closed my eyes and relaxed.

Ren's mood reminded me of the sun-and-moon story from the other night. During the day, the elf was stoic and stubborn, headstrong. At night, the darkness allowed her to show her softer, emotional side. Nothing like a near-death experience to remind you how fragile you truly were.

And what of me? Had I learned anything?

Before my brain had a chance to gather up the script for an already prepared response, I let out a deep sigh and sank into a well-earned sleep.

CHAPTER FORTY-EIGHT

Into the Light

Things often seemed to progress in chunks, like the toothed blade of a saw. After danger, you had a period of conflict, then some time to recover. Tension led to further danger, and the cycle repeated. Sawing someone in half was a classic magic trick, but when it was reality trying to split your existence into different parts, it stopped being such a spectacle. The issue with realizing the movement of the waves was any lull just felt shallow when you knew the change was coming. Still, less chance of getting swept away if you were always prepared.

"Max? Max."

I awoke, briefly unaware of where or when I was. Why my mornings had devolved into someone calling my name to wake me, I didn't know—but any brief annoyance quickly fizzled out when I saw that it was Ren. The elf was already dressed and looking bright-eyed and energetic.

"How are you already this *alive*?" I groaned and covered my eyes with my forearm. It felt like another week and I might be ready to face the world. *Might.*

"Elves need less sleep than humans, it seems." There was some mirth in her tone, a life to her I'd rarely heard previously. "But it's been fifteen hours or something ridiculous, so get up, trickster."

I relented to sitting up, my muscles aching with every movement. A grimace crossed my face as a sharp pain flashed up my injured side. Healed but complaining from the trauma. Good morning to me.

"I'm actually going to take Wolf and do a bit of shopping. Try not to die while I'm gone? Meet us at the Town Board when you're ready."

My head nodded, and I watched her leave. She turned to chuck me the key before shutting the door. Not only did she have the energy to be up before me but also to make plans for the day—and look *happy* while doing it. As happy as she ever looked anyway. The blanket had been removed from the window, and bright morning sunlight illuminated the room. I shuffled my aching body up against the headboard and sighed.

[Health Report]
[No reported injury]

If only I could bounce back from the trauma that easily. The thoughts of turning into a demon had played on my mind, even though the long sleep had made me question how much of yesterday was real. The flare of pain in my side told me the answer was too much of it. There was some worry about letting them out of my sight, but I couldn't allow myself to live in paranoia like that. Despite the dead bodies that hopefully weren't still littering the other room, the town in bright daylight seemed like a safe enough place.

Better check the skills from my level up, at least.

<Stacked Deck> had the shortest description, which easily made it the first target of my dreary morning eyes. Ten percent bonus to <Pick a Card> damage. It should hopefully allow my magic cards to stay relevant against more than unarmored or exposed opponents. Time would tell. The amount of Intelligence I was stacking was certainly helping too—alongside my apparent ability to funnel more Mana into the skill than intended. Or perhaps it was intended? It was hard to tell with the System.

I left <Bloodletting> for last because the name alone gave me the chills, and I wasn't keen on seeing the path the System wanted to drag me down just yet. I switched my focus to <Vanishing Act>.

[<Vanishing Act>: Make a medium or small object that isn't being held or equipped invisible for ten seconds]

I prickled with delight. The conditions were fair enough—it would be wild to make my opponent's held weapons invisible or obscure a runaway wagon as it careered toward my foes. I wondered if it counted things I was holding, or rather, could I briefly let go to do the action before grabbing it again?

Not wanting the question to go unanswered so early in the day, I rose from bed onto the wooden floor and switched to my Cosmetic outfit—my suit now perfect and unblemished. Into my hand my dagger went, and I held it limply.

With a quick flick, I spun it into the air and used <Vanishing Act>. The weapon immediately evaporated from sight. A moment later, a sharp pain scratched across my fingers, drawing blood, before the metal clattered to the floorboards.

Lesson learned—I couldn't see invisible things, nor did I have the option to stow them in my Inventory. After a few more seconds, the dagger reappeared on the floor. "Et tu dagger?" It didn't seem to feel any guilt for its role in my injury.

I wouldn't be able to use it on my summoned demons either, so despite it being a potentially powerful aide to my trickery—I'd need to have a good think on the best-use cases.

Now that I had bloodied myself, I relented to checking out <Bloodletting>. Nothing overtly sinister. I hummed to myself as my eyes darted across the text. I could expend 10 percent of my maximum Health to use instead of Mana if I was fully exerted. More temptation to ruin myself, it seemed. How that translated to actual card damage I wasn't too sure and wasn't about to beat myself up about working it out. Despite that being the key point of the Passive.

The card that I had used to sever the arm of the man had been empowered by the Treant curse—even with using <Bloodletting> and my full Mana reserve, I wouldn't be able to repeat the act at this stage. Ha—*act, stage*. I shook my head, and then the rest of my body followed. Limbered up to meet the day ahead. Perhaps I should have gone shopping with them.

With a sigh, I left the room and traveled down to the tavern proper. A couple of patrons, all of them dressed in generic Villager outfits. None of them turned their gazes to meet me, but I drew a fine line across the room with my glare. I was supposed to be good at Illusion Magic, and if anyone was in disguise or keeping eyes on us, I would hope to know. Nothing tingled at the back of my mind.

"Hope you had a good evening, adventurer. Fine day out."

I raised an eyebrow at the barkeep. "Nobody tried to murder us last night, so it was better than last time." Briefly I considered whether the way my heart had pounded in my chest last night was a coy attempt from Ren to off me but brushed those thoughts away. *Focus on the show, Max.*

"Glad to hear it." He took me from the careening thoughts.

With a shrug, I went to the door and waved him off. It was a fine day out. Whatever gloom of the day prior had equally been satiated by the long sleep, and now a soft warmth lit the town. It burned at my eyes, but I couldn't let that ruin the moment. All the hardship seemed so far away once more. As if there was no danger to our lives ever present. I smiled and walked over to the Town Board.

New Quests that had replaced the ones prior. I wondered if Ren had glanced them over yet, but while I was here, I might as well put in the effort to keep the Party on the ball. I had agreed to, of course. Seemed rude to go back to old habits so soon, especially after she put so much trust in me.

[Wanted: Reggie Drake. Smuggler, Murderer, Tax Evader. Dead or Alive.]
[Cull Enraged Dire Elk]
[Investigate Suspected Witch Coven]

I nodded slowly, as if I was getting any useful information out of the requests. Go to place and kill things. These were all challenging, however—so perhaps we should be talking around town to try to get some less terrifying options. Then again, we rose to any challenge leveled our way so far. Knowing the Lady was in the next area made me keen to go a little rougher on the Quests to level faster.

Movement in my peripheral caught my attention, as the unmistakable mass of Wolf drew closer. I turned with a smile, confusion passing over my face to see whom he was with.

"Ren?"

Her eyes were alight—smiling, even if her mouth hadn't budged. "What do you think?" She gave me a brief twirl, some awkwardness in her face at the out-of-character act.

No longer in her usual Ranger garb, she had changed into a totally different outfit. A white blouse partially covered by a soft pastel-blue waistcoat. Matching slacks that went down to smart boots. Atop her golden hair was a top hat, slightly shorter and wider than mine, with a black ribbon around it.

"You have that tailored? It looks like it fits you perfectly." I was as amazed as I was confused. It was always a struggle to get my suits to match my figure, which was why I always stayed so lean. Ren had a lot more going on in that department and yet it looked like it was designed with her in mind.

"System shenanigans," she said as she rolled her eyes. "However, I couldn't deal with the dress shoes."

"Honestly, I'm . . . at a loss for words." I was trying to take it all in while also not trying to stare too much and appear rude. "Just very confused as to *why*."

Her eyes softened. "Let's take a walk down to the coast. The breeze is nice."

I nodded, shooting a look at Wolf as she walked beside me. He looked like he was off in his own world, perhaps trying to work his STAR.

"I had a think about what you said last night," she began as we walked down the street toward the beach. "About my Ranger outfit."

My head was nodding still, agreeing with the words but unsure where this was leading to. It had mostly been an off-the-cuff observation, not meant to jostle some change in her outlook on life.

"My heritage . . . My family . . . It all means a lot to me. Always will. But they're gone now, and I've been trying to cling to them in the hope that they don't fade away." She sighed and looked out toward the sea now that we were getting closer. "This morning I realized that to get stronger, I needed to learn to let go of some of that."

"Then, what's with . . . this?" I gestured to her outfit. Our feet hit the sand, and we kept on going until our full 180-degree vision was open sea and horizon. Wolf had sat back at the edge of the road, not too keen on getting sandy paws.

We stopped, and she turned to face me, crossing her arms over her chest. "The only other outfits were slutty nurse and some kind of dinosaur."

I opened my mouth, but the light in her eyes gave me pause. Instead, I settled for a tired smile and allowed her to explain.

"I realize it's pretty weird to mimic your style, but the truth is, I want to *learn*. I want to bullshit like you can." Her eyes tried to read my face, searching for something. "We're meeting halfway, right?"

My hands rubbed at my temples. "I don't know if . . . I don't know what I *am* yet. Whether I'm even safe to be around." I turned from her to look out at the gentle waves that extended to the horizon. Admitting that to myself was exhausting. What if the violent me took over from the pleasant me, and I was no better than the scum working for the Lady?

With a sigh, I sat down on a conjured chair, the legs sinking slightly into the sand. "I feel like I'm on a destructive course that will only be filled with hardship and loss."

She stepped up behind me and put her hands on my shoulders, which did more to make me tense up rather than relax. "When I met you, Max, I told myself not to care about you. Everything I cared about was taken away from me. I didn't want that to keep happening. Yesterday you, Wolf, and I could have died."

"Very true." Especially if I had made any mistakes.

"So I don't want to live without *living* if death could take us at any time."

I saw her reasoning. The shadows might be safer, but what use was allowing our enemies to keep us miserable and where they wanted us? We might burn out twice as fast, being twice as bright, but it would be a life better lived. We'd still have enemies either way. I was mostly trying to avoid the subtext that she cared for me. Then again, I couldn't deny I cared for her—*and Wolf*—after yesterday.

Perhaps she was right. "Alright, I relent to your reasoning. But why dressed up as my assis—*Ah!*" Her fingers pinched into my shoulders.

"We don't use that word. You're not just acting your assigned Class; you are bullshitting beyond what the System should allow. I want in on that—we need every advantage as we grow in power."

My jaw worked as I stared at the waves wetting the sand at the edge of the shore. I felt unequipped and unqualified to do this. A danger to the group if I truly did turn into a demon and lost control. Could I be responsible for our abilities going forward? I didn't feel enough to hoist up my own ego that I had falsely inflated all these years.

Ren leaned down beside my ear, the brim of her hat pressing against mine. "Max. Just think about how great a show you could pull off with a protégé."

I shivered. For a variety of reasons. Perhaps she was right though. She might not have the capability to manipulate her Inventory—but with two of us, or even with Wolf too, the possibilities grew exponentially. Ideas bubbled up within me.

The elf backed away from me, and I stood from my chair to face her. Her arms crossed again, but those brilliant blue eyes had a life to them that radiated beyond her impassive expression.

I smiled, and as the chair vanished, I stepped up onto nothing. Seemingly hovering in midair, I flourished my cape and gave her a bow.

"Welcome to the first day of becoming *insufferable*." I grinned widely.

CHAPTER FORTY-NINE

Taking Stock

Another blank page lined my journal at this juncture, aside from a few stars I had doodled. I remembered it clearly, even without the visual reminder. That outfit. Her intention to become part of the show. Despite the slideshow of horrible images that ran through my mind, that time on the beach shone out among them. The sound of the waves lapping at the shore. Warmth of the sun. How radiant and full of hope she was. How we both were. The System had ways of correcting that, but it could never shake that memory.

I dropped to the sand once the chair reappeared and went into my Inventory, my grin maintaining. "My new Ability lets me make things invisible for ten seconds."

"Not clothes, I hope?" She narrowed her eyes at me.

"Nothing . . . equipped." Somehow, I managed to maintain eye contact, my grin only slightly wavering.

She turned her head to look back at Wolf. "We should make a move soon. But first, you should teach me something."

I screwed my face up in response. Although I wanted to ascertain some key principles of the order of magic and ease her into the whole journey, I also didn't want her glaring me to death all day. My fingers rubbed at the bridge of my nose. "I suppose, first off . . . You're an Oathwarden—you never mentioned what your oath was to ward."

"You," she stated plainly and didn't change expression.

My brow furrowed, but I didn't have much to say, slightly caught off guard by the simple and rather personal answer.

"What?" She scowled. "You think you can tank a sword through your guts without some kind of divine intervention? I'm already embarrassed enough about last night. Let's not dwell on the details."

Quickly, I nodded, if only because I was keen to not address anything to do with any of that until necessary. Today had already been a roller coaster, and I was beginning to feel like my heart had given out in the night and this was a last dream before I headed into the light. It made a change from getting my skull broken, I supposed.

"Okay." I shook my head to get the train back on the tracks. "What about <Smite Shot>—is that specifically a bow ability?"

Her brow furrowed as she looked through her System windows. "It says . . . it's a projectile attack."

I smiled. *Silly System.* "And what is a projectile attack?"

The simple answer popped into her head before the more out-of-the-box ones tumbled in. I handed her a knife.

She turned to the side, a scowl of concentration along her face as she held the weapon's sharp end between her fingers. It would probably take more effort than the way she had been doing it innately, but . . .

Ren leaned back and then launched the dagger, a radiant light illuminating it as it careened over the beach before landing in the loose sand with a small pulse of energy.

"Holy shit, trickster." She turned to me, either impressed or perhaps expecting that to have been more difficult.

"Obviously not as damaging as an arrow would have been." I held up a finger. "But . . ."

I turned away and walked to the water sloshing up the damp sand as she watched me. Empty bottle came up, and I filled it with seawater, putting a cork in the end. Humming to myself, I stepped over and held it out for her. Some apprehension in her face but understanding the process.

"<Entangling Shot>," I offered.

She repeated the same actions, this time the green-and-golden light swirling around the thrown bottle before it broke on the sands ahead. Vines wriggled about the empty area and then sank away amid a wet patch.

"Now imagine that bottle was filled with poison gas or oil." I grinned.

"Root them and cause more damage." She cupped her chin in thought, looking out to where the skill had landed.

Again, not as damaging nor as far-reaching as an arrow would have been— but the spark was lit, and I could see the possibilities whirring around in her head. I held my hand out for her to shake. "To being the greatest magician duo in the world."

She eschewed the extended offering and moved in for a brief hug. Already, she had moved away before I had a chance to process. She dipped her hat to hide half her face as she stepped back. "Embarrassing acts come in threes. Better to get it over with. Ready to go see how we'll die today?"

My brain clicked into place, still unsure as to what was happening. "I don't know. I'm starting to get a taste for living." Rubbing at my eyes, I turned to face the road, where a familiar figure was slouched against the wall and talking to Wolf.

We exchanged glances and walked back across the sands toward Hannah.

"I knew it'd only be a matter of time." She clicked her tongue and grinned.

"That Ren would become my protégé?" I blurted out before anyone else got a word in. "It was inevitable. Did *you* want to join us?"

"Pass." The shape-shifter pulled a face and frowned. "Wolf was telling me you ran into some trouble yesterday?"

There had been the thought that Hannah may have tipped the Crimson Shadow off to our position, but even with her confidence, she wouldn't be so overt and in our faces about it if that was the case. Mostly, I felt I just didn't want to be wrong about her.

"Group of five ambushed us outside the Dungeon exit." Ren crossed her arms.

Hannah whistled. "Shit, yeah, that sounds like a death trap. But you managed to escape okay? You lost them?"

"We killed them." I shrugged at her visual disbelief. "Mixture of our luck and their arrogance."

"Good eating though." Wolf shrugged and lay back down on the warm stone road.

She stood, working her jaw and trying to chew through the truths she had trouble accepting. Eventually, she had no reason to think what we were saying wasn't true, and she shrugged it away. "I've got the coordinates on Hadrian's camp, if you can pay."

Ren raised an eyebrow at me, and I nodded. She withdrew the token and handed it over as the shape-shifter sent the location to our maps.

"I'm warning you that I don't know their full numbers and power. This is just where the rat is holed up. I couldn't hang about for too long because they have magic that could detect what I really am." She rubbed at one of her cat ears. "I'm going to stay away, probably head west to see what's going on there."

"I understand. Staying safe out there is the most important thing." I looked past her to the road leading up to the town. It would have been very impressive if a new Player had teleported to the beach when I was faux floating atop the invisible chair. Another time, perhaps. "We know that the Lady is past the Golden Fields now, but we want to clear up the area here before moving on."

Hannah pulled an even more exaggerated face. "You'd risk death for what? When your prey is—"

I held up a hand. "How are we supposed to grow an audience with the trash here killing them off?"

She scowled and looked between my devious grin and the stoic glare of the elf. "Whatever." She threw her arms up. "Just follow through. I could use the continued tokens and to breathe a little easier in this area. *Maybe* if you can really do it, then I'll follow you west over the bridge."

With a nod, that was the end of our business meeting. The woman transformed into a cat and scarpered up the road to the town. I watched her leave, for some reason expecting something to happen—but nothing did.

Ren sighed and leaned against the bear, patting him on the shoulder. "I tried to get Wolf to wear a little hat too, but he wasn't having it."

I beamed at them both. Despite the danger on our doorstep, the day had been . . . good? I had never considered having an understudy before. While Ren didn't really have the natural gifts that the System was keen to give out, there wasn't anyone else I'd rather have as my equal. We'd already built the trust, killed for each other, saved each other's lives . . . and hugged a few times—my fuzzy brain was quick to add. The performing-tricks part was the easy bit once we had more time to workshop.

"You two check out the Quest board?"

They shook their heads. "Oh, I did spend some of your share of the gold on supplies." Ren tilted her head. "Health Potions, bandages, and so many bullshit things."

I frowned and tilted my head. "You have my attention, Ren."

She sucked her teeth and looked upward, narrowing her eyes to try to remember everything. "Nails, parchment paper, a hammer, pliers, three different colors of paint, caltrops, rope, yarn, a shovel—"

I held up my hand. "You had me at whatever the first thing was. My brain will literally explode if you give me too many options to think about . . . But thank you."

Her eyes smiled. "Shall we go murder some of the Shadow, then?"

With a sigh, I nodded. It was a shame to leave this snapshot of idyllic comfort, but greater things drew us to harsher times. Even hiding out here and enjoying our time, there was a chance they'd track us down and send people to kill us among the town. Again.

"See any other Players here?"

She shook her head. "Either they have moved on or . . . *moved on*." She drew a finger across her neck, just in case I didn't catch the difference. I did.

"Let's go then, and you'll need to tell me every Skill and what their exact description is along the way." She nodded as I continued. "We'll have you full of bullshit in no time."

Wolf groaned as he stood to his feet, shaking himself off. "If you expect me to do tricks, then you are . . . Well, you best have enough food to convince me."

I raised an eyebrow at the elf, and she nodded eagerly to let me know she'd stocked up on provisions too. Ren had thought of everything.

Other than to hand in her thief Quest and level up apparently. It seemed as though meeting halfway also meant she would be a little slacker on things. We did so and took the three from the noticeboard. Even if we had no intention of completing them at this stage, it would be handy to have them ready in case we stumbled upon the targets. Plus, we could equally be dead soon anyway.

With one last glance at relative safety, we set back out into the woods as Ren began to list off her current Abilities and Passives. They certainly didn't have the intentional flare that mine did.

"Hmm." Eventually, I rubbed my chin in consideration. "Not a lot to work with there. The System has you pegged to your role quite well."

Ren looked glum at my take on it. "The Ability I received at level seven lets me imbue a projectile with an elemental bonus but only one time per element per day."

My brow furrowed. "So you could throw a bottle of oil *already on fire* to explode where it lands? Probably plenty of other interactions I'd have to think about."

She nodded and looked around. We had traveled a decent distance from the town, and as beautiful as the woods were in this weather, we were only stepping ever closer toward the fight against the Shadow.

"Small breakfast stop? I picked up more coffee too." From her Inventory, she withdrew a full jar of the stuff to hand toward me.

"Oh." I stepped back from her. "You best look after it—I, uh, will overindulge otherwise, and you don't want to see me when I'm super wired up."

"Delegating your coffee making to me, huh?" Her eyes narrowed as she set up the grill before her face then softened at seeing my brief panic. "We have a saying in elvish that means 'bound by trauma' or 'death forged.' I believe it's common for adventuring groups to grow tight-knit due to this."

I nodded and looked over at Wolf, who sat down after a stretch and a yawn. That certainly seemed possible. We had shared the near-death experiences, the bloodshed, and rising above odds. It certainly beat out the surface-level conversations I'd have with my previous colleagues or acquaintances.

Maybe this could be even more.

"I have a bear saying," Wolf added, "that means 'feed me or become the food.'"

"Poetic." I smiled.

Ren withdrew some meat and threw it toward him, the slightest of smiles at the edge of his muzzle.

"Say, before we all go off and die . . ." I drew out a chair to sit on as the kettle started to boil. "What's one of the best memories you have of your previous world?" I gestured toward the bear first, as he had been quiet as of late and I didn't want to distract Ren from making my coffee.

He scratched at the underside of his chin for a moment as he finished chewing on his snack, trying to cast his mind back to when he was a normal bear. "When I was a cub, I had two siblings. A sister and a brother. My sister was poorly and passed at a young age, but I recall a time when we were all together, snuggled against our mother. Warmth and safety."

I gave him a soft smile. Perhaps one of the reasons he didn't mind us using him as a bed to rest up against in the night. My eyebrow raised to the elf as she passed me over a mug of steaming salvation. "Ren?"

"Probably my family dog I had as a child. Apparently, I never smiled so much as when she was around. You, Max?"

My mind was still trying to imagine the younger elf beaming at whatever type of dog she had. It was hard to parse and set me back in coming up with my own memories. The flap of pages only half filled brought up a few of my shows or points in my career before the inevitable settled into my mind.

"My grandparents on my dad's side were always into the weird and occult. They had an old book on magical tricks—somewhat taboo back in the day as magicians were quite tight-lipped about their tricks." I stared down at my drink. "But I picked some things up, and my first ever performance was for my mother. Still remember the sparkle of . . . joy and pride in her eyes even as I did just a handful of basic things unsuccessfully."

Ren nodded at me. "Just imagine how impressed she'd be with you now." She handed me a bread roll that she had put cheese in and melted on the grill.

I tried to imagine it. Remembered her smile and the kind words. But it still didn't feel like I was doing enough.

CHAPTER FIFTY

Crimson Flag

Going into a situation with only half the necessary information was a cue to have the gaps labored with whatever the System deemed the direst. A glass half full was all well and good until fate used your blood to top it off. Unfortunately, knowledge was scarce at the best of times, limited by time or untenable emotions. Work with what you had and hope that what you gained was greater than what you lost. Learn the hard way, as long as you actually *learned.*

The rest of our journey was done in near silence. Both from the weight of the task ahead, alongside the reflections of our past memories. Growing closer as a Party. Friendships and proper emotional connections that I hadn't had previously in my adult life. Every step up that ladder making the inevitable fall all the more dangerous. How would I even deal with Ren dying if I survived?

I supposed the answer should be no different from all the other people who had died in my life. But, despite knowing the elf only a short time, she had left a bright mark on my life. Part of me . . . cared deeply for her. We had become each other's coping mechanisms. She accepted my flaws, tolerated me when I wavered, and pushed me to be better. Harsh mentor but now eager protégé. I could hardly imagine any joy in this world where she was no longer by my side. Not that I'd ever tell her as much.

"I regret having to tell you this," she began as she walked beside me. "But I respect you a little more for wearing this kind of outfit constantly. It's not the most comfortable."

"You get used to it." I grinned. "Eventually. Formfitting clothing is more for the appearance than comfort. Short term."

She gave a dull glare out at the woods. "I'll get used to it."

I found it an amusing thing for her to be so stubborn about. Even though her reasoning had some basis that made sense—she wanted us to look like more of a team, and it might help with my performance tricks—it seemed to make her somewhat uncomfortable in more ways than one. I felt on edge, so I opted to rock the boat.

"Good. Confidence is part of making the act seem authentic."

She scowled at me in my peripheral as I looked ahead. "Dickbag. You know I'll never do the fake-smile thing though."

I nodded and turned to look her in her eyes. "That's fine. I'll never ask you to do anything you don't want to do. This is all your choice."

Wolf sidled up beside us with a huff, a small bowler sitting atop his head. Black, with a purple ribbon around it. "This is my choice too." He looked up at me with his amber eyes, looking more like he wanted us to be quiet than anything else.

A wide grin spread across my face. Even Ren looked a little amused.

The expression slowly wore from our faces the farther we traveled. Despite my unbridled joy at our shared theme now, those coordinates were getting closer. Some distraction along the way would have been nice, but it was as if the System saw the route we led ourselves down, and we saw barely a woodland critter. Better not to arrive tired and bloodied, however.

Wolf stopped, his snout probing the air as he sniffed. "Close. Group of smells, but no Hadrian or horse."

I nodded. The Map said we'd be there soon. The bear seemed to have as good a nose as the elf did eyes. Perfect, as I had good taste.

My jaw worked, already knowing some of the answers to the impending question. "Does our plan change if he isn't there? How should we approach?"

We paused to gather ourselves. Ren removed her hat to rub at her head. "We'll just kill whoever is there then. So, either we just charge in, try to be stealthy and pick them off from range, or . . . try to get information from them." She narrowed her eyes at me as if that was certainly my plan out of the three.

"What?" I shrugged. "You were thinking I was about to suggest I go in disguise and try to join them to see if they give up anything useful?"

Neither of them said anything, but their expressions told me that is exactly what they thought. It would have been *such* a good plan too. Maybe when there was less at stake. "I was actually going to say a bit of both should work. If we can attack from range at one angle and they hunker down behind cover, we'll get Wolf to charge in from a different way and disrupt them."

"Sounds good to me." The bear nodded.

"Rather than head straight on then . . ." Ren unfocused as she looked at her Map. "We'll circle to the east slightly and then split with Wolf and go toward the northeast more?"

"Perfect," I agreed, and we started walking again. A plan agreed upon with no arguments. It was too early in our career to fully lean into my way of doing things. It was slightly more important we all lived, unfortunately.

Although the Shadow might not be expecting combat, the route straight from the town would be the most likely direction people would appear from. Their camp would be designed with that in mind. If they were smart enough or thought it was a threat anyway. We had experienced nothing but reckless arrogance from their members so far.

It would be nice to know more about their purpose and how the Lady was gathering such forces in so little time . . . but if she had left the area, then cleansing it of their evil was the second-best thing. They did no good for the area, and if the System was going to bring in new Players, we didn't want them falling to the Shadow—or joining them. It was dawning on me that I might not be the only Player with broken or unexpected Skill interactions. It seemed rude that the Lady would be even more overpowered than me and use that power to be so destructive.

Before I could busy myself with any further distractions, we had a visual on their camp. A loose gathering of assumed stolen wagons with a perimeter lined with spiked wooden constructions.

"Cheval-de-frise," Ren muttered, somehow filling in my mental blank for the correct term. The fact that she even put on the accent when saying it did odd things to my internal organs. Thanks, System.

We backtracked a little so that we were out of sight and left Wolf. The signal was simple—when things went bad, come and join in. He was already licking his lips in anticipation. With the inclusion of the bowler, it was somehow more unsettling a visual than normal. I wondered if the defenses were made with the bear in mind, but they surely didn't expect us to assault their camp. They might not even know about the dead group from the previous day yet.

Ren and I circled around. My mouth felt dry, and the low murmurs of our targets' conversations were just in earshot as we kept ourselves out of line of sight. It was hard to not feel like a bad guy when we were actively stalking people we intended to murder. I had once thought the System would have certain walls up to prevent this sort of thing, but it turned out to be more brutal and real than the casual video-game-esque experience it had originally waved in front of my eyes.

We stopped at the helpful cover of a small bulge in the ground where a tree sat, a minor hill blocking our visuals as we peered over to observe our prey. I could see at least three figures, maybe four. Awake and alert. Two of them conversing beside a grill. One a little ways off on a chair, a mug in her hand.

"Four to six targets, unknown levels or Classes. Most defenses are wooden in nature. Two of the wagons offer cover against our position." Ren reeled off some information so that we were on the same page.

"Eliminate biggest threats first. Healers and any casters before breaking cover down." My response was shrewd, but I understood the basics. Destroying the cover first gave us an advantage, but taking out a key target or two before they could act left a lot of danger in the dirt rather than leveled at us. Despite my predilection for getting into the thick of danger, pelting from a distance sounded preferable in this instance.

She nodded and withdrew an arrow. She whispered a word in elfin that the System didn't care to translate, but with the swirl of blue around the projectile, I assumed it was *water*.

I threw an Imp card out to our right farther away to have him appear hidden among some trees. Mentally, I told him to target wagons once Ren had fired. His little arm waving in response told me he understood. Then I drew a magic card and split it in two. At this distance, I wouldn't be able to pick out necks or other soft spots, so solely dealing what Damage I could would have to do.

Ren aimed and then let loose the magical arrow. I could see her intent—hit one by the grill in anticipation that the water might splash onto the hot metal and cause steam to rise up, obscuring their vision. If only I had something to appear from the cloud, that would have been perfect.

Instead, a flash of light blue rolled over the camp as her arrow struck a previously invisible barrier. The now-inert arrow felt to the dirt, down the domed wall of the Ability.

"*Fuck!*" she whispered and dropped to the ground beside me.

"*Enemies!*" a voice growled out.

"Who's out there? Show yourselves and we might allow you mercy."

"Looks like it came from the northeast," a third voice offered.

The sounds of spells and buffs being cast and weapons being drawn were soon accompanied by boots on dirt.

"Don't wander too far from camp. Three of you guard Gustov so the barrier stays up. You three come with me."

Eight in total then. The spellcaster defending the camp was the biggest issue and the one probably hardest to reach currently. Wolf hadn't jumped the gun, which was great. I just had to think a little harder. Imp vanished, and I brought out the last glass bottle of oil. Needed to stock up on these when we had the chance.

Footsteps drew closer, and one of the opponents was humming with energy. No more jeers or offers of mercy; they were tense. Somehow, I remained calm. Ren's jaw was clenched, and an arrow was clutched at the ready, but she was waiting it out. These people weren't likely to be caught in trying to duel me for their ego. We'd be killed on sight. Crossbow into my right hand, left holding a card I was empowering. Ren waited for the signal.

"*Fuck! Fire!*" a voiced yelled back from the camp.

Good. They had left the grill out in their hurry, and my demonic dove had delivered the oil without being spotted. The magical dome only blocked actual attacks—that was good information.

"We're being played for fools here," a nearby voice growled. "They must be nearer the west." There was a pause, as if they were surveying the area one last time, before they staggered off farther to the right.

With their backs turned, this was our best chance.

I leaped to my feet to peer over the hill and let my card off, pulling the trigger of the crossbow. Ren followed suit almost as my shadow, the green-and-gold <Entangling Shot> arcing through the air just behind my shots.

A Knight in crimson armor turned to block my bolt with a flare of red, my card passing beyond him to strike a robed figure across the face. The <Entangling Shot> rooted the wounded spellcaster and a slim man in leathers but didn't affect the Knight or a woman in a padded gambeson.

With a yell, said woman went for us immediately. She was faster than the Knight, a blur of red around her feet as she rushed toward me. The handprint of crimson across her angered face a contrast to her short blonde hair. Her held weapon—an axe—burst into flame as she prepared to strike when she got close enough.

Her footing stumbled as she tripped over thin air, falling to the ground and sliding down the slight incline toward us. The wooden chair appeared back into view as she tried to get the air back into her surprised lungs. My Hellhound leaped from behind me and immediately tore at her throat.

Heavy plated footsteps thundered right after as the Knight was close behind, a radiant arrow causing him to have to lift his shield up to block the Damage. Full helm, but this one only had a mess of small circles rather than a handy eye slot for my cards to burrow within. The symbol of the handprint was on his shield in deep black. I didn't really have much to deal with heavy armor, so I just stood in place.

The roar of Wolf came from our side. Those four in the campground were about to have a very bad day. We needed to get in and support him.

"Stop," I told the Knight. Seeing if I could just bluff my way into another Dazzle icon.

He reached for me and swung his sword. With a flash of incandescent light, it cut through my suit and into my skin—straight from my left shoulder to chest.

"Stop. I mean you no harm," I repeated with a friendly smile. My right eye twitched from the pain, but I was already twirling a bandage in my hidden left hand.

He hesitated. Ren fired off an arrow, and he didn't have the reaction time to block it. It wasn't aimed for him, however, but for the injured spellcaster—who took the unopposed arrow through his head as he tried to heal his face.

I threw up a blanket and went to dive away, but the Knight shot out a beam of blue light that struck me through it and drew me closer to him like a fishing line. My feet caught on the ground, and I stumbled backward, right as his sword came down to meet me.

<Card Fan> blocked the slash, but I felt pain across my back. An elfin word whispered across my ears before the sound of shattering glass hit the plated figure. I turned away to face him, seeing some of his metallic armor melting away. Acid. Some manner of fantasy stuff, as I didn't think it worked so effectively in my world.

Magic card out, and he raised his shield to block it. I stopped it before it struck and circled it around him. Humming to myself, I let it orbit him before splitting it. He was briefly dumbstruck, trying to avoid the attack or anticipate when I'd pull them in against him.

"Go help Wolf," I told Ren. "I've got it here."

She nodded and was off. No doubt in her mind that I believed what I said. The other combatant was out of the entangle now and was being harried by the Hellhound.

"You've been great." I grinned widely at the struggling Knight. "But now it's time for the curtain to fall."

CHAPTER FIFTY-ONE

Sparkling Turncoat

One of the impressive things about fighting other Players was how slow they seemed to use their Abilities. For the longest time, it perplexed me—as if they had some manner of a mental block like Wolf and could only use things innately and didn't have a proper grasp of their Classes or how to interact with the System. Could it also be that they were inferior Classes and had worse Ability options? Maybe. It sounded cruel of the System to put others on unequal footing, but even by now I had established that the System—or whoever had built it—just didn't care.

As the Knight continued to stand waiting for my attack to land, I didn't even send the cards to him—he was starting to suspect they wouldn't do a lot of Damage and he could just empower some Ability to skewer me with little Damage to himself instead. So I pulled them toward him and let them vanish; instead I threw one of the blankets over him.

He slashed about wildly, getting it out of his way just as Roger slammed a rock into the side of his helmet.

"Knock, knock, fucker!" The demon grinned as the Knight fell to the ground before leaping atop him. The puppet body of the woman I had slain now sporting two purple ears from her skull.

I turned to the last of the group as my pact summon tried his best to be a can opener, just as the fourth member ran my hound through. He gave a look to the carnage and then back to the camp—weighing up his options. He didn't look like the type to think he could take on the man who had just destroyed the rest of his group. Sweaty and pale, going to get reinforcements was his ultimate decision. He turned from me and ran toward the main camp.

Poor choice.

From my hand, I split my cards and sent them through the air. The magic one cut into his lower leg, causing him to stumble. An Imp one struck the ground just behind him. *Wagons*, I commanded. The escapee didn't get much farther as an arrow appeared out through his back, his route clearly taking him straight toward the elf. I grinned but immediately regretted the action as a surge of electricity pulsed through the left of the camp, light flickering against all the wooden objects obscuring my vision of the other two.

"Don't take too long," I yelled back at Roger as I ran. An increasing tempo of repeated clangs from behind me was the only response I received as he plied his rock against the armor to get at the meaty part inside.

Another explosion bloomed in pale-green light from between the wagons and spiked defenses. I swore under my breath. Despite her arrow coming over from there, I couldn't see where she was. A fireball headed off from my Imp to the right side of the camp where the grill fire was still burning away at some wooden crates. It struck a wagon, and flames stuck to it, lapping around and growing in ferocity by the second.

I slid into the camp to see Ren leaning up against one of the wagons, breathing heavily. The left sleeve of her blouse had been charred off and etchings of red ran all the way up her arm. Wolf looked equally as injured. Patches of fur had been burned off, and a limp, robed figure lay bloodied in his mouth.

"Lightning spell," Ren hissed, healing herself with radiant light. "Spellcasters are *motherfuckers*."

"Mfmff," Wolf agreed before spitting the corpse to the ground. "Taste weirder too."

Probably not the right time to remind them I was some form of spellcaster. Whatever Classes the other three here were, they didn't have the necessary defenses to stop Wolf crumpling them like cardboard. One lay several feet away from a severed right arm. The other had a crushed skull, a sight that sent a twinge of pain through my own head.

"You two get healed up and let's pick the camp clean and move on?" I rubbed at my temples. Something wasn't right, but I couldn't think what. Adrenaline was draining away, and I felt unaccomplished, barely a handful of Dazzles in that brief fight. Didn't get to pop the <Finale>. Did that mean things weren't over yet, or was I holding the wrong end of the stick? I caught the eye of the elf.

"Max, you need healing too." Ren scowled at me as the redness on her arm faded away.

I looked down, briefly surprised to see how much of my front was soaked with blood. There was some pain there, but I hadn't really focused on it.

"Use some bandages? And probably next time, don't just stand in front of people attacking you." She rolled her eyes. "Even if it did look badass."

"Careful." I grinned. "Shouldn't encourage me with compliments." My eyes turned away from her glare as Roger stumbled over in a suit of dented crimson armor.

"Hey, boss . . . and witch and big dog, I guess."

"Wolf," the bear corrected, as the elf narrowed her eyes.

"Roger." I nodded. "Thanks for your help. How have you been?"

He awkwardly moved over and leaned on one of the spiked walls, the sharp-ened wood scraping against his metal side. "Can't complain. It's nice to get away from the wives and kids every so often though, you know?"

"*Wives and kids*," I repeated, slowly looking back at Ren.

"Yeah." His head shuffled like a nod, purple ears atop the helmet waving. "Seven wives, twenty-three kids. Couple more on the way. The gals always dote on me more after some time in this plane, and the kids love the stories."

My imagination was working overtime but couldn't keep up. "The stories of you murdering people?"

"In a way." He leaned over and creaked further against the spikes. "They see me as an adventurer. Being summoned by you is an honor."

I bowed, not really knowing how else to process all that information. "Always a pleasure to have you assist us, Roger."

"Well, I'll be going now, boss. Florentine is cooking today, and her caramelized mash is to *die* for." With that said, his body slunk lax as his energy faded away.

All of that was pretty unexpected and hard to accept. For a variety of reasons. There was a brief moment of awkward silence before I turned back to my Party. "Is it bad I wanted to ask him to bring us some of the mash?"

"Get looting, trickster," Ren said with a sigh, hoping to move on from that odd conversation. "This place already gives me enough of a bad vibe."

Glad that it wasn't just me that felt it, I nodded and began looking around as she healed up the bear. As much as it tempted me to take everything not nailed down, the more I cluttered my Inventory, the longer it would take me to cycle to what I wanted—even with the speed I could currently do it.

I whistled. "This Wizard was *stacked*. Rare equipment with Intelligence and spell Crit Chance, some with elemental Damage too. You'll probably want the ring with that?" I turned and spun it in the air. She easily caught it and turned away from us.

Wolf watched her walk off to the corpses back in the woods before looking up at me. "You've both exchanged rings now."

"Huh?" My brain froze for a second, unsure as to how he even knew that tra-dition. "Oh. No, that's not . . ."

"You share the same sleeping quarters and dress the same." His amber eyes bored into me.

For some reason, my brain felt like mud. "I think you are reading too much into it, Wolf." Technically speaking, we had all shared sleeping arrangements at some point—and he too now wore a hat denoting his place in our troupe. No need to grasp for anything further.

He stretched out and looked idly over to the woods where the elf had gone. "The details do not concern me. I only wish to ask that you do not leave me behind wherever the path leads."

I knelt down on one knee to look him in the eyes. "You have my word, Wolf. Whatever happens, you are part of this team."

With a grunt, he nodded. "I'm glad I didn't eat you before."

"Me too." I stood back to my feet and grinned before picking the Wizard clean of what I wanted.

[Mad Mage Hat: +2 INT, +5% spell Crit Chance]
[White Magic Gloves: +3 INT]
[Slippers of Magic: +2 INT, +5% magic Damage]
[Belt of Magic: +2 INT, +5% magic Damage]

Ten percent more Damage already, even without the extra Intelligence. Seemed like it didn't do the Wizard much good though. He had gotten a few spells off and damaged the Party. Probably holding the barrier up during most of the start of the battle weakened his effectiveness. Then, once you had a bear in your face, your options were limited. I went through the other bodies as Wolf yawned and lay down. Some gold and consumables but no gear that was worth upgrading what I had. A couple Strength and Constitution things for Wolf to go through later.

The smell of burning caught in my nose, distracting me from ruminating any further. Imp had departed, but not before setting some tents on fire. My eyes moved around the campground, looking for the most prime sources of loot before everything was consumed by flame. A journal lay sprawled on the worn dirt, pages gently moving about in the slight breeze.

I relented to checking it out, despite time being a precious resource. Information was perhaps more valuable than the new Equipment I now sported, if it could keep us alive. The pages flicked across in front of my eyes as I leaned against a crate. Thankfully, this hadn't ended up on the currently burning side of the camp.

My brow furrowed. Nice of them to document things. Recruitment attempts. Oddly enough, it sounded like they were all . . . willingly joining this charade. The process of how all of this had been brought forth . . . The dead Wizard and the red Knight appeared to be in charge of . . .

As Ren approached, I turned around and kicked over the crate I had been leaning against. The clatter of glass was accompanied by the lid popping off, dozens of bottles pouring out into a pile on the ground. Most empty but some full.

"What are those?" the elf asked with her own furrowed brow in full effect.

"Blood."

Ren knelt down to inspect one, not willing to touch it with her hands. I joined her by the side of the crate. She flared her nostrils and shook her head. "I suppose the two questions are whose and why?"

I met her questioning gaze with nothing but a blank expression.

"*Fuck*," she whispered. "She's a blood mage or vampire or something?"

All I could do was nod slowly. The information was still trying to worm its way through my brain, and I'd need some quiet time to properly dig through the journal to get an accurate grasp on what it was all about. A rough formation of the bigger picture took shape, and I squinted to make it out.

Whatever her level-five skill had been must have granted her this Ability. Using her blood, she had somehow offered them power or an end goal that was too good for them to pass up. Either way, it had enabled her to gather up or kill the majority of Players in this area. It didn't read like hypnosis, possession, or corruption. But I hadn't the time to fully inhale the words into my head.

Ren sighed and stood again. "At least that gives a little more exposition to what we're up against. Seems you're not the only one bullshitting the System." She moved past me, placing her hand briefly on my shoulder as she moved over to Wolf. "Let's get moving. I hate the smell of burning wood."

I wondered if she had found anything useful on the other figures. Something to go over somewhere safer. "Just have a couple more boxes to check and then we're good." My Inventory now had three bottles of blood and five more empty within it as I turned and stood. Again, not intending to be deceptive, but I had a knack for knowing what might be useful. Until we knew better, the Lady's blood could be used to our benefit.

"I doubt there's anything else worthwhile." She gave Wolf a pat on the head. "There's some new gear for you. That'll be great, huh?"

The bear nodded but didn't seem too enthused. We had managed to get him into the bowler, which was the biggest win we were likely to have on that front.

Shame the Shadow camp wasn't filled with unused Power Tokens. I was still sore that the Dungeon only gave us two. Ren was probably right though. We had achieved our goal here, and there was no sense getting greedy by trying to scour every last container for scraps of loot. If there was a treasure chest, maybe—but the boxes not on fire didn't look like they'd be filled with anything important or valuable.

"Alright, you've won me over with your sound reasoning." I walked over to join them. "Where should we head to next?"

"I was thinking north," she replied. "Wait for the area to cool off and see if we can hit a couple of Quests until we have more information on where we should strike next."

That made sense to me. We were fast becoming the biggest thorn in the side of Crimson Shadow. They were not likely to give us this kind of chance again to act so unopposed, if there were any actually left in the area. Hadrian sure, but there couldn't be . . .

My mouth opened and closed to signal my agreement, but no words came out. Even as their eyes widened, a numbing pain flooded down my neck. As a radiant heal pulsed through me, the bloodied arrow fell from my neck. My eyes blurred briefly, death avoided by a sliver of luck.

From the woods, Hadrian, mounted atop his horse and followed by four others. Some spell had silenced their advance, I was sure of it. As I went to move, ethereal chains appeared around me, keeping me in place. Their Archer fired a skill into the air, an arrow bursting into two dozen more, ready to pepper the area like a rain of projectiles.

If we took shelter from the spray, their melee fighters would be upon us before we recovered. Number advantage was theirs. Too risky for us to attempt to overcome, any hubris I once held melted away as my need to protect the others overrode it.

"Both of you run, *now*." My eyes blazed with anger, and they didn't hesitate. Around one of the wagons and through the barricades, an aura burst around Wolf as they sprinted back toward the woods. Was it the right call to make? I wasn't used to this kind of leadership, but I was willing to risk sinking with the ship if they made it away on the life rafts. What mattered most was that they heeded my word without hesitation. Something frightening, if I had the time to process it at present.

The lobbed arrows began clattering around the camp, and I crossed my arms. None of them struck me, more from luck than anything else—but my indifference had an effect on the approaching five. Slight confusion and amusement on the face of the wild-eyed man at their front.

I leveled a stern gaze at the mounted man. "Let them go and I'll join the Crimson Shadow." Either he would buy it, or I was about to lose my head.

He grinned as his halberd glinted in the sunlight, his decision already made.

CHAPTER FIFTY-TWO

Once More with Soul

I kept reminding myself every so often that I wasn't a gambler. Or rather, I tried to convince myself that was true. While I liked my tricks to have a certain amount of sureness to them, it seemed that time and time again I would put my life on the line and see how highly fate regarded my continued existence. Perhaps I was just writing these memoirs as a ghost. The fading thoughts of a man lost to the endless sea. Sure felt that way more often than I cared to acknowledge.

Hadrian pulled back on the reins to make his horse stop before me. Gestured for two of his lackeys to pursue my Party. "Trail 'em but don't engage until my signal. They're tougher than they look."

His scowl then turned back to me as he dismounted his steed and strode over to me. He was a large man, a good half a foot over me, and overtly muscled in a way that wasn't normal. More like something you'd see in a comic book. Wide shoulders, barrel chest, and arms that could surely snap me in half. Nothing like a superhero though—a wild mania blazed in his eyes—he looked unstable. Perhaps that was rich coming from me currently. Or at any point in the last week.

The two companions remaining were an odd pair. A Wizard in deep-red robes, his face shadowed by a tall peaked hood. A gray beard spilled out from the darkness, and his clothing was painted with eye shapes all over. The Ranger was a female dwarf, a heavy crossbow in her thick arms. Short mohawk of bright-orange hair and a smudge of dark war paint across her bright-green eyes beneath the traditional handprint denoting their allegiance to Lady in Red.

"Got some huge fuckin' balls on you, eh?" Hadrian moved up to my face, rubbing at his stubbled chin. "Thinkin' acting the hero will save yer little Party?"

"I was thinking of switching sides anyway." I continued to stare at him impassively. Although I wasn't an actor, I could fool myself into playing a part. Suspend my own disbelief. "You seem like you could use the help."

He glared at me, then looked around the camp. "Aye." He slowly nodded. "You're a competent asshole, at least. You the one that killed the scouting party too?"

"Greasy dickbag with the dark metal sword?" I raised an eyebrow.

Hadrian grunted in response and began to walk slowly around me. The dwarven woman took the reins of the horse and moved it to our side, gave it something to eat. While the Wizard stood with his face still covered, focusing on the chains holding me in place. How inconvenient. Channeled spells seemed to put you at a disadvantage, yet I could see the benefit.

"The Lady *is* always on the lookout for promising recruits," the man began from beside me. "You should see the size of the new fucker she left in charge of this area. *Was meant to be me.*"

A clear sore spot, but he seemed willing to give up this information. One step more on the ladder for us to climb to get across and find Lady in Red. As much as I wanted to probe him further, if I was caught digging, then it'd put my ruse under question.

"However . . ." he continued, moving behind me. "She doesn't like little shits like you and the frigid elf prancing about and killing off parts of the gang."

I had *hardly* pranced. "You'd rather have a gang of weak fighters then?"

He stopped behind me. Perhaps deciding whether lopping my head off would stop my smart mouth or not. It would—unfortunately. I knew my time here was limited, but there wasn't a way to seal the deal against all three of them. *Improvisation.* The internal me paled. Something I was meant to be decent at. Look where it had gotten me currently.

"You make a point, smart-ass. But do you know what gives us our power, our unity?"

"Blood. From the Lady herself." I heard him exhale behind me. The Ranger returned to the position in front of me with her crossbow readied, the horse now satisfied to look over at the fire or something. I daren't turn my head to see, lest it fall off.

Hadrian moved his mouth close behind my ear, the warmth and smell of his body washing over me. "Done me a little favor, in a way. Less competition means more blood for me."

He made it *sound* like vampirism. They needed the blood to maintain their strength and whatever bond they had with the Lady. Perhaps a little too hopeful to think he'd just lay it out and tell me exactly what it did. Probably not something I should find out firsthand, however. I wondered what withdrawal did to them.

"How about a toast then? I looted a couple if you wanted to celebrate your new member joining?" I licked around my teeth. Felt like my brain was overheating. Using up all my bluffs and about to fall down a painful path. Not thirsty for what was potentially about to occur but dry enough to walk toward the danger.

Slowly he continued around me, back to the front. I could see the hunger in his eyes. The mania and desire for the sweet juice.

"Show me." He narrowed his eyes.

I made the show of reaching for my side pouch, drawing two of the blood bottles from my Inventory. They knew some things about me, but I was unsure as to what degree they knew I could manipulate my items. Extending my arm slowly, I offered them both to him. No tricks yet.

He took them both and held them up in the air, gave them a little shake. Another grunt and he placed them back in my open palm. Halberd stabbed downward into the dirt, he then wiped his hands off on his dark leather leggings. He turned to his two companions with his hands open in the air, making sure he had their full attention as if they were children.

"Any objections to this man joining and we celebrate with our extra rations?" The only response was heads shaken in the negative. I assumed they just wanted the extra blood rather than to welcome me with open arms. It must be good stuff.

Hadrian turned back to me and snatched back up a vial. "To the Lady then."

"To the Lady," I confirmed, popping the cork of the one remaining and lifting it to my lips.

He stared me down as he did the same action to make sure I wasn't bluffing. His brow furrowed as he downed the contents of his own. I removed the empty bottle from my lips. Barely a trick at all, I probably could have done this with normal sleight of hand if given a bit more time. Too eager to watch me do the deed, it took him a couple of gulps to notice what he held. Then again, something was telling him to drink it, even after he knew something was amiss. A draw that I had resisted for the few seconds that he had his back turned.

The man took a step back from me, confusion on his face. He raised the remnants of his drink, the odd bluish hue of the water reflecting in his widening eyes. Anger flashed over his face as he turned back to me right before a fireball flew past and struck the mage, disrupting the man and freeing me from his spell. My patient Imp had almost run out of time, the card having followed behind the bear as he escaped and landed on the other side of the wagon, hidden from my opponents.

Hadrian panicked as one hand clutched at his throat. His eyes looked around wildly for his halberd that he thought was just beside him but now appeared vanished. Invisible for a handful more seconds. A little closer and I could have put it in my Inventory instead. He started coughing as the Ranger stepped forward and let a bolt off toward me.

The fresh dove rose from a magic circle to be impaled immediately from the shot, taking enough force out of the projectile for me to deflect it with the dark sword, which I drew into a flourish. As the wizard recovered, he leveled a spell toward me, a ball of cold blue energy that blew apart the wooden chair I kicked toward him.

<Finale>.

Lights crackled in the air behind me as I rose both hands into the air, sparklers streaming amber lights from around where I stood. They were stunned. I had pulled it off. Not a great amount of Dazzle icons, but I was playing it by ear here—bringing out everything but the kitchen sink during the brief chance I had to overpower them with their leader out of action.

Roger came leaping from offstage to brain the Wizard with a rock, knocking the man to the ground. Purple card cut the cable off the crossbow and severed some fingers of the Ranger. Purple electricity arced from my body as anger and elation filled me. Invincible. Immutable. *Infamous.*

As the dwarf recovered, she saw her inert weapon and didn't fancy her chances trying to draw a second out in the open. She dove to the dirt and rolled as my follow-up card scored a line against the ground. The horse was spooked but hadn't bolted. Probably tamed to be calmer around battle, I imagined, but it wasn't important right this second.

Hadrian dropped to his knees, clutching at his throat. I could have ended him there. Didn't want to. He deserved to suffer. All of them did. Alarm bells rang inside my head. Locked doors inside my core buckled and cracked open. *Get rid of the Ranger and take my time with the man.* Crossbow in hand, the bolt blew up dirt by her feet, while my card cut grass passing her before I drew it back into her side. She *was* fast. Hellhound card went out. He could chase her.

I turned back to the choking man, my eyes burning with energy. Perhaps I could get some questions—

"Nice try, motherfucker."

My head barely turned in time as I received the metal horseshoe of one outstretched leg from the now-apparent Player horse, straight to my dome. I probably had a Dazzle icon from that twist, if I could see it from the bloodied ground, which I couldn't.

There weren't many other thoughts after that. Muffled sounds, odd sensations, and barely any vision. Finally, my time to shuffle from this strange world into whatever was beyond. Even if nothingness was the answer . . . it had been a reasonable last show. I could even vaguely hear the crowd calling my name. Or at least, someone was. *Max.*

A large shape, warm brown fur, went across my dim vision. Some sounds of violence. Two orbs of purple came down before my face before being pushed away. Warmth and my head was lifted slightly. Warmth again and softness. Some of my senses started to filter back.

". . . It's not working . . . Max? . . ."

Preaching to the choir. Many things were not working for me now. Most of my muscles, for one. The rest of my body, for two. I closed my eyes as my brain was about to combust. Couldn't have that; it was too valuable. Needed to temper those flames, lest they consume me.

As if hearing my inner monologue, it started to rain. Although, it was only a handful of drops, located on my face. Warm drops.

"Fuckfuckfuck!"

"Is he going to . . . ?"

"Boss?"

I wanted to assure the shadows waving around me that I wasn't dead, but my mouth wouldn't work. Perhaps it would be better if I just slept for a while instead. *Good idea*. Gradually, the light slipped away.

There was darkness.

And then there I was. Standing in a pitch-dark room of unknown size, ankle deep in water illuminated with a shimmering purple light. Not the worst place to go after death, I supposed. Only, I wasn't alone. That familiar feeling, the one who had pursued me in my previous dream. Here he was.

Across from me was . . . *me*. Another Max with his hands in his pockets and a grim smile.

"Looks like you got us into a little pickle, Max." He pouted and sighed.

"Did I die? Did *we* die?" My mouth felt sore even in this space.

"It's touch and go. Apparently, you have a habit of dropping our brains all over the place." The other Max rolled his eyes. "Only Ren's Oathwarden Ability is keeping us from becoming worm food right now."

"So, why am I here with you?" I looked around in the hope of seeing some manner of clue or landmark. Other than having wet feet, I was none the wiser. "Is this a dream, a hallucination?"

"Here's the thing, Max . . ." He began to walk slowly toward me. "The System said it merged our souls, but we both had such a force of personality that it was incomplete." He gestured to show himself off, a clear separation of two people.

"Who were you before this?"

The other me smiled and shook his head. "Short answer is a warlock, bound to a demon. Long answer has your brain leaking over Ren's lap as we talk backstory."

"Fine. What's your suggestion?" My patience was wearing as thin as my skull. He had cards up his sleeve, and for once I hadn't caught the thread of the explanation.

"We merge fully. I don't know enough for sure, but it might jump-start the System into thinking you're alive again."

"Shame. And we've only just met." Not that I wanted to have a series of talks with myself, but the System could have really done something with this and dragged it out further. Made a real *thing* of it.

"You'll still be you, but you'll also be me. And I'll be you, and *blah blah*. You were the stronger soul for some reason, so you'll inherit all my memories and life experience. Or it's the other way around, but there's no way of really knowing." He shrugged. "I don't *really* know how this works."

"We'll just be *Max*." We already had been, in a way. Just lopsided. He, a cold demon-adjacent killer. Me, a people-pleasing performance artist. Perhaps the other way around. But there was no time left. I couldn't keep the crowd waiting. "I'm ready."

He nodded and walked up to me, right hand extended to be shaken.

One of the books that my grandparents had in their collection had a section on demons. It had said they often left it to the last possible moment—when you were most desperate—to offer you a deal. Something you couldn't refuse. This *could* be a demon masquerading as my other soul, but at this stage, it made no difference. I had to let him in to survive, no matter what the long-term cost. It could also be the waning fever dream of a man dying from his own hubris.

My own right hand extended, almost a perfect mirror image of the other Max, and I took his.

We shook, and it was done.

[Soul split detected . . .]
[Pending . . . Pending . . .]
[Partial merge detected. Correcting.]
[Complete—Soul Merge accepted]

CHAPTER FIFTY-THREE

Horsing Around

This page of my journal is just a crudely drawn picture of a horse with a cross through it, a little angry face with a top hat on the side. That might be me.

I took a gasp of cold air as pain and waves of numbness pulsed through my body. Immediately, I was enveloped in warmth. My ears still rang, but context clues told me this was Ren beside me.

[Health Report]
[Extreme head injury (Fracture)—Healed 40% (Ren)]
[Major trauma]
[Exhaustion (3)]
[Nerve damage (Temporary)]

Vertigo hit me, and I leaned into the elf. "Sorry," I slurred, wanting to fully apologize for being so forward but unable to hit more than one word at a time. She righted me and rested me against the warm fur of Wolf. Still not quite able to see or understand where I was or what had happened. I lived, maybe?

Whenever my heart was empty, the System found a way to fill it. If my soul reached its breaking point, the System would mend it. When I became nothing more than a bloodied bag of internal parts, the System became the world's best puzzle completer. There was an underlying suspicion that some Players were meant to be heroes, that the strongest and most capable were favored by the System to carry out a cleansing of those who were weak enough to corrupt the status quo. That or I was just lucky.

My eyes found their purpose, and it looked to be nighttime already. Ren's face was illuminated by the glow of a fire to the side. She looked stressed, worried, and like she had been crying.

Wolf's face circled around beside her, his eyes drab but sparkling with something in seeing me active.

"Max?" the elf asked. "Can you hear me?"

"Loud . . . and clear," I managed, attempting a nod but collapsing back onto her, unable to hold my own weight. "Sorry again."

"Just ask if you want to be held, dickbag."

"Please." I sighed and felt my own eyes blur up. No use putting on an act anymore. I didn't think my brain was capable of such ego at present. She put her arms around me and held me against her chest. I'd never really listened to someone's heartbeat before. Not this closely. It was remarkably humbling. Also, it was giving me a headache. That might be me finally feeling the damage my skull had earned.

"I ate that horse for you, Max," Wolf offered, already providing his furred flank as a comforting recliner seat for my numb body.

"*Fuck horses*," I murmured. The elf shook slightly, a relieved laugh inaudible but soul crushing in its own way. That they had cared so much for me. Talking horse, though, who'd have guessed that? The look on my face must have been something. The first trick played on me and it almost ended my career. Something was poignant there, but it just hurt to decide on what.

"You had us so worried." Ren sniffed and ran her fingers through the back of my hair. "My heals wouldn't fix you. We couldn't get you to drink a potion. Even Roger looked distraught."

"I tried licking your face," Wolf added.

"That might have been what saved me." I smiled, wondering if he cleaned the horse gore from his face first. Somehow I felt content, despite the agony flaring back down my nerves. My muscles tensed from the pain. "*Ah*. Try healing me now."

Ren did, and this time it worked, to a degree. I sat against the bear, relinquishing the generous hug now that I had a bit more of my normal sensibilities. I groaned and sank back into the warm fur.

"Coffee?" she asked.

"You are a literal angel," I murmured, trying not to let sleep take me away. I didn't see her reaction to that statement, but she stood, and her shadow crossed my vision as she went nearer the fire to set up the kettle. They arrived just in time, and I needed the story there to believe it. "Tell me what happened on your end."

"We ran for a bit and saw two were chasing. We laid a trap and killed them. Ren's idea." Wolf's deep tone vibrated through his body as I listened.

Ren continued. "Did you know Wolf is excellent at climbing trees? It was simply a matter of getting him up one once we were out of sight, then when we drew them under it, I fired an earth arrow to distract them with disturbed dirt."

"Then I dropped down. Squish." Wolf shook as he chuckled.

That warmed my heart. "I would have liked to have seen that."

"What did you get up to on the main stage?"

I opened my eyes against their will to narrow a glare at the elf. Despite the number of emotions that had been wracking her face, her eyes were smiling.

"Pretty simple actually." I sighed and looked up at the night sky. How beautiful and perplexing the stars were. "Bunch of bullshit they fell for."

"Details please, Max," Ren requested. Of course, they had more of a vested interest now. They were learning.

"Said I'd join them. A little social engineering to play their egos up and make myself seem worth it. Switched the blood vials. Empty one to look like I had drunk the blood. Treant water one for Hadrian. I had already hidden a card to follow you both and land behind the wagon. My Imp struck the Wizard in the confusion, and the spell holding me was dropped. Quickly let out a dove to block the Ranger's bolt. Sent off Roger's card and conjured a chair to block a spell. Roger took the Wizard. I disarmed the Ranger and had a hound chase her down. Then the horse kicked me."

There was silence for a few moments after. Perhaps it was all too much bullshit to sound believable. It could be that getting mashed in by a horse was a pretty miserable way to go after all that effort. They'd had a trick up their sleeve the whole time, and I hadn't seen it. It would be more humbling if it weren't so amusing.

"Wow," Ren eventually said, moving her free hand to the side. "I suppose that explains that then."

I looked to see where she was gesturing, to find that there was a Treant bound and gagged at the outskirts of our little camp. Some fury in his eyes. So now we knew what drinking that water did.

"Can he talk?" I asked.

"No, not really." She shook her head and glared at him. "We kept him alive just in case there was a way he could . . . bring you back."

"Hate to disappoint there, Ren." I smiled. "I survived purely through bullshit too."

The kettle whistled, and I almost sat up straight as a Pavlovian response. Well, if only my spine were capable of it.

"Explain," she demanded, holding the preparation of the lifesaving liquid hostage.

"My Soul Merge . . . It wasn't properly completed before, and I suppose clicking it in place reset my life a little." She seemed reluctantly content enough with this response. The brief conversation with my alter ego I'd keep to myself—I didn't want to sound *crazy*. "But it was your Oathwarden Ability that kept me alive, so the most thanks goes to you."

She feigned a brief curtsey before pouring herself a coffee too. She came over and handed me a mug, ensuring that I was able to hold it before sitting close to me. "It's my job to keep your dumb ass alive. I should've been there."

"You're here now." I smiled at her. "Although I have something to admit. I've been holding out on you."

She narrowed her eyes at me, having to lean slightly away to not be right in my face.

I raised up my free hand, two sweet cakes in my palm.

"There are a lot of curse words I could call you, Max. But instead, I will graciously accept your gift."

"Kept them for our darkest hour. At least you could have looted them from my body had I died. You'd have *two* then."

She glared at me, mouth already half full of the cake. "I'd punch you if you weren't holding scalding liquid."

If only our enemies were so considerate. But then they wouldn't really be enemies, I supposed. We sat in silence as we drank coffee and ate the cakes. Took me a little longer, but I savored it more than usual. Pain decreasing, but I felt spent. Too many head injuries in such a short period. And now a really mixed Max?

"You thought you lost me, huh?" I stared at the fire as it waved and crackled at the wood.

"Yeah."

I wished I could say something romantic or cliché about how my last thoughts were of her, or even of the Party. But they weren't. I had considered the show and how I had performed. A broken man chasing something adjacent to what mattered but not hitting anything that really built to something greater.

"Max?" The remnants of my coffee sloshed about as she leaned against me, head against my shoulder.

"Hmm?"

"We won't part ways after killing the dumb vampire lady, right?"

"No. I'm here as long as you want me." I placed my mug away and withdrew a blanket to pull around us both.

"Good."

Too traumatized and exhausted to feel awkward about the situation. I accepted it for what it was. In truth, I hadn't thought too hard about what came after defeating Lady in Red. This didn't seem like the sort of world where we could just buy a cottage and settle down into a normal life. Always power to gain, some danger ahead of us to fight. If she wanted to invite tragedy by us growing closer, then that meant we just needed to get stronger to protect our bond.

She turned over, away from me to get more comfortable. Wolf was already asleep, snoring every so often.

My tired eyes stared at the Treant Hadrian. Cold malice sank through me, even against the warmth of care around me. I pictured myself standing without waking the others. Dragging the bastard deeper into the woods, hands clenched around his thicker branches above the impassive face. I'd throw him against a tree in the pale light of the moon. Withdraw the hammer and nails from my Inventory . . .

Hmm. Best stop there, lest I get too excited. My brush with death and physical trauma had left me a little unhinged—a dim view of those who opposed me. Certainly it wasn't the part of me who was . . . now *me*.

I dug about in the fresh earth of the memories once buried. The other *me* used to hunt demons in hell on his own world. That joined a few dots together. He was also a magician and was bound with a pact to a demon who appeared as a white rabbit. It had been so easy for the System to mash the two things together. I had even read books on demonology and the occult during my life, so some of the edges were easy to smudge across the gap between us.

What did that really mean for me now? Any tangible benefits to the proper merging of my whole being? The System hadn't sprung up to tell me I had any new Abilities or powers. Other Max had used a portal to escape from certain death against pigmen demons, wounded—which explained the healing done by the System at the start. Maybe the immediate head injury was what caused the merge to be offset. Came to this world by chance the same time that I did and perhaps bore the brunt of the sharp rock that greeted us, so that I may continue on.

Gradually I worked my way through the menus of the STAR, each change of menu a short stab of pain in my mind.

[Soul merged]

There it was, a Passive Ability at the bottom of my list. I couldn't press it for more information, and there was no obvious change to my Stats or Abilities. Did that mean that it did nothing but signify the process had been completed? Perhaps the true ramifications wouldn't reveal themselves until the right moment? Why did I think the other Max was cooler than me? Which Max was thinking that?

I chased far too many errant thoughts deep into the darkness of night until my mind was too exhausted. Allowed to rest fully, no dreams dared cross my path.

"Max?"

I opened my eyes. Daylight that burned at my retinas. I groaned as I looked up at the elf. "One day, I'll wake up without you prodding at me."

She rolled her eyes. "I doubt it. You'd sleep all day if allowed."

"He did lose half of his brains." Wolf came to my defense, turning his head. He looked like he had been awake awhile but had stayed put to aid my rest.

I held up my arm. "In my defense . . ." My brow furrowed, and I lowered my arm back down. I couldn't actually think of much to say. Maybe I did lose half my brains.

Ren tilted her head and sighed. "Come on, Max. I can't be soft on you night *and* day. You know how this works. What's your health Status?"

[Health Report]
[Medium trauma]

Medium trauma. Reminded me of the time that Reggie thought we needed a psychic as our opener. My skull seemed to be in one piece, even if bruised and sore still.

"It says I've contracted horse-ism. I have three days before I turn into a centaur."

Wolf gasped. Ren worked her jaw, not willing to budge an inch until I gave her a proper answer.

"Minor trauma." I shrugged. "What's new?" I clenched my hands into fists. "Actually . . . No, sorry. It's medium."

"Fuck, Max. But thank you for being honest."

I could have lied and even wanted to at first. Be *fine.* Pretend to be *fine.* We were slowly peeling off the layers around each of our damaged cores; the sunlight burned away and cleansed. I smiled at her as I grunted and stretched up to my feet, only wavering slightly as I was lightheaded. Wolf was just too comfortable for his own good.

"If I pretended and got myself into trouble, you'd break me in half."

"It's not that." She frowned and shook the tongs at me as her grill started to cook up some meat. "You just need to make a choice about how strong you want this partnership to be. Lies will cool my drive, make us less effective."

I nodded. Understandable. She would give it her all if I gave it mine. Got to learn how each other fought so we could enact plans without needing to speak. It made sense for survival. Reading into it any further was not something for a day where a growing headache threatened to pulse my mashed brains out of my ears.

The kettle was already boiling, the question not needing to be asked. Wolf stretched out and yawned, licking his muzzle in anticipation of the cooked meats.

I turned my gaze over to the bound Treant still lurking at the edge of our happy space. A haunting shadow we didn't deserve to have darkening our flickering candle. Something cold prickled inside of me. The need to go to any length to protect our troupe, the need to kill any demon not allied to us, even if it was just figuratively.

"Make sure to keep the embers of the campfire going," I said with a grin, maintaining eye contact with our captive.

CHAPTER FIFTY-FOUR

Brain Waves

There's a marked changed in my notes from the . . . horse incident onward. Whether it was due to the brain injury, the near-death experience, or part of my apparent soul merge, I wasn't sure. I still felt like myself and acted like myself. Well, that was the crux of it—some of my actions were slightly skewed. One half charming showman, the other ruthless combatant—the resulting mix was a boon to both sides. As if my very being had been hit with a power token. Max+.

Ren sighed. "You can't torture information out of him."

I raised an eyebrow at her, unsure if she meant morally or because he couldn't speak. Probably the latter. Not that I particularly *wanted* to torture him and get bad information in the process. There was a part of me who wasn't sure if he had suffered enough yet. Not that I knew his crimes, but he couldn't be much better than the gang who had destroyed the outpost. Complicit, at the least. An eye for an eye left me with a smaller audience, however.

Hadrian continued to glare at us with the impassive yellow eyes that Treants were known for. Based on that one encounter. He had remained remarkably still during the night, and I wondered how the System saw him now. Surely not as a Player, otherwise it would translate his speech. Had he somehow become a Monster but with his memories intact? Not something I wanted an answer to. Maybe it was just a curse that needed lifting.

I turned back to Ren and rubbed my chin. "Do elves have something like good cop, bad cop?"

She blinked, the System doing the hard work of smoothing over the idiom. "Yeah."

"Alright, I'll be the bad cop." I grinned.

"Unfair. That's kind of my thing." She pouted and made a show of possibly wanting to argue over it but relented with a sigh. "I'll follow your lead."

Bad cop wasn't exactly my thing either, but I was feeling off my normal game due to the cracked skull, and it might put off the Treant enough to work better. Maybe demon Max could carry the burden for me. Unfair to name him that, when he was me. I withdrew my lit torch, and we walked over.

"Morning, Hadrian. If that is still you in there. Ren here is insisting that we untie your little tree arms. Personally, I'm against that . . . but if you try anything, then I'll be illuminating your internal organs." I waved the torch in front of him, and he winced away. "I'm fair though—I'll let you decide from which end."

Ren knelt down to work on the bindings. "Best behave. He's been getting gradually more unhinged every day. He'll listen to me, okay? I won't let him hurt you if you play nice."

I watched Hadrian for any kind of reaction, but he remained impassive. If he was a Monster he'd probably attack immediately. One arm came out, and he kept it to himself. Wolf came and sat behind us to watch. I tilted my head over my shoulder. "Don't worry, bud, you might have your new chew toy soon."

Second arm out and he rubbed at his wooden wrists with his little claw hands but continued to glare. Some part of him must remain.

"You're doing well," Ren said to him in a hushed tone beside his head before rejoining me for the interrogation.

"Alright!" I began, louder than necessary to cut him from that comfort. "Now we'll see how useful you are. Raise your right hand if you understand me."

After a brief pause, he did.

"Lower it. Now left arm." The process was repeated, and he understood me. "Right hand is for yes; left is for no. Do you understand?"

His right hand raised with hesitation.

"Just answer honestly," Ren added. "Things will be okay."

She was selling it too well; *I* almost believed her. "Let's start off easy." I worked my jaw. "Are you still Hadrian?"

Right hand, he was still in there. Part of me paled at that reality and how close I had come to drinking the stuff in the Dungeon. Would this have been my life? At least I wouldn't have gotten kicked by the horse—I doubted Treants had proper skulls to crack. Those thoughts aside for now, I went back to the questions.

"Is this a permanent transfiguration?" Left hand. "A curse that needs lifting?" Right hand.

"I have an antidote I could give him!" Ren offered, being ever so helpful.

Hadrian seemed to perk up at this, wanting to nod if his current physiology allowed it. His right clawed hand rose up eagerly.

"Hand down," I demanded. "That wasn't a question. Your honesty *may* earn you lenience, but I need further questions answered first."

An outside observer may wonder why we didn't turn him back into a human first and get the information in its fullest form. Have an actual conversation about it. Well, a magician never revealed his secrets. We kept him desperate.

"First question. Are there any other groups of the Crimson Shadow in this area?" Right hand. "There is one by the bridge over the river?" Right hand.

Ren leaned toward him. "Is that the only one left?" Tentative right hand.

That filled enough of the gaps for me to be contented. We had killed just over a dozen of the gang. It'd be hard to imagine there were many more lurking around, given how quiet the woods had been in terms of Players. One last group to prevent people gaining access to the Golden Fields and beyond seemed reasonable.

"Are there more than five members there?" I narrowed my eyes. Right hand. "More than ten?" He paused, raising both hands slightly—unsure. It looked as though Parties were often the maximum of five people. They had three scouting groups causing havoc throughout this first area. Probably a group or two would be at the bridge.

The three of us might have an issue. I wondered how they would respond if I suggested stowing a corpse on Wolf for easy Roger access. I wondered if he'd enjoyed his mash. Suddenly, I felt very hungry. I'd need to bring him back soon to let him know that I was okay. Would he even be worried? Probably busy making more little Rogers. Why was I so hungry?

My eyes scanned through my Inventory as the other two waited. Just needed something to snack on really—why was so much of it raw meat? I was just about to settle for some plain bread when I scrolled to the consumable bottles.

Into my hand, one of the vials of blood. "This pique your interest, firewood?"

He almost went to leap from his sitting position to grab for it before a calm hand from the elf kept him seated. I rolled my tongue around in my mouth, wondering how it tasted. Probably worse than my own blood, which I wasn't too keen on—based on way too much experience to be healthy.

"Addiction is a terrible thing." I swirled it side to side. It was fair to assume he probably didn't know how the Lady's Ability worked or couldn't explain the nuance of it even if he did. "Perhaps we can cure you of this, as well?"

He shook, and his left hand went up. They seemed reliant on it, or at least desired it more than was reasonable. A knife I could use to twist.

I popped the cork, watching the panicked reaction on his wooden face. Slowly, I started to tip it until the first drop escaped and fell to the uncaring ground.

Hadrian squirmed and shook as though I had plunged the torch into him.

"Wait," Ren interrupted. "Maybe if he *really* helps us, then you can give that to him?"

I clicked my tongue and watched her bright-blue eyes. It was hidden far below her surface expression, but there was the hint there that she was enjoying this. It *was* fun; I was enjoying it too. "Well, it'd have to be something *very* helpful for me to reconsider." I didn't tip any more, but I held it at a threatening slant. Maybe it should be worrying we found joy in tormenting someone, but then again, the history between us all . . .

"You can do that, right, Hadrian?" Her eyes searched his yellow orbs. "Do you know where the Lady is going?"

Despite his lust for the liquid I held with such contempt, he wavered before slowly raising his right hand.

"Somewhere in the second area, past the bridge?" Right hand. "The Mills?" Left hand. "One of the towns?" Right hand.

I raised my eyebrow at Wolf as the elf went through all the towns in the second area. Sitting there with his little bowler on, he looked quite the character. I gave him an are-you-okay nod, which he answered by rubbing his stomach with a large paw. With a grin, I acknowledged his desires. We had already had breakfast, but there was no law against a second one. *Did* we already eat? Things were starting to blur, and an ache spread through my head. I *was* hungry.

"Candlekeep! Perfect, thank you, Hadrian." Ren didn't have it in her to fake a smile, but at least her voice sounded happy to have gotten an answer.

With a minute gesture to her, I wanted to see if she had anything to ask—which she declined with the slight shake of her head, reading my intent loud and clear. Being on the same page felt good.

"Alright, Hadrian. I guess you've earned this then." I chucked a bottle to his rootlike feet.

Immediately, he dropped to the ground to scrabble for it, his sharp fingers digging through the dirt. He got it in his clutches with some effort and lifted it up into the air to see that it was just an empty container instead. One singular sad Dazzle icon. A shadow passed over him as Wolf stomped down upon his body and began to tear him to pieces.

"Shame we didn't have any antidotes, huh?" I watched the carnage impassively.

"Oh, I did." Ren shrugged and looked at me. "But I wasn't about to waste something we might need."

I nodded and then winced as a sharp pain radiated up the front of my head. My hand held it to make sure I didn't have a trapdoor about to open and spill my brain matter about. Fertilize the soil, see what grew from my mind. Probably something remarkably impressive to look at but structurally flawed and liable to leap beneath the first hoof that came near it. *Foot*, not hoof. Although . . .

"You okay? You need to rest." Ren put her arm around me and walked us away from the sound of Wolf chewing wood into shrapnel.

"Need to sit and maybe eat. Definitely eat actually. And sit." Conjured up a chair—my last one. I'd have to steal more. I sat, and she gave me a squeeze on the shoulder before moving away. My eyes held closed, I tried to will away the pain.

"No adventuring until you're recovered. I know you're burning up to go get maimed at the bridge, but this is the first time we've got the upper hand, right?"

She *was* right, on all accounts. Her chair moved across the dirt and stopped beside mine. If we had taken out most of the gang here, then they couldn't afford to try to chase us around. They'd hold the bridge at all costs—if that was truly their plan. That put them in one place that we could assail at our leisure. When I was a little healthier.

I turned my tired head to see her beside me. "You're a great good cop."

"Thanks. I was impressed by your bad-cop routine." Although her eyes narrowed, there was no tension in her face. "You do the unhinged thing really well."

"Hardly had to act at all." I smiled and looked at the sky. Cloudy but pleasant. I closed my eyes as Wolf padded over to lie down near us. The trauma and the merge had left me feeling both not myself and too much of myself. An odd mix that didn't seem to have settled yet.

I felt Ren's hand on my arm. "Hey, Max. Take a break from being full-on today, okay? Let me be in charge."

"My life is in your hands." Too tired to open my eyes, I tried to tune out most things. She asked the bear to collect wood, specifying clearly that it shouldn't be wood from Hadrian. The campfire was renewed. The sound of cutting. Pouring water. I fell asleep with a complaining stomach.

I awoke, briefly concerned, sometime later. By my own volition and not at the behest of the elf. My vision blurred as I tried to click everything back into place. Still daytime, so just a nap. There was a smell that was . . . divine. I leaned forward to see Ren stirring an almost cauldron-sized metal pot hanging over the fire. Wolf was lying on his side against my chair, asleep, like an oversize dog.

"Sometimes it feels like I did die and went to heaven." I smiled softly at the elf as she turned to me.

"Smells good, huh? My aunt used to have a plot where she'd grow vegetables. In the colder months, we'd hunt rabbits and then make stew." Her eyes unfocused as she dug around at those memories. "Just a hot meal, a fireplace, and warm blankets against the unrelenting cold."

"Sounds like the perfect day." I furrowed my brow. "I seem to have mixed memories now. Although, only at a certain point do things diverge. Same childhood. The love for magic . . . also similar. Mother passing, then it gets a bit murky."

"It's kind of spooky in a way." She began ladling some stew into bowls. "Like there must be other versions of me somewhere? Ones where I didn't come here?"

I grunted. "No point worrying. You're you, and this is your life and existence."

"I suppose." She walked over to hand me a bowl before sitting on the chair beside me with her own. "You wouldn't want to be a different Max, in a different time? Somewhere less dangerous?"

My tired eyes looked at the raised spoon, and I blew the steam away and cooled the stew. Put the chunks of cooked vegetables in my mouth. Heavenly.

Glancing at her bright-blue eyes eager for my response, I shook my head with a smile. I didn't know whether it was the comforting food or something about the way she was looking at me, but the answer was a clear page in my otherwise clouded mind.

"I'm right where I want to be."

CHAPTER FIFTY-FIVE

Wand Waving

Rest and recovery were always worth the time spent. There was the temptation to go full speed constantly, but that just led to stretching yourself too thin. In this world, there were dozens of things waiting in the wings for that to happen, just to snap you in half or pierce you through. On the flip side, you didn't want to get too used to the easy times, lest you found yourself a pincushion for the hard times eager for a share in ending your existence. A balance had to be struck.

We ate the amazing stew. Several helpings, in fact. Just sat and enjoyed the moderate weather and some time not being under constant threat. I dozed off a few times, always waking to see that Ren was nearby. It comforted me as much as I felt guilty about my current predicament. Was I holding us back? Could I look after her just as well if something similar happened to her? I hated to think she may get as injured as me. As if I could choose to solely take on the burden myself.

Now that my mind was closer to being in one piece, I withdrew the journal taken from the Crimson Shadow camp. Given that it had only been a handful of days, it wasn't exactly information dense. The start was a few weeks prior. A group of them had been an adventuring party, and they were . . . disillusioned with the System. Not a particularly villainous take. I would admit that I held my own disdain for the world I now found myself in. Well . . . parts of it. I gave Ren a sly glance before returning to the pages.

There was a marked change in the tone and language used after the point where they had met the Lady. For a moment, I considered someone else had written the rest of the few entries—but no, same idioms and structure, just . . . less concise. My tongue rolled around in my mouth as I tried to read the bigger picture that the writing wasn't really telling me. Eventually, I sighed and snapped it shut, returning it to my Inventory with no accompanying trick.

"What is it? Mind control? *Is* she a vampire?" Ren had been patiently waiting for me to finish, not wanting to rush my brain and turn it to slurry. I presumed, at least.

I rubbed at my forehead. "No, it's not something so . . . cliché? Uh, do you remember when you first came here, there was a Soft Landing buff?"

She nodded. "To smooth over our initial acceptance of the System."

"Imagine if there was an opposite, something that took your rejection and amplified it. And then someone came along and told you—"

"That there was a way out. If you followed them?"

With those sharp blue eyes, she had no issue reading between the lines. I looked into them for a second longer than I intended before I nodded. "If my assumption is correct, it reduces some Stats as well. Unless the author was an anomaly, his writing simplified after the . . . change."

"Lower Intelligence and Wisdom would certainly explain their reckless actions. And how easily they fall for your tricks." She narrowed her eyes, testing the waters. It mostly reminded me of how close I was to success before the equine interruption.

"I'm never going to live down almost dying to a horse, am I?" I groaned and sank into my chair farther. On my to-do list, I added stealing a more comfortable chair to the bottom.

"Probably not. But you also almost died from falling out of a tree, so . . ."

"Touché." It seemed as though I could overcome any odd danger aside from things that would be anticlimactic ways for me to die. No doubt, after besting the rest of the Shadow, I would slip off the bridge and drown myself after hitting a rock in the river. That said, I did come into this world with a head injury. Perhaps the System liked to repeat things like that. I was doomed to slowly batter my brain on the regular until I couldn't survive it any longer.

I rubbed my fingertips on the wooden chair arms, feeling the texture. "Where are we?"

There was brief concern on her face, as if my traumatic brain injury may have knocked something loose. "We went north from their camp. Wolf carried you in a sling I had fashioned until we felt we were far enough away."

I smiled, unsure why I didn't just check my Map. That prompted my lagging brain into action, however. Thoughts spinning back up as if I had never been down for the count at all. "Perfect. We can hit a couple of Quests on the way back to town. Level up and then make plans for our assault." Things were really coming together now. Knowledge was indeed power.

"How is your recovery?" Her words a damp blanket on my ablaze ambition.

[Health Report]
[Minor trauma]

"Down to minor now. That stew is powerful stuff." I gave her a grin, and she rolled her eyes.

Wolf returned to our camp having been out patrolling. He had seemed fulfilled enough to sleep and laze most of the day away, quiet and content. Ren had helped him with his STAR at some point during my on-and-off napping schedule, using the same sausage-pointer method. Got some items equipped on him, and even used some of the tokens we had saved for him—although my brain was too mushed up to hear what they had settled on.

"There's some System-created to the northeast." He yawned, now in close proximity to our fire again. "And to the northwest there's a house that smells bad."

"How bad?" I raised an eyebrow.

"Like bad magic."

Ren removed her hat to place it on her lap and scratched at her hair, which was tied up. Still radiant, as always. "Sound like it could be the witches for that Quest?"

I didn't even have my hat on and hadn't for a while. No wonder my brain felt so exposed—it was definitely that and not the broken skull. "Could be. Was it made of wood?"

"We should probably double-check first before we go immolating random buildings, trickster." She tapped at the edge of the wide brim. "If we are careless, then we'll end up falling to the bad side."

She had a point, even if I was reluctant to agree. As much as I trusted Wolf's nose to determine danger, it could easily be something unknown. Still, a fire arrow to the building followed up by an entangling arrow through the window seemed like a decent way to approach witches. Of course, I didn't really know much about them to say—it was a decent way to kill anyone with an allergy to being burned alive.

Some of the books I had read as a child mentioned witches, for all the good that was. Often just female spellcasters when wizardry was seen as a more masculine title. Some were like hags—demented and cruel—whereas others were closer to druids and crafted potions—based around nature. If the Town Board wanted the witch killed, then she was probably more likely the former and quite likely not to be so easily taken down with a little fire.

"Are you truly embarrassed about the horse thing?"

"Huh?" Her question took me out of the pondering, and it didn't look like she was teasing me. "Ah. Not really. It's okay to fail sometimes, right?" I grinned. "There were a handful of moments I could have died if things didn't work out perfectly. Can't plan for everything."

Ren smiled.

It briefly alarmed me, and my heart skipped a beat—probably just due to the shock. My brain tried to reverse to see what I could have said to elicit such a reaction.

"You must have really hurt your head, trickster." Her face softened to a normal neutral expression as her eyes focused on her STAR menus. "There is something I needed your help with, speaking of planning."

Despite the initial surprise, I settled into a comfortable smile too. I watched her eyes look around at the unseen screens as she gathered her thoughts. She had some ideas, and I was all ears.

We spent the rest of the late afternoon and early evening going over Skills, Inventory uses, and Equipment. It was nice to have time to sit and mull over problems rather than be constantly traveling between battles. She was earnest in her attempts to learn, and I tried not to gush at having someone to share all the details of my tricks and illusions with.

Her brow furrowed as she looked at the pack of cards in her hands, the glow of the fire illuminating one side of her as the light of day faded away. Working her jaw, she withdrew the top card and held it up. Three of clubs. "Is this your card?"

I shook my head and smiled. "No, I'm afraid not."

"Ah." She wrinkled her face up. "I think that's because . . . you already have it."

"Oh?"

She looked toward my chest, and my eyes fell to my jacket pocket. I reached a hand in there and felt the shape of a card. Out of the pocket and into the light. Nine of diamonds. "That *is* my card." I grinned. "Very impressive."

"I learned from the best." She stuck her tongue out and returned the deck to me.

"You'll have to introduce me to them," I murmured, eyes focused on shuffling through the deck. One of the cards had a slight defect, as expected. Very minor, yet I assumed easy for her elfin eyes to pick up. No Dazzle icon for me. As I turned it over, it was also a nine of diamonds. "Placed the card in my jacket earlier and forced my hand into picking the same one from the deck."

"Makes it less impressive when you explain it." She pouted and leaned back in her chair.

"No, no." I smiled and waved the card at her. "This is very solid. I *am* impressed."

She raised an eyebrow. "Impressed but not fooled?"

"Magic is my life's work, and *you* are never fooled by what I do. We are both too perceptive for such tricks."

Ren shrugged but took the compliment without wanting to argue about it. "What about you, Wolf?"

"I am easily fooled. Everything Max does is beyond my understanding." The bear rested his chin on his crossed paws as he watched us.

"What about the trick I just did on Max?"

"I saw you place the card when he was asleep, so I already understood the deception."

Ren screwed her face up in defeat. I wasn't sure if it was due to my injury, but she was a bit more relaxed in showing her emotions. Somewhere between the scowls, unrelenting showmanship, and bloody murder, we had become somewhat inseparable. My brush with death had prompted the part of her scared of losing everything again into perhaps cherishing the time we did have before something really bad happened to one or both of us.

And what of me? I had accepted that it was okay to be a little broken. To have a day off and not be so focused on perfecting my tricks. Failure and being miserable. Took a split skull to finally release the built pressure, but I felt . . . calmer than I had in years. Happier even, despite the hardship. My eyes settled on the grumpy elf. It was hard not to be totally enamored with her. If anything, wanting to carve out a space in this world where she could be happy and safe was worth a dozen kicks to the head.

"What are you thinking about, Max?" Her head was tilted as my eyes had glazed over in thought.

"Nothing." I smiled. "You have any Magic Wands?"

"I think a couple?" She sat back up and started looking through her Inventory.

I avoided certain thoughts by getting back to work. Ironic given my inner monologue just now, but I didn't have the heart to address certain things yet, even as they swelled within my chest. "Wolf, could you grab me some . . . chunks of the Treant, please?"

"Okay." He yawned as he stood up and left for the pile of Hadrian parts.

My eyes spun through my Inventory as I started planning my next attempted bullshitting maneuver. The System would end up regretting my existence, I was sure of it.

I spent some time cutting, carving, and attempting to sew parts together out of whatever junk I had managed to accumulate over the adventure so far. It wasn't exactly perfect and probably wouldn't last more than a few days—but for a prototype it'd do.

"Here, hold your arm out." I gestured for her to show me her right arm, which she did. I frowned in thought. Outside arm would probably be best so that it didn't get in the way of drawing arrows. With a shrug, I placed my contraption on her forearm and began to tie it around her. An awkward, weighty silence sat in the background of the act as she watched me patiently.

"Only slightly less charming than the flowers you gave me," she eventually said as I finished tying the last knot.

"Don't." I sighed and sank into my chair. "Another thing I'll never live down."

"You will." She looked up from the roughly created apparel to me before gathering her composure. "So, what's this thing you've burdened me with?"

"Probably something overengineered that doesn't work. But you can slot wands into it, and depending on how strict the System is, you should be able to focus and use them from this arm-mounted thing rather than solely holding one out."

Her furrowed brow returned, and she gave it a look over. "So if it works, it'll give me some pseudomagical powers essentially?"

"Essentially," I said and nodded. "Either that or I just spent my evening making an ugly bracelet for you that does nothing."

"If it's the latter, then it doesn't need to do anything. I'll keep it as something you spent time and effort making." Her eyes moved from it to me. "And I'll keep it nice and safe in my Inventory where it can't be seen by anyone."

I waved her off. "Yeah, yeah. Give it a try already." If it didn't work, then I had other ideas, but if it did, then it opened up a whole can of worms for me to dig into. "It should fit Spell Scrolls in too, barely."

"Don't want to waste those on a test though." Her eyes were unfocused as she was looking through her items. "Here's a plain Zap Wand. Does hardly any Damage, but ten charges that replenish every day."

My head nodded slowly, trying not to think of what I could do with that. Ren withdrew it and slowly inserted it in the grooves on the bracer. She flexed her fingers back and forth a few times and then leveled her fist toward the fire.

Wolf and I widened our eyes in expectation.

Nothing happened, and I began to deflate. Worth a try, but back to the—

A zap of yellow light arced from the wand and out into the fire, briefly causing it to flare up brighter before it simmered down.

"It's not superintuitive," Ren said, focusing on the bracer. "But . . ." She fired a second and then a third soon after, her face a scowl occasionally illuminated by the magic fired. She nodded slowly after the third shot dissipated and turned to me with a raised eyebrow. "Not bad, trickster."

"I would bow, but my head would roll from my shoulders and crack on the ground." Instead, I smiled and closed my eyes, looking up at the night sky. The amber light of the fire illuminating the darkness. "Best stick around," I said, mostly to fill the silence, "because the show is just getting started."

"I intend to," she said quietly.

Which I couldn't reply to, as I had fallen asleep once again.

Or was just about to anyway and could pretend that I didn't hear it so that I didn't have to address it.

Possibly the least commendable show of Deception yet.

CHAPTER FIFTY-SIX

Just a Spell

Down to business. The System certainly expected you to want to continue to grow in power. Do Quests, level up, unlock new Abilities, and travel to new locations. There were Players who had given up the rat race to varying success. Tried to settle into normal jobs or whatever closest proximity to it they could get. Some lucky ones even had the System on their side to facilitate some normality. Others were punished and flung from whatever safety they tried to shroud themselves in. Attempting to understand what the System wanted from you was to court madness.

"Max?"

"Huh?" I awoke, standing up by reflex. "Ow . . ." I groaned and tried to flex my back out. Morning light blinded me as I recovered into the waking world.

"Serves you right for falling asleep in your chair rather than being comfortable with me and Wolf." Ren stood with arms crossed, a scowl leveled my way. "Health Report?"

I blinked twice, still trying to process everything. The information popped into the side of my vision while my brain caught up.

[Health Report]
[No injury]

"Clean bill of health." I smiled, rubbing at my eye sockets.

"Good, get packed up. We're leaving soon."

I let my eyes free again to see her walking off. Wolf sat beside me, and I gave him a grimace. "Ren okay? She seems . . . annoyed at me." While that was hardly irregular—at least visually—it made our closeness over the days of rest seem like something I had only dreamed.

"No. She is more annoyed at herself. But it is your duty to take the brunt of it until she can come to terms with her feelings." He looked up at me with his amber eyes.

"Is it?" I yawned and stretched out again. Sleeping in the chair *was* a real mistake. Couldn't deny her that, whatever feelings she was having issue with.

Wolf yawned in response, a louder echo of my own. "I'm certainly not going to. If you are to be her mate, then—"

"*Ah-ah.* None of that, please." I tried to push him away. He was very heavy. "Let's just go murder things and not get ahead of ourselves."

"You are both impossible." He rolled his eyes and moved away to catch up to the elf.

Having an intangible Inventory meant there wasn't really much to pack away and everything that I did need to was a simple matter of getting close enough. So eager was I to catch up, I didn't even flourish about as the chair, blanket, and some of my crafting things vanished into nothing. Not everything had to be a show. I shuddered. *Who was I?*

I relented to a little jog to up to catch them, as they were just on the outskirts of our safe area. The cardio wasn't necessary, but at least my head didn't feel like cracking like an egg under the pressure, which made a nice change. Not a bad idea to make sure I was in top form before submitting myself to violent combat once more.

"No funny business until we know you're top form again," Ren admonished me as I approached, seemingly catching the tail end of my inner thoughts.

"Of course." I nodded, although I wouldn't call it *funny business*. "Everything okay?"

She opened and closed her mouth before exhaling from her nose. "Yeah. Just spent too much time in my own head last night." She narrowed her blue eyes at me. "Sorry if I snapped at you. We'll talk later, okay?"

"Promise?"

My persistence seemed to relax her more than annoy her further. "Promise," she confirmed. "Now, we going for the witches?"

"Yeah. Tough magical opponent, but it'll be useful loot. Hopefully." Who knew with the System—we might get nothing for our efforts. Plus, magic users seemed to get the short end of the stick when faced with the long end of Wolf's claws, so if we could get close enough, it might not be such a hardship. Knock on wood. I tapped the closest tree.

Ren nodded. "Confirm target, then burn the house down?"

"I was thinking about that." I leaned against Wolf and crossed my arms. "We're looking at this a little too simply."

The bear turned his head. "How so? House was small. I could probably knock it down."

"Wolf also upgraded an Ability that allows him to absorb magical damage," Ren added.

I stretched my neck out. Spending most of the day on the wooden chair had really done me a disservice. "Witches might not be Players, but I've been thinking about what I would do in their situation. Like a Dungeon."

The elf nodded slowly. "So, traps and passive spells in the area—like that dome over the Shadow camp?"

"Exactly." I snapped my fingers. "I might just be overthinking it—but it was on the challenge board, so it is supposed to be difficult for a whole group." My right eye twitched. "You think we'll ever be a full Party?"

The elf shrugged, and the bear had nothing to say. At this stage, I didn't care to add anyone else—it would just mean more voices clogging up the poor bear's brain. But when the default was five, we were less effective as three. Of course, that would just mean we'd need to try harder. Our Class rarities might pull us through.

"So," I continued, glazing past that train of thought and lukewarm reception. "I expect that our presence will be known as we get closer and that we should be on guard."

"Your suggestion is to knock on the door and see if they answer?" Her eyes narrowed.

Witches would be System-created Monsters, so I couldn't exactly rely on my charms. In fairness, I wasn't feeling too mentally spry anyway. "Magic users are weakest at close range, for the most part. I feel if we engage from afar, they will have more use of whatever spells they have."

"Sounds good to me." Wolf grinned. "Although if they taste as bad as they smell, then my view is more neutral."

Ren sighed and looked out into the woods, drumming her fingers on her belt. "As much as I'd like to burn it down from afar, I think you're right. Any good witch would have protection from that, and then we'd be on the back foot. Plus, we haven't even confirmed it's them yet."

The Quest just gave a vague region where they might be found. The house was within the region, but then a lot of things could be. It had also said "suspected witch coven," which could mean two to . . . five or six witches, as far as my knowledge took me. "In the event that it *is* more than one witch . . ." I frowned and rubbed my head. Maybe not so perfectly recovered. "I don't know. It's not really a nuanced encounter, is it?"

"I trust your judgment. Confirm targets and then deal accordingly." The elf nodded to sign off on the conversation. The die had been cast.

We started walking, and I felt better about it. Not really less achy—but the ball had been pushed down the hill, and all I had to do was keep the momentum. Back to adventuring. Dipping toes into the violence to get stronger, to go be violent somewhere else. The group at the bridge worried me, but I wasn't sure why yet. Maybe it was just that it was an end point. The final part of the tumor to cut out of this first area before it could be deemed safe. Or *safer*, perhaps.

Ren walked up beside me. "Here, peace offering." She held out a sandwich.

"Thanks." I took it, realizing how hungry I was. No breakfast, as I had over-indulged on much-needed sleep. I took a bite and smiled at her, swallowing it down before responding. "All is forgiven. It'll be my turn to cook tonight."

"Oh?" She raised an eyebrow. "I look forward to that then."

"Temper your expectations." I grinned in response. "Let's just survive the day first."

Wolf turned his head to me, a smile at the edges of his mouth. "I'll keep an eye out for any horses."

I groaned but was secretly thankful.

It helped to keep us in better spirits, in fact. I didn't mind a little levity at my own expense. Not unlike me to be a spectacle, of course, so I could be the butt of the joke to keep the mood light. And it *was*, at least up until the point that the house came into view.

A small cottage by any description. The mixture of cobblestone walls and off-white plaster broken up by a deep-brown wooden frame made it look like something from a storybook. Perhaps I *was* living in a storybook. Was I the main character? Maybe Wolf was. He was much stronger and looked rather dapper in his bowler. I should just be thankful to be his assistant.

Ren nudged me, and the growing mania fell off my mental shelf. Her glare of concern told me she could see me losing focus. Despite the System giving me the go-ahead, my mind was still reeling from the . . . accident. In the real world—my real world—there wouldn't have been a recovery from that kind of injury. At least not without months of rest, and even then, to have bounced back like I had would be unheard of. System be damned for the unrelenting violence, but a shaky thumbs-up for being able to put its toys back together again after they broke into pieces.

Her ability to read me so well might be part of her Oathwarden Class, or she could just be perceptive, and I had a terrible poker face when losing control of my mind. Back on track, I focused on what lay ahead. The thatched roof looked like it could go up in flames easily. With enough of a running start, the whole thing could be leveled by the bear if he charged it down. More fool us if it turned out to be the quaint home of an elderly grandma or young family trying to make a start off the grid. Although there was no grid, only violence.

"Let's go," I said, more to get out of my own head than wanting to get into the cauldron looming ahead.

I stopped as we entered the clearing that surrounded it. About sixty feet away. Little wisps of smoke waved from the brickwork chimney. Magic surrounded us.

I could feel it. Steeped into the ground. Something odd about it—not familiar, but perhaps adjacent. Definitely present, and something to be cautious about.

"You were right," I murmured to the bear, "there *is* the taste of bad magic here."

Even from the outside, there was a sense of foreboding, as if the sky were darkening as we approached. Still not enough of a clue to destroy the building—it could just be cursed. I wondered briefly why I was talking myself out of the easy option. Was it part of the spell? Maybe I was just too worried about becoming like the Shadow and leaving nothing but ruin in my wake. The points where compassion and warmth won over along our journey were few and far between. We couldn't let that be an excuse to fall down to their level.

Twenty feet away, and the door opened. We stopped.

A short figure emerged into the light of day. An old woman with silver hair wearing an aged yellow sundress, a circle of flowers as a belt. Simple leather sandals and a crocheted white shawl around her. A matching yellow ribbon in her hair and a small wooden cane in her hand.

"Hello!" Her voice was cracked and shaky. "Are you adventurers? I've been waiting for my daughter to visit, but she has been missing for two days."

Tension filled the air. Apprehensive, sure. But I wasn't so easily dissuaded from my gut feeling. System-created ran from a loose script, and I wanted to skip to the last page.

"How many are in your coven, witch?" I glared at her.

"What's that, young man? I didn't quite hear you." She made the motion of cupping at her ear, eyes narrowing in concentration.

I ran my tongue across my teeth. "You see it?" I murmured to Ren. She returned a slow nod.

Good. I wasn't going crazy. Perhaps rude not to ask Wolf, but I could see his fur was on end—he could smell it even if he couldn't see it.

A smile crossed my lips, and I pulled my cloak tightly over my arm. Perhaps you could catch more flies with honey, after all. "I said it's chilly out. We'd be glad to help you in exchange for some warmth."

"The stove is on." The old lady smiled. "I can make tea."

"Delightful." My fake smile widened as I started walking closer.

Her eyes narrowed, and she glared at all three of us one after another. "You are *nice* adventurers, right?" Smarter than she looked, she wanted to see behind the curtain more than we did.

"No," I said, flinging back my cape to reveal the Imp tucked under my arm. His fireball went out immediately.

Amber light obscured the witch as the attack blasted around her, the flickering of a purple shield painting the flame in a foul hue. A radiant arrow went out from beside me and burst into the shield just as the fire faded away.

"Miserable shits! You'll pay!" the woman hissed, now dressed in a dark robe with scratchy black hair, the life present in her pleasant appearance replaced with the grimace of something more evil. Ren's arrow was embedded in her shoulder.

Wolf charged forward, blazing energy around his feet as he surged toward the small cottage.

And then, with a click of her fingers, it was gone. Or rather, we were now somewhere different.

Darkness loomed overhead. Underground. A chamber, roughly the same size as the clearing around where the cottage had been. Dimly lit by a few candles melting atop of skulls. A little too on the nose, but I admired a little cliché when it came to appearances. Tables strewn with a random assortment of jars, ingredient containers, and potion-crafting apparatuses. The smell of damp earth and a twinge of bad smells—foul magic, warmth, and untoward ingredients.

A few skeletons chained to one wall, probably not-skeletons at one point, and if I had the time I would have pondered over whether those were captured Players or just System dressing to set the mood. The second-most-important thing in this new space was the large cauldron in the center of the room, heated by a glowing fire that flickered between the expected oranges and a strange green. It bubbled and steamed in a way most displeasing, yet remained enthralling despite that fact.

Of course, the most important thing to note was the three figures. The old lady with an arrow in her shoulder was now accompanied by two other witches. One tall and lithe, her curly ginger hair a contrast to Skill being prepared that was almost green in hue. Their third was portly and covered in necklaces and jewelry made of dried insect parts. Her tongue didn't seem to know its place and writhed around the outside of her mouth as she glared at me hungrily.

"Fresh meat!" the first cackled as the other two readied spells to be cast.

My feet dug into the soft earth as I tensed to move, a wide grin across my face as purple electricity arced along my arms. There was a new show to be put on.

A contest of magical prowess, mine for the winning.

CHAPTER FIFTY-SEVEN

Powered Up

I wasn't a demon, at least not in the traditional sense. There was some manner of blurred lines where I certainly had demonic abilities, but I still had a tight grip on my humanity. No growing horns or wings bursting from my back. Not so far anyway. For the purposes of these memoirs, imagine that I just knocked on wood. That phrase might not even be a real thing in any world other than my old one. But neither were demons, or at least that's what I told myself.

Spellcasters were bad news. Three of them, as we found ourselves stuck in a near-open space, were even worse. Still, I was fresh off a day of rest and eager to put on a good show. Other Max was a combatant and where I believed I had previously drawn my competency and cool head in regard to violence. Now fully formed, it felt even more natural. Born to perform, to live at any cost. To erase any that threatened me.

Even as their spells were about to be cast, my cards went out, split. Purple one burst along a shield on the insect witch, while the second flew off behind them all. An energy flooded the cavern as Wolf activated an Ability. There was a loud hiss, and some darkness filled the area as Ren hit the fire that was beneath the cauldron up with a water arrow, extinguishing it. Pragmatic. I seemed to have made myself the primary target by rushing forward already.

The tall witch had begun casting a dark spell but had to switch to the bear as he launched himself toward her. The smell of something arcane sank through the chamber as blazing light flickered through the darkness where the two clashed. I had to focus ahead and trust he was fine.

Behind the cauldron, the older witch had her arms raised. A pulsing orb of black energy formed and then launched out toward the center of the cavern. As soon as it had been released, an arrow impaled her thin arm. Other than growling out loud, the witch didn't even flinch. The card thrown earlier burst out a

Hellhound from behind her, the flaming canine drawing some focus away from her next spell preparation. The dark orb rose above the cauldron and burst, sending shards of pointed black energy throughout the area. One scoured through my left thigh, a second along my back—narrowly missing my neck.

Insect witch sent a spell at me. A curse. I suddenly felt very slow and sluggish, now unable to get any closer, as if I were dream running. In anger, I sent a single imbued card out. I didn't need to get closer, more fool her. The pain and feeling of warm blood running down my leg cooled my need to show off. I wanted nothing more than to get revenge. Purple energy crackled along my arms as the flare of her shield glowed brightly in the darkness. But I didn't drop the card—I held it there, keeping it powered. She dropped her follow-up to focus on keeping her flickering shield up, pouring her Mana into it. I just poured more of my Mana into my card in return.

The card glowed bright purple at first before starting to turn white as it grew in power. The smell of something burning filled the air and overpowered all the other odors in this underground cavern as our two magical energies fought against each other. I didn't even pay attention to anything else going on in the room. Card stayed energized. Card overpowered all. *Card always won.*

As electricity continued to arc along my arms, I held my right wrist with my left hand. Both soaked with blood. Pain throbbed through my head as the card shone brightly, constantly pushing against the shield. Mana exhaustion hit, and the purple arcs around my arms turned crimson. The card breached the struggling magic shield slowly, carving into it gradually, right before her spell failed.

It was difficult to control the blazing card at such a sudden change of velocity. As soon as it sprang forward, I flicked it straight vertically into the ceiling and let it drop. Mud fell from the ceiling onto the witch's head as she stared at me impassively. Not very flashy, I'll admit—no wonder she wasn't impressed. Part of me wanted my strength tested to find out my limits. My attack had gone halfway through her before I shot it upward, slicing through most of her insides and out of the top of her head. Her hat fell in two halves as she dropped limply to the floor, dark blood and worse leaking from the wound.

My tired eyes scoured the rest of the room. Probably shouldn't have worn myself down just in the first fight. Three on three was good odds for us anyway. The crunch of bones from the growling bear was proof enough. A spellcaster's weakness was usually melee, and Wolf was a force of nature just on his own. I looked at the older witch, who was promptly head shot with an arrow, her spell fizzling out. They had more than one weakness, I supposed.

The Hellhound, happy with his contribution to the fight, padded around from behind the cauldron and went over to the elf, who bent over to give him pets.

"It's sweet of you to always have them come to me." She didn't look up at me but continued to stroke the demonic dog.

"Oh? I don't do that. Not since the first one, really." I flexed out my fingers, wondering if I had a better way of cleaning my hands rather than marring my suit.

"Really?" She looked up at me now, a raised eyebrow as I looked back at her. "Max, did you know your eyes are glowing purple?"

"No?" I looked around to try to find a mirror or reflective enough surface. "Have they done that before?"

Wolf coughed and sneezed. "Ugh, they *do* taste as bad as they smell."

"Only once before, when you lost control that time outside the Dungeon."

I caught her glare as I stepped around to try to find something to look at. "I'm not possessed or anything." My eyebrows raised toward her, and I held up my bloody hands. "I feel totally normal and calm." Perhaps not the most convincing show but hopefully enough to not meet the sharp end of her evil-destroying Ability. It must just be an aftereffect of pushing my magic too far.

She rolled her eyes and returned to ruffling the ears of the hound.

"I suggest we loot and find our way out as soon as possible. This place gives me the creeps worse than the Shadow camp." I narrowed my apparently purple eyes at the tables filled with all sorts of things that I could use—or at least clutter up my Inventory with.

"In my world, witches gain power from their cauldrons. It's like the focus for the coven, so that's why I put out the fire." She stood from the hound to approach one of the bodies.

"I figured it was something smart like that, thank you." The occult books that I had read weren't so instructive, and witches were not actually real in my world— so her knowledge was appreciated.

She whistled. "Two Power Tokens, some scrolls and wands."

I checked the body near me.

[138 Gold]
[Power Tokens (2)]
[Fleet Boots of the Strider]
[Necklace of the Wise]
[Wand of Frost Cone (1 use)]
[Odd Skull]
[Emerald]
[Witch's Pride]

I whistled at the boots. Three Dexterity and 5 percent movement-speed increase. One of the better things we had found so far, in terms of Stat distribution. "What do you have on your boots currently?"

"Just two Dexterity."

"Here, have these then." I grinned. It annoyed me that the pure-Intelligence suffix seemed to be *of the Wise* when really that should be for Wisdom. Perhaps it was the Intelligence that made me think that. Witch's Pride fit in the vague Accessory slot, and increased spell-casting speed and magic Damage both by 5 percent. As if I needed more excuse to push my cards to the limit.

Wolf threw up part of the witch he had eaten. "That's better." He smacked his lips together in disgust. "My body here also has items to loot, but I keep accidentally closing the blue box every time I go to read things."

"Did you try imagining a sausage?" I raised an eyebrow.

He shook his head and then furrowed his brow in concentration. Bizarrely cute, if not for the blood covering his face and bowler. After a moment, elation struck his face, and he smiled, tongue hanging out. "I got the two tokens, but I'm not looking at the rest."

"Good enough, bud. Nice effort." I gave him a pat along his flank, mostly as an excuse to wipe my hands off on his fur rather than my own clothing. I helped him out by looking at the loot on the corpse he had created.

[155 Gold]

[Ruby (2)]

[Warrior's Breastplate]

[Normal Skull]

[Sword of Fire]

[Headband of Woe]

I blinked slowly. Surely not? That was a lot of loot and not particularly useful for me. Except for the orange border around the headband item . . .

"Everything okay, Max?"

"Oh, yeah," I said, as I stood and turned to face her. "Just found my first legendary item, is all."

[Headband of Woe: Magic Damage increases 5% per 5% Mana spent]

She returned my gaze impassively. "Is it a bow?"

"No."

"Will it stop your hands from bleeding?"

"Uh. Maybe the opposite." I grinned sheepishly. <Mana Manipulation> allowing me to funnel the stuff into my card made this a potentially broken item in terms of increasing my card damage—it was worth dropping the Intelligence and spell Crit Chance for the extra boost, even if it didn't click with my summons.

She sighed and threw her arms up in resignation. "I give up with you. If you're done stealing everything, let's find our way out?"

I watched her pace about, looking for a switch or magical device to flip us back up to the surface. There were certainly no obvious doors or stairs out of here. "Are you just disappointed we didn't get to do any magic?"

She crossed her arms and bit her tongue. "Am I becoming that easy to read?"

"Sometimes overpowering enemies the normal way is just safer. If you can put a threat down from a distance, then that's less of a headache." With a smile, I leaned against a table. I knew that the combined-trick stuff would come to us slowly, being how it wasn't such a natural thing for them—but it was great to see she remained eager. "That said, I am also disappointed."

"Good. I'd hate to think we'd swapped ideals."

Wolf sniffed and looked up at me. "I thought you said you weren't—"

"That's not what that means," I interrupted, waving him away. "This cavern sure is stuffy, huh? Let's find the switch."

[Witch's Brew]
[Empty Bottle (3)]
[Incense (4)]
[Sapphire]

Most of the table-bound loot looked a little too gross to want to carry around. Small body parts once belonging to animals, dried leaves and herbs, or mysterious liquids that I didn't like the look of. Useful if I wanted to poison someone, maybe, but my cards seemed to be quicker at getting people dead. The Witch's Brew was a potion that the System wouldn't even describe the purpose of—but it looked *evil* and reminded me of the Treants' transformation water.

Given that I could barely stand the thought of drinking Health Potions, there wasn't much chance of me casually taking a sip to find out what it actually did. A sudden guilt sank into me, as I realized that Roger was still out of the loop on everything. Walking over to the witch that looked the least maimed, I threw down the <Demonic Pact> card.

The figure rose, ears cracking out amid the wiry hair of the puppet. "Boss? Boss!" A wide grin twisted up from under his glowing purple eyes.

"Roger." I grinned back. "Just wanted to let you know I still live."

"Thank fuck!" He leaned the body back against one of the tables. "I was worried as shit after seeing how fucked your head was. *Absolutely fucked.*"

"You're telling me." I tried not to think about it, lest my head start hurting again in reliving the moment. "We have a superimportant gig coming up tomorrow. More people killing."

He nodded, an awkward expression for the puppet corpse. "That's, like, my second-favorite thing to do. Big dog and the gargoyle will be there too?"

I winced. "The team is still together, yes."

He looked past me at the surrounding area for the first time, seeing where we were and undoubtedly catching the glare of the elf. "I'll get to training then, boss. I'll be ready to crack skulls as soon as you call me."

"Thanks, Roger. Give my best to your family."

As he sank away and the body dropped to the floor, I turned to the expected furrowed brow of the Oathwarden—but there was none. Either she hadn't heard it or had just moved on and not taken it to heart. I rubbed my eyes, already tired of the gloom of this place.

With everything now scoured for what looked vaguely useful, I assisted with finding a way out. It took some awkward prodding around, and some interesting revelations that made it look like the coven might have eaten people at some point, before we eventually found the spell artifact that swapped us back to the surface. Thanks to my apparent magical training, I was able to understand and activate it, otherwise we would have lived down there forever. Or at least until Wolf ate us.

"Fresh air!" Ren breathed deeply as we stood in the clearing once more, among the grass and beneath a clouded sky.

I grimaced toward the building. The witches were System-created, so might respawn at some point. Should we destroy the house? Was there even a point? Futility pressed down on my sore brain, and I attempted to shrug it off. Quest was done. That's all that mattered right now.

"Did you get any lightning-based Spell Scrolls?" I stretched my neck out as I gestured for us to leave the area.

"Yeah, one. Arc+." She withdrew it and handed it over.

"Thank you. Keep any others; use them for devising tricks."

She narrowed her eyes but nodded. I practiced putting it into my Inventory and then into my hand a few times before putting it away. Scrolls were something I should look into more. There was a slight delay to activating them that made it obvious I was doing so, but not everything had to be an act of deception.

Oh, how I'd changed.

Ren sent across some Map information, which I brought up as we walked.

"Assassinate the target, do the Elk repeatable twice, and then head back to town to return Quests and level up?"

The route looked fine. We were still quite north and heading to the west. Bridge was far west straight from the town, along the road, so we weren't in any danger there. "Sounds perfect. I know it said dead or alive, but I think the less time spent there means getting through the Elks quicker."

"Agreed. If the timing is right, we might be able to get a night in at the tavern before heading to the bridge."

One last night of some comfort before our imminent demise. Almost sounded too good to be true, and my brain was hesitant to even play out the actions in my head. I looked at Ren to find she had been gazing at me, her blue eyes piercing through my distracted skull. A shared room seemed like a given, and if I were honest with myself, then I—

"Oh!" Wolf pushed in between us, breaking whatever conversation was going unspoken. "I worked out how to use the tokens by myself!"

"Great job, bud. That's super helpful actually." I raised an eyebrow in thought. "I suppose I should decide on mine too."

With so many Abilities and Passives, it would take forever to eventually upgrade them all, so I'd need to make a shortlist. I wasn't able to upgrade my keystone, <Demonic Magician>—it appeared to be something innate for the Class that increased in power automatically.

I had already upgraded my most useful Passives with <Sleight of Hand> and <Mana Manipulation>. Perhaps it was time for something else. <Vanishing Act>, <Finale>, <Card Fan>, <Demonic Pact>, <Summon Demon>—all still at base level. Tough choices.

After some humming to myself, and almost tripping over a tree root, I made the decision.

[<Summon Demon>: Demons are more powerful and last longer.]
[<Card Fan>: Card fan is larger and can absorb more damage before
breaking.]

I used both of these skills all the time—and while they weren't as flashy or trick adjacent as the others, they increased the base efficiency of how I worked. Unable to let my curiosity go unsated, I dropped a Hellhound card to the floor.

A slightly larger summoning circle of crimson runes, and then the hound himself appeared. Slightly taller and much more muscular. His wide head turned to me as dark red flames lapped over his body. His tongue stuck out as he panted at me as a greeting.

"You're a handsome chap, huh?" I knelt down to give him a rubdown. "No heavy lifting for you, my friend, but tell all the others I'm proud of them and can't wait to see them again."

He huffed in my ear, a half bark of acknowledgment, before I let him fade away back to hell. I looked up at Ren, who had her face screwed up into a pout.

"Sorry," I said with a grin. "I'll share next time."

CHAPTER FIFTY-EIGHT

Last Scraps

Things felt good when you were on a roll. And roll we did. In a different timeline where the Crimson Shadow wasn't a constant threat, we would have easily run circles around everything in the first area and sucked every mote of good loot from any Quest offered. Our time there was shorter than necessary, and we would fall into the habit of scraping by with the bare minimum power needed. Bad habits died hard.

I sank into the thick grass, itching as it tried to prod me in the nostril. Ren slunk up beside me, and we peered over the ridge. A small encampment a good three to four dozen feet below. Some wooden structures, including a basic shack. Dozen or so people idling around. One of them looked less generic and more like the mug shot on the wanted poster.

"Reckon we could just pop him from here and be done with it?" I murmured.

"If he stopped twitching around. Looks like he's on something."

He was rather . . . energetic, to say the least. As if he had forgotten where he left five different things around the camp and switched which one he wanted to go find every three seconds. Erratic and unpredictable. A missed shot could potentially draw the whole camp up to our position—which we could handle, I didn't doubt, but that sounded very tiring. A direct kill shot would save us a lot of headache.

"I bet I could kill him in one hit from here." My eyes narrowed.

"Oh yeah, what do you bet?"

"If I'm successful, then you owe me"—I turned my head to her to see that she was lying a lot closer than I had realized—"something."

"Deal," she whispered. "If you mess it up, then you owe me . . . *something.*"

I looked away from her blue eyes and back to the target, letting the building steam flow out of my ears. Couldn't have just said something simple, could I? With a deep breath, I cooled myself and focused. Pushed myself up a little so that I wasn't so buried in the grass and let a card appear in my hand.

Held it, the Mana pooling from me and empowering it, and it grew brighter. Hit the exhaustion and my Health started to drop, blood running from my hand and down my sleeve—which was rather unpleasant. A quick glance at Ren showed she had a dim view of my casual attitude about harming myself for more power. The System *let* me do it, although that sounded like a poor excuse.

I hit my limit, the card pure white and crackling with pale electricity. Exhaling through my nose, I took aim and let it fly through the air. The man moved. So I turned the trajectory, my hand shaking at trying to control the amount of power as it flew farther away. It was just about there, and he turned again. The card narrowly missed lopping off an ear as it went past his head toward the ground.

Ren exhaled and pushed herself up to see better, perhaps more in surprise than celebrating her win.

But it wasn't over.

"*What the—*" His voice came out from below.

My fingers clenched into my palms, and pain radiated through my head, but I brought it back like a boomerang. A struggle with how much power was soaked into it, like a lead weight on the end of a fishing line. As he looked down at the slim card of white light, it then appeared from the back of his head and vanished into nothing. His body toppled over, to a lot less concern from his group than I had expected.

I dropped back down into the grass with a gasp before holding my breath as I let the pain wash away. Probably shouldn't push myself so hard just yet, but I wanted to see how well my new headband worked. I rolled onto my back and exhaled, finally letting the air out as my senses calmed. No shouts or sounds of pursuit from below, so I counted that as a win.

Ren loomed over me. Her face, way too close, was shadowed against the day-lit canopy above. "Looks like I owe you *something*, trickster."

"Have mercy," I groaned and waved her away before clarifying. "The mercy isn't the *something*, just a normal request."

She snorted and moved away to stand while I took a few seconds to compose myself. My brain just needed to refresh and reboot since my blood was all the way . . . across my hands. With a sigh, I sat up and brought out a linen sheet to wipe them on. Not the most hygienic, but it beat using my suit. I stood and walked over to her where she was now watching Wolf roll around in the dry dirt on his back.

"Fascinating how his hat stays on," she noted.

The gears in my head were still spinning without the teeth engaging, so I didn't have anything to say to add to the conversation. Nothing that didn't taste like a foot, at least. Other than crushing me with awkwardness, Ren seemed to be in a better mood this afternoon. Two Quests down and a couple of Power Tokens each—that should put a smile on anyone's face.

I enjoyed the moment for what it was. The humor in her eyes as she watched the bear wriggle around and get all dusty. A little snapshot for the future when times were difficult. This seemed like one of those cliché moments where I could turn and open my emotional hatch. Shower Ren with everything going on within me. But I didn't. Not yet. There were things still guarded that I was . . . scared to reveal in case the Crimson Shadow came and took everything away. When they were gone, I could breathe easy.

"What are you thinking about, Max?"

Thoughts popped like bubbles, and I watched the bear right himself and shake off the dust from his fur like a dog out of a bath. I raised an eyebrow at the elf. "Nothing."

"Bullshitter." She rolled her eyes and sighed. "Let's go kill some Elks?"

They weren't too far away, and before I knew it, we were doing exactly that. It felt too strange to try to Dazzle the wild beasts, so we played it straight. Wolf mauled them while Ren and I did damage from range. No need for Roger or other demons, really. Once we got into a routine, the first Quest was completed, and we handed it in to repeat it.

[80 Gold]
[Regeneration Potion]

Slow healing over five minutes. Could be useful if it didn't taste like alcohol and vomit. I knew now that part of my aversion to the stuff was due to the other Max. While I wasn't a drinker in my normal life due to the negative effect it had on my work, the pact my other half was bound with restricted him from imbibing the stuff. Still, I could hold my nose if it meant not dying. Currently, I was thankful I'd been able to get by mostly on bandages and Ren's healing.

"Hey, Max." Ren stretched out her back as we took a breather. "If I asked you a direct question, you'd answer honestly, right?"

I narrowed my eyes at her. "It might depend on what you ask."

"What kind of answer is that?" She frowned and crossed her arms.

"Alright, alright. I would be honest with you."

"Then . . . I have a question for you." She shuffled her feet on the floor, some eagerness mixed with apprehension.

My right eye twitched. "*Okay*, go for it."

"Do you have any sweet cakes left?"

I worked my jaw and stared at her impassively. This is why it depended on what she asked. We held eye contact, but I didn't respond.

"Max . . . Why aren't you answering? You're holding out on me, aren't you? Dickbag!" She strode toward me.

"I never said I had any!" I started to back away.

"You aren't denying it! I can't wait till the next time you almost die to have another."

I stopped and pulled a face, and she stood a couple of feet away to glare at me. Wolf was almost audibly rolling his eyes from a little distance away, and I saw his point of view on how this looked.

"*Okay.*" I raised up my hands in resignation. "I have one left. I was waiting until I had two to share. But since you're so insistent . . ." It popped up into my hand, and I moved it toward her.

She took it without hesitation, snapped it in half, and pressed part of it back into my palm. "You make things too complicated when the answer is right in front of you." The elf stared at me as she practically inhaled the pastry. The fact that she hadn't managed to find any when they went shopping the other day was perhaps in the top five worst things to happen this week.

"Guilty," I managed with a tied-up tongue. Her intensity today had been more disarming than usual, and I wasn't sure if that was my fragile mind just being more malleable or . . . I stopped, realizing we had been staring at each other while my brain tried to hastily put matching shapes together. "Elks!" I said, unceremoniously shoving the cake into my mouth and walking away.

I approached Wolf and shook my hand at him as I exhaled. "I know. You don't need to say anything."

"She was smiling." He raised an eyebrow at me. "I don't understand your rituals, but it's easier to be happier before you're dead, rather than after."

My mouth opened, but he turned around to get ready to charge the next Monster. The greatest tragedy was the other Max being just as much of a dweeb with women as I was. A sigh drew away those thoughts. I should focus on the enemy before us, *then* gather the pieces. If there was actually something between us, I could deal with it once the dust had settled. Too much danger and the unknown in the way. So many things to plan, and so little—

"Are you ready, Max?" Ren called, arrow up to her bow as her default scowl was back.

"*Almost.*" I grinned slightly maniacally, dealing damage to my own mental fortitude.

And then we were back into it. The killing cooled me down, which was possibly not a good sign. I enjoyed the artistry of swirling the cards around, avoiding Wolf, as Ren peppered the beasts from slightly farther back. Our team skills had been a little rusty from where we had mostly been focused on high-stakes Player combat. Now that we were grinding through System-created like nothing, there was a peace to it. A comfort that there wasn't much personal danger. The slightest hint of safety that I was loath to accept at more than face value.

Before long, we had finished off the Quest requirements a second time. Lots of meat to feed to Wolf, but no gold or useful equipment, which was disappointing after a couple of good spates of luck in that department.

[Quest complete]

Same Reward as before. I yawned and stretched out. Some of the meat I considered cooking later on, if we had the chance—which was a nice thought. My hands ached, but I'd kept things under control and hadn't exerted myself. No more blood.

"Must be our lucky day." Ren whistled as she looted through the last group. "Two more tokens."

I nodded and sat down on my conjured chair. Exhaustion seemed to be hitting me harder, even though the System said I was fine. "Give one to Wolf, save another for Hannah?"

"Shape-shifter can go without. I doubt she has a lot of information with the bridge being the last bastion of the shitbags." She flicked one through the air toward me. "You and Wolf can have them."

I didn't move. The power token just vanished once it got into my perimeter. "You sure?"

"Do I make mistakes?" She narrowed her eyes and crossed her arms. Narrowed them further as my mouth opened to respond.

It closed without objection. While I didn't want to start getting greedy and getting all the power myself, I also didn't want to argue with her. Back to looking at upgrade options then.

<Finale> upgrade lowered the number of Dazzle Stacks for the greater effects, whereas <Vanishing Act> would allow me to hide two objects at once. There was also <Mana Extension>—having a greater Mana pool meant more strength for my cards. Last time I went for the useful combat skill, so on this occasion I'd go for the pizzazz. Especially with the looming production, I wanted to really make it memorable for whoever's corpses remained afterward. Maybe my own.

[<Finale>: Decreases the Dazzle thresholds for certain effects]

Somewhat vague, but I imagined it would just stun things for longer or let me do it with fewer icons in play. Let's see if I could get it going before I died.

"What did you pick, Wolf?" I glanced toward the bear who had been lying down and licking his fur clean.

"Some sort of extra damage when I'm hurt." He yawned, widening his maw before smacking his lips. "So many words annoy me."

"And you, trickster?" Ren raised an eyebrow.

"<Finale>. If there's a group we have to break, the area stun seemed useful."

She nodded. "Let's get moving to the town. We should get there by dusk if we don't get distracted."

I groaned and got back to my feet, waving my cloak over the chair as it went into my Inventory. There we go, getting some of it back. My eyes closed, and I focused on my breathing. Not enough practice recently. With a smile, I turned to the waiting elf and held a gold coin up.

"Call it for who gets the bath first?"

"I wasn't born yesterday, Max. You can just change it to what you want."

I ignored her and flicked it into the air, raising an expectant eyebrow.

"*Heads*," she said with a sigh.

Caught it. Onto the back of my hand for the reveal. Heads it was.

Ren rolled her eyes. "I'm not sure what that was meant to prove, but I'll take it. Let's head out."

I smiled as she walked away, Wolf following alongside her. I didn't often do a setup to be called back on later, but it was there to draw on if the situation ever arose. A little preplanning might go to waste 90 percent of the time . . . but when it hit, that's when magic could *really* dazzle.

Too caught up in living, I almost forgot what I was best at. Rest and violence had drawn a cover over the showman waiting to reemerge like a butterfly from a cocoon. There were things I needed to practice before the main event. I followed slowly behind them as we walked south, drawing and switching between things in my Inventory to prepare.

Our harshest critics lay in wait for the curtain to open and the lights to come on. Eager for the best, and last, show of their lives.

I wouldn't leave them wanting.

CHAPTER FIFTY-NINE

Life and Death

Another gap in my journal here. I knew why and liked to pretend it was the looming battle for the bridge. I didn't care to put into writing the actual reason, lest the unfaltering text alter the memories that I held close and ruin the illusion.

As soon as the town came into sight, part of me relaxed. The amber sky as the sun started to depart calmed me, despite the creeping danger of the next day.

"From the book, there's one high-level guy in charge of their defenses. Half giant or something, full plate and bad attitude. Rest of the group is a mix of ranged focused, some melee, from what I can gather. There's only some vague records because Hadrian was jealous over it." I sighed and rubbed at the back of my head.

"Not very fun for us then," Ren agreed. "Plate is tough to crack."

Wolf grumbled. "Metal, gross."

Melee was *usually* easier for us to deal with. Rooting them in place and doing damage from afar while Wolf chewed everyone up. More arrows and spells meant we would be taking a lot more hits without being able to contest them. Maybe not something to worry ourselves over right now. The large metal opponent might be the exception to the usual rule, unless Roger fancied putting some dents in their helmet too.

I felt like I had walked enough for a lifetime over the last few days and hoped there were carts and possibly horses that didn't want to maim me in our near future.

Our mood was rather subdued as we slunk into the perimeter of the town. It was quiet, as it usually was, with the System-created starting to pack up and get ready for the evening themselves. It was odd, and the promise of a warm bed was the only thing stopping me from standing around and taking it all in. Still no

Players that stood out. Aside from our enemies, this whole area had felt disjointed, like a ghost town. A one-woman apocalyptic event had rolled through and bathed the world in blood.

The misery sank in as we walked into the tavern. It looked near identical to the other day, down to all the System-created in similar positions. Again, a few patrons that Wolf shoved out of the way to settle down beside the fireplace.

"Greetings, adventurers. How can I help you this evening?"

"One room. En suite." I gave him the plain details. Anything else was just set dressing he wouldn't care for.

"Of course." He put the key on the counter. Same room as last time. "We have full vacancy tonight. Enjoy your evening."

I gave him the gold as I raised an eyebrow at Ren. A fully empty tavern again wasn't concerning in and of itself, but it added to the dramatic air. I had come to the conclusion that on the first night, the assassins had bought out all but one room to guarantee where we'd be. But now it felt like the world was devoid of normal Players. Well, we couldn't know that for sure, but it was the impression we were being presented. "Sleep well, Wolf. Same security measures as before."

He grumbled his acknowledgment.

We headed to the room and locked it behind us. A little shrine of safety. Immediately, I went and sat on the bed. Then I just flopped backward onto it and sighed, unable to hold myself back from truly relaxing. Heavenly.

"Don't get the bed dirty. I'm going to bathe."

I closed my eyes and smiled, listening to the door close before the taps started up. *Next time,* I mused and sat back up. Put the gold coin back away and rubbed at my eye sockets. Time to hand those Quests in while I waited my turn.

"Take as long as you want," I called to her. "I'm going through my new Abilities."

"*Gladly.*"

The blue boxes appeared, and I got rid of them immediately, not particularly interested in whatever terrible Rewards the System wanted to give me. The STAR glowed golden as all the experience filtered in as the Quests were completed. I exhaled, hoping for something overpowered to make the next day easier.

[**Level up—<8>**]
[**Stats increased**]
[**New Ability: <Demonic Transposition>**]
[**New Passive: <All Hands>**]
[**New Passive: <Top Deck>**]

I clicked my tongue and brought the ability up immediately. <Demonic Transposition> allowed me to swap places with one of my summoned demons.

Decently long cooldown, certain restrictions on distance and such, used a lot of Mana . . . Hmm. It seemed the System was listening, after all. There were plenty of noncombat-related scenarios where that would be exceedingly good, especially considering I had a demon that could fly. Despite being dragged through the prickly bushes, I almost felt like the System's favored pupil.

<All Hands> was nice too—for every ally that assisted me in gaining a Dazzle debuff icon, a second one would be added. How the System determined assistance was just another part of the vague way it worked. This meant that Ren and Wolf could actually help me out with my tricks, probably my demons too. More icons meant a more effective Max. I smiled, wondering how much our life choices really changed the course of our progression or if it truly was coincidence that we were one step ahead of the design.

<Top Deck> allowed my <Pick a Card> magic attacks to crit at my normal spell Crit Chance—after a bit of swapping through screens, it turned out that it was pretty low. It was at least helpful enough to tell me a critical card would be red in color and do extra Damage. Couldn't really argue with Passives like that. Previously, it didn't look as though it could have crit, which I thought was unfair. Yet . . . I shouldn't complain when two out of three Skills were winners.

I stood and walked around the room. Covered the window with a thick blanket even though it was heading to nightfall anyway. Put the lantern on medium. Placed my chair by the door with my hat and jacket on it.

Eye of the storm.

The bathroom door opened, and Ren stepped out.

"Good news." I grinned, pausing in brief surprise as she was already in her nightgown.

"Sorry, we were heading to sleep anyway, and I didn't want to squeeze into that waistcoat again." She wrinkled her face up and headed for the bed. "It's all yours—but what's the good news?"

"Oh—uh, I can now teleport, and when you help me with tricks, it gives me Dazzle icons."

She walked across the room and got under the covers with a yawn. "All my efforts won't go to waste then. I haven't done mine yet. I hope I get some bullshit too."

I smiled and waved her off as I went into the bathroom and shut the door. Taps on, stripped down, and sat in the warm water as quickly as possible as it filled. I grew tired of my own dried blood getting everywhere—it wasn't exactly very becoming of a great showman to look like he had rolled out from a fistfight in a butcher's shop. I scrubbed down fully. All the sweat and grime from the day, my hair matted from being stuck under my hat for hours. Just fresh, clean, and ready to be served up on a platter tomorrow.

How did one even assault a bridge? Taps off, I sank into the hot water and tried to relax my brow rather than furrow it. Neither part of me was particularly well-versed in siege warfare, but the hope was that it'd just be a bunch of goons standing about preventing access and we could just hit them with everything we had with the intent that they buckled before we took any serious Damage. Never that easy though, was it?

I had a few tricks on the sidelines but needed to think of more—just in case. Might even lose a little sleep in thinking up potential new plans. Ultimately, improvisation in situ would just be me clicking the practiced skills into place. What would fit and give me the win—or at least a few Dazzle icons?

With a sigh, I left the warmth of the water. Despite how much I needed it, the soft bed was too big a draw, and I yearned for the comfort of a proper sleep. Sleepwear on as the water filtered out. I yawned and rubbed my hair backward. Needed a cut soon enough. A little time roughing it out in the wild, and it wasn't as sharp as it used to be.

Into the bedroom, and the lantern had been lowered to almost nothing. Enough for me to see around my side of the bed, however, and I climbed in eagerly. Completely melting between the cover and mattress once again.

"Max?"

"Yeah?"

"Can I ask you something?"

I turned over, expecting her to have something to bring up about her new Ability—or even just ask for me to hold her again for comfort. I hadn't realized she was facing my way in the bed already, and I rotated to be face-to-face with the elf. A lot closer than anticipated. "*Ah, of course?*"

"Are you worried about tomorrow?" Her voice was soft, and her eyes stared into mine, not scowling but perhaps concerned.

My jaw worked more than my brain did. Always at nighttime, she came to crack me open and see what emotional response she could get from me. Safety in the dark. Well, I was about to test that theory. Maybe some of the bathwater got in through my ears, as my brain felt like soup.

"You want my honest answer?"

She nodded slowly. "Always."

My heart caught in my chest, but I allowed the truth to come out unabated for once. "The only thing I'm scared of . . . is losing you."

Her eyes widened slightly and searched my face to see if I was trying to pull a fast one. "You're not bullshitting?"

"No." No tricks, no deception, and no illusions.

A soft smile crossed her face. "Good. I'm scared of losing you too."

I raised my hand and brushed the blonde hair away from her face. Leaned forward to kiss her, and she reciprocated. She wrapped her arms around me as I pulled her in closer.

Just as I had known all along, magic *was* real.

My eyes flickered open. Daytime, but the sun struggled to get through the blanket covering the window. Briefly, I panicked at not being woken up by the elf before I turned to see her still beside me in bed, smiling.

"Ren, I—" My words stopped as she put her finger to my lips.

"Today is going to be noisy, trickster. Let's just enjoy a little peace while we can."

I nodded and lay back down. She put her arm over me and rested her head on my chest while I idly rubbed my fingertips on her back. More to live for. More to die for.

My brain felt empty. For the first time in a while, I let it stay so. Enjoyed the moment for what it was. Two flawed people just existing despite the odds. It was maybe ten or fifteen minutes that we stayed like this, although it felt like hours. I wished it could have been. She gave me a pat on the chest and rolled out of bed, throwing the covers to obscure my vision from her escape. As they dropped, she stood, fully dressed in her magician's outfit.

"I was about to do the same . . ." I grinned. "But realized I'd probably crack my head open on the bedside table."

She rolled her eyes, but a soft smile stayed on her face. "Too preoccupied with trying to feel me up that you didn't even ask about my new Ability."

"Unfair." I threw back the covers and stood, changing into my Cosmetic outfit in the least flashy way possible. "I seem to remember—"

"Ah!" she interrupted, holding her hand up. "*New rules*. Mild flirting is acceptable, but no pillow talk during the day."

"Acceptable." I crossed my arms.

"Let's survive today before we go any further, okay?" The smile faded from her face as cold reality cooled the new flames we were trying to stoke. "My new Ability is another arrow attack. Like <Entangling Shot>, but it . . . makes targets more susceptible to debuffs."

"Like Dazzle," I said with a nod. "System really knows, huh? About the Party dynamics, I mean."

"Perhaps," she replied and shrugged. "Let's get Wolf and start making the journey? If we don't leave now . . ."

"We might never," I agreed. Too easy to sink into comfort. We needed to keep the fires lit.

The room was unlocked as I donned my hat and jacket keeping guard, chair back into my Inventory. I also stole the lantern but forgot the blanket over the window—so it seemed a fair trade at the end of the day. We walked down the stairs to see Wolf waiting for us. The bear stretched out and yawned.

"Ready to meet the day, bud?" I grinned at him.

He looked between me and Ren and raised his eyebrows, his amber eyes twinkling beneath the bowler.

I raised a finger and wagged it at him. "Don't even start. I just want to know your new Ability, and then I'll go die of embarrassment. Or head trauma, as is tradition."

"No dying before you've cooked for us." Ren sidled in beside me. "You were supposed to yesterday."

I waved off the System-created barkeep as we exited and headed for the western road. "I did say that, didn't I? Sorry, my mind was quite preoccupied."

They both raised their eyebrows at me.

"With the whole battle thing." I rolled my eyes. "Let's grab food from a shop and I'll cook later if we survive."

"*When* we survive," Wolf corrected. "Positive attitude manifests what you want in this world."

Somewhat true, I had to relent as I deflated. The System certainly gave me the Skills I needed to succeed. I just had to do the hard work myself.

Soon enough, we were back on the road eating meat pies. They were adequate—filling enough to keep the nerves from shaking at my stomach. The day had started sunny, but gray clouds were looming from the east, and the breeze was carrying them straight toward our path. Typical that gloom would know where some tragedy was about to take place.

We rounded a hill, the cobbled road rough and overgrown in parts. Odd, considering it was the main way over the river to the next area. A dark shape loomed into view as the trees slid along the sidelines.

"Is that some kind of sign?" I narrowed my eyes at the cross shape, like a large *X*, sitting on the side of the road.

"No," Ren said, her face paling before she ran to get closer.

We followed suit, more of the picture becoming clear as we neared the logs tied together. It didn't take elfin eyesight to see what it was now.

A body.

Tied to the shape by hands and feet, the man was long dead. The elements and nature having worn away at his frame already. There wasn't much to signify whether it was a System-created or not, but the pit in my stomach told me it was a Player.

"They are Monsters." Ren worked her jaw, cold anger burning in her blue eyes.

I looked beyond, eyes darting to the road leading toward the bridge. There were more of the crosses, every so often. Some had blurred into the woodland around them, making them harder to spot at the outset, but now that I knew they were there . . . There were dozens along the part of the road we could see.

Ren stood beside me and narrowed her eyes. Her hand gripped my forearm as she pointed at the next one along.

"Max, that's Hannah."

CHAPTER SIXTY

Sandbagged

They say to fight fire with fire, but the best method was to smother it. Deprive it of oxygen until the flicker of light died out. That was my dim view of how the Crimson Shadow should be dealt with. Violence was a part of my daily life now, but the cruelty and barbarism they showed toward their fellow Players was beyond me. Beyond acceptable. Beyond my mercy.

We ran toward the cross, my card in the air well before our feet arrived. It cut the ropes around her wrists, and her limp body fell into Ren's arms. The shape-shifter was beaten and bloodied. Unresponsive.

The elf poured some healing into the woman, the glow of radiant light fading and nothing. I cut the ropes around her ankles.

"It's not . . . *Come on, you fuck . . .*" Ren exhaled and closed her eyes, deflating. "She's . . . gone, Max."

She laid the shape-shifter on the ground. Anger burned within me as I saw her impassive face. I knelt down and put my fingers to her neck. Pointless, but I was a loss as to what to do. Her skin was cold to the touch. No heartbeat. Guilt mixed with the rage. She must have been caught trying to find out information for us. I withdrew my hand and clenched it into a fist.

"Look at me, Max." Ren was stern in her demand, and I met her eyes. "I feel that too, but the only viable solution is revenge. We kill them, and they pay for what they did." Her eyes were watery, but there was the same burning inferno behind them that I felt.

"Agreed." My jaw was clenched, but she was right. Beating ourselves up was just doing the Shadow's job for them. I raised an eyebrow at Wolf.

He gave a sad nod, already knowing what I was going to ask. In the softer area of mud, he began digging a grave. Shallow for now, but if successful in avenging her, we would return to put her to rest properly. Maybe all of them, if we had the heart for it. I helped Ren move her, and then Wolf covered her over with the churned mud. We hadn't known her long, but we had built rapport. She was the only Player we had met that wasn't one of *them*.

"Why are they even doing this?" I narrowed my eyes to look down the road at more filled crosses. It was a warning, but why was the Lady so intent on building a ruthless gang to squash out any other possible Player? Why was it join her or die?

"Your eyes are purple again, Max."

I took a deep breath and looked toward Ren. Being that they were my eyes, I couldn't see when they were doing that, but she gave me a nod to let me know they were calming down.

"You can ask them yourself when I tear their arms and legs off," Wolf offered, glaring out down the road.

Not only to provoke fear, the bodies were presented to ignite an emotional response. Our anger and sadness were valid, but we couldn't let that drive our attack. As much as I wanted to pry apart their jaws in search of answers until the cracking of broken bone deafened me, a clouded approach would get us pegged up to one of these crosses ourselves.

I rubbed at my eyes and wondered if we could just rewind a little from this impending horror show. No. The show must go on. We had our parts to play. "I'm sick of these assholes. Sick and tired and angry as fuck." My fingers flexed into fists and back. "So let's go."

We fell into step, back to the road. If they'd caught Hannah, then they might have some manner of detection magic. It would be fair to assume they would be well prepared to deal with any manner of Player type. They'd never come across a Party like us though. I let my ego elevate me above their degeneracy. It didn't matter who they were; we would win over them and continue chasing down Lady in Red.

Ren put her hand on my shoulder, which startled me from my thoughts.

"Win, escape, die. We will do it all as one. We're not leaving you behind again."

I nodded. There could only be one outcome. I wouldn't allow anything aside from the win. A couple more levels or Power Tokens would have been nice, but the sooner we could remove the festering tumor clogging up the start of this world, the better. New Players might be on the island already, and the least we could do was allow them a normal System to thrive in. They were potential fans, after all. I ground my teeth at the dual parts of me wanting control. Wanting to kill, wanting to impress.

As we passed each dead body on display, it did little of the intended effect. If anything, we grew colder and more hardened to the macabre displays. Barely started to register them. The shape-shifter had been a gut punch because we had a connection and a brief relationship with her. Although the rest were Players too, it was easy to disassociate. Think of them as just more System-created for a suddenly very grimdark area as opposed to most of the forest.

"Hey, forgive me for breaking the new rules . . ." Ren wrapped her hand gently around my left forearm. "I wanted you to know . . . Last night wasn't just because we might die today."

"I know." I smiled at her. "And I forgive you." With my right hand, I took her hat off, allowing what remained of the sunlight to illuminate her blonde hair with an almost unnatural radiance. I felt tired, even though the day had hardly begun. My eyes looked over her face, taking in her piercing blue eyes, soft features, and glowing hair. She smiled, and I plopped the hat back onto her head.

My luck had been a pretty mixed bag since arriving in this world. On the rare few occasions I would catch her smile, it washed away all the bad. The only things remaining were the scrawls in my journal saying how terrible Bandits were. Allowing my heart to be open, knowing it might get broken, made me stronger. Not weaker.

Typical that I'd have such a breakthrough right before dashing myself on the rocks below, but such clarity was often born of hardship. Tell that to the broken figures we were still passing. My internal self rolled his eyes. Their hardship was at least over.

I stopped and turned on the spot, my eyes scouring the road behind us. Ren already had an arrow up and readied, reacting to my sudden movement.

"Hear or see something?"

"No . . ." I flexed my fingers. "But if I were them, I'd have a scout on the road." Maybe it was paranoia or the dead lining our route, but something definitely felt off. My Illusion Magic sense was tingling, and I had hoped Ren would be able to pick up something that I couldn't. They wouldn't let the route go unprotected and had a way of detecting the shape-shifter. The throbbing in my head started up again. "Something isn't adding up."

"You're . . . right . . ." Her eyes narrowed. "But I'm not sure what. Wolf, can you smell anything?"

"Only death." He sniffed the air again for good measure but shook his head.

I blinked my eyes slowly and calmed my breathing. It couldn't be invisibility to last this long, and we weren't close enough to the woods on either side for someone to properly stalk us. Not without being detected. What would I do, as a magician? A little bit of trickery, naturally.

My eyes went to the backs of the two crosses we had just passed. One was a good twenty feet away on the left, the other closer to sixty on the right. Slowly, I turned my head to the other two and raised a finger up to my lips. I had seen the deception now, hidden on the side you wouldn't normally see. With weary and distracted eyes, I didn't doubt that it would go unseen by most. I nodded toward the pair as I imagined a card. They nodded in return.

From the inside of my jacket, a dove. Into the air I sent it off to the closer wooden-beamed cross. Into my hand, I flipped my dagger. So *tired*. I turned to face away from the cross.

As soon as the demonic dove flew up through the underside of the structure, I hit <Demonic Transposition>. A blur of light and I had taken its place. I swung my dagger into the thigh of the body held in position.

"Ow, you fuck—"

Only the body wasn't held in position and wasn't dead. The man brought down his fist at me as I dropped to the ground, leaving the dagger in his wound. Some manner of horn dropped to the dirt, fumbled, as he went on the offensive. My card came up in my left hand and empowered, slicing through his fingers as they punched out at me. Took a lot of force from the hit but sprayed me with his blood. He went to move, and an arrow pierced through the thick beam and into the back of his leg.

He growled in pain, now unable to move.

"Hello." I smiled widely as my dove flew over and sat atop my hat. "I have a few questions and seem to have lost my moral compass."

He was covered in fake grime and dried blood. Stage makeup to appear bruised and dead. A round and wrinkled face beneath the mask grimaced in pain. His leather cap barely held in a messy mop of hair. Although his eyes were an odd yellow color—which I assumed meant he wasn't human—the rest of him was otherwise as expected. Dirty clothes to fit in and not look like part of the Crimson Shadow.

"I'll not tell you fuckin' shits anything!" He spat and growled, writhing against wounded legs that didn't want to associate with him.

"You killed one of our friends. There are at least five things I can think of that would have you *praying* for us to kill you." I ran my tongue across my teeth, trying to maintain composure. Letting off steam on the first bad guy to fall into our laps might feel good in the short term, but we had to remember not to lose sight of who we were.

I raised an eyebrow to Ren, hoping she would play good cop and not just encourage me. A beautiful partner in crime almost sounded nicer than being heroic. Thankfully, she got the hint.

"I'd listen to him. I was only able to stop him from killing Hadrian because he cooperated."

"Lies." The man continued to growl his admonishment. "Hadrian hasn't been heard from in days."

Ren walked around in front of the cross and folded her arms across her chest. "I told him to run, gave him some vials of blood to keep him safe as long as he stayed out of our way."

"Hey, Wolf," I interrupted. "Come here, bud." I waited for the bear to come up beside me. "You said you were after some legs, right? You think you could take one without killing him?"

"Yeah," the bear said as he licked his lips. "He might bleed out slowly though. Or quickly. I'm no surgeon."

"I'm in no hurry. We can find out together." I tilted my head and stared at the scout impassively.

"Empty threats won't scare me, heroic fucks! Once Jokkar hears about this, he'll—"

"Please!" Ren begged, her eyes wide. "He isn't bluffing. You don't know him like I do."

That almost got me to break character. Although, I wasn't sure how much of it was character now and how much was the real me wanting to extract some pain on someone possibly partially responsible for the ache in my heart.

"Get fucked, elfin whore!" He writhed and tried to move away from the arrow holding him loosely to the raised wooden structure.

"*Wolf.*" I gestured. Not just because he insulted Ren, of course. Partially but not entirely.

The bear moved up to him, sniffing at the grass first and lapping up the severed fingers to chew them down. He looked up at the scout with amber eyes. "Appetizers, yum." He licked his lips slowly.

Ren shot me a glance. It wasn't to dissuade me from letting the bear have a snack, but I understood what she was getting at. Some grievous bodily harm would put any subsequent information extracted into question. I nodded back at her, but I couldn't call off the bear without looking weak.

"What about if we gave you some of the Lady's blood?" She grimaced. "We just need some information, and we'll let you go."

The man was wavering a little now that Wolf was sniffing around his lower leg. "H-how many do you have?"

"Three," I answered. "But it'd have to be good information for more than one."

He licked his lips, weighing up his options. As Wolf opened his mouth wide, the scout lifted his bloodied leg away gingerly.

"Alright, alright. Call the fuckin' bear off. What do you want to know?"

"Wolf." The bear sighed and sat down, disappointed. "What's at the bridge? How many people? What do you plan to do after we let you go?"

That was a little trick—to end with the phrase about letting him go, let that sit in his mind. All he had to do was get rid of the pesky prior questions. It worked way too easily on a man eager to scoot himself away from the looming jaws of our third.

"They've built up a shantytown—more of a fort really. Maybe twenty-odd there now. I suppose . . . I'll run away and try to live a good life?" His desperate facial expression gave away how likely that was.

A fort with more people than we had expected. I rubbed my chin in thought.

Ren added her own questions. "That's so helpful! I bet they have magical wards or protections too, right?"

"The main building has an anti-attack dome, and the road itself has traps." He grinned nervously, now eager to squeeze his way out of this problem.

I withdrew two bottles of blood into my hand, pretending they came from a pouch. "Assuming you haven't lied, then that's enough for two, I suppose."

Greed illuminated his eyes. "No lies, I promise! Jokkar even has a weakness to elemental damage—but I don't know which. Maybe all?"

"Ah, eager for that third. Well . . . I hate to disappoint then." I raised my hand up, and the bottle changed to a crossbow. Bolt to his neck. He convulsed, trying to clutch at it, but his motor functions were already failing. Leaning forward, he dropped from the cross onto the grass. Better than he deserved.

"A mercy, really," Ren complained, giving his body a kick.

"Method to the madness, sorry." I gave her a glum smile and withdrew a large linen sheet from my Inventory. Just because his tongue held no further use, it didn't mean the rest of him couldn't serve us still.

CHAPTER SIXTY-ONE

Opening Act

It always amazed me how productive evil could be. When you cut corners and didn't care whom you had to step on to steal materials or labor . . . anything was possible. The knowledge that the Crimson Shadow had managed to produce some manner of fortifications in however many short days was as impressive as it was tiring. Breaking things down didn't seem like the good-guy thing to do. They were trying to clog up the System and cause errors in the process of things, and it was up to us to destroy their foul machinations at any cost—in the hope the System might notice and reward us.

We switched to traveling off the side of the road. It was slower going, but we would hopefully avoid any potential traps. Ren was still a little sour at being called names, despite being the good cop. I was a little sour at not taking the man apart limb by limb, despite being the bad cop. Truth was, I let the sensible Max take the reins. Show to run and *yada yada*. Other than giving us the brief satisfaction of hurting someone who had hurt us, the man had a greater role he could play being intact. I could be cold, but to let sadism in was a short road into staring into the abyss.

I told Wolf it was a one-time thing, but I don't think any of us truly believed it. The heavy sling at his side was a testament to how macabre things truly were. How *I* truly was. If we got through this day, then it just meant the cycle would repeat, surely. Bigger problems for our stronger hands and harder hearts. Perhaps I was giving this more noir overtones than it deserved, but as the dark clouds rolled overhead and brought gloom to the sight before us, I figured the set pieces were pretty on point. Had to stick to the theme, naturally.

Once again, I found myself shuffling over dirt and wild grass like a worm, attempting not to dirty my suit right before the opening act. It had already been bloodied by the scout so seemed like a moot point. A small rise in the terrain would offer us a glimpse of what loomed ahead—even though the rough battlements were starting to show between the trees. Normally I tried not to peek out into the audience prior to a performance, but when they held something more dangerous than a poor review over your head, it paid to be well-informed.

Ren writhed along aside me—although farther away than usual. Whether that was to try to conceal our rather overt costumes better or she just wanted us to go into this with cooler minds . . . I didn't know. Perhaps I should invest in a more covert outfit if we found ourselves the saboteurs on the regular. Put purple hand-prints on our foreheads.

The bridge came into view as we crept to the crest of the muddied embank-ment—or rather, it didn't. Hastily constructed, a ramshackle fort had been built up around it, obscuring the path across the river. The latter being much wider and faster flowing than I imagined—putting the more sensible option of crossing it elsewhere to bed. The System had designed a funnel, and the Shadow was now blocking it. We were up on the right-hand side, looking down at the construction at an angle.

A barred gatehouse sat in front of the bridge itself. Perhaps they intended to ferry materials, or worse, across the border. There was a higher floor above it to look out over the road, with a roofed area open to the air that was empty aside from one small awning where two figures sat playing . . . cards, I hoped. I still didn't have a full normal deck. Either side of the central gatehouse were two extensions with two or three floors each. Slim openings instead of windows, enough to fire arrows through. As we were peering over to the right of the struc-ture, I couldn't see the entrance to the left side—but on the right there was an open doorway almost at the back of the building, nothing too easily breached. A grand structure, in some ways, even if it did look like a stiff breeze would col-lapse it.

Three figures stood around the back opening, discussing something, while a wagon and several crates sat beside them. Not only did it not look like the sturdi-est of buildings, but it was entirely made from wood—aside from the gatehouse bars. They couldn't be so blind as to not have something to protect against fire. Surely? The scout had mentioned a barrier or something, so any attack we attempted by range was likely to be thwarted. I imagined a dome held up by some spell-caster in a similar manner to the camp we had attacked. That left us one option. Well, actually, two . . .

We slunk backward out of sight again. Back to the waiting bear as he watched us patiently. Although they might not be on high alert due to their scout not report-ing anything, it'd be a big disadvantage to be spotted before the show had even started. Especially if there were almost two dozen Shadow members in there—or more. We needed every upper hand we could grab hold of.

"Thoughts?" Ren whispered to me as the three of us gathered, sitting down amid the darkening woods.

"We need to kill any spellcasters first, reduce their defenses." I rubbed at my chin. "My guess is they'd be above the gatehouse."

Ren scowled at me. "With the barrier up, I can't protect you. Not from range and not if you are indoors."

"We'll get bogged down in melee if we try to do it head-on from the outset." I understood her frustrations. My option put me out of reach, alone, to fend for myself. Foolish? Perhaps. Bullshit? *Inevitable.* "That's why I need to take the spellcaster out before anything else."

"*Fine.* Assuming you don't throw your life away playing hero, you'll give us a signal when the barrier is down? I can then hit it with a flame arrow, and Wolf can start mauling through the confusion?"

"Sounds like a plan." I grinned.

"Sounds like *bullshit*," she murmured in response.

There was a calm that sank over me. Normally there would be a brief moment of elation before stepping out on stage, the overwhelming brightness of the overhead lights and roar of the crowd sending adrenaline and dopamine flooding through my system. Nothing now. I didn't want to impress my audience. I wanted them dead and for me to be flourishing above their surprised corpses. Manifesting.

I turned my gaze away from the pouting elf. "You okay with that, Wolf? Ren will help you get into the building, and then you have free rein."

He nodded. "Don't die, Max."

"Ah." I stood up and stretched my back out. "They didn't appear to have any horses, so I'll be practically invincible."

"Don't try to fist fight Jokkar either." Ren stood and admonished me. "If he is built like a tank, then trying your tricks will just get you turned into mincemeat."

Wolf licked his lips.

I withdrew a crossbow into each hand and gave her a tired smile. Despite agreeing to keep things cool until the day was done, part of me still wanted to give a cliché goodbye. Hold or kiss her and tell her I'd be fine. That would be unfair to us both, not knowing truly what was in store. Her eyes were full of concern, and I could see things were going unsaid behind her eyes too. I gave her a nod. We were both smart enough to read behind the lines.

"Break a leg," I said with a brief bow to them both.

And then I vanished.

An abrupt rush of air, and then I was atop the battlements. Crossbow triggers pulled toward the shocked faces of the dazzled guards sitting under the awning as they were trying to catch a glance at the odd-colored bird that was just there. The first one took the bolt straight through the neck. The second had a defensive Skill that activated just in time, and he moved, taking it to the shoulder. In panic, he stood to draw his weapon and went to lean on the chair to come toward me.

Chair went straight into my Inventory, and he fell forward, now supported by nothing. Got a good view of my dagger—a little close-up magic that left him wide-eyed. Well, one of them anyway.

I withdrew it from his socket as he dropped to the floor. Scooped the playing cards into my stash to arrange later. They had a different back design, which was frustrating. There was a downward staircase behind me, nearer the back of the fort, which should lead to the floor above the taller gatehouse. I dismissed the dove and narrowed my eyes. Couldn't see the others out in the woods—which was good. They needn't get involved until the alarm was raised.

Into my hand, the lit torch, which I dropped to the floor. No oil or other accelerant, unfortunately, but the match was struck. Burning the place down from afar and then picking through the rubble had been a consideration—but if they had a mage or other way to put out the fire, then that would be a losing battle once more. The only option was to go all out. Get as close to the danger as our mortality would allow.

Speaking of which . . . I dropped an Imp card and was briefly shocked to see that instead of the pudgy ball demon, they were now a foot taller and in better shape. Still deep-red skin, a little tuft of black hair between stubby black horns. Long tail with a barbed end, pitchfork in one hand. I gave him a brief bow and gestured toward the far side of the battlements. *On my signal.* He nodded and plodded over.

Roger burst from the corpse of the one I had given an impromptu eye exam. He opened his mouth but quickly closed it in seeing my finger to my lips. From my Inventory, I withdrew his mace and handed it over. With a gesture, he followed as I walked over to the stairs. Murmured voices could be heard from below. The quick scuffle up here hadn't alerted them, and I hoped a short burst of violence could silence those below just as easily. Shouldn't wish too hard. I took a breath and powered up a card in my hand.

We descended and came into a wide room dimly lit by a sparse number of wall-mounted lanterns. A handful of figures, two in robes by the far wall looking out the front of the fort—both seemed to be holding a spell each. Another leaned against the wall on the far left by a doorway where someone else was standing and relaying some information. Each of them in drab clothing with crimson handprints on their foreheads. The final figure, dressed in thick leathers, was right by the bottom of the stairs. He didn't seem to be too pleased with my unannounced presence.

His brow furrowed in brief confusion. "Intruder!" he yelled, pushing forward and slashing out at me with an Ability.

I backed against the wall of the stairs, <Card Fan> illuminating my vision as the shield of larger magical cards barely absorbed the blow. Any brief thanks to my foresight for upgrading that Skill was interrupted as Roger leaped down the stairs and struck the man with his mace. The pair of them both crumpled to the floor in a mass of struggling limbs.

The card I had fired off had gone astray during the interruption, and as one panicked male Wizard went to move behind the two Shadow members near the doorway, the other spellcaster stood in shock. A crimson gash across the side of her face. I flung a split card toward her as I dove over Roger and his opponent, landing into a roll across the wooden floor. The woman had recovered enough composure to bring up a shield to protect from my attack, and they were deflected.

I spun back up to my feet with a twirl of my cape, blocking the sword swung by the approaching fighter from the door as my spear appeared into my hands.

"You got some fuckin' balls trying this," the man growled from behind a thick red beard.

"*Oh*, you don't even know." I grinned as purple electricity began sparking along my arms. The man stepped back, a Skill empowering his weapon for the follow-up. Panic flashed across his face as his footing slipped—the floor by my feet now full of marbles.

Dagger in hand, I went to step toward him before my feet burst into ice, pinning me to the floor. I raised an eyebrow at the female spellcaster to the right. "Really?"

Either this meant that the male Wizard was holding the protective enchantments up, or they had dropped them in favor of killing me. I couldn't take either assumed answer as fact.

"Brett, go raise the alarm," the red-bearded man growled at the other combatant who was trying to get a gauge on me with a ranged weapon.

I also couldn't allow that. Clapped my hands together to vanish the spear and instead I held a blood vial in each hand. Immediately caught all their attention as there was no denying that I held what they coveted most. They could almost sense it, like hot meat to a grizzly bear. I started juggling them. All eyes on me. I held a small hessian bag out as the glass bottles flipped through the air and caught them with a slight clink. Threw it over toward the stairs.

No eyes on me. Lots of Dazzle icons though. *What a great crowd.* The man closest to me stepped forward and bent over toward the small bag. It had been fun, but now it was time for a brief <Finale+>.

As lights illuminated and crackled through the room, I rolled across the back of the hunched man. Poured all my remaining Mana into a card in the process and flung it at the stunned Wizard by the door. Straight into the middle of his head. As he dropped, I ran at the one meant to be raising the alarm, leaping from a conjured chair to come down on him with the black-bladed sword. With what meager Strength the System told me I had, I slammed it down through his chest. Shocked that I found a place between ribs and into his internal organs but not as much as he was.

I turned to see the bloodied and broken Roger slam his mace into the head of the bearded man, the stun wearing off a second too late for the Shadow to react. His body convulsed as he dropped before my demon gave him a second strike to the back of the head, finishing him off. Behind him, the bloodied eye sockets of the prior combatant gave away he had taken in his fill of the show. And Roger's thumbs.

With a thought, I unsummoned him from this plane, his energy evaporating just before a spear of magical energy pierced the puppet's skull.

"Rude." I tutted and shook my head. A card of bright purple blazed in my hand as I glared at the woman. "No interruptions during the show, please."

As the magical card turned a bright white, I gave the Imp+ the signal.

CHAPTER SIXTY-TWO

Consistency

This section of my memories always gives me a headache. The smells, the sounds, the violence. Makes my brain feel clogged and smoky, desperate for fresh air. A prison of my own making, perhaps.

I wiped my hands off as I walked back up the stairs into the open air. Briefly, I had looked through the bodies for Equipment, but it was just a scan for the high-rarity stuff. Stakes were too high to sit and deliberate over all the corpses I was about to make. If we survived, then the spoils would be ours, the second-best prize next to our lives at the top.

My stomach felt uncomfortable, so I looked down. Some blood. I was unsure at how I got the cut across my side, but it was shallow and didn't really hurt—I was already halfway through a bandage, in fact—it just felt awkward. Still, just made a mess of my suit, as was apparently tradition now. The Imp+ was already readying a second fireball to throw down at the other side of the fort, and I was just in time to see the arc of an arrow blazing with fire emerge from the woods and also strike that side of the building.

Wolf burst from the woods toward the grouped figures now to my left. The sling that held the dead scout dropped from his side and rolled down the hill. Quite the distance, but I was a natural by now. With the flick of my wrist, the card was out, traveling the large distance before striking into the corpse. Roger emerged, grabbing at the lantern and sword I had left in there with the body. A moment to gauge where he was, and then he was following the bear.

Ren emerged from the tree line and fired an arrow out toward the Shadow members shouting at the approaching bear. <Entangling Shot> hitting them mere seconds before Wolf would. Even from this distance, she was radiant and looked quite the part in our team uniform. I grinned to myself and looked at the lower floor of the next section of the fort. Imp+ vanished, so I summoned another and told him to repeat the same actions, still focused on that side. Disable the middle barriers, set the far side ablaze, fight through the closest side. Push the rats into the waiting maw of the bear.

A small fire had started where I had left the torch on the floor. Nothing major, but the smell of charring wood was starting to become oppressive. Not a fan. A glance over my shoulder and most of it was coming from where the Imp+ had scorched many places, and dark smoke was now waving into the air. They must know something was awry by now. It was only a matter of time before the main stage was crowded by potential volunteers.

I leaped from this building to the next, intending to join my Party somehow. A linen sheet into my hands like a parachute to try to soften the blow slightly as I hit the wooden roof of the side section and rolled. Brief pain, but nothing that I couldn't live through. I popped the cork of a Rejuvenation Potion. Tasted warm and like cherries. Still disgusting, but at least there was a brief soothing—

A large creak and groan drew my attention to my feet. It turned out that whoever had been the designated carpenter for this section of the fort had—

The roof collapsed, and I dropped into the room below, among a clatter of split planks and broken furniture. Something had broken my fall but pierced through my side as a show of its disdain. I winced, although the potion should slowly fix that up. A figure silhouetted against the dust cloud and scant daylight stepped into view.

"Jokkar?" I narrowed my eyes with a grimace.

No, only his head was encased in metal plate, strange horns jutting in the air from where his ears would be. A dark metal flecked by a red paint job that looked like it was wearing off. The rest of him was pretty much stark naked, aside from a chain mail loincloth covering his modesty. Lean but muscled, two chain-wrapped pipes ran from the back of his helmet into the handles of the two shark-toothed swords he held. Almost looked like—

"*Nope,*" he growled, the helmet muffling his voice. A burst of harsh noise accompanied the whir of the jagged edges of his weapons as they spun around the main shape. *Chainswords*, my panicked brain helpfully finished the sentence.

He stepped toward me, and I aimed a drawn crossbow. Metal-encased head snapped back as the bolt struck it but ricocheted straight off. I pushed myself away, crawling backward across the debris as he recovered. The illusion of the fantasy world was partly shattered, before I considered he may have come from a post-apocalyptic world. The System wasn't picky where it drew Players from, after all. Now it looked like I had run out of goons and had dropped right into some of the more proficient members of the gang. *Chainswords*, my inner monologue repeated, slightly higher pitched this time.

The saw-wielding man went to leap at me and immediately stumbled, tripping on something with a curse. A clang of metal as hot coals were spread across the wooden floorboards toward me—the damage breaking the invisibility as my grill came into view.

"Wise guy, huh?" He seethed. As he went to step forward again, a Hellhound+ burst out from the side wall and latched on to his bare leg.

Purple electricity worked its way around my arms as I stood. The yelp of the hound as he was struck filling me with cold anger. I unsummoned him before the man could level a follow-up, the saw blade instead chewing into the floor briefly, sending splinters into the air.

"Looks like I'll have to use my ultimate attack," I seethed at him, my eyes aglow and three tomatoes in my hand.

He turned to face me, cutting the first thrown fruit out of the air with his blade. I lobbed the second, which he didn't even bother to dodge, his overconfidence allowing it to burst across his toned torso.

The third left my hand instead as a bottle. The Witch's Brew from the coven, the dark liquid that felt too evil to consider drinking. If the System wasn't even keen on telling me the contents, then perhaps the latest attraction could assist me. A hands-on experiment seemed to be the best way to tick off that mystery at hopefully no danger to my own well-being.

He went to block it too late, only realizing it was not a tomato halfway through the air. With a blur, he activated some manner of dodge, but it wasn't enough to fully avoid the projectile. The glass burst on his shoulder, and the liquid splashed across his right arm. This seemed to displease him, and he launched toward me.

A sword appeared in my hand. I blocked the initial swipe, but the toothed blade flung the weapon from my hand and bit through my upper arm. <Card Fan> went up for the follow-up, the cards shimmering and bursting almost immediately. Thankfully, the diverted thrust slid to the side and slammed into the wall instead. I dropped to the floor and sent a pair of cards up at him. He leaped backward with surprising agility, my attacks just drawing lines up his stomach and chest before vanishing.

He paused slightly at the sight of his left arm where the potion had hit. His skin had swollen up and looked bulbous and discolored. Whether he was in any pain was hard to tell with his encased head, but dark smoke had begun billowing out of the horns, which I now saw as exhausts for his macabre living machinery.

With the buzz of sparking metal, he clashed his blades together before lunging toward me. I threw up a blanket and rolled to the side—his swords bursting straight through the wall and carving a chunk out of the thin wood as he withdrew them. He hadn't seemed to notice the room wasn't as strewn with loose debris as before. Just as I was considering some options for the final part of the act, the door at the end of the room swung open, and a woman with bright-red hair and a silver crossbow stepped in, leveling the weapon at me.

"I'm afraid I must bow out," I said, purple energy crackling around me. The floor where I stood collapsed, my cards having weakened a circle of the wood during the fight. I dropped to a roll and ran for the opposite door, leaping to slide across a table and knocking paperwork all over the place. Behind me, I dropped all the planks of wood from the above room I had sucked into my Inventory. Not really enough to stop a man wielding two chainswords, but it'd waylay him a little and give me time to prepare the next attempt to wow.

I slammed through the door and almost ran straight into one of Ren's arrows as she turned her bow toward me. Relief painted her face, and I felt a little more comforted too. Wolf blew through one of the walls to my right, a warrior with a large shield being pushed along as he blocked the charge. Roger hobbled along in the broken body of a different goon, giving me a brief wave as he went to assist the bear.

"Two behind me," I yelled and jerked a thumb backward. My eyes went upward as rays of light bloomed through the wood floor. *Above me*, rather than behind, perhaps. I flung my body to the side just as the wood burst downward, the heat of the attack warming me even through my clothes. Among the clattering debris, the chainsword man jumped down and started toward me.

I groaned and struggled to push myself back up on my left arm. It was numb and didn't want to cooperate. I must have landed on it oddly. An arrow struck him in the good shoulder, and he stopped to look Ren's way with a growl. Small flames flickered out of his exhaust. Behind him, the cloaked woman with the silver weapon dropped down and aimed toward the elf, a volley of five bolts firing out in quick succession.

The purple, swollen arm of my attacker had worsened by a large degree by now. It was a wonder he could even move that arm, and as he turned back to me and took a step, the agony was clear in his body language. Just as his weapons buzzed up with energy again, his infected arm burst. Like a water balloon, flesh and muscle spread across the surrounding area, leaving just a limp skeletal arm that relinquished hold of his weapon.

He was stunned—as was I. The other woman had moved to where I couldn't see to chase down the rest of the Party. The metal head turned to observe his spent appendage. He couldn't move it, and that weapon weighed heavily to the floor, holding him back. With the whir of his good blade, he raised it to himself, chewing through the bone near his shoulder and then the tubing holding the weapon, allowing both useless arm and weapon to drop to the floor.

I wasn't even sure what to think at that point. Despite how hardened to violence I had become, the act was coldly pragmatic and yet utterly horrifying in every way. My right hand raised, bloody, as I held a card of bright white. Straight for his neck.

He blurred as an Ability let him dodge the attack, the beam of my attack traveling straight through him ineffectively. He readied his good sword to pounce on me, and then I brought the card back, bursting out from where his heart was. With another step, he paused and then slowly tipped over, blood draining down his bare torso. I had to give it to the System—while I didn't like the Stats side of things, where my cards used to struggle against tough skin, I could now burst through people with enough stacked damage.

With my right hand, I applied a quick bandage as I stood, and then I could use my left arm again. Needed to find the others to make sure they were okay. I picked up the chainsword he had severed from the tethering machinery. My brow furrowed at it as I turned the corner. There were crossbow bolts across the wall and blood on the floor. Holes through the structure where Wolf had just pushed through on a destructive path. The whole building was groaning and creaking now, thick with the smell of smoke and death. Warm too. I rubbed the back of my neck. Roger would have smashed the lantern at the start of this side as intended.

I paced through the destruction with clenched teeth and stopped at the circular hole to the next room.

A figure lay on the floor. Ren's cloak. Blood had soaked through it where crossbow bolts had pierced. The elf's bow was lying on the floor nearby. The woman with red hair stood, leaning over the body with a smile on her face. It didn't seem like she had noticed me, and I paused, my eyes narrowed.

"Can't run from me, little elf," she cooed, pushing the cloak from the figure's face.

"*Surprise, fucker!*" Roger beamed back up at her.

Ren stepped into the room from the opposite doorway, throwing a dagger that burst into radiant light. It struck the surprised woman in the chest, and the elf followed up with several zaps from her wrist-mounted wand holder, causing small chunks of flesh and clothing to burst from her target. The woman dropped her weapon and toppled backward as Ren gave a twirl and a bow.

"Hope I didn't have you worried?" She grinned.

There were no Dazzle icons over my head, but I was still *very* impressed. I returned the smile. She hadn't been wearing her cloak previously, so I knew something was off. The woman had only seen her as she fled from fighting the chainsword guy, so it was believable enough. I wondered if Ren could see the Dazzle icons she had inflicted on the woman. That would be a good confidence boost. As I went to ask her, I paused—something still felt off . . .

I ducked just as a blade passed over my head. My elbow shot back, catching the assailant in the leg, and then they hopped back into the other room. My boots spun on the wood, and I launched myself through, straight into a clutch of thrown daggers.

Deflected two with the inert chainsword. One scratched across my head, almost catching my eye. One to the side and one to the thigh. Painful. Also possibly poisoned.

The female figure darted away, her clothing a dark blur against the mixed browns of the ramshackle wooden building. She wanted me to chase, but that wasn't happening. My right hand had already cast the die, while my left bandaged me. A tune played in my head, and I hummed along while I waited for the audio cue. I heard her yelp out in pain, and then there was a growl and the sound of gnashing. *There we go.*

I shook the blood from my hand as Ren and Roger came over.

"You okay, Max?"

"Antidote, please." My pained smile was enough to convince her to do so immediately. I probably had one myself, but I had a single-minded focus. Revenge.

Against the warmth of the burning building, I strode off around the corner, downing the contents. Almost as gross as the regeneration one, this tasted like grass. The assassin was bloodied, limp from where my Hellhound+ and thrown card had struck her. Unable to run now, panic and sweat covered the part of her face that wasn't masked.

She attempted one final, last-ditch attack against me that I blocked with <Card Fan>.

"This next trick is quite the classic . . ." I smiled coldly, purple light illuminating my eyes as I flooded my Mana into the held weapon.

After a small amount of hesitation, the saw blades spun up and screamed rapturous applause.

CHAPTER SIXTY-THREE

Smoke and Pressure

I could almost taste the blood as the sounds vibrated through my skull. Even now, the first time I had . . . It had always been something that could happen. The moment I stepped through the portal, my fate had been decided. The death, the blood, the suffering I would both enact and overcome. Would I change any of it? No. Every step had brought me to where I was now.

Excessive," Ren noted after a brief pause to take in what I had just enacted. "The real tricky part is getting the two pieces back together again." I dropped the gore-soaked weapon to the floor.

Any longer and my arm muscles would have burst from the bone. I wasn't meant to use a weapon like that. The single word from the elf repeated in my head, echoing around. There was some nuance to the whole thing that was more of an ironic joke that would be a lot less funny if I explained it to her. Not that this was currently very amusing. "Sorry." It *was* excessive, unlike me. But it *was* me, so I was apologetic. I felt cold, withdrawn.

"I know what you are and can do. These are no friends of ours." Her bright eyes turned to me, and her hand raised to fill me with radiant warmth, a needed heal that only felt uncomfortable at first due to her insinuation that I was a demon. Well, I was reading between a few lines there—perhaps a little self-realization. "Just, don't lose yourself."

I nodded. The current atmosphere reminded me of hell or at least the new memories I held. It wasn't very healthy for my mental state; I was able to admit that much to myself. Not a demon, but I had hung around them and done demon things. The situation sank back into me as the anger cooled. "Let's go find Wolf."

Roger had found a new home in the red-haired Ranger, and I flung him his mace as we went back through the ruined rooms. It didn't take long to find the large bear a couple of rooms down, which must now be back up against the gatehouse wall, if I were to guess. The fort seemed bigger on the inside, but that might just be because all the rooms were similar in design and oddly devoid of furniture or decor.

Wolf had a number of arrows in his right shoulder and flank and a gash that ran over his eye. His little bowler was also mostly cinders. Worse could be said for the remains of the warrior he was currently chewing on, the scraping and cracking of armor vibrating around the room. Another figure, a female spellcaster, lay dead, slumped against the opposite wall—mostly disemboweled.

Ren ran over and healed him as I tried to focus. My hands were sore already. I needed to pause and let my Mana regenerate fully, otherwise I'd be running on empty for the rest of the fight. I hovered over the option to fix my outfit. While I would no longer feel any embarrassment to be in my underwear, I doubted we had five minutes where I could get away with being so vulnerable. I wanted to look my best for the big piece at the end, but perhaps just crossing the finish line would be the better outcome.

"How you holding up?" Ren came over to me, concern across her brow.

I'd freely admit the heat and smoke were getting to me, my senses numb to it. We were long past being *fine*. "I feel like I am in hell."

"Is that why you're smiling?" She raised an eyebrow.

"It is close," Roger added from behind. "Hell stinks a lot fuckin' worse though."

I hadn't even realized I had been smiling this whole time. Something that was potentially worrying. Maybe dissociation from the violence. "Are my eyes purple?"

"A little, yeah. They get more intense when . . . things are more intense."

"Just in combat, right?" I narrowed my questioning gaze at her.

She rolled her eyes. "Yes, dickbag. Now, what's our next move?"

We had probably killed most people in this section of the fort, along with a good amount of those defending the gatehouse. All sections were on fire and liable to collapse eventually. Being outside would be beneficial but might put us in danger of the rest of the Shadow members.

"How many have you three killed?" I asked, rubbing at my eye sockets. Briefly clocking that I, a humble magician, was currently going on a killing spree through a fantasy-gang hideout. Humble magician *and demon hunter* apparently.

"These two, red hair, three outside . . . Oh, there was one other. Seven?"

"Nine for me then." I clicked my tongue. "That shouldn't leave too many, if the scout was well enough informed."

She raised an eyebrow. "Not that it's a competition, but nine is impressive."

"I had help from Roger and my demons, of course." Plenty of luck and exploiting how brainless a lot of the gang was too. "Perhaps we can just go through the walls and into the other side? They'll be expecting us to use doorbs."

"Doorbs?" She tilted her head.

"Doors. Sorry, this smoke is making me woozy."

She nodded but looked concerned. Wolf dropped his current chew toy and backed up, ready to go through the wall. Red light pulsed around him as he charged and blew through the wood into open space. He slid across cobblestone and waited for us.

The middle of the gatehouse, caged bars blocking the road to the left and the bridge to our right. From beyond, the sound of the running river was almost calming. But only almost. It wasn't the most well-defended fort. If you reinforced a wagon, you could probably slam through the large metal gate by the process of shifting it from its wooden hinges—or however it was attached. If we were a little more selfish, Wolf could have just run us straight through and over the bridge, and they'd either have to chase us down or let us go.

A thought that was cut short as the bear repeated the process and blasted a hole into the next building. The figure inside was trampled in surprise before Wolf crunched down onto their skull. With how powerful he was, I didn't doubt we could slowly take on a whole city of bad guys, just going room to room without them having the opportunity to do much. Not that I wanted to put that out into the world.

We entered in behind him. The smoke was thicker here, the heat more oppressive. Perhaps not the best idea to enter the more damaged side of the fort, probably the most damaged thanks to my Imp+. However, we did need to clear out all the Crimson Shadow members and had some manner of advantage in restricting range. Couldn't leave any behind to poison the area once we had moved on past the river.

The door on the right side burst open, and a robed figure leaped out, a spell prepared in his hands. He took an arrow to the leg and immediately stumbled straight into the bear's face. Wolf glared at the man, and he recoiled just as my card slit across his throat. Chest crushed straight after by a massive paw. Roger stood behind us, fingers tapping on his mace as though he had something on his mind.

"See, does that count as mine or yours?" Wolf raised an eyebrow with a grin.

I gave him a bow. "All yours, my friend."

Ren nudged me as she walked past. "Been looting?"

"Ah, not much. I figured we could circle back to it if we lived." I scratched the back of my head and smiled. "Picked up a couple of Crossbows, just in case."

"They work well with your Dexterity and the fact that you can swap through them quickly." She nodded.

"I just have to remember to reload them." In saying that, I hadn't so far today. Three loaded ones, the rest were spent. Prep work was important, but I had been rather distracted lately.

I peered through the next room, card in hand. Everything had an amber hue to it, with the flames licking at the rooms above us. A few tables and chairs, but nothing—or rather nobody—untoward in sight. Then again, invisibility was a thing. I threw a conjured plank of wood into the room. As it arced toward the floor, a figure appeared as their crossbow bolt fired prematurely from down the end of the room by the next doorway.

"*Shit!*" the person hissed as the plank impaled by their shot clattered to the floor.

"Mine!" Roger pushed past me and ran awkwardly after them, mace in his hand. I let my card vanish. Although I had a good sense for it, I was still partially likely to impale him in the back of the head with it rather than the opponent.

"When we get out of here . . ." Ren removed her hat to wipe the sweat from her forehead. "We need to design more comfortable outfits."

As much as I liked our ensemble, perhaps if this was going to be a full-time thing, we could make some adjustments. "And Wolf could do with a little bow tie," I added.

The bear grunted and glowered at me. "No, I don't think so." He shook his head as he tried to wipe his muzzle on his thick forearms. "But some armor would be nice."

I grinned. We had started painting a picture of success already, even while things were still in progress. Ambitious? Maybe. We had cleared through the majority of the fort. The Crimson Shadow lay in ruins, save for wherever Jokkar was hiding. The building itself was being burned away. Even if we were to fail now, we had set them back by a huge margin in this starting area.

But . . . would there be any other Parties that would come along and do the same as we had? Eventually, perhaps. It was the nature of adventurers to rise up against evil, of course. By that time, the Lady may have achieved whatever mad plans she was trying to put in motion—and that could prove detrimental to any who stood opposed to her. We needed to find more information.

After surviving the day, of course.

Roger came back into the room, now in the body of the figure he had chased out into the next. Their masked head was dented inward, but the purple ears that had burst from their skull probably didn't improve that situation.

"Today has been fun as fuck, boss. Super glad you didn't die." He stepped over and rubbed the viscera from his spiked mace across his clothing. "Oh, I wanted to apologize." He turned to Ren and gave her a bow. "I treated you like shit before because I only recently realized you are an actual person."

"That's . . ." Ren furrowed her brow. "How did you *not* previously?"

"Just like . . . the way that you are." He waved his free hand up and down toward her. "I just didn't believe something real could be like . . . *that*. But now that boss—"

I raised my hand. "That is too many threads of discussion I do not want to get into, especially not in our current situation." I gave an exasperated shrug toward the elf, and she rolled her eyes in response. She had an arrow against her bow still. Things were tense, despite the moment of brief manic levity between the odd bunch that we were. Aching fingers flexed, ready to draw another card.

My brow furrowed as a vibration shook through the wooden floor. Was the building starting to collapse already? We'd need to get out as soon—

The wall beside us exploded, showering us with splinters and wooden shards. A huge figure stepped into the room, easily ten feet tall and completely covered in thick plated armor painted bright red. Atop the helmet, a white handprint decorated the forehead, blazing eyes peering out of darkened recesses. There would be no points for guessing who this could be.

"You dare question the Lady?"

Immediately, he swung a large mace around, pure force surrounding it. Ren fired off her arrow, but I didn't have time for a magic card. The next few seconds were a slideshow. He struck us all. My <Card Fan> hardly appeared before being immediately erased. The walls exploded. We were sent tumbling across the hard cobbled road. Light rain began pelting me. Refreshingly cool, almost a blessing compared to the hellish insides of the fort.

I blinked slowly. Still alive but in a lot of agony. The echoes of a stunning attack faded from me as I pushed myself up. Turns out it wasn't fun being on the receiving end of one of those. Broken ribs pained my breathing, slowly healing as I idly bandaged myself despite the disorientation. My eyes darted around the outside as realization brought panic to the forefront of my brain, chilling me further.

Wolf off to my left. His breathing was heavy, and his tongue lolled out of his mouth as he lay with eyes closed. Maybe just the effects of the stun, but I couldn't see that kind of icon to be reassured. To my right, the corpse Roger had been in was empty. Killed in action. I couldn't bring him back for a while. It was either disperse him or raise my shield up.

I craned my neck back to see Ren. She lay still, blood matting her blonde hair and running down her face. The slight breeze took her hat, and it rolled across the road toward the embankment. I couldn't tell how injured she was, but either she hadn't recovered from the stun or she was unconscious. Couldn't be dead. Just . . . couldn't. I wouldn't allow it, not at this stage.

Fear and anger filled my insides, burning for control. The pulse of purple electricity shuddered through me as energy arced around my body.

Jokkar stepped out of the ruined building and onto the road. His plated boots ground against the stone as he struck a martial pose.

"Look at how easily those who stand against her fall." His booming voice filling the open space, the only other sounds to oppose it being the light pattering of rain and the crackle of burning wood as the fort degraded in the background. He spun the cylindrical mace around in his hands. It was studded at the end.

Pearl-like teeth. It had the slight mar of crimson across it. Ren's blood. Above his head was a new icon I hadn't seen before. A question mark of black upon light gray. I knew what it was by instinct. Ren's new ability, making him more easily debuffed *and dazzled.*

A parting gift, setting up the main event so I could really shock and awe him. Even if she wasn't awake to watch it, I couldn't let her down now. I slowly rose to my feet, which seemed to amuse him.

"You dare stand? Stronger than you look. <Max Stun> usually puts most down for *much* longer."

The interlocking parts of the anger and power within me found their purpose. Pain and adrenaline flooded through me in waves as the crackling energy that pulsed around my body grew wilder and more intense.

"*<Max Stun>?*" I grinned, blood running from my mouth. "Don't mind if I do."

CHAPTER SIXTY-FOUR

Critical Reception

The bigger they are, the harder they fall. That's what they say anyway. The problem for me was that my ego had gotten pretty big. I was under no illusion that my time was coming, and indeed there had been some close calls. You would think I'd be humbler after being nearly bested by gravity, or a horse, or even hubris. The trouble was, I had gotten away with it. Time healed all wounds, as if the System was keen on showing all the different types of injuries I could amass yet still hold myself together in one piece.

Jokkar chuckled, a deep rumbling thing that did little to improve my own mood. "My stun usually makes it easy to smash people into paste. I'll have to kill you normally before your friends wake up."

He was in thick plated armor, and even the joints looked like they were padded with something difficult to pierce. Other than the shadowed circle areas where his eyes were and thin vertical slits where his mouth would be, he was totally covered in metal. Not great for me. Yet, before I knew it, my feet were taking me toward him. Self-preservation was out of the window. I wanted to keep his focus away from the others even at the cost of my own mortality. All eyes on me. I was the showman, after all.

I slid across the cobbled road as his mace swung over my head, the gust of displaced air taking my hat off. A pair of cards scraped across his arm but did very little. As he went for a backhand follow-up, I threw a conjured bag at him. A blue shield flared around him as he jumped back. The bag fell to the floor, and an onion rolled out from the opening. Testing the waters, seeing what he was made of.

As his helmet turned back to me, my crossbow bolt was already in the air, denting the metal just to the side of his right eye. His arm went up and blocked the second. While he was distracted, I ran around him. He had Strength, but his movement speed was terrible. I rolled past his leg, and he shoved the end of his mace downward, cracking the stone road. Another card went out and scratched around the side of his helmet, doing little more than removing some of the paint to show brighter silver. The ground around him burst with a shock wave, and I stumbled backward.

He swung in a wide arc, and I jumped atop a chair and into the air over it, my beloved furniture piece shattered in the process. As I dropped back down, a cloth went over me. I rolled forward as he swiped at it, catching the head of the spear that I used to prop up the fabric in lieu of it being my head. Dazzle icons were doubling up at an impressive rate, my tricks mostly for survival at this stage but working all the same.

His mace came around in another wild swing as his boot stomped toward me. <Card Fan+> took the brunt, the excess force still sending me tumbling to the floor. I turned over on my back and fired off the last primed crossbow. The surprise caught him off guard, and the bolt found his eye. He growled out in pain and yanked the offending projectile from the socket. Crossbow away, I went to move back to my feet just as he raised up a glowing hand. There was a swell of power beneath me, but I couldn't escape it in time. A circular platform of the road burst upward, taking me with it as it rose to meet his downward-swinging mace. I had just used <Card Fan>, so I—

It collided with me, and for a brief moment, I felt dead. The warmth of the healing charm broke at the same time as most of my bones, and the worst of it snapped back into place right after. My body slunk from the raised stone onto the ground. Still exhausted from the trauma of it, my body struggled to function against the draw of having a peaceful nap.

"Nice try," he growled at me as he looked down and saw the rope tied around one leg, now visible. I hadn't the time to do anything more with it before the invisibility wore off. "For taking my eye, you can watch me kill your Party first."

He turned away and started walking toward Ren, mace slung up onto his shoulder.

"*No*," I seethed, pain wracking my body.

His plated feet stopped, and he looked over his shoulder. "So stubborn. Do you not know when you have lost?"

"It ends when *I* say . . . that the show is over." I wavered as I stood to my feet. My eyes felt as though they were on fire. Beneath my cape my left hand worked through a bandage. Just a few more seconds of inaction, *please*.

"Oh, a show is what you want?" He turned back to the prone elf and raised his mace into the air.

A blur of a dark shape brushed in front of his helmet, and then I was in the air in front of him, switched with the hell bird. From my hand, I threw a handful of nails into his face. As I hit the ground, pain flaring up my tired legs, I held out my hands and cast Arc+ from the Spell Scroll. Lightning pulsed from my hands, sharp yellow electricity arcing across from his body to the conductive nails and back to him again. He staggered back, clutching at his face and convulsing.

"Bastard, y-you'll pay for this." He dropped his mace to the road and held his head as he absorbed the last of the magical damage. As he went to pick the weapon back up, it vanished into my Inventory.

"Looks like that's *mine* now." I grinned from beside him, the glow of my purple eyes reflecting off of his armor.

He turned and punched me, <Card Fan> causing me to slide across the rain-slick road, my back slamming up against the embankment. I coughed up a little blood as he ran toward me, anger blazing in his one good eye. I grinned and crossed my arms. A blanket suddenly hung over me as he launched his next punch, striking something that burst out bright red across the muddy embankment. I had left the can of red paint in the way as I dropped and rolled forward between his legs.

As he tried to turn, he got caught on a couple of chairs that I had ejected from my Inventory to get in the way. Too heavy to fall over such small obstacles, he crushed his way through them. When he gained his footing, I was juggling three blood vials again. There was a tune playing in the back of my head. Pleasant. Complimentary. Soothing.

"That won't work on me, mewling shit. I get that stuff by the jug load."

"Huh? No, this is just to distract you."

He glared to the sidelines too late as a fireball from my Imp struck him on the side of the head. The red paint cracked and flaked away from the armor as he winced. From near the woods, the Imp+ was starting up a second attack already. There was no way he could go out there to kill the demon while still trying to kill me. I had thrown that card as far as I could while he was busy punching dirt.

"Tell me the Lady's plans and I won't kill you." I spoke calmly, despite the energy pulsing through me. Vials away, my hands hung low.

"You're not getting a word out of me, shitstain. She'll be sitting in the palace long before I'm done torturing you. My regeneration will heal these wounds once I get more blood, no problem."

That was enough for me. Minimum threshold for everything reached.

"Any last words?" Any humor was gone from my face. I felt cold now, almost wanted to shiver. Needed to keep him busy. Blood ran from my nose. I wavered as I became lightheaded, eyes burning as if they might bleed too. It all needed to escape. I had pushed too hard. Sometimes you had to give the show your all and then some.

"Fuck your tricks."

Amusing, in its own way. I probably couldn't have thought of anything more poignant if I was in the same situation, really. The cobbled road was littered with small indents of all the times during the fight when I had attempted to get this one specific card . . . and as fresh blood ran from the rest of my suffered wounds, I wondered if it would be enough. Well, I wouldn't have to worry for much longer if it wasn't.

He launched himself toward me, and from underneath my cape, I withdrew the card.

Not purple and not even white. Bright red, crackling with energy. The fabled critical card that the System promised me. Had taken a lot of attempts during the fight to get it, but as soon as it bloomed into my hand, I knew it. Could feel the difference immediately. It was beautiful, in a way, to my tired mind that was so bored with blood and flame. Something radiant yet hellish at the same time, perfect for my demonic side. Even time seemed to slow as I performed my final trick.

One last calm breath and then the card was out, a trail of bright crimson illuminating the path as it cut through the air. Turned it vertically, then at a slight slant, even as blood dripped from both my hands. So much practice in using my cards, all for a moment like this. I exhaled as I made the last adjustment before . . . Oh, yes. <Finale+>.

Among the gloom and light rain of the battlefield, show light illuminated me. The sounds of applause and cheers overrode the burning fort, filling my ears with something so comforting and familiar despite this new world. Small fireworks blossomed with color into the air above me. Reds, greens, and blue. I was almost sure some bouquets were thrown at my feet. A risk to let the card go uncontrolled as I cast the showstopping spell. But now he couldn't move. Frozen in place by the greatest and last performance he'd ever see.

I threaded the needle. Despite all the odds and the risk taken by the man who never gambled, the card passed through one of the thin mouth slits in the helmet. Red light briefly illuminated the insides of the metal before flesh and bone burst out of the eye holes.

Blood sprayed across me as his body stumbled to the ground, right before a second fireball hit him, warming me. The perfect execution, in more ways than one.

"How's that for <Max Stun> . . . *fucker*?" I slurred as my tongue and brain hadn't quite gotten back on the same page yet.

As his life and Dazzle icons faded away, so too did the elated glow of appreciation. I popped the cork of the second Rejuvenation Potion and stumbled over to the prone elf.

Her eyes flickered open slowly as I knelt beside her. With my bloodied hand, I pushed the hair from her face. "Sorry," I murmured, painting streaks of my own red across her cheek, "that made it worse."

"Max?" Her brow furrowed, and she struggled to push herself up. "Shit! *Ow*. Think I dislocated my leg. You okay?" Panic flashed across her face as she tried to read me before looking at the dead-Jokkar situation behind me. "You did it?"

I handed her a Health Potion and sat beside her to prop her up. "I guess. To all three questions." I didn't feel the elation of success. Even the finale showering me with brief adoration hadn't brought me the dopamine it used to. The bear yawned and began to come to as well.

She took the potion with a grimace and grunted as her leg popped back into place with a loud click. Wolf got up to his feet shakily, noticed us, and padded over, still lightheaded and dazed.

"Sorry," he grunted. "I think I napped through the battle."

"You're good, bud." Warmth flooded me as Ren healed me before she cast a second one onto the bear.

He sat beside us, and we watched the fort aflame. A section collapsed, sending embers up into the sky. They faded as they cooled in the air, dropping again as soot and ash. The largest campfire I could imagine. I was enthralled.

Ren leaned her head against me. "You look like shit. Was it a tough fight?"

"Nah," I lied. "I've fought tougher horses."

She exhaled through her nose. "I suppose he wasn't the talkative type?"

I looked over at the bear, who was just idly licking around his maw as he stared off at the burning building. He didn't seem too much worse for wear, probably the toughest out of all of us. Despite how things turned out, I wasn't sure whether I was the lucky one not taking the full stun length when these two did. It would have been the Oathwarden Ability that kept me up; my shield only stopped Damage. No use worrying about the what-ifs. Instead, I rested my aching head against the blonde hair of the elf.

"He might have just been posturing, but he mentioned something about the Lady taking the palace." Lofty ideals—it seemed clear she wasn't getting her levels the traditional way.

"There's a palace?" Ren sat up away from me. "Oh, where's my hat?"

I pointed over to a muddy area near the woods where it had gotten caught on a branch. "Here." From my aching hand, a Hellhound+ went out, and the large canine grabbed the hat softly between its teeth and brought it back. Ren gave the demonic dog a hug in thanks, and I let him hang about with us until his time was up.

We took the time to heal up properly but barely moved. There was something about the large building slowly burning away and collapsing in parts that captured our full attention. Possessed us almost. The whole left side went down, having sustained the greatest amount of fire damage alongside Wolf and Jokkar breaking most of the lower floor structure. There wasn't much to say, really. I was tired and had endured enough hardship for one day. It was nice just to see what we had accomplished. Somehow defeating greater odds because why? We were stronger? Smarter? Luckier?

Eventually, I sighed. "We should head back to town." It seemed obvious, but we had been sitting out in the light rain for a good twenty minutes. Rushing headlong into the next area in our state was just asking to get knocked into the river by a trap—or we'd find there was another fort on the other side. Or worse.

Some rest and relaxation allowed our enemy to get a couple of steps ahead, but better than us putting more feet in an early grave. Then we wouldn't be able to help or save anyone. Not that I felt like a hero at present.

"Alright," she agreed as I helped her to her feet. "Let's go."

Despite the journey along the road being arduous enough on the way to the fort, it was even worse on the return. Drab showings of the corpses on display were not facing toward us, but moving past the blank sides didn't make it feel any more like a victory parade.

Even the rain picked up as the breeze pushed in our faces to harry our return. We hobbled and winced. I helped Ren walk some of the way; Wolf helped us both when we needed to stop and rest. It had taken a lot out of us. Even with all the healing we had, our bodies were just aching and sore. If the System had something hidden away that dealt with all the minor traumas, I'd be spending half my gold on stocking up. Not injured, just worn down.

We entered the town once more, and it felt the same as usual. As if our actions hadn't even moved the needle. While it was nice to think there would be handshakes and celebrations for the adventurers who thwarted evil, the System-created didn't know and didn't care. We had fixed the area for future Players, maybe, but there was no fame and fortune granted to us for our self-imposed heroics.

The barkeep didn't pay too much notice to how bloodied and beaten we looked. Gave us the key for our usual room. Nobody else in the tavern, save for the mindless patrons that Wolf nudged out of the way a little more forcefully than usual.

Ascending the stairs felt like agony, and as Ren locked the door, I sank to the floor, my back against the side of the bed.

"Flip for the first bath?" I asked, a tired smile across my face.

She rolled her eyes. "Sure, go for it."

A coin in my hand, I flipped it in the air for her to call it.

"Heads."

Caught it, flipped it onto the back of my hand. I slid my hand back to reveal two coins, one heads and one tails.

"Smooth, trickster." She smiled and shook her head in exasperation before gesturing for me to follow her to the bathroom.

After all, what good was being the best showman around without an audience willing to suspend their disbelief?

CHAPTER SIXTY-FIVE

Crowd Goes Wild

That was the beauty of it all, really. Struggle, resolve conflict, then rest and enjoy your life. Repeat. I wasn't too keen on the repeating part. That's what made us adventurers though. Drawn to danger, wanting to overcome odds and carve a better world for everyone. It involved a lot of over-the-top violence sometimes—assuming this wasn't just me going over the drab point in the future, then you read the part where I sawed a woman in half, right?—but our intentions were always good. The road to hell may be paved with such, but I had enough dealings with demons for that to feel like home.

I groaned and rolled from the bed. Three days of bliss. Altogether too much and yet not nearly enough. Wiped my bleary eyes to see that Ren was not there. One day I'd get used to her waking before me. She'd mentioned heading out for supplies the night before.

There hadn't been as much to worry about in terms of imminent danger since breaking down the fort, so having her out with Wolf and me here alone wasn't a cause for concern. I switched to my magician outfit and adjusted my hat. Although, this was probably one of the few times I had been alone in the past three days. Being around the pair had become so normal that I couldn't imagine how I used to live such a solitary existence before.

I had spent a lot of time in bed, eating food, and generally just living for these few days. Cooked for Ren as promised. Got Wolf some padded armor—and a bow tie, as much as he grumbled about it. Made some slight adjustments to our outfits so that they were less torturous to fight in. Checked the shops every day for anything new to add to my repertoire.

Aside from avoiding anything that looked like a Quest, we had been enjoying the System experience as it was probably intended. Peaceful. Three days seemed like the perfect amount of time to fully recover from our injuries, both physically and emotionally. Any more than that, then we'd run the risk of wanting to stay.

Part of me did, despite the prickling knowledge that something untoward was happening a few steps ahead of us.

We had learned that the continent was ruled over by a King and Queen, several areas away. My best guess was that the Lady wanted to become Queen and take over control of everything, if not the System itself. It seemed a big stretch, but given how easily she could convert people to her cause, I could see it happening. Just because she could make people despise the System and the proper experience of it, reject their place and humanity . . . it didn't mean she had the power to control or change it. Least of all escape it.

From the bedside table, I picked up my journal and flipped it into the air to vanish into my Inventory. Ren had watched me scrawl in it the night before. Her question had been why all my notes were so dire, and was I really that miserable? I had given her a nonanswer that made her roll her eyes, but the truth was, this was my coping mechanism. Allowed me to scream into the void and vent out the trauma so that my brain was left with the good memories only. Sure, it painted our travels in a dimmer light than what we truly lived, but I hoped one day to look back and scoff at the notion things had been so bad. Thieves and Bandits still sucked though.

With the first area soon to be a distant memory, I relented to checking my stats one last time. A brief record of what I had accomplished, without seeing any of the corpses and ruined scraps of my suit that had gotten me to this point.

[Stats]
[Strength—6]
[Constitution—7]
[Agility—6]
[Dexterity—20 (15 + 5)]
[Intelligence—29 (15 + 14)]
[Wisdom—6]
[Luck—12 (11 + 1)]
**[Other—+10% Mana, +20% Mana regeneration, +15% magic Damage,
+5% magic Damage per 5% Mana spent, +5% spell-casting speed]**

I sighed and left the room. My Knife of the Trickster put my Intelligence over double the base amount. Didn't actually make me feel any smarter, but at least my magic cards could do more than scratch tougher opponents. Was I powerful? Perhaps. Killing other Players seemed to come down to striking first and getting lucky most of the time. I'd save some of those musings for my diary. My legs took me down the stairs and into the main tavern.

"Hope you had a great evening, adventurer," the barkeep greeted me.

"Was alright." I waved him off. Didn't want to give him all the details, and I only responded because it seemed rude not to—even if he didn't actually listen or respond in kind.

Outside, the sun was bright, and the day was warm. Pleasant. With my eyes closed, I could hear the ocean lapping at the beach. Something I'd miss when we moved farther inland. Maybe on better days we could return here, like a vacation. Relive some of our better moments, as few as they were.

"Morning, Max."

I opened my eyes to see the burly man with a handlebar mustache and a large axe over his shoulders addressing me. A Player.

"Morning, Sven. Off questing?" He had come to the island yesterday, the fifth new Player we had seen since recovering. It was like the System was healing.

"Yeah, some bullshit about getting lumber from trees. Easy experience though."

I nodded, and he went off. The other four had been equally as amiable. Bright-eyed and bushy-tailed after having survived the starter island under a lot less pressure than I had. After another deep breath, I went off toward the town center where the shops were. At least, I assumed the rest of my Party would be there—certainly would be handy to have a way for us to communicate when we weren't together. I wasn't sure if there were any tricks I could do to help us there.

Before I reached my destination, I stopped at the Town Board where the challenges were posted. There was now a fourth page that wasn't part of the System messages. Something we had placed across the wooden planks. A warning about the Crimson Shadow, painting them as the danger and enemy that they were. We hadn't heard of any activity in this area during our rest, but it was better to be proactive. Early days, after all. The area was large. It wasn't impossible for a few to have been missed, and we could only hope that without the main recruiters, they would soon die out.

Any fears of losing my Party members soon melted away as I turned to see Wolf sitting in the town center looking bored out of his skull. His padded armor resembled a waistcoat, which he didn't find as amusing as we did. Certainly made him look the part though. His nose twitched in the air as he turned to me.

"Morning, Max."

"Wolf." I nodded. "Today's the day."

"Shame," he grumbled. "Getting used to lazing around and eating good food."

"I hear that. World won't save itself though." I grinned at him. "Plus, the next area might have even *better* food."

He licked his lips in anticipation, and then his nose twitched.

Someone stepped up behind me, and something metal pressed against my spine through my suit.

"*What now?*" a soft voice said.

I smiled and vanished, appearing back up the road by the Town Board. My grin widened as the Hellhound+ jumped up at Ren in excitement, trying to lick at her face.

"*Ah, Max!*" she complained as she turned to me with her face wrinkled up. "*Bullshit* that you foresaw that!"

I walked back down to the square with my hands in my pockets. "What?" I shrugged my shoulders. "If I tell you how I knew, it'll ruin the mystique."

"Ass." She knelt down and gave the hound pets. "Did *you* tell him, Wolf?"

The bear shook his head. "No, never!"

Perhaps if they knew how often I sent out a just-in-case demon, then it wouldn't sound so wild. You only had to hit once to make it seem like a miracle if they didn't see all the misses. Plus Wolf had the tell. He knew our smells and reacted when we got close enough by twitching his nose.

Not that I was about to tell them either of those things. I had been teaching Ren some more magic in our downtime, but some secrets had to be kept. If only for my own ego at being the best showman in the System. Perhaps the next area would have enough Players to throw a proper performance . . .

I smiled at the elf as she stood and returned a grin. Still no closer to getting a Dazzle icon over her. I often wondered what it would take . . . but then again, I was close to letting it slide. Personal growth? Sure, we could go with that.

"Look what I have." She extended her arm to show a device of polished wood and leather that matched the gray blue of her waistcoat. "I took the prototype you made and had it constructed. One of the Players, Petra, has some crafting abilities."

It was beautiful, a lot more practically functional than what I had managed to cobble together. Plus, it wasn't made out of parts of Hadrian. "I am amazed. You just got the one?"

She narrowed her eyes, but a sly grin went up at the side of her mouth. "Hell no. I have one for the other arm that fits scrolls better." She showed me an equally well-made one, now appearing on her left arm.

I wrinkled up my nose, feeling rather green.

"And if you're good . . ." She adjusted my jacket to make me look a little tidier. "I got you a pair as well."

Three wands and three scrolls at my beck and call. I might be able to swap them at will too. Not as powerful as a real mage, but the possibilities . . .

"Let's get going," Wolf grumbled. "Otherwise, Max will spend all morning thinking of new ways to get us into trouble."

"Yeah, you're right—ready, Max?"

I nodded, although my brain was still trying to process in the background. We'd need to hit up the next area for better magic shops—if we can get new wands on the regular, then that would be a huge boost. Scrolls too, although—

"Here." Ren tipped the table containing my thoughts as she handed me a sweet cake.

"Thanks, Ren." I smiled at her as we left the outskirts of the town. "I thought we'd get tired of eating these by now, but they're still just as good."

"Mm-hmm." She nodded, her mouth already full.

Our comforted elation became somber silence the farther along the western road we traveled. The giant warning crosses were toppled now. It had taken us a while, and it was perhaps disingenuous to say the first day of rest was just that. Bodies were buried best we were able to without being able to carry them too far.

A graveyard of our own making, on our right-hand side. Small plots that grass would probably overtake in no time. Flowers we had gathered and left. It all felt so . . . disjointed from reality, yet still the right thing to do.

We hadn't gone as far as the fort. Even with the partial recovery, it stuck out like a sore thumb on the horizon as we approached. Most of it was a burned-out and collapsed shell, hardly recognizable compared to its former shape. About the only good thing I could say about it was that it didn't look like it had been looted, nor anything recovered.

"Still stinks like charcoal." Ren scowled at the surroundings.

"You're telling me," Wolf grumbled.

We picked our way across the debris, moving past the dead bodies and ruined furniture. I didn't much care to loot them, all things told. If it were possible, I wanted nothing to do with them anymore. Most of them didn't even give the option to. Either left too long to spoil or the fire had ravaged them, just like those in the outpost. Even my memories brought a bad taste to my mouth of the fight from three days ago. So much blood and suffering, and for what? So someone on a power trip could rule over everything? It seemed too basic.

Therein lay the reason why it was so evil, perhaps. Uncaring about the lives crushed or changed by her path. Still, all it would take was a crossbow bolt or two, and this thing could be over. I was too clever to fool myself into thinking it could be that easy, unfortunately.

We stepped over the ruined gates, charred black in places from the fire. Wolf pushed them to the side, the large metal beams creaking from the movement, causing small chunks of wood to clatter from the decaying floors above. After he relented when we moved ahead, we found ourselves on the edge of the bridge.

It was long. Several hundred feet, by my rough estimation. As we moved from the shadow of the broken fort, the daylight illuminated the river, and everything seemed vibrant again. I'd never seen such a large and fast-flowing body of water before—it was mesmerizing. All the way to the north, it seemed to come down from a mountainous region, and off in the other direction, it eventually flowed out to the near-endless sea.

"It's both beautiful and humbling at the same time," Ren said, her eyes wide as she was also enthralled with it.

"Makes me thirsty," Wolf added, peering closer to the edge.

"The sooner we get across this, the better I'll feel." I grimaced, and with a nod, we began walking.

It wasn't so much that I had a phobia of water, but there was something about this that unsettled me. The intrusive thoughts wanted me to hop in and see how fast I could flow down and find out what was at the end. Nothing healthy or helpful for our current task, I told my panicked brain.

Thankfully, it listened, and while we remained on guard . . . nothing terrible happened. We reached the other side and were officially in the second area of the continent.

Ren narrowed her eyes at her Map. We had gone over it a few times already, but it was always worth triple-checking to be sure. "There's a small village just to the north. We should stop there and see what's going on. Maybe pick up a couple of Quests?"

I nodded. "Perfect." In among the struggles against the Shadow, we still needed to focus on dancing to the System's tune in gaining new powers and keeping up. Usually adventurers would hit the second area at level ten, but I considered the fact we were punching above our weight. Wouldn't take us long to catch up.

In fact, I almost allowed myself a chance to cheer up. The sun was shining, and I had some amazing company. I grew more proficient by the day, both in combat and magical ability. For the most part, we were on top of things. That was plenty to be content about. I even allowed myself to look forward to finding better Equipment in the new area, where things would be scaled for higher levels. What heights could I reach if I just put that extra effort in?

We rounded the curve of the road as it rose up a hill, to be greeted by a signpost dug into the ground. In the distance behind it were the shapes of cottages all gathered together among farming fields.

"Warning," it read, "this area under control of the Crimson Shadow. Trespassers will be killed."

Atop the signpost, lending some streaks of crimson to the notice, were three impaled heads.

Any vibrancy to the area immediately dimmed, and the optimism froze in the pit of my stomach. I glanced between the others, and they had the same drab expressions on their faces.

My right hand clenched into a fist as we strode toward the village.

I hadn't considered an encore so soon, but the crowd wouldn't be told no.

About the Author

Kleggt is the author of the Death of the Party and Demonic Magician series, originally released on Royal Road. Upon clawing his way out of the depths of Scheduling Hell as a Forever DM, he began writing web novels, channeling his love of world-building and oddball characters into his own LitRPG and progression fantasy stories.